A SEASIDE AFFAIR

Fern Britton is a household name and the presenter of iconic TV shows such as *Ready Steady Cook* and *This Morning*. Fern's warmth, humour and compassion have made her incredibly popular and she has become a much sought-after presenter and participant in shows such as *Have I Got News For You* and *Strictly Come Dancing*.

Her autobiography, *Fern: My Story*, was a huge bestseller and her novels, *New Beginnings*, *Hidden Treasures* and *The Holiday Home* have been published to great acclaim. Fern is deeply committed to a number of charities, in particular the Genesis Research Trust founded by Professor Robert Winston to help create healthy families.

She lives with her husband Phil Vickery, the well-respected chef, and her four children in Buckinghamshire and Cornwall.

By the same author:

Fern: My Story

New Beginnings
Hidden Treasures
The Holiday Home

The Stolen Weekend (Short Story)
A Cornish Carol (Short Story)

Fern Britton

A SEASIDE AFFAIR

HARPER

Harper
An imprint of HarperCollins*Publishers*
1 London Bridge Street
London SE1 9GF

www.harpercollins.co.uk

This paperback edition 2015
1

First published in Great Britain by
HarperCollins*Publishers* 2014

Copyright © Fern Britton 2014

Fern Britton asserts the moral right to
be identified as the author of this work

A catalogue record for this book is
available from the British Library

ISBN: 9780007947645

Set by Palimpsest Book Production Limited, Falkirk, Stirlingahire

Printed and bound in Great Britain by
Clays Ltd, St Ives plc

MIX
Paper from
responsible sources

FSC
www.fsc.org   **FSC® C007454**

FSC™ is a non-profit international organisation established to promote
the responsible management of the world's forests. Products carrying the
FSC label are independently certified to assure consumers that they come
from forests that are managed to meet the social, economic and
ecological needs of present and future generations,
and other controlled sources.

Find out more about HarperCollins and the environment at
www.harpercollins.co.uk/green

ACKNOWLEDGEMENTS

It's a very cold day in January and the rain is lashing the Cornish coast as I type. The storms are so bad that ancient, landmark pieces of coastline are being torn down by the powerful waves.

If this book were real, the much-loved Pavilions Theatre of Trevay would be in deep threat. Built up on the cliffs above the beautiful fishing village, the dressing rooms would be leaking and the orchestra pit under a foot of water.

Dear Piran, Penny, Simon and Helen would roll their sleeves up and gather together a staunch work party to bail it out, though . . .

In *A Seaside Affair*, our old friends battle to save the theatre from a rather different, but no less destructive, threat. I have spent the last year immersed in thoughts of Trevay and its people; it has become so real to me, and to some of you, that I hope you enjoy this next bit of their story.

I grew up in the theatre and worked as a stage manager when very young. A lot of what I describe here has happened or certainly could happen given the right circumstances!

As always, I couldn't have got through the emotional maze of characters and plot without the immense wisdom of my editor Kate Bradley and the calming influence of my agents John Rush and Luigi Bonomi. I may not always look as if I am taking on board your steadying hands, but boy, do I appreciate them. You three are the tops.

Liz Dawson, you are the best publicist and the best of women too.

Thank you, Phil, for bringing me endless cups of tea and listening to plot dilemmas while you're trying to watch the football.

And thank you to the kids who keep me from going completely up my own bum, and the cats who always make me laugh.

Finally to my parents who are both ninety this year. You are incredible and I owe everything to you.

Fern

To Harry and your exciting future, with all
my love, Mum xx

Part One

Part One

1

'You should've woken me, silly.' Ryan Hearst ambled into the sunny kitchen, scratching himself somewhere inside his rumpled boxer shorts.

His girlfriend, Jess Tate, glanced up from reading the paper at the kitchen table and allowed her eyebrows to wrinkle briefly in distaste.

Ryan bent down and gave her a kiss on her freckled nose. A small gesture he was prone to, which always managed to irritate her.

'What's for breakfast?' He stretched out his muscular arms, then straightened up and yawned. His armpits gave off an unpleasant odour.

Jess pushed up her reading specs, sweeping her loose brown curls off her face, and gave him what she hoped was a relaxed smile. 'If your fans could see you now . . .'

'Yeah, don't tell them. Anyway, baby, I'm all yours.' He placed his hands either side of her head and thrust his hips and crotch towards her, mimicking a male stripper. She pulled a face and turned away. 'You pong. Go and have a shower and I'll make something to eat.'

'You love me, baby, you know you do.' He scratched his chest and yawned again. 'I've missed you, Jess. I really have.'

She looked into his dark, almond-shaped eyes, even more sexy with the tanned creases of crow's feet at their edges.

'Yes, and I've missed you,' she murmured, closing her eyes and forming her full lips into a shape for kissing – but he was already on his way to the bathroom.

With a sigh she got up and made her way to the fridge. There were plenty of eggs, a slab of cheese and some mushrooms. Ryan hadn't touched a carbohydrate since the third person in their relationship, Cosmo Venini, had entered their lives.

'Will an omelette do you?' she called. But he couldn't hear her over the sound of the shower.

Two pairs of beady eyes popped up over the dog basket next to the dishwasher.

Jess bent down to tickle a brace of plump tummies. 'Daddy's home, girls.'

Elsie and Ethel were miniature dachshund sisters. Ryan had brought them home nine months ago, the day he had landed the title role in *Venini*, a TV series about the exploits of a globe-trotting classical conductor who moonlights as an MI5 agent. The show had been an overnight success and as a result the tabloids had given Ryan the dubious honour of dubbing him 'the thinking woman's brioche'.

Jess recalled that cold January afternoon when he'd poked his head round the living room door, the smell of frosty air clinging to him. She was huddled on the sofa in front of the TV, swaddled from head to toe in their duvet to combat the lack of heating, watching *Deal or No Deal* and wondering whether she should apply to be a contestant in the hope of bringing home some prize money. One look at Ryan's face told her his audition had been successful.

'Oh my God! You got the job?' The icy temperature forgotten, she'd thrown off the duvet and leapt up from the sofa.

'Yep. Call me Cosmo!' He pushed the door wide open and stood in front of her, smiling self-deprecatingly, still wearing the huge misshapen tweed overcoat that he'd bought in the charity shop the previous winter.

For a moment, Jess could only jump up and down on the spot, beside herself with happiness, then she ran across the room, hugged him tightly and kissed him. 'I'm so happy for you! This is *it*, Ryan! This is your big break – oh my God, oh my God – we can pay the gas bill!'

'I think perhaps we can!' he laughed, pulling her closer to him. 'Oh . . .' He loosened his grip on her and created a little space between them. 'Almost forgot – I've bought you a present to celebrate.'

She smiled, wide-eyed with excitement, thinking of the silver earrings she'd pointed out to him the previous weekend. 'You mustn't, Ryan. We don't have any money yet.'

He opened his coat and rummaged in the deep poacher's pockets within.

'Ta-dah!' His hands emerged clutching two long bodies with impossibly short legs.

'What the hell . . . ?' These were not earrings. 'Who are they for?'

'You.'

'Why?'

'Present.'

'I don't need a present. My present is you getting this great job.' In spite of herself she reached out and tickled a pair of silken ears. 'When does shooting start?'

'In a couple of days.'

'Gosh, that's quick. Where?' Jess asked.

'Northumberland.'

'A bit of a schlep from Willesden.'

'Yeah . . . Then Milan, New York and Hong Kong.'

She stopped the tickling and looked at Ryan.

'For how long?'

'Six months.' His eyes dropped to the two warm, wriggling pups.

Jess pushed her hair behind her ears, suddenly feeling all of her pleasure at the news drain away. 'Six months? But you will be coming home, won't you? Backwards and forwards?'

Ryan shook his head, 'Probably not.'

'Oh,' said Jess, suddenly deflated.

He held the puppies up and spoke to them: 'So that's where you two come in. You're going to look after Mummy while Daddy's gone.'

Now she got it. The dogs were her consolation prize. A way of keeping her occupied while Ryan was away having the time of his life.

'So you get to swan off and I'm left holding the fort here, on my own? And it isn't only that, Ryan – pets are such a tie.' She was aware of the whining note that had crept into her voice. 'Suppose I get a job that means *I* have to go away? Who'll look after them then?'

He set the dogs down and she heard their little tappy claws on the tiles as he put his arms around her. She clung to him and inhaled the distinctive smell of his coat, burying herself in his neck.

'Don't be like that, Jess. I'm really trying here. Don't spoil it for me.'

*

Ryan ran the soap over his body and revelled in his newly honed physique. His personal trainer, insisted upon by the production company, had worked him hard but it was definitely worth it. Biceps, triceps, abs, quads, arse. Not bad for a forty-two-year-old. There was no doubt about it: men were luckier than women. The older they got the better they looked. George Clooney, Richard Gere – even Sean Connery in his eighties. For women it was tougher, and everyone in the business knew it. Helen Mirren and Meryl Streep were the exceptions. Poor Jess; she would struggle to find work now, unless it was playing a worn-down mum, or a character role.

Ryan got out of the shower and wrapped a large bath sheet around his waist. He checked himself out in the mirror then pulled the towel a little lower to show off the muscled definition of his hips, stomach and groin. Donning his 'Cosmo' face he gave his reflection a seductive grin and growled, 'Down, boy! It's only me, silly.'

*

Ryan loved going out in public. He always wore his film-star-in-disguise sunglasses and a baseball cap. The thrill of being recognised hadn't left him yet. Today, walking the dogs on a busy Hampstead Heath, he felt as if he owned the world. *Venini* was top of the ratings, his face was on the cover of *Esquire* magazine, he had just been voted the Sexiest Man in Britain and it looked as if the Best Actor BAFTA was sure to have his name on it. Beside him, Jess was recounting what he thought was a rather tedious and seemingly interminable story about her agent and a part in a commercial she'd been put up for the previous week.

'. . . I wouldn't have cared if she'd told me they were looking for actresses ten years older than me. I would have dressed the part. But then to go and be told that I looked *too* middle-aged, without even trying, it was just so humiliating . . . Ethel, come away from the ducks! I mean, do I really look middle-aged? My CV says thirty-eight! Where do these advertising execs, fresh out of junior school, think middle age begins? Twenty-five? . . . Elsie, come away from the Labrador, he's too big for you! Honestly, Ryan, maybe I should start thinking about a bit of Botox or getting my hair cut or dyed. What do you think?'

But before Ryan had a chance to respond they were interrupted by something that was becoming an ever-more regular occurrence.

'Cosmo! Cosmo Venini! It is you, isn't it?'

An over-made-up woman in her fifties was power-walking towards Ryan, who had stopped and was taking off his sunglasses, wrinkling his beautiful eyes into a smile. He held his hands out in a gesture of surrender.

She arrived, puffing slightly, and all but elbowed Jess out of the way in her eagerness to accost Ryan.

'I knew it was you! What's your real name again, I've forgotten?'

Only Jess knew the slight tightness at the corner of Ryan's lips signalled annoyance.

'George Clooney,' he replied, oozing charm. The woman laughed hysterically as if this was the funniest thing she'd ever heard. He held his hand out to her. 'It's Ryan, Ryan Hearst. And you are . . . ?'

'Gilly. Gilly Lomax. I live over there –' She pointed to a pretty pink house just outside the railings of the park. 'You're always welcome to pop in.'

'I'm afraid he's very busy.' Jess stepped in. 'I'm his partner.'

'The kettle's always on . . .' Gilly continued talking to

Ryan. 'I think you're marvellous, and all those gorgeous locations you film in. Venice is my favourite. I've been to the Teatro La Fenice, it's so romantic!'

'Ryan, we must go, the dogs are getting tired.' Jess tugged at his jacket sleeve. Not some old charity-shop jacket, but a Prada summer collection number that had cost thousands.

'Sorry, darling.' He smiled at Jess and draped his arm across her shoulders in a show of ownership.

'Oh.' The woman swept a look over Jess, from top to bottom, then returned to Ryan. 'Perhaps your friend wouldn't mind taking a photo of us both on my phone.' She pulled it from her pocket and pushed it into Jess's hand. 'Take a few. Close up.'

'Of course.' Jess watched grimly as the woman cosied up to a willing Ryan, and then proceeded to take a series of photos where she knew the woman either had her eyes shut or her mouth at an unflattering angle. Just for good measure, she made sure the last couple of snaps were out of focus.

'Oh, they're perfect!' she announced, quickly turning the phone off and handing it back before the ghastly Gilly could look at them. 'Lovely to meet you. Come on, Ryan.'

*

They arrived at the park café during a lull between waves of pushchairs, toddlers and exhausted-looking parents. Having bought their coffees they steered their way through the plastic tables until they found a relatively unsticky one in the sunshine. Jess tied Elsie and Ethel's leads to her chair and sat down gratefully.

Ryan took a sip of the scalding and bitter cappuccino

then reached over and squeezed Jess's hand. 'That poor woman. I can't believe you could be so mean. You'll have ruined her day.'

'Well, it made mine. Rude cow. I'm invisible to your fans. They push past me and tread on my toes to get to you. No wonder casting agents reject me – I'm invisible.'

Ryan had heard this lament often enough to know where it was going. He tried to head it off at the pass.

'Not to me you're not.'

'Really?'

'You're my girl.'

'Am I?'

'You sure are.' He took her other hand and gazed soulfully into her eyes, hoping it would have the desired effect.

'Even when you're away with all those gorgeous actresses?' Jess peered at him intently. 'You can tell me the truth, you know. Are you sure you're not tempted?'

'No,' he lied. 'You know me better than that,' he protested, as if wounded by the accusation.

'I thought I knew you,' she said, her voice wavering, 'but that was before . . .'

Oh, not this again, thought Ryan. He pulled one hand away from hers and swept it through the floppy long hair he'd been cultivating for Cosmo.

'Darling, that was five years ago. We are over that, aren't we? I can't believe I was such a fool and nearly lost you. Besides, can you imagine the bad press if I did that now and someone found out?'

This time it was Jess who pulled her hand away.

'That's nice. You're more concerned about the damage to your image than the hurt it would cause me.'

'That's not what I meant,' Ryan sighed, tired of Jess's insecurities. 'What you need is a job. A good job. One that will give you back your confidence. You're a great actress – the best. You're beautiful and clever and—'

'Unemployable.'

Knowing he would have to choose his words carefully or else this would escalate into a full-blown row, Ryan tried to buy himself some thinking time by picking up his cup and taking two large mouthfuls of coffee. Clearly in no mood to let him off the hook, Jess fixed him with a flinty glare and allowed the uncomfortable silence to drag on, broken only by the tap-tap-tap of her foot against the chair leg.

A sudden inspiration came to Ryan's rescue: 'Look, I've got two weeks off before we start filming the second series of *Venini*. Suppose you and I take a break . . . ?'

'Where?'

'How about Thailand? Stay in one of those wonderful spas. Beauty treatments, exercise classes, sunshine . . . We could rent a little hut perched on stilts over the sea, just the two of us, no distractions.'

'I can't afford it.'

'My treat.'

'But I hate living off you.'

Ryan sighed in exasperation, 'Can't I treat you?'

'We'll have to put the girls in kennels, and that's expensive.'

'Oh for God's sake, Jess! The two of us are going on a bloody holiday and you'll bloody well like it – OK?'

2

A balmy breeze was drifting in off the sea, ruffling the hair of the two friends perched on Trevay's old harbour wall. Helen Merrifield and Penny Leighton sat in companionable silence for a moment, luxuriating in the late afternoon sunshine. Cornwall had endured a rotten summer, endless days of cold and wet. Holidaymakers had remained admirably stoic, but the sun waited until late September when the last people-carrier crammed with pale-skinned tourists in soggy anoraks had left the county before putting in an appearance.

Penny stretched her long, tanned legs out in front of her.

'I'd forgotten how good a real tan looks,' she said.

'You look marvellous, Mrs Canter, as always,' Helen replied admiringly.

'I keep telling you: less of the Canter, if you don't mind. No matter what the fuddy-duddies in the parish might think, I'm determined to stick with Miz Penny Leighton – running a successful production company in my own name is my one excuse for not getting sucked into the duties of a vicar's wife!'

Helen found it hard to imagine anyone brave enough to shoehorn Penny into the stereotypical vicar's wife mould. The two of them had met when they were in their early twenties, both working for the BBC; Helen had never progressed beyond secretarial level, having fallen in love and fallen pregnant in short order, but Penny had worked her way up the ladder to director, making her name with an historical drama that became a hit both in the UK and America. Capitalising on her success, she'd set up Penny Leighton Productions and her drive and energy had ensured that even the recession could not prevent the company going from strength to strength. On the romantic front, however, she'd been a disaster, lurching from one unsuitable man to the next. Until she met Simon. The shy, gentle, decent vicar had seemed an unlikely soul mate for Penny, and initially Helen had harboured misgivings about the relationship, but she was delighted to have been proved wrong. The couple had just returned from a holiday to celebrate their first anniversary, both of them positively glowing with happiness.

'Simon was so sweet on the cruise – so romantic. This time yesterday we were just flying out of Venice,' sighed Penny.

'Lucky you. Piran and I could do with a holiday, but he's so busy. All the holidays with Gray seem to have blended into one. I remember usually being the one managing the children while he was off ogling all of the young bathing beauties!'

'Ah, Gray – how is that ex-husband of yours? Any news?'

'According to the kids, Dahlia Dahling is still giving him the runaround. A glamorous grand dame of stage and screen is an entirely different proposition to good old reliable me. I gather it's come as quite a shock to him, being in a relationship with a woman who's accustomed to having her own way.'

'Quite!' Penny smiled at the thought. 'And what have you been up to while I've been gone?'

'You're going to be very impressed with me. Remember what I said about trying my hand at a few articles for the local press? Well, after I'd submitted a bunch of homes and gardens pieces, the *Cornish Guardian* turned round and offered me a weekly column! They want me to write about what's on locally: arts and crafts, shopping, eating out . . . The pay's not great, but it's a start.'

'Oh, bravo you! That'll suit you down to the ground – you've always had a genius for finding the best little cafés and galleries and boutiques, and spotting what's going to be the next big thing.'

'Well, I'd like to think I haven't completely lost my London cool,' Helen returned with mock modesty.

'Better not let the locals hear you say that – they'll hang you out to dry!' They both laughed, but then Penny asked, 'Speaking of locals, how are things with Piran? Still the embodiment of brooding male?'

'Yep.'

'Things are OK, though?'

'Yeah. I know he loves me and I know that if we lived in each other's pockets, or under the same roof, we'd drive each other mad . . .' It struck Helen that she was trying to convince herself as much as her friend. She let out a small sigh and admitted, 'All the same, I wouldn't mind a bit of romance every now and again.'

'I thought he was your dream man – Marco Pierre White and Heathcliffe rolled into one. All broody moody and drop-dead gorgeous with it?'

'He is gorgeous, and my heart still flutters and all those things, but he's just so . . .'

Penny chimed in on the final word: '. . . Piran.' They both grinned.

'He wouldn't be seen dead on a Mediterranean cruise,' said Helen.

'Hardly surprising. One look at Piran and the crew would have him swinging from the yardarm!'

'True, true,' Helen laughed. 'He hasn't had a haircut all summer and he's starting to look even more like Bluebeard than Bluebeard himself!'

'I've got you a present, by the way.' Penny rummaged in her voluminous handbag. 'Here –' She passed over a duty-free carrier bag.

'Ooh, a treat!' Helen pulled out a bottle of her favourite perfume: Cristalle by Chanel. 'Oh, Pen, thank you.' She threw her arm round her friend's tanned shoulders and hugged her. 'I'm going over to Piran's tonight. I'll splash plenty of this on.'

'Who's cooking?'

'Piran. Dinner will be whatever he catches this afternoon.' Helen tucked the bottle of perfume safely into her straw shopping basket before asking, 'By the way, where's Simon?'

'Back at the vicarage. He's going through all his post and emails, and then he's got his sermon to write for Sunday. I thought it better to leave him to it.'

'Did he wear his dog collar on holiday?'

'It took some persuading, but no – thank God. It seems being a vicar is a bit like being a doctor: the minute people find out your profession, particularly in a confined space like a boat, they start coming to you with their problems. He'd have had everyone asking him to marry them, or cast out demons or whatever.'

Helen couldn't suppress a snigger at the thought of Simon casting out demons on a cruise liner. She shook her head in mock reproach. 'Penny, you're an awful vicar's wife.'

'Tell me about it! I keep reminding him that I married him for who he is, not because of his job. The Worst Vicar's Wife in Britain – that's me. Hey, that's a great idea for a programme, let me write it down.' Penny pulled out her iPhone and spent a few moments typing. When she'd finished, she couldn't resist checking her emails. Thanks to the huge success of *Mr Tibbs*, a series based on Mavis Carew's popular crime novels – filmed locally and starring Dahlia Dahling – she was being fêted by TV executives worldwide, eager to get their hands on a second series. She was also being inundated with screenplays and requests from writers and their agents, convinced that Penny Leighton Productions had the Midas touch.

As she checked her emails, the phone rang and she answered it.

'Hello, Simon. I'm in Trevay with Helen . . . No, I haven't seen the paper . . . The local one? . . . OK . . . I'll get it now . . . Why? . . . Oh! What do they expect you to do? . . . Me? . . . Let me look at it and then we can talk later . . . Love you too, bye.'

'What was that about?' asked Helen.

'Something about saving the Pavilions. Let's get a paper and I'll buy you a coffee . . . maybe even a glass of vino.'

*

Piran Ambrose was in his office at the Trevay Museum, hurrying to finish the day's tasks so that he could get out in his boat and catch the tide for a spot of mackerel fishing. He swore under his breath when the phone on his desk rang, his hand hovering over the receiver indecisively before picking up.

'Yes.'

'Piran? It's me, Simon.'

Piran breathed a sigh of relief. He and the vicar had been friends for many years, supporting each other through some difficult times.

'Simon! Welcome home, how was the holiday with your maid?'

'Simply wonderful. Marriage is to be recommended, Piran.'

Piran decided to ignore the obvious implications in this comment. 'How can I help you, Simon?'

'It's the Pavilions – there's a report in the paper that the council are about to sell the place to a coffee chain. Possibly Café Au Lait.'

'Good idea. The building is falling apart. It needs money spending on it, or knocking down.'

Simon was shocked. 'You can't mean that? You're our local historian – surely you of all people want to save the old place?'

Piran put one leg up on his desk and tipped his chair back, glancing at the clock on the wall. If he didn't get a move on he'd miss the tide. 'It's an eyesore, Simon. We're not talking about some Frank Matcham theatre of distinction here. The Pavilions is a fifties, flat-roof, jerry-built dinosaur that hasn't made any money in decades.'

'But the Sea Scouts and the WI and . . . the Trevay Players . . .'

Piran sniffed with disdain at the mention of the local amateur dramatic company.

'. . . and the Arts and Crafts Show, and . . . er . . .'

'Exactly. It's not exactly a top-drawer venue, is it?'

'Piran, please. I've already had emails from all sorts of

people asking me to be on the board of an action committee. I thought you might want to lend us your support, maybe dig out some facts of historical importance.'

Piran scratched his beard and pulled on the gold hoop in his ear. 'OK. Let me think about it.'

'I knew you'd help.'

'Hang on, I haven't said I'd help. I've said I'll think about it.'

The men rang off, each hoping the other would see sense. Swinging his leg off the desk and springing to his feet, Piran hurried out of his office before the phone had a chance to ring again.

Down in the lobby, Janet, the museum receptionist, was so engrossed in her newspaper that she didn't look up until he called, 'Bye, Janet. I'm finished for the day. See you tomorrow.'

'Piran, sorry I didn't hear you. I was reading this –' She held up the front page so he could read the headline:

THE END FOR THE PAVILIONS?

'I'd be ever so sad to see the old place go. My parents used to take me there every summer to see the big shows. Remember when Morecambe and Wise had a season here? Sold out every night. They were on the same bill as . . . oh what were they called . . . The Bachelors, that's it! Lovely boys, they were. Great music.'

'Not exactly The Beatles, were they?' sniffed Piran, unimpressed. 'Not my thing, Janet, see you tomorrow.'

Janet persisted, 'But it's heartbreaking. There'll be a lot of people with a lot of memories.'

'It's a white elephant and an architectural mess.'

Leaving Janet shaking her head in disbelief he stamped

out of the door with Jack, his devoted Jack Russell, scampering behind him.

*

Out on the balcony of the Sail Loft, the new wine bar overlooking the inner harbour, Penny was reading the paper too, with Helen squinting over her shoulder at the photos.

'It's rather a sweet building, isn't it?' she said.

'If you like the garish fifties Festival of Britain look,' snorted Penny.

'That was a great era,' protested Helen. 'The war was over. Rationing was coming to an end. Women could wear full skirts and feminine clothes again.'

'And Trevay built the Pavilions.' Penny began to read aloud. 'It says here, "*The opening summer season in 1954 ran for twelve weeks. Local man, Walter Irvine, was the first theatre manager. He called in favours from stars he'd worked with before the war, including top comedian Max Miller. Miller, best known for his risqué jokes, topped the bill and made the theatre one of the most successful entertainment venues of its day. It's hard to imagine that now. The building is succumbing to half a century of Atlantic gales battering it from all sides on its prominent position on the Trevay headland. It is thought that the new owners may be Café Au Lait, the coffee chain well known for buying up buildings of interest and investing multimillions in redevelopment. Could they be the Pavilions' saviour? Have your say: email your thoughts to . . .* blah blah blah."' Penny closed the paper and picked up her glass of wine. 'Another lost cause for Simon to get involved with.'

Helen chinked her glass with Penny's. 'Welcome home!'

They sat without speaking, enjoying their own thoughts and easy in each other's company. Helen's eyes wandered up to the headland and the familiar outline of the Pavilions. From this distance it looked rather grand. Onion domes either side of the grand entrance, silvered central cupola above the auditorium and the tall fly tower behind. The building was still painted in its sugared-almond colours of pale blue, pink and yellow, albeit now cracked and faded. It was in a good location, away from the ancient narrow streets of Trevay, with the spectacular backdrop of the Atlantic Ocean behind it. With all that open space it had the benefit of a large car park (now used for car boot sales) and no neighbours to complain about noisy late-night exoduses.

Helen sipped on her chilled glass of wine and shifted her focus back to the harbour. The tide was high but on its way out. She looked along the floating pontoons to the spot where Piran kept his boat tied up. It was still there. He'd better hurry if he was going to catch supper and get back before low tide. Then she saw him; his familiar gait, slightly bow-legged in his faded, shabby jeans, but very attractive. His arms hung loosely by his sides, the wind ruffling his long dark curls, lifting them to reveal the grey at his temples. His hands, nut brown, were pulled from the pockets of his salt-stained fisherman's smock in order to pick up little Jack and help him into the boat. Helen smiled as Jack went straight to the bow and put his paws up on the ledge, almost like a living figurehead.

'Look, there's Piran,' said Penny.

'Mmm, I saw him. I wonder what he'll say about this Pavilions business?'

'He'll be all for saving the place, I should think. As the local historian, he's bound to be part of this action committee Simon was talking about. I've a sinking feeling that this campaign is going to be the bane of both our lives if we're not careful.'

*

'Hi, honey, I'm hoooome!' sang Penny as she shut the front door of the vicarage behind her.

'I'm in the kitchen, Pen.'

'I hope the kettle's on.' Penny walked into her kitchen and had the wind taken out of her sails when she found several familiar, if not entirely welcome, faces round her table.

Penny furrowed her brow slightly at the sight of Audrey Tipton's determined features peering at her sternly over a teacup.

'Audrey, Geoff, what an unexpected pleasure!' Penny oozed, with as much sincerity as she could muster, only to be greeted by a tight-lipped nod from Audrey.

'Pen, Queenie, Geoff, Audrey and I are debating what, if anything, we can do to save the Pavilions.'

Penny dropped a few teabags into the pot. 'I guessed as much.' She nodded her head slowly. A woman of indeterminable age (somewhere between fifty-five and seventy-five was Penny's best guess) and indomitable disposition, Audrey Tipton was a powerhouse in tweed. She was chairwoman of the Pendruggan village Women's Institute, the church flower committee and the Village in Bloom committee. Her husband, Geoff, was widely referred to behind his back as Mr Audrey Tipton, due to his total subservience to his wife.

Next to Geoff sat Queenie, owner of the only shop in the village and a gold-medal gossip who couldn't bear to be left out of anything, which explained her presence at the table.

'Hello, Queenie!' Penny stooped to give the friendliest of the faces a kiss, and got a damp whiskery one in return.

''Ello, me duck. Coo, you look like you've caught the sun. 'Ow was yer second 'oneymoon?' She gave one of her crackly tobacco-induced laughs and nudged Simon's elbow. 'She looks like you gave 'er a proper good time, an' no mistake!'

Simon turned a deep shade of pink at this, but Penny merely grinned and set about filling the kettle. 'Don't you go embarrassing my husband, Queenie. You are a very naughty woman.'

Desperate to steer the conversation away from his personal life and back to the matter in hand, Simon cleared his throat. 'As I was saying, we're having a meeting about what can be done to save the Pavilions.'

Audrey Tipton fixed Penny with a challenging stare. 'You got here at just the right moment. We've decided that you are critical to our campaign.'

'Oh?' replied Penny coolly.

Audrey was not to be intimidated. 'Yes. As you move in the world of "celebrities"' – this was accompanied by an unpleasant little smirk, which her husband dutifully mirrored – 'you can organise a troupe of actors to come down and put on some sort of event to raise the profile of the campaign.'

'Ah, I see. Would you like me to phone Judi Dench and David Attenborough now, or shall I wait until tomorrow?' Penny gave a sweet smile and plonked a plate of HobNobs on the table.

'This is no laughing matter, Mrs Canter. May I remind

you that without the co-operation of this village, your *Mr Tibbs Mysteries* series would never have got off the ground.' She turned to her husband and commanded: 'Geoffrey, pour me a cup of tea.' Then her icy gaze returned to Penny. 'If you weren't the vicar's wife, the whole exercise would have been doomed to fail.'

Penny gritted her teeth and reminded herself that as the vicar's wife she had a duty to be civil to parishioners, no matter how trying they might be. 'Audrey, the series was conceived long before I became the vicar's wife. There's more to a successful series than—'

'That may well be the case,' Audrey cut her off huffily. 'But without the goodwill and co-operation of the villagers, you would find it very difficult indeed to do your shooting. I do have some influence, you know,' she added ominously.

Penny felt anger rise in her. She was vaguely conscious of Simon and Geoff holding their breath, and Queenie leaning forward as if she was hoping Penny would give in to temptation and crown Audrey with the teapot. Instead she set the teapot carefully on the table and enquired in a calm, cool voice, 'Are you blackmailing me, Mrs Tipton?'

'Not at all, not at all!' trilled Mrs Tipton, pushing back her chair and standing up. 'I'm just stating the facts, that's all. Come along, Geoffrey, it's time for your dinner.'

As Audrey swept out regally, her submissive husband trailing in her wake, Penny turned to Simon and threw her hands in the air, 'Oh the life of a vicar's wife!'

'For better or for worse, darling,' Simon reminded her.

'Don't push your luck, sunshine!' growled Penny.

3

Ollie Pinkerton was feeling good. The gym was buzzing today and his pre-breakfast workout had gone well. He zipped up his jeans, checked his gelled hair in the changing-room mirror and hefted his sports bag onto his shoulder.

Out in the members' lounge he queued for a skinny mochaccino.

'Hi, Ollie. What can I get you?' asked the smiling woman behind the counter.

'The usual, please, Lou. You still on for tonight's show?'

It was Lou's silver wedding anniversary and he had given her a couple of complimentary tickets for *The Merry Wives of Windsor* at Stratford's RSC.

'Oooh, yes. Graeme and I are really looking forward to it. You sure it's OK?' Ever so kind of you. We couldn't afford those prices.'

'My pleasure.' Ollie gave her his winning beam of a smile. He hadn't bothered to tell her that the tickets were comps. 'We'll be nicely warmed up for you after this afternoon's matinee,' he said, opening his wallet to pay for the coffee.

'No, no, Ollie. On the house.'

He trousered the five-pound note speedily and thanked her. Just because he was an actor with the Royal Shakespeare Company didn't mean he was minted.

Collecting his coffee he threaded his way through clusters of tables and chairs to an empty two-seater brown leather sofa in front of a huge television screen showing highlights of a tennis tournament.

On the seat next to him was a copy of the *Daily Mail*. He flicked through it, only half engaged, until he saw a large photo of himself with a girl who wasn't his girlfriend. *Shit*. The headline blared '*Still Seeing Red, Ollie?*' Shit shit shit.

His phone began to vibrate in his back pocket. He pulled it out, wincing when he saw the caller ID, his pocket rocket rock star girlfriend, 'Red'.

'Hi, babe,' he said, trying to keep his voice neutral. 'Didn't expect to hear from you this early. How's Sydney? How's the show?'

'How am I supposed to do a show when my boyfriend is shagging around?' was Red's blisteringly chilly response.

'What are you talking about?'

'Henrik just showed me the Mail Online.'

Ollie resisted the urge to swear. Red's smarmy PA seemed to think the best way to ingratiate himself with Red and worm his way into her good books was to make her suspicious of everyone else. Unfortunately, he'd succeeded; Red wouldn't hear a word against the little creep. When Ollie had been unwise enough to joke that Henrik was more PITA than PA, she'd turned on him, demanding, 'What the hell's that supposed to mean?'

'You know, Pain In The Arse – PITA. It's a joke.'

'Another of your stupid public schoolboy jokes, eh? Well, forgive me and my Wolverhampton comprehensive school denseness. Oh no, hang on – I'm not that dense, am I? I'm sixty-seventh on the *Sunday Times* Rich List,

I'm number one in fourteen countries and I have an entourage of eight, including Henrik my *PA*.'

As a result, Ollie kept his opinion of Henrik's latest helpful gesture to himself and instead tried to explain, but Red wasn't listening.

'I'm going to have to cancel the show tonight,' she wailed. 'I can't go on stage knowing what an unfaithful shit you are.' She was so loud, he held the phone away from his ear. Noticing people on nearby tables casting curious glances in his direction, he tried to muffle the sounds coming from the earpiece while holding the phone close to his mouth.

'Red, honey, I love you. It's just a picture of some girl who saw the show last night and was waiting at the stage door for an autograph. She was with her fiancée. He took the photo.'

'Oh yeah? Then how come it got into the papers?'

'I don't know. Maybe he uploaded it to Twitter or . . . maybe he sold it. I don't know, honey. You have to believe me – I don't even know her name. An autograph, a photo and then it was home to bed, on my own, dreaming of you.'

'Yeah?' she snivelled.

'Yeah.'

'So, you'd be pleased to see me if I jumped on a plane tonight and came home?'

He felt a tap on his shoulder and looked round. One of the young actresses in the cast of *The Merry Wives of Windsor*, damp from a swim, was miming a cup of coffee. He shook his head, pointed to the phone and raised his eyebrows in despair. She nodded, pulling the corners of her mouth down comically, and went to the bar.

'Ollie, are you still there?' Red's shrill voice boomed from the earpiece.

'Yeah, yeah, sorry, there must have been some dropout on the satellite . . . I missed what you said.' He hoped she'd forgotten what she had said.

There was a pause while she smothered the mouthpiece and spoke to someone at the other end. He couldn't catch what she was saying, and was straining to make out the words when her voice suddenly came back loud and clear: 'You don't know the pressure I'm under here. There's thirty-two thousand people out there, and just because they've had to wait a bit they're booing. They don't know how you're breaking my heart.'

'How long have they been waiting?'

'Not long. Maybe two hours.'

'You've kept them waiting two hours?'

'No. *You've* kept them waiting two hours by being such a shit to me.' Someone was calling to her in the background. She muted the phone for a moment, then came back on the line. 'OK, OK, I have to go. I'll Skype you later. We need to talk.'

'Yeah, honey.' He groaned inwardly. 'I love talking. Now go get 'em, tiger!'

Gemma, his actress friend, thumped down next to him, licking a splash of coffee from her wrist.

'"Go get 'em, tiger"?' She arched a sardonic eyebrow. 'Sooo rock'n'roll.'

'Oh, Gem, this long-distance, high-profile relationship stuff is not for cissies.'

Gemma took a sip of her cappuccino and wiped the froth from her lips with the tiny paper napkin. 'Any kind of relationship would do me at the moment.'

'Look at this.' He handed her the newspaper.

'Ah.' She read the text. 'Nice photo.'

'Thank you.'

'Not you. The mystery girl. She's very pretty.'

He snatched the paper from her and dropped it on the floor by his feet. 'You're not being very helpful.' They sat and watched the tennis players on the screen for a few moments, then Ollie asked. 'Are you a jealous person, Gemma?'

'I haven't had enough boyfriends to find out. Maybe I haven't loved anyone enough to care. Don't you get jealous of Red? All those male groupies hanging outside her hotels and following her around the world?'

'No.'

'You don't love her enough then.'

'It's not that. I'm just not the jealous type. She wouldn't do anything. She doesn't get the opportunity on tour, anyway. She's surrounded by her hangers-on and hustled from airport to hotel to stadium to hotel to airport. I've seen it. Our first date was at the O2. I went to watch her from the wings.'

'Great date. Intimate.'

'Shut up.'

'Just saying.'

'Yeah, well anyway, I watched her give her heart and soul to the audience. The way she worked with the band and her dancers, she blew me away. Then the minute she's sung her last note she takes her bow and runs off stage. Her dresser is waiting with a big warm dressing gown to wrap her in. Her assistant dresser is waiting with a huge towel to wrap round her sweaty hair and then she's just like, whoosh, straight through a path made for her by Security, past all the backstage crew and out into a blacked-out limo. The band will still be playing. The crowd will still be chanting. The police will have closed the exit roads for a five-minute window to get her out, and in ten minutes she'll be in her hotel room watching a late-night movie, all on her own.'

'No wonder she's bonkers.'

'It's tough on her. She's only twenty-four. She's been a star for three years, since she blew the world away on *The X Factor*. The world wants to know everything about her.'

'And you.'

Ollie's face clouded over. 'I hate it.'

'Lots of actors would give anything to get their profile as high as yours. Why not go with the flow and enjoy the ride?'

'I don't want to be famous as a "celebrity boyfriend". I want my work as an actor to speak for me.'

'Get over yourself! We're all a bunch of children dancing in front of our parents: *Look at me, Mummy. Look at me!*'

Ollie couldn't help but laugh. 'OK, perhaps there's a bit of that. But I still want a private life and a private relationship with my girlfriend, but that's not likely to happen when there's a fortune to be made selling photos of us. The irony of it is, while the paps are cashing in, I'm skint.' Gemma nodded with understanding. You worked for the RSC for kudos, not cash. 'Red expects me to fly out and join her whenever I have a break, but the transatlantic flights and hotels are cleaning me out.'

'Have you told her that?'

'I can't – she'd offer to pick up the bill, and I don't want that. I could never be a freeloader.'

Gemma patted his knee. 'You're too noble for your own good, that's your trouble. Want to walk with me back to the theatre?'

'No, I've got some stuff to do.'

'OK see you later.'

Ollie watched as Gemma made her way to the exit. The 'stuff' he had to do – calling in at the dry cleaners for his shirts, stopping by the cashpoint to draw some money – wouldn't have prevented him walking back to the theatre with her. The real problem was that he couldn't risk being photographed with Gemma; that would only lead to another row with Red.

Outside, the sun was surprisingly warm and tourists were wandering happily along the Stratford-upon-Avon high street, stopping, with little or no warning, whenever something in a shop window took their fancy. Ollie cursed under his breath as he employed all his navigational skills to avoid tripping over them.

His call with Red had annoyed him. Lately, all his calls with Red annoyed him. She was a great girl. Funny, pretty, great body, talented, never there. It was the *never there* bit that messed things up. They'd met when she'd come to see him in a fringe production of Joe Orton's *Loot*. He'd had the best reviews of his life and it was a game-changer for him. The production was the hottest ticket in town. He'd heard backstage that Red was in the audience; she was already huge in the UK but hadn't quite gone global. Back then it had just been a matter of dodging the paparazzi, which meant she was still able to enjoy the odd night out.

After the performance, he'd received a sweet handwritten note in red ink on the back of a fag packet:

Fancy dodging the paps with me after the show? Rx

They'd slipped out of a side entrance, just the two of them, and managed to hole up in a tiny bar, blissfully unrecognised, while her minders parked up nearby. She made him laugh, she seemed kind, genuine, in touch with her roots. The connection was instant. She told him about her upbringing in the Midlands, how hard it had been on her family, enduring the constant attention after *The X Factor*. He told her about his father walking out when he was just a kid, how he'd never really fitted in at public school, and how much he wanted to become a good actor. Their lives were different but something really clicked between them that night.

But no sooner had they got together than her star had gone stratospheric.

Ollie was twenty-eight. He loved life. Fifteen months ago he'd had a great social life, but all that had closed down for him. Thanks to Red and her fame. A big fat problem. Did he love her enough to accept it? Was she The One? He knew that she was the most exciting woman he'd ever known . . . so far . . . But in the time that he'd known her, she'd changed. The stress of her lifestyle had taken its toll. And the initial excitement of their relationship had been replaced by a kind of prison . . . That was it, he had lost his freedom . . . and she was losing herself.

He stopped walking and stared at the swans floating elegantly on the river by the theatre. They were free. Free and wild. One of them got out of the water and waggled up to him, hoping for food.

'Sorry, mate. Nothing for you.'

He stood still while the large bird pecked fruitlessly at the chewing gum stains on the path, then stood tall, looking at him in disappointment, before giving a shake of its feathers and wandering off forlornly. Ollie saw the tag round one slender black ankle.

'Not wild after all, boy, eh? Tagged, same as me.' He shook his head. 'Oh, to be free again.'

*

The matinee went well. The audience of GCSE students were attentive and seemed to enjoy the story. At the curtain calls one young female voice called out, 'Ollie, I love you' as he took his bow. He smiled and gave a wave, which provoked another shout: 'Send my love to Red!' One of the grander old actors sighed with utter disdain and walked off before the curtain came down.

*

Back in his dressing room, Ollie was sitting with his head in his hands, wondering how he'd got into such a mess, when there was a knock at the door.

'Ah, Ollie – may I have a word?' Nigel the company manager licked his wispy moustache.

'Yeah, Nige. Come in.' Ollie leaned over and took his costume off the spare chair. 'Sit down.'

Nigel carried on standing.

'This is a bit awkward, but . . . your young fans. We appreciate you can't, *we* can't, stop them from calling out, but could you not acknowledge them?'

Ollie slumped back in his chair. 'Who's complained?'

'Er, it's not a complaint as such. More a request for some respect towards your fellow artistes.'

'Sir Terry? Is that why he walked off before the tabs came in?'

'I'm not going to name names, that would be too sordid. The fact is you're a young actor sharing the stage with colleagues who deserve your respect and that of the audience.'

'Sir Terry it is then.'

'Possibly.'

'The Knight', as he was nicknamed, was a grand old gay actor; charming, knowledgeable and with a seemingly bottomless fund of outrageous stories. He'd first joined the RSC in the early fifties, working with Olivier, Gielgud and Richardson. He was theatrical royalty and if he found a company member to be *upsetting*, that company member would never work with him again. Sir Terry had been considered the box office draw of the season, but as the weeks went by it was becoming clear that young Ollie Pinkerton, hitherto unknown jobbing actor but now a celebrity as a result of his relationship with rock star Red, was the one pulling in the punters.

Ollie took a deep breath and stood up. 'Nigel, I quite understand. And, as a matter of courtesy, I shall apologise to The Knight right away.'

'Thank you, Ollie. You will make my life, and indeed your own life, much happier if you do so.'

4

Piran, gutting half a dozen fresh mackerel with a vengeance, was clearly in a bad mood.

'I'm an historian. Anything after the Second World War is of no interest to me. The Pavilions could slide into the sea and I wouldn't give a toss.' He slapped a fillet into a plate of flour. 'Unless it uncovered an Iron Age settlement or bloody King Arthur's Camelot – which doesn't exist, by the way – I'm not interested.'

His two cats, Bosun and Sprat, were winding themselves round his feet waiting for scraps. He chucked down a couple of fish skins.

Helen, who had rolled her shirtsleeves up and was busily covering the fish fillets in flour, patting them gently before placing them on a clean tea towel ready for the frying pan, turned to him crestfallen. 'I hate that Camelot wasn't real. Are you sure?'

'Aye.'

'But there was an Arthur, wasn't there?'

'There's no evidence, no.' Piran carried on focusing on the job in hand, his curls bouncing over his forehead as his strong weathered hands dexterously removed the last remaining bones.

'So no Guinevere?'

Piran slapped the final fillet on the plate in front of her and pushed his hair out of his eyes with the back of his wrist. 'No – thank God. She was supposed to have broken his heart, wasn't she? Ran off with his best mate. Typical bloody woman!'

'Typical chauvinist comment.'

He stuck his sharp knife, point down, into the wood of his kitchen table so that it quivered like an arrow. 'I'm making you supper, aren't I?'

Helen opened her eyes wide and cooed, 'You are one hundred per cent new man! Would you pour me a glass of wine?'

He glowered at her for a moment then kissed her nose. 'Don't go pushing your luck, maid.'

*

The mackerel were delicious, served simply with hunks of buttered crusty bread and large tumblers of local cider. Helen got up, threw the bones in the bin and made a move to put the plates in the sink but Piran reached up and stopped her. 'Don't bother with those. They'll keep till the morning.' He found her hand and she felt the roughness of his skin on her palm. 'You smell nice. Are you staying tonight?'

'Would you like me to?'

'I'm not going to beg. Your decision, Helen.'

'Sometimes I'd like you to beg.'

'I thought you didn't want to feel crowded, that you liked your independence.'

'I do . . .' An image of Gull's Cry, the dream cottage that she'd made a reality, flitted through her mind. Once the children had flown the nest, she'd realised that she couldn't go on sharing a Chiswick townhouse with her philandering husband. So she'd asked Gray for a divorce and uprooted herself to Pendruggan. She'd settled in so well, it was hard to believe only two years had gone by since she moved in. And after years of playing housekeeper and homemaker to her family, it was a luxury to be free to do her own thing.

She was brought back to the present by Piran squeezing her hand. 'Something tells me there's a "but . . . " coming,' he said.

'No – well, sort of. I do like my independence, but that doesn't mean I wouldn't appreciate a bit of spontaneous passion now and again.'

'Why are women so bloody contrary?' growled Piran in mock exasperation. 'If it's passion you want, maid, I'll sling you over my shoulder and carry you upstairs.'

'Oooh, would you – right now?'

Her laughter echoed up the stairs as Piran made good on his threat.

*

Piran's bed was a big old wooden thing, made, he said, out of the wreckage of a fishing boat that had run aground years before. It was the most comfortable bed Helen had ever known. She stretched herself out then curled herself around Piran as he slept with his back to her. Bosun and Sprat lifted their heads as they were gently bobbed about on a sea of tartan blanket, waiting for her to settle. When she was finally still, they put their heads down and curled their tails round their noses. Piran mumbled something.

Helen lifted her head slightly, the better to hear him. 'What did you say?'

He spoke a little louder.

'I said, What time is it, cloth ears.'

'Seven fifteen.'

'Want a cup of tea?'

'Yes please.'

For a big man he moved with a fluidity that never failed to amaze her. She watched as he bent down and picked up his discarded T-shirt from the night before, then sat on the edge of the bed to pull it over his head. As all men do, he looked faintly ridiculous and even vulnerable as he stood up displaying his naked lower half. He checked his testicles unconsciously, before shuffling his feet into an ancient pair of leather slippers and reaching for an equally ancient dressing gown that had been draped over a chair.

Bosun and Sprat's ears pricked up, their eyes watchful in case this was a false alarm or whether it was looking good for breakfast. At the words 'Come on, boys' they both sprang off the bed and followed their owner downstairs.

Helen sank back into the tangle of soft cotton sheets and blankets (Piran was never going to be a duvet man) and closed her eyes. She could hear him talking to the cats and the scrape of their food bowls as he placed them on the tiled floor of the kitchen. She could hear the whoosh of the water from the tap as he filled the kettle, and then the radio came on, tuned to the local news. With a sigh she snuggled into the pillow and was almost drifting back into sleep when she heard a loud 'Oh, for chrissake!' and the sound of Piran's footsteps marching towards the bottom of the stairs.

'Helen, come down here. They're on the bloody radio.'

'Who?' she called back, but he had returned to the kitchen and was out of earshot.

Hurriedly pulling on one of Piran's old shirts, she made her way to the kitchen. He was standing at the counter, staring at the battered radio and listening intently.

'What . . . ?' she asked.

'Shhh.'

She shut up and listened.

It seemed to be a phone-in. Pam, the show's presenter, was talking to a female caller:

Caller: The point is, Pam, this is an important and much-loved part of our heritage. The community still uses the Pavilions building and it mustn't be allowed to fall into the hands of some global coffee chain.

Pam: This wouldn't have anything to do with the fact that you run three of Trevay's cafés and you don't want the competition?

Caller: It's not about money. It's about what the Pavilions means to us as a community.

Pam: And when did you last go to the Pavilions?

Caller: That theatre is a piece of Trevay history and should continue to be so.

Pam: When did you last buy a ticket to attend an event there?

Caller: That's irrelevant. It's not a matter of when I last went or when you last—

Pam: I last went six months ago, to an antiques fair. I was shocked at the state of the place. It reeks of damp, the window frames are rusted, some of the panes of glass are cracked and boarded up. It needs a lot of money spending on it. Café Au Lait taking over might just be the best thing that could happen to the Pavilions. Let's see what the caller on line two has to say.

Second caller: Good morning, Pam. My name is Mrs Audrey Tipton. I have lived in Pendruggan for the last forty years. It's a quiet, unspoiled village with a strong community—

Pam: Audrey, do you think the Pavilions should be preserved as a theatre?

Audrey: Well, yes, that's my point. Trevay is a ten-minute drive from my house in Pendruggan and offers everything I need for shopping and entertainment. The Pavilions should be fully restored by the council so that it will once again be the top attraction for our summer visitors.

Pam: The council say it's a white elephant they can no longer afford. Café Au Lait promise that their redevelopment of the site will not only attract more visitors to the area, it will guarantee jobs for local people. That's a good thing, surely?

Audrey: I have started an action group with several high-profile local supporters and we will fight the council all the way.

Pam: You've got a fighting fund, have you?

Audrey: We are establishing one right now with the help of a local television producer – Penny Leighton. She's our vicar's wife and very hands-on with local issues. Also Piran Ambrose—

Pam: A local historian we know well here at Cornwall Radio.

Audrey: Indeed. Piran has assured the action group that he can prove the historical importance of the Pavilions and—

Audrey was cut off mid-flow by Piran pulling the plug. Pointing at the now-silent radio in frustration, he turned to Helen. 'That bloody Tipton woman! I have assured her blasted action group of no such thing – I haven't even been approached by them. And if she had bloody well approached me . . .'

Leaving him ranting at the kitchen sink, punctuating each sentence by slinging one of yesterday's dinner plates noisily into the bowl, Helen picked up her coffee and tiptoed back to bed.

*

Piran wasn't the only one left apoplectic by Audrey's comments. Over at the vicarage, Penny was pacing up and down the kitchen in a fury.

'How can she be allowed to say that stuff? Now she's put my name out there, people will think I'm committed to the cause.'

Simon ran a hand over his balding head and ventured tentatively, 'I know she's put you in a terrible position, darling, but . . .' his chocolate eyes took on a pleading look. 'I'm sure you could phone a few of your actor friends to help, couldn't you?'

'It's not as simple as that. These people have lives of their own and busy diaries. Plus they're swamped with requests to do something for nothing. No – I can't do it. I won't. Besides, what time do I have to get involved? We're about to start filming the Tibbs series – I won't have a moment to call my own until that's done and dusted.'

'I see.' Simon's expression hovered somewhere between expectation and disappointment.

'Now don't give me that look.' Penny hated letting down her loving and devoted husband, especially when he asked so little of her.

He turned away. 'Well, I must get on. Things to do.'

Penny could feel the hot itch of guilt and duty creeping

up the back of her neck. Bloody Pavilions, what did any of it have to do with her?

'Oh, all right,' she sighed.

Simon's face lit up and he stepped forward to kiss her, but she restrained him with a gentle hand on his chest.

'No, darling, I'm not saying I'll do it. I'm saying all right, I'll think about it.'

'Really?' He beamed at her in delight. 'Oh, Pen, I knew you wouldn't let us down.'

'No promises, Simon. This won't be easy and I'm not a miracle worker.'

'Oh yes you are,' said Simon, giving her a hug before heading off to prepare for morning service.

'And don't forget,' Penny called after him, 'I'm doing this for you, not Audrey bloody Tipton!'

*

In the Tiptons' kitchen, Geoffrey was dutifully congratulating his wife. 'Well done, Audrey. You were magnificent.'

'Thank you, Geoffrey.'

'When did you get Piran on board?'

'I haven't actually spoken to him – Simon was supposed to do that, but he went about it in his usual wishy-washy way and got a wishy-washy response in return. He can't go backing out of it now though, can he!' she announced smugly.

'Aud, you're a genius!' Geoffrey was about to say more but was interrupted by the phone ringing. He lifted the receiver: 'Good morning, Tipton residence – Geoffrey Tipton speaking.'

An angry voice growled, 'Is your meddling wife there?'

'Excuse me, but who is calling?'

'Piran Ambrose.'

Geoffrey felt a squirt of fear in his stomach. 'I'll just get her for you.' Thrusting the phone at his wife as if it were a hot potato, he whispered, 'It's Piran – he wants a word.'

Audrey's lips, stained with carmine matte lipstick, curled in something approximating a grin. 'So, the mountain has finally come to Audrey Tipton,' she said, sotto voce, holding out an imperious hand for the receiver.

*

Piran's truck rattled loudly as he hit a lump of dry mud, left by the tyres of some long-gone tractor. 'That woman thinks she's Margaret Thatcher. She's touched in the head! "No, no, no, Mr Ambrose –"' Helen was reduced to giggles by his booming attempt to emulate Audrey Tipton's dominating voice – '"We are not going to let the Pavilions go without a fight, Mr Ambrose." I'll give 'er a fight, all right.'

Despite his protestations, it looked to Helen as though Audrey had indeed got the better of Piran – for now.

They were on their way to the Pavilions, where Audrey had organised an emergency press conference.

They pulled up in the car park, its once smooth tarmac now a craze of cracks, rudimentary repairs and an astonishingly lovely display of willowherb gently going to seed.

A small crowd had formed on the steps to the theatre. Audrey was standing on the top step, and as Helen and Piran approached they could hear her penetrating voice, hectoring the group and one man in particular.

'Councillor Bedford, you call yourself a man of principle, a man of Cornwall – nay, of Trevay. We, on the other hand, call you "Liar"!'

'Now steady on, Mrs Tipton.' Councillor Bedford, a pugnacious man in his forties, squared up to her. 'This is all a storm in a coffee cup! I want the best for the community. If the council comes to a satisfactory agreement with Café Au Lait, the Pavilions will have a new lease of life and there will be many more jobs for local people.'

There was a smattering of applause from the crowd. Audrey quelled them with a look. 'So, we have traitors in the ranks, do we? We think a few jobs and the loss of an important community facility is OK, do we?' The crowd shuffled and looked at their feet.

Helen, standing a short distance away, was distracted by the arrival of a small white car containing the journalist from the *Trevay Times* and a photographer. She nudged Piran, but failed to get his attention as he was listening to Councillor Bedford, who was beginning to lose his rag.

'*Mrs Tipton*, if you or any of your followers had bothered to look after this building, to use it and support it over the last decades, we wouldn't be in this situation. People like you are hypocrites. If you hadn't sat idly by, this theatre could have been saved years ago.'

'How dare you speak to my wife that way, you insolent pipsqueak!' Mr Audrey weighed in. 'I demand an apology.'

'You're not getting one,' snarled Councillor Bedford. He turned to the wider audience: 'You have five weeks from today to come up with a viable business plan for this place. After that, the council's negotiations with Café Au Lait enter the formal stages of agreement. Good day to you all and good luck.'

''ang on a minute, Councillor.' Piran moved to bar his way. 'What will you and Café Au Lait be agreeing on? There are rules to follow about this sort of thing –

planning applications, consultation with local businesses and residents, public hearings . . . Seems to me like Café Au Lait are being given a fast track through the back door.'

Councillor Bedford looked Piran up and down with contempt and spoke at a level only the two of them could hear. 'Oh dear,' he hissed. 'She's got our eminent local historian involved now, has she? You'll find, Ambrose, that there are no flies on me. Oppose our plans and things could get tricky the next time you want the council to do something for you. Without easy access to archaeological sites and public records, you might find it that much harder to do your job. So think twice before you try making my job harder.'

'Are you threatening me?' growled Ambrose, moving in closer, fists clenched. 'Mess with me and I'll soon sort you out.'

'First slander and now threats,' trumpeted Bedford. 'What a charmless bunch of no brainers this "Save the Pavilions" brigade is turning out to be.'

'I'm warning you, Bedford – any funny business over this Café Au Lait deal and I'll be on to you so fast you won't know what's hit you.'

Councillor Bedford leered up into Piran's face.

'Watch. This. Space. Yokel.'

The punch was so swift it took everyone by surprise.

As Councillor Bedford sprawled on the moth-eaten tarmac, Piran, rubbing his knuckles, turned to address the wide-eyed bystanders.

'Sorry about that. Just tidying up a bit of unwanted rubbish. I'll do some research on the old place and see if it is worth saving.' He turned to the *Trevay Times* reporter. 'Wayne, can we count on you to dig around and find out what this little shit' – he pointed at a winded Councillor Bedford, who had picked himself up and was now tentatively checking his nose for damage – 'and his cronies are up to.'

Wayne grinned and gave him the thumbs up. 'You can count on me, Piran. Nothing like a bit of local dirt to boost circulation!'

But as soon as Bedford saw the reporter making a beeline for him, he did a sharp about turn and began trotting in the direction of his car. Wayne was immediately waylaid by Audrey Tipton, who launched into a lengthy diatribe about multinational conglomerates riding rough-shod over small communities. By the time he'd managed to extricate himself, the crowd had dispersed and there was no one left to interview. As things stood, the best he could hope for was a couple of paragraphs on page seven – or so he thought, until his photographer excitedly beckoned him over.

'Hey, Wayne, look at this!'

Wayne leaned over his colleague's shoulder and peered at the LCD display on the back of the camera. It showed a perfect shot of Piran's fist connecting with Councillor Bedford's nose. Wayne's face lit up.

'Looks like we got our front page!'

5

Helen hurried through the front door and made straight for the telephone, not even stopping to take off her coat. As she hit speed-dial and waited impatiently for an answer, her eyes fell to the bag of shopping dumped at her feet with that week's edition of the *Trevay Times* resting on top.

'Hi, Pen. It's me,' she announced in a shaky voice, staring miserably at the photo of Piran on the front page.

Penny groaned down the receiver. 'I thought it might be. I've got your bruiser of a bloke here right now. Simon's pouring the sherry. Want to come over?'

The wind was picking up as she set out across the village green, and Helen felt a nip in the air that told her autumn wasn't far away. The sun, so warm earlier, had dipped low in the sky, and the temperature was dipping with it. She could smell woodsmoke on the air, and there were plumes of smoke coming from three or four chimneys dotted around the green, one of which belonged to the vicarage.

'Come in – he's in there,' said Penny, pointing to the sitting room.

Helen went through and found Piran sprawled in an armchair, fire-gazing.

Simon had taken his glasses off and was polishing them on his handkerchief, a sure sign that he was feeling anxious.

'Whatever were you thinking, Piran?' he asked, shaking his head in dismay before putting his glasses back on.

'I just saw red, that's all. The way he was goading me, so cocksure – like he was up to something and there was nothing anyone could do about it. I've a feeling in my water the council are trying to pull a fast one. There is no way Café Au Lait should have got this far with their application before anyone knew about it. It's not that I care about the bloody theatre – I don't. But I don't like being had. Something—' Catching sight of Helen, he broke off, his mouth forming a tight line. Barely acknowledging her, he returned his gaze to the fire.

Helen ignored him and went to give Simon a kiss, then took a seat on the sofa and accepted the large glass of red wine that Penny had poured for her.

'Thanks, Pen.' She lifted her glass and took a deep swallow before announcing, 'I've been thinking . . .'

Piran looked across at Simon and raised his eyebrows. 'God 'elp us.'

Simon frowned at Piran and turned to Helen. 'And . . . ?'

'We've got to move on from looking like hysterical idiots' – she stared fixedly at Piran who stared equally fixedly into his glass – 'who talk only with their fists.'

'Hear hear,' concurred Penny.

'We need to start looking like credible opposition to Café Au Lait instead of making the headlines thanks to your loutish behaviour!'

'Exactly,' said Penny.

'We have only four weeks to prove ourselves to be serious about saving a building that many locals feel passionate about.'

'Ppff' or some such sound escaped from between Piran's teeth.

'Piran,' she reminded him sternly, 'you have said you'll see whether there's a case to be made for saving the Pavilions on the grounds that it's historically important. Agreed?'

Piran rubbed his sunburned hand over his chin. 'Aye. But that's all I'm going—'

She cut across him. 'And that journalist . . .'

'Wayne. Good lad, he is,' mumbled Piran.

'. . . Wayne is going to root about for any underhand dealings between the council and Café Au Lait. Yes?'

'Yes,' said Penny and Simon.

'So those are two good, positive things to put into action immediately. Yes?'

'Yes,' said Penny and Simon again.

'And you, Penny, my dearest and bestest mate . . .'

Penny looked at Helen with fear and suspicion. 'Ye-ess?'

'You, Penny, are going to open your very hot address book and get some big names to support us.'

'Oh, but . . . it's not that easy – I'm in pre-production for the *Mr Tibbs* shoot and I don't like to ask people for things and these people trust me not to impose this sort of stuff on them and—'

'Good. That's that sorted out,' said Helen, patting her friend's leg.

'Noooo, I won't let you guilt me into this, Helen.'

'Come on, Pen. Your empire is big enough for you to delegate all the Tibbs stuff – I should know, I was your PA for the pilot episode, wasn't I?'

'Yes, but—'

'And isn't it true that if you don't ask, you don't get?'

'Yes, but—'

'Pen, you're our wild card – the one woman who can really make a difference. This is too important to leave it to Audrey Tipton – she'll only end up alienating everyone. There's only one person who can save the Pavilions and that's you. We're counting on you.'

Penny felt three pairs of eyes boring into her as she sat staring at her hands. She knew that once she met those three pairs of eyes (well, technically two, because Piran was still brooding by the fire), the combined looks of hope and anticipation from her favourite people would be too much for her already shaky resolve. Oh bloody hell. How was she going to get out of this? She looked up . . . and knew it was too late – she'd been had.

'Excellent!' Helen clapped her hands together as Penny sighed theatrically. 'Tomorrow you are going to go through your address book and we'll draw up a list of possible names and then hit the phones.'

Piran barked a laugh of admiration. 'Well done, Hel. I like your style!'

She turned her gaze to him. 'And you, my boy, will be in the archives as soon as the office opens.'

'What about the vicar?' complained Piran. 'What's 'e going to do – get down on his knees and pray?'

'Yes,' said Helen. 'And then he can gather together a committee of sensible, clued-up people who we can rely on not to get into any more fistfights.'

6

Brooke Lynne was on her way to her agent's office in Mayfair when she spotted her face on the side of a London bus. *Brooke Lynne and Café Au Lait: the stuff of fantasies* said the slogan. She liked the photo. The photographer had gone to town on the touching up, and her legs, hips, breasts and scarlet shiny lips, sipping suggestively from the steaming coffee cup, were nothing short of Jessica Rabbit. She pressed the button to open the blacked-out rear window of her chauffeured Lexus and, holding up her phone, took a snap of the poster. Thank God for Twitter she thought, sending the picture out to the world with the message *Fabulous coffee, fabulous me xxxx #CafeAuLait.*

'Hey, Brooke, how's it feel to be the face of coffee?' Her agent Milo James hugged her. 'I saw your tweet. Good work. The guys at Café Au Lait will love that. Sit down.'

Brooke sat down on a state-of-the-art ultra-modern plastic moulded chair every bit as uncomfortable (and cold on her derrière) as it appeared. Milo sat at his clear Perspex desk, which was completely empty of anything other than a slender matte black phone that looked exactly like a sex toy.

'Now, babe . . .' He stretched out his arms and interwove his manicured hands. 'How do you fancy a trip to the seaside? Little place called Trevay – have you heard of it?'

She shook her head.

'Neither had I, but we will. It's the new St Tropez, only in Cornwall. Pretty harbour, quaint locals, good food, sassy restaurants and Café Au Lait are opening a big flagship café-cum-bistro there. They want you to go down there tomorrow and smile for the cameras. Tell me you're free.'

Brooke knew that Milo was well aware she had nothing else in her diary so there was no point in dithering. 'I'm free.'

'Good girl.' His phone rang. 'Excuse me, babe.' She nodded as he picked up the ridiculous receiver. 'Yes?' He listened as his secretary, Bunnie, spoke. 'OK, hon, put him through.' Milo looked over at Brooke and mouthed, 'Won't be a minute' before taking the call.

The distraction gave Brooke the chance to study her extraordinary surroundings. Milo's office occupied the corner penthouse of a building overlooking Hyde Park. Two walls were floor-to-ceiling glass. Both opened out onto a wrap-around balcony styled as a Japanese garden. A young oriental woman, no more than twenty and chewing gum, was slowly raking a patch of sand into a pattern resembling the ripples of the sea at the water's edge. There were several maple trees, now clad in their gold and scarlet autumn mantles. Water trickled from the open mouth of a snarling copper tiger into a deep pool full of koi carp. The fish lingered languidly in the shadow of the wooden hump-backed bridge crossing it. The oriental woman palmed her chewing gum and chucked it into the water before collecting her rake and disappearing round the corner of the building and out of sight.

Milo was deep into his phone call and held a hand up at Brooke to let her know he wanted her to stay, before spinning his chair round to look at the view of garden and park.

Milo James. Brooke wasn't sure whether she liked him much, or indeed trusted him, but he'd taken her on and the least she could do was play along nicely.

Brooke was an actress. What no one seemed to realise was that she was a rather good one. She had trained at the Bristol Old Vic and then gone to New York to take a course at the Actors Studio. It had opened her eyes to how much work Americans put into making it in the industry. They had to be able to sing, dance, act for stage, act for television, act for film, take fitness classes every day and constantly put themselves through the agony of 'cattle calls' – their name for mass auditions – to land the one big break.

She'd arrived in New York knowing only the British way: go to drama school, get an agent, sit about waiting for a job. Her new college friends had laughed at her.

'Girl, you gotta get off your white ass and go to the world! It sure ain't gonna come to you! And what's this shit name? Ain't nothin' sexy about Brenda Foster! We gotta find you a new name, girl. Look out the window – whaddya see?'

Brenda had obediently got to her feet and gazed out of her grimy Manhattan window. 'Errm . . . a yellow taxi.'

'What else?'

'A man with a peacock under his arm.'

'That fool still there?' Laverne, her flatmate, pushed Brenda out of the way. 'What *is* his vibe? OK, forget him. Look again. To the right and up a bit.'

'The bridge.'

'Ah-hmm. What's that bridge called, honey?'

'The Brooklyn Bridge.' Brenda turned and looked at her flatmate, nonplussed. 'Why?'

'That's your new name.'

'Brooklyn Bridge?'

Laverne laughed her deep and wonderful laugh. 'That'd get you some attention, but not in a good way. No. Play a little. Brooke Bridge? Brooke Lynne? Oh, hey, that's kinda Beckham, ain't it? Brooke Lynne. I like it.'

So Brenda Foster was put away and Brooke Lynne was born.

Not satisfied with restyling the name, Laverne had gone to work on the look too. The mouse-brown hair was cut short, highlighted and curled. Her eyebrows were marshalled into two bold works of art. Her make-up became ethereal with smoky eyes and coral lips. Her wardrobe went from jeans and T-shirts to bodycon dresses and towering heels.

It seemed to work. Her tutors started to take notice and in the end-of-term play she was given the role of Hedda Gabler. She earned herself two or three good reviews in the smaller artsy publications, including one that described her performance as *fluid and believable. Another chip off the old English acting block. Classy. Remember the name.*

The day after graduation, Brooke had to return home. There had been tearful goodbyes at JFK airport, with Laverne hugging her one last time and telling her, 'Now, girl, you go get the world, OK?'

'OK. You'll come and see me soon, won't you?'

'Sure. Now go.'

They'd hugged again. Brooke turned for one last wave as she went through security, but Laverne had already gone. Brooke had little family. She'd never known her dad and her mum had ended up with a man who'd have preferred it if little Brenda Foster didn't exist. Her mum had sent her to live with her Aunt Sheila, who was practical, loving and instilled in Brenda an appreciation for hard work.

'No point dwelling on what might have been,' she'd say. 'Best to go out and make your own luck in this life, my girl.' This advice had stood Brooke in good stead.

Her mother had died when Brooke was in her teens and she had found it hard to grieve for a mother who had shown her so little love. Instead, she locked her feelings of insecurity and abandonment away for another day and focused on being a success. Her aunt had left her a small legacy when she too died a few years later and Brooke spent it on her airfare to the States, knowing it was what her aunt would have wished for her.

Back in London she'd found a room to rent in a smart flat in Barons Court and a job as a waitress in Covent Garden.

In her spare time she went to as many acting/dancing/fitness classes as she could afford and scoured *The Stage* for open auditions. One of the restaurant regulars was a photographer who got chatting and offered to take some head shots of her to send to agents, etc.

As she walked to the address he'd given her, she planned what she would say and how she would escape if he even suggested that she take her top off. The building, when she got to it, looked bona fide. A renovated warehouse in the West End with a batch of bells and names beside them. She rang his bell. His assistant, a friendly skinny blonde, opened the door and introduced herself as his wife. Brooke relaxed.

After three hours of fun and some fabulous photos, she went back into the tiny changing room to collect her make-up bag and pack her case of clothes. She heard the door bell ring and a few moments later a man's voice. When she came out from behind the curtain, she was confronted by a tall, muscled, bronzed Adonis. She stopped in her tracks.

'Ah, Brooke – this is Bob. Bob Wetherby. Bob, Brooke Lynne.'

She shook the huge calloused hand. 'Hi,' she said, noticing his beguiling smile and the little scars above his right eye and his . . . cauliflower ears?

'Hi,' he said, gaping at her as if in awe.

It turned out he was *the* Bob Wetherby. Captain of the England rugby team, current holders of the Rugby World Cup. A genuine sporting legend.

That afternoon he insisted on driving her to work in Covent Garden and sat all night waiting for her to finish. He drove her home. Kissed her on the doorstep and phoned her in the morning. 'Hi. It's me, Bob. Bob Wetherby?'

'I guessed.' She smiled down the phone.

'Want some breakfast?'

'Sure. What time? Only, I'm still in bed.'

'I'm right outside, so open up and I'll cook while you shower.'

How was a woman supposed to resist that kind of attention and thoughtfulness from a living god who also happened to be world famous? Brooke couldn't. She fell head over heels in love.

Bob couldn't go anywhere without a pack of paparazzi following him and she was really impressed when the Beckhams texted to warn him that there was a group of them hanging about outside Scott's restaurant in Mayfair.

'How do Victoria and David know where we're having supper?' she asked.

'Because I told them.'

'Oh.'

'Didn't I mention – we're having dinner with them and my agent Milo?'

Assuming he was winding her up, Brooke laughed. 'Ha! Good one, Bobby. I'd die if I met them.'

'No, seriously, we're all having supper together. It might be a bit boring because Dave and I will probably talk sport, so he said he'd bring Victoria along so that you and she could talk girl stuff.'

For a moment Brooke sat with her jaw hanging, then she said urgently, 'Turn round. I need to go home and change.'

'No time. Here we are.'

Even though Bob had parked his Range Rover in a side street and they went through a rear entrance, a lone photographer managed to get a shot of them. Next morning it was headline news:

SHE LOOKS SCRUM-MY, BOB!

It had actually been a wonderful supper. David, utterly gorgeous, was polite and interesting. Victoria was funny and kind. She had loved Brooke's Topshop dress and had laughed when Brooke told the story of the origin of her name. The only one she'd hadn't been entirely comfortable with was Milo James. Although he'd joined in the conversation, she sensed he was constantly scrutinising her and evaluating how well she coped in this rarefied company. It unnerved her. She felt as if he was trying to decide whether she was good enough for Bob, whether she'd tarnish his image.

Apparently she passed the test. At the end of the evening

Milo had handed her his card saying, 'Call me in the morning.'

His secretary put her straight through, as if she was expecting the call.

'Hi, Brooke. So, how did you enjoy last night?' said Milo's oily voice.

'I enjoyed it very much.'

'Have you seen the papers?'

She looked at the handful of tabloids spread over the duvet. 'Erm, yeah. Bob picked them up this morning.'

'Do you like seeing yourself on the front page?'

Brooke hesitated before answering. It had shocked her to see the extent of the coverage, but once that had subsided, she had to admit it gave her a bit of a thrill. 'It's a bit strange, but at the same time quite nice.'

She heard him stifle a laugh. 'Got an agent?'

'Not yet.'

'Get Bob to bring you over to the office later. Ciao.'

*

Milo had promised to raise her profile and make her a star. And that's what he had done. She and Bob had become celebrity darlings. She had a beauty column in a glossy magazine – ghost-written for her, of course. A cosmetics company were launching a line of make-up in her name. She even had a handbag named after her. The Café Au Lait deal was huge, both in terms of her bank balance and the publicity it generated, and yet . . .

She didn't want to seem ungrateful after all Milo's hard work in getting her these deals, but sometimes it was as if he'd forgotten she was an actress. She'd come to his office today determined to remind him of that.

'Milo—' she started the moment he finished his call, but he cut across her.

'Brooke, I'm sorry, something's come up. Are there things you want to discuss?'

'Yes.'

'OK, how about we talk on the way down to Cornwall tomorrow morning? We'll be uninterrupted in the car. Four hours to ourselves. Can it wait till then?'

'Yeah, I suppose it can.'

'Good girl.' He stood and ushered her towards the door. 'Bye, babe.'

Before she knew it, he'd gone back into his office and she was standing on the smooth marble of the reception area, wondering how he always managed to head her off before she had a chance to say what was on her mind.

7

Penny and Helen were on fire. Penny's address book had names not just dropping out of it, but bouncing round the floor laughing at them.

'Oh my God, Pen. Samantha Bond, Pierce Brosnan, Judi Dench, David Cunningham, Dahlia Dahling, Ryan Gosling – *Ryan Gosling?* Are you kidding me?'

Penny laughed and shook her head. Helen high-fived her friend and continued, 'Philip Glenister, Miranda Hart, John Simm, Maggie Smith, Quentin Tarantino – Tarantino! I'm almost impressed . . . David Tennant. Stop! You've got Dr Who? Now I am impressed.'

'I'm a very important person, you know.' Penny held her hands up in front of her. 'Guilty as charged. What can I do?'

'You can get on the flipping phone and start ringing these buggers up!' cried Helen.

*

Simon called the meeting to order. He had chosen the church hall in Trevay because it was bigger than anything in his own parish and because he wanted to get as many people behind the campaign as possible. For the umpteenth time, he checked his watch. Two minutes to eleven. He'd wait those couple of minutes in case anyone was having trouble parking. Another quick head count. Fifteen. He offered up a silent prayer. As if on cue, the double doors at the back of the hall squeaked open and in came the local eccentric. Seen at all hours of the day briskly walking the lanes and coastal paths, forever poking his walking stick into interesting piles of rubbish or using it to test the depth of puddles, he was affectionately known as Colonel Stick. The spritely octogenarian was wearing his usual shabby tweed trousers, highly polished but down-at-heel brogues, frayed shirt, MCC tie, shiny navy-blue blazer and his ever-present gnarled stick was clutched in his equally gnarled right hand.

'Welcome, Colonel,' called Simon as the old boy came forward to shake his hand. 'Glad you could come.'

The Colonel stood up as straight as he was able and saluted. 'I've never missed a show in my life and I'm not about to start now.' His voice was plummy and surprisingly strong. Simon supposed it must be the result of many years barking orders on the parade ground.

'Come and sit next to me, Colonel.' Queenie patted the chair next to her. 'I've got some aniseed twists to keep us going.'

'Thank you, madam. How very generous,' beamed the Colonel.

Simon returned to the front of the hall and started proceedings: 'Welcome, everyone, and thank you for sparing the time to come and help with this most import-ant and urgent issue. I am grateful to Audrey Tipton for agreeing to take the minutes, and—'

Audrey stood up and immediately took charge. 'I need a roll call of all attendees. Please state your name and occupation when I point at you.'

Simon sighed and sat down. He was the first to be pointed at. Wearily he said, 'Simon Canter. Vicar of Pendruggan.'

Scribble, point.

'Queenie Quintrel. Postmistress, Pendruggan.'

Scribble, point.

'Colonel Irvine. British Army. Trevay.'

Scribble, point.

The scout master and his wife, the leader of the amateur dramatics society, four members of the chamber of commerce and three local residents.

When the scribbling and pointing was finally done, Simon once again got to his feet and stated the case for action.

By the end of the sixty-minute meeting they had all agreed to post fliers in every window and write letters to the council and their local MP. Mrs Audrey Tipton volunteered to draft those letters, assuming, possibly rightly, that she and Geoffrey knew better than anyone how to compose an important epistle. They would certainly be awkward customers for the council to deal with. Never in her life had Audrey been content to take 'no' for an answer, and her husband could vouch for that – out of her hearing, obviously.

*

Piran was hunched over his laptop at Helen's kitchen table, an enormous pile of ancient copies of the *Trevay Times* stacked at his elbow.

He'd been sitting like this, growling and grumbling, for a couple of hours. 'Bloody wild-goose chase. The Pavilions ain't old enough to have any history.'

Having left Penny to make her entreaties to her famous

friends, Helen had come home and made a coffee for Piran before abandoning him to his growling and whingeing. She was now ensconced in her cosy sitting room with Jack, Piran's devoted Jack Russell. The pair of them were snuggled on the sofa, absorbed in an old black-and-white film on the television. It was just getting to the bit where Bette Davis's character would utter the famous line 'fasten your seat belts, it's going to be a bumpy night' when there came a shout from the kitchen:

'Helen – come 'ere.'

'Just a minute.'

'Come 'ere now!'

'What's the magic word?'

'Oh, for God's sake!' His chair scraped on the floor and he marched in with a yellowing newspaper in his hand.

She paused the film. 'What?'

'Look 'ere. It's a review for the opening night of the Pavilions back in 1954.'

She read silently for a moment or two then looked at him. 'And . . . ?'

'Look at the photo.'

She looked. It was a picture of two men on stage. One wearing a loud checked suit and a trilby jammed on his head, the other with a monocle and a swagger stick under his arm. The caption read:

Marvellous Max Miller and Pavilion theatre manager Walter Irvine delight audiences at the opening night of Trevay's latest attraction.

She looked up at him, wrinkling her brow. 'I still don't get it.'

'Look carefully at the man with the stick under his arm. Does he seem familiar?'

She peered closer. 'Erm . . . no . . .'

'Walter Irvine?'

She shook her head.

'Better known as Colonel Stick?'

She gasped and looked again. 'Really?'

'I'd bet Jack's life on it.'

Hearing his name, the terrier lifted his head from his paws and wagged his tail.

*

Simon parked his old Volvo outside the vicarage. The large bag of fish and chips on the seat next to him smelled enticingly of warm paper, hot grease and vinegar. He tucked the package under his arm and got out of the car. Immediately the front door opened and Penny flew out, wrapped in a huge beige cashmere poncho and carrying a fat plastic documents folder. She locked the door and kissed her husband.

Simon never failed to be blown away by the fact that this glamorous, exacting, talented, lovely woman was his. He returned her kiss and, blinking soulful chocolate-coloured eyes through his spectacles, he held out his free arm for her to take. 'Evening, Mrs Canter. Good day?'

She arranged her chic sunglasses on the top of her head and beamed up at him. 'Great! You? How did the meeting go? Audrey unbearable?'

'Not bad. Meeting pretty good. Audrey rather helpful.'

'Excellent.' The two set off down the vicarage path to walk the short distance across the green to Gull's Cry. 'Thanks for getting the chish and fips. Helen wouldn't tell me what's going on, but she sounded so excited I reckon Piran must have found something.'

*

'Pass the ketchup would you, Pen? Thanks.' Piran squirted a large pool of sauce on the open packet of chips. They hadn't bothered getting plates out, preferring to eat them straight from the paper wrapping.

For a while the only sound was satisfied munching as everyone tucked in. Then Helen wiped her fingers on a piece of kitchen towel and kicked off the conversation.

'Simon, you start – how did the meeting go?'

He told them about the plans for fliers in windows, leaflets through letterboxes and letters to the council.

'Good for Audrey and Geoff. That'll keep them busy. Who else was there?'

Simon duly listed the attendees, finishing: '. . . and Queenie, of course. She took Colonel Stick under her wing – kept him quiet with aniseed twists.'

Helen paused with a chunk of cod halfway between her plate and her lips. She darted a look at Piran, who shook his head as a warning for her not to say anything just yet.

'What?' said Penny, immediately spotting what had passed.

'All in good time,' Piran answered infuriatingly. 'Penny, your turn – any of those actor types in your address book come good?'

Penny clapped her hands together, thrilled with what she had to tell. She moved her fish-and-chip paper to one side and opened the document wallet that had been sitting underneath.

'I think you're going to be very pleased!' She beamed at them, waiting for murmurs of wonder and approval, but kept them waiting a moment too long.

'Get on with it, woman!' barked Piran.

'OK, OK.' Penny took the papers out of the wallet. 'Let's see . . . I started by emailing the cast of *Mr Tibbs*; seeing as the series is being filmed locally I thought they'd be supportive. Both David Cunningham and Dahlia Dahling' – the actors who played the two lead roles, bank-manager-cum-sleuth Mr Tibbs and his secretary Nancy Trumpet – 'have agreed to help in some way.'

'That's jolly good of them,' said Simon, patting Penny's arm affectionately.

'There's more. The Arts Council are launching a new campaign to get people to support their regional theatres, so we can get some publicity on the back of that. *AND* – ta-dah! – dear Julian Fellowes has said he might, *might*, can't promise in blood, but might . . .'

'Yes?' Helen was on the edge of her seat.

'. . . be able to persuade Hugh Bonneville and Maggie Smith to join him for a special *Downton Abbey* night where they share a kind of behind-the-scenes gossipy chat with the audience.'

'What's *Downton Abbey*?' asked Piran, frowning.

'Shut up!' Helen punched his arm. 'I'll tell you later.'

'*And* . . .' Penny continued, 'it looks as though we'll be getting some memorabilia from *Doctor Who*, signed by cast members, past and present.'

'David Tennant?' swooned Helen.

'Yes, David Tennant. *And* my man in Hollywood is going to ask Quentin Tarantino's office for anything the great man can sign and send us too.'

Penny sat back looking very pleased with herself. Simon

and Helen could only gaze at her in astonishment, their eyes like saucers.

'Wow,' said Helen.

''oo's Quentin Tarantino?' asked Piran.

After it was explained exactly who Tarantino was, and Penny had poured out the last of the bottle of red wine, Piran pulled out the newspaper cutting he'd shown to Helen earlier that day and passed it to Penny and Simon.

''ave a look at that.'

Simon and Penny hunched together and looked. It was Simon who got the connection first.

'Piran! This is Colonel Stick, isn't it?'

'Yes.'

'So the man who first took charge of the theatre is still in Trevay?'

'That's right.'

'And he was a music hall performer who knew Max Miller?'

'Give the man a cigar!'

'He was at the meeting today. He told me he'd never missed a show, but I thought he meant a military "show", that he liked nothing better than to get stuck into a battle. But he meant—'

'I should think he did.'

Penny was listening hard and had finally put two and two together. 'So *he* is the piece of historic interest we need to save the Pavilions?'

'Correct.'

'But how exactly? What can Colonel Stick do that could possibly help us save the theatre?' asked Helen. 'I mean, I'm sure he has lots of interesting anecdotes about the old days, but how many people really care about music hall now? And why would they be bothered about a retired theatre manager?'

Piran leaned back in his chair and drained his glass. 'If you birds would finally stop your incessant twittering, I might be able to get a word in and enlighten you.'

Penny and Helen exchanged looks but fell silent.

'I've been doing a bit of digging. This Colonel Stick isn't just famous for his music hall act. He was also an avid adopter of amateur film-making back in the day. Judging from all the old theatre press cuttings I've dug out, our Colonel was rubbing shoulders with the greats – not just music-hall greats, but the biggest stars of the theatre world. He was friends with the likes of Laurence Olivier and Vivien Leigh, John Gielgud and Richard Burton. And seeing as he was so keen on capturing everything on film, I reckon those old home movies of his could turn out to be some very rare and highly desirable footage.'

Helen, Penny and Simon were agog.

'And people would be really interested to see this stuff, wouldn't they?' said Helen.

'Film memorabilia is highly sought after. There'll be collectors out there who would pay a fortune for that sort of stuff,' added Penny, ever the businesswoman.

'Right then, I reckon one of us needs to have a chat with our Colonel,' said Piran.

All eyes turned to Helen.

'You're such a people person,' cooed Penny, nudging her friend in the ribs.

8

Brooke was in the back of yet another silent, blacked-out limo, speeding down the M4 towards the West Country. The driver was super professional, smart and polite.

'Good morning, Miss Lynne. Have you any bags you'd like to put in the boot?'

'Just these, thank you.'

He'd lifted the large heavy aluminium suitcases with a barely audible grunt while she checked her bag for her keys, phone and sunglasses, then locked the front door of the flat and made her way into the sunshine, glancing around quickly for photographers. All clear. The driver was already waiting for her with the door open.

Brooke glanced inside, ready to give Milo a cheery 'good morning', but the car was empty apart from a selection of newspapers and a bottle of water standing in the arm rest separating the two back seats.

As if reading her mind, the driver said, 'Mr James sends his apologies. He's in meetings all day today. He'll be travelling to Cornwall this evening.'

He settled her in the car, making sure the skirt of her dress was clear of the door as he shut it and then got in himself.

'Would you like the radio on, Miss Lynne?'

'No thank you.'

71

'Just let me know if you get too hot or too cold.'

'Thank you.'

'If you need to stop for anything, just say the word.'

'I will.'

He hadn't spoken after that. The car moved smoothly and efficiently, gliding through the London traffic and out on to the westbound M4. It gave her time to think about Milo.

She really did need to talk to him about getting her some acting work. He'd certainly made her a 'celebrity' – whatever that meant. Thanks to the gossip columns, she was now mononymous: known by her first name alone. The 'Lynne' was seemingly superfluous. (Laverne back in New York would be thrilled.)

More often than not though, when she featured in the media it was as half of BobBro – thanks to some 'witty' journalist who'd come up with the idea of combining her name with Bob's. Dear Bob . . . the perfect boyfriend. He worshipped her and she adored him. But were worship and adoration the same thing as love?

Was being the face of a coffee company the same as being a respected actress?

The answer to both questions was clear.

Brooke was stuck. She enjoyed being a 'name'. She enjoyed being ferried in stretch limos to restaurants and photo shoots. Watching the money pouring into her bank account and being showered with celeb freebies was a welcome relief after waitressing to make ends meet. And yet . . .

She wanted to act. Proper acting. A chilling thought entered her brain and send a shudder through her. Oh God: she was acting. Brooke Lynne was just a part. A character she had created. Had created so successfully that no one could see or remember Brenda Foster. No one wanted Brenda Foster, but they loved Brooke Lynne.

She needed to talk to Milo. Face-to-face. Tonight.

*

Ollie woke with the King Daddy of hangovers. He lay still, waiting for the thumping in his head to subside. As of ten thirty last night he was officially out of work. The end-of-season party had been a very boozy affair. The Knight, Sir Terry, had made an emotional speech to the assembled company, recalling his glory days with 'Darling Larry, Ralph and Johnny' before following Ollie to the gents' and making a clumsy pass at him.

Ollie groaned, recalling the heartbreaking look of humiliation on Sir Terry's face as he gently turned him down.

'Oh, dear boy,' The Knight had blustered. 'Please don't think that I . . . I would never do anything so . . . please don't mention this to anyone . . . I'd hate to give the wrong impression.'

Ollie's response had been to give him a firm hug and plant a kiss on his wrinkled cheek. 'Sir Terry, I'm flattered.'

One thing The Knight had said to him later that night, as they said their final goodbyes had stayed with him and it now rattled around in his brain like a painful ballbearing.

'My dear boy, you are indeed a pretty face, but you're a bloody fine actor, too. Never lose sight of that. Make that your focus and don't get sucked into all the other flim-flam.'

'By flim-flam, do you mean Red?' asked Ollie.

'I mean the fame game, my dear. I'm sure your Red is a wonderful girl. But fame is a fickle mistress. You need to be known for *your* talent, not for hers.'

His thoughts were interrupted by the shrill ring of his smartphone on the bedside table. He fumbled for it and saw it was Red wanting FaceTime. He pressed the accept button and held the phone up so that she could see him. Her face came into view on the screen.

'You look like shit,' she said.

'Hey, thanks. Good morning to you, too.'

'Let me see round the room.'

He held the phone up and turned it a full three hundred and sixty degrees.

'You're on your own?' she demanded.

'Yes. As always.'

'How was the party? Anyone make a pass at you?'

'Yes – The Knight.'

'You turned him down?'

'What do you think?'

'Dunno. I haven't seen you for so long, for all I know you might have turned gay.'

He closed his eyes and didn't bother to reply. She was getting more and more demanding, and irritating.

Red spoke again: 'So, now you're not working, when are you coming out to see me?'

Even if he could have afforded it, especially now that he was unemployed, the last thing he wanted to do was jump on a flight and travel halfway around the world. He longed to get back to his flat in London and hang out with his mates. Sleep a bit. Drink a bit. Have a break. Then look for another job. Despite the constant attention from the media, his new-found fame had yet to result in any big new job. He thought about what Sir Terry had said. Thanks to all the 'flim-flam' most directors probably saw him as a liability rather than an asset.

'Ollie! Have you fallen asleep? Can you hear me?'

He opened his eyes and tried to smile, 'Sorry, babe. I'm a bit hungover.'

'So, do you want to come and see me or what?'

'I would love to, but I really need to sort some stuff out here. Get back home to London, pay the bills, do my washing . . . You know . . .' He trailed off lamely.

Her expression turned sour and she spoke to someone Ollie couldn't see: 'He says he's tired.'

'Put him on!' shrieked a German-accented voice. Henrik's overplucked eyebrows and satsuma tan filled the screen. 'Why are *you* tired, Actor Boy? Do *you* perform to hundreds of thousands of people screaming your name every night? Do you give your entire soul to the world, every second of every day?' He didn't wait for Ollie to answer. 'No! Yet you whine about being tired. You don't know the meaning of the word, Actor Boy.'

Ollie's headache suddenly got a whole lot worse.

*

Ryan reached for Jess's hand across the armrest of their first-class seats. She was sleeping. The elastic on the left-hand side of her eye mask had forced her hair into a loop, exposing a freckled ear. She was making little pppfff noises through her slack lips. He forced down a desire to pinch them shut.

The Thai holiday had, to all intents and purposes, been a great success. Ryan had spoiled Jess rotten. He'd sunbathed on the beach or sweated in the gym while she indulged herself in the spa and availed herself of Rick, the resort's not unattractive, and infuriatingly straight, personal trainer. Between Rick and the crack team of beauty therapists, Jess had dropped ten pounds and fifteen years.

Ryan had enjoyed the best sex with her that he could remember. The old Jess was back.

He tweaked her hand three times, the shared code meaning 'I Love You', one word per squeeze. She stirred and gave a snorey snort before lifting her eye mask and wiping a dribble of saliva from the corner of her mouth.

'Hello.' He leaned forward and kissed her.

She smiled sleepily at him. 'What time is it?'

'We're about an hour to landing.'

'Great.' She stretched extravagantly, extending her hands above her head, and marvelled at her tanned and streamlined arms. She hadn't felt this good in a long time. The lines across her forehead had vanished. The crevasses either side of her eyes had softened to mere culverts – and attractive culverts at that. Her hip bones had fought their way out of her flesh and her legs were showing signs of muscle definition. Ryan couldn't keep his hands off her and had actually shown signs of jealousy when Rick, the trainer, had paid her a few compliments in front of him.

'That bloody man fancies you,' he'd huffed, having had the uncomfortable experience of watching Rick put his hands all over Jess as she lifted some very heavy weights.

'Who? Rick?' Jess had asked, genuinely astonished.

The next day, during their gym session, Jess had flirted gently with Rick and, to her amazement, he had definitely flirted back.

A few days into their holiday, the *Venini* press office had arranged for a photo agency to grab some 'caught unawares' photos of Ryan looking hunky on the beach. Jess and Rick happened to jog past at the moment the shots were taken, and the magazines back home had been full of photos showing 'Ryan Hearst's long-term lover working hard to keep her man'. To Ryan's annoyance, those photos had appeared in a considerably larger format than the ones showing his toned body.

The camp elocution of the purser came over the intercom: 'Ladies and gentlemen, we are due to land at London Heathrow in approximately forty minutes. Can we ask you now to adjust your seats to the upright position, put your tray tables away and fold any blankets or pillows ready for the cabin crew to collect. Thanking you.'

Ryan handed his blanket to Jess and stood up. 'I think I'll just stretch my legs.' He stepped over her, leaving his newspapers and his leather gladiator sandals in a heap on the floor, and set off down the aisle towards the bathroom in his flight socks.

Jess started clearing up the detritus of several hours in the air. She suspected that Ryan didn't really need to stretch his legs; what he needed was some public love.

Sure enough he had made his way down the aisle and pushed aside the coarse and scratchy pleated curtain that separated the wealthy from the hoi polloi. Giving it a count of twenty, he stood there gazing deeply into as many eyes as he could lock onto, waiting patiently until the signs of recognition began. It started with a few elbows nudging the ribs of their neighbour, then eyes widening and broad smiles, then a ripple of sound as his name was murmured, with row after row picking up the refrain like a Mexican wave of whispers.

Only then did Ryan step forward and walk amongst his fans.

Twenty minutes later he stepped over Jess and sat back in his seat, noisily clipping his seat belt.

'Sorry I took so long. You know how it can be. Someone in goat class spotted me. Got recognised. Had to do the right thing. Chatted, had a few photos. God, it's so tedious, but it goes with the territory – ya gotta do it.'

The chief stewardess approached, smiling. 'Mr Hearst. Thank you so much for taking the time to talk to other passengers. You've made their day. If only all celebrities could be so generous.'

'It's my pleasure. After all, it's the fans who have given me so much. It is they who have made Cosmo Venini so very popular.' He feigned humility.

The stewardess turned to Jess. 'You're Mr Hearst's girlfriend, aren't you?'

Jess extended her hand. 'Jess. Yes, I am. Pleased to meet you.'

'Those photos of you on the beach were amazing! You look super hot! Certainly don't look your age.'

Ryan took Jess's hand and kissed her fingers. 'She doesn't, does she? She needed a treat, what with me being away so much.'

'Oh, Mr Hearst!' The stewardess clutched her pussy-bowed neck and turned to Jess: 'How lucky you are to have him.'

As soon as the stewardess had walked away, Jess's bright smile dropped like an Acme safe tumbling off the side of a cliff in a *Road Runner* cartoon, 'Hmph – she can fuck right off.'

'What?' said Ryan, running his hands through his well-cut hair and gazing out of the window at London spread below them.

'Saying I look good for my age!'

'Don't be so sensitive. She's a charming young woman. Do you have any chewing gum? I haven't had time to clean my teeth.'

Jess rootled around in her bag and passed him a half-empty packet.

'Thank you. You could do with some too.'

Chewing on her gum furiously, she rummaged through her bag for a hairbrush and ran it through her hair. She found a mirror and gave it a quick polish on her T-shirt. Her reflection did look pretty good. Her glossy brown mane of curls framed a tanned and freckled face that enhanced the blue of her eyes and the whiteness of her teeth. She had definitely lost a bit of chub from her cheeks and chin. She dared to tell her reflection that she was happy. Now if only she could get a job. Pay her way. Feel useful. Talented.

Maybe it wasn't too late . . .

9

The limo pulled smoothly up to the steps leading to the wide and welcoming entrance of the Starfish Hotel. While the driver helped Brooke out of the car, a couple of linen-clad flunkeys raced to collect her bags from the boot.

'Good afternoon, Miss Brooke. Welcome to the Starfish. I'm Toby, this is Marc.'

'Thank you.' She gave the young bronzed man a warm appraising glance.

His colleague stepped round from the back of the car carrying her Hermès valise.

'I love your luggage,' he said in a deliciously fruity voice. 'Very stylish.'

Her driver straightened his tie and asked, 'Anything more I can do for you, Miss Brooke?'

'No, thank you. Do you have any idea when Milo – Mr James – will be arriving?'

'I'm waiting to hear what flight he's on. I'm heading to Newquay Airport now to pick him up.'

'OK. Thanks.'

As the car drove away, the two young bellhops escorted her up the steps and into the hotel lobby. She was gratified to see that her super sexy Marilyn wiggle was attracting much attention along the way.

The Starfish Hotel was the smartest of Cornwall's hotels.

Built to coincide with the completion of Brunel's revolutionary train line from Paddington to Trevay, it had offered suitably luxurious accommodation for the wealthy Victorian and Edwardian travellers who flocked to the pretty little fishing village in search of sea breezes and sunshine. With Dr Beeching's cuts, however, the hotel had lost favour and business, sinking into unloved shabbiness throughout the sixties and seventies. During the eighties and nineties, surfers from all over the globe had used it as a form of cheap hostel. And then in the noughties a wealthy widow, Louise Lonsdale, had stepped in and saved it from decline.

Now the Starfish was the epitome of twenty-first century beach chic. Lots of glass, sunlight, luxury bathrooms and excellent food.

Brooke was swept up to her penthouse suite in the decadently ironic beach-hut lift. As Toby opened the door for her she was dazzled by the early October sunshine, blessing the drawing room with a drench of rosy gold. 'This is fabulous!' she said, kicking off her shoes ('Louboutin!' Bellhop Marc swooned appreciatively) and let her feet revel in the deep pile of the sky-blue carpet as she walked to the big bay window and looked at the harbour below.

As soon as Toby and Marc had finished running through all the instructions for the air conditioning, satellite TV, electric curtains and waterfall shower, she tipped generously and they left her to it.

For a couple of hours she pottered around happily, testing the bed, unpacking her case, phoning Bob and trying out the super-comfy outsized sun lounger on her balcony-cum-deck. This was definitely the life. After a quick shower she slipped on some skinny jeans, tied a headscarf over her famous blonde hair and covered her eyes with a pair of huge sunglasses – a gift from Victoria Beckham. She was ready to explore Trevay.

It was the end of the season, so the town was quiet as Brooke plunged into the narrow back streets lined with smart shops selling local art, beach fashion and desirable home accessories. She spent a happy hour entertaining herself with a bit of retail therapy, enjoying the recognition of the shop assistants and the admiring looks of the men she passed in the street.

When at last she emerged from the maze of little streets she made a beeline for the seafront. Leaning on the railings overlooking the harbour, she took in the view. The tide was out and several boats were lying on their keels, the mooring ropes draped with curtains of green seaweed. Taking a great lungful of the warm, damp air, Brooke turned her face to the watery sun. She had to make the most of this. She'd be back in London by tomorrow night. Reopening her eyes, she scanned the headland to her left as it stretched out towards the open sea. A vast silver dome in the distance was reflecting the sun's rays, forcing her to squint in order to make out details of the ice-cream-coloured building beneath. It looked like a theatre. Curious, she started to walk towards it.

As she got closer the signs of age and neglect grew ever more obvious. Several windows were broken, the brass handles on the main doors had a patina of verdigris from exposure to salt air and damp. Glass cases that had once held play bills advertising the shows now housed a miscellany of typed notices warning of the cancellation of the Scouts' Gang Show or requesting volunteers to help out at the next pensioners' bingo night. She cupped her hands over the glass aperture in one of the main doors to see what the foyer looked like. A face suddenly loomed into view, staring at her from the other side of the door. She gave a shriek of surprise and jumped back. The face remained in the window, his lips moving. He was saying something to her.

She composed herself. 'What?' she mouthed.

The door opened and a head popped out. 'Did I startle you? Do forgive me.'

'I didn't expect to see anyone, that's all,' she replied.

'Would you like to come in and look around?' he asked.

'I . . . erm . . .'

'Don't worry. I come up here all the time. I have the keys.' He patted the pocket of his worn tweed jacket.

Brooke stayed where she was and looked about, hoping that she wasn't alone up here with a strange old man. Bad news: she was.

As if he guessed what was going through her mind, he said, 'Or maybe you'd like to come back another time? With a friend, perhaps?'

'Well, I . . .' she hesitated. 'I . . . yes, I'd love to. I'm an actress actually.'

'Are you? How marvellous! I used to run this place, you know. That's why I have keys – I never handed them back.' He smiled naughtily and twinkled his milky brown eyes at her. 'Come on in. Where shall we start . . . ?'

*

Brooke was in her element. The old man's stories, full of the romance and history of the place, kept her spellbound. It was as if she could hear the laughter of bygone audiences filling the auditorium as she looked out over the ripped and worn red plush seats. She could hear the band playing in the dark of the grimy orchestra pit. The old man told her to wait in the stalls while he disappeared through a door to the side of the stage. It was dark and cool as she waited. The only light came from the dome above, as the sun forced its way through the peeling silver paint.

From the wings she heard the old man's voice announce, 'Ladies and gentlemen, the Pavilions proudly presents the one and only Colonel Walter Stick!' He marched on to the stage, head held high, his walking stick under his arm. Stamping to a smart halt, he turned to address her. 'What ho, chaps.' For the next seven or eight minutes he beguiled her with a stand-up routine that was word perfect. He finished with a little song and a soft-shoe shuffle before bowing deeply.

Her heart-felt applause soaked into the empty space. 'That was wonderful!'

'Prehistoric humour,' he said humbly. 'It used to go down quite well in the fifties. People could relate to stuffy Colonel Blimp types in those days. I called myself Colonel Stick. Many locals still call me that – behind my back. But they don't remember why.'

'So did you run this place *and* perform here?'

'Yes. The last of the old actor managers, I suppose. Wonderful days and happy memories. Would you like to see my dressing room? I'd give it up whenever the really big stars came down – Max Miller, Morecambe and Wise, Petula Clark . . .'

'I'd love to see it.'

She climbed the steps to the stage and he escorted her through the wings into an echoey corridor, down a short flight of steps that opened into a large space with doors leading off in all directions.

'This was the green room. A great gathering place for before, after and during shows. All these doors surrounding us are dressing rooms.' He led her to one where a star had once hung, leaving behind a faded imprint to prove its existence.

'This was mine.'

He turned on a light switch and the room came to life. Turkey carpet on the floor. A huge cheval mirror in the corner. A rail holding two bent metal coat hangers with a shelf above for shoes or hats. A gilt mirror with at least a dozen light bulbs round it sat above an immaculate dressing table laid with several sticks of grease paint, a magnifying mirror, two silver-backed gentleman's hair brushes and a small box labelled 'moustaches'.

Brooke stepped into the room and ran her fingers over the make-up sticks. She turned to the old man. 'Is this all yours?'

'Yes.' He looked at his feet, shame-faced. 'I keep it here for old times' sake. You must think I'm a silly old man.'

She shook her head. 'Not at all. Who owns this theatre now? Why is it in such a state?'

'The council own it. Always have. They're selling it though. Soon it will be no more. That is what's called progress. A few of us are banding together to fight for its survival, but I fear defeat is inevitable.'

'Who's buying it?'

'Some coffee chain or other.' He waved her to a chair and sat down to tell the whole story.

*

Helen was at home googling, trying to find out as much as possible about Colonel Stick aka Walter Irvine.

It seemed he had been born into a family where acting and music hall was in the blood. His father, Tommy Irvine, had been a well-known theatre manager and performer in his own time, best known for his ventriloquist act with an aristocratic, bad-tempered dummy called Claude. Tommy had famously retired from performing after Claude drunkenly insulted Queen Mary during a Royal Command Performance in 1931 and ventriloquist and dummy had to be bundled off the stage by Flanagan and Allen.

As a young man, Walter had carried on the family tradition. Thanks to his father, he knew many of the stars of the day, including Max Miller, but Walter didn't confine himself to music hall alone. A comic actor of some talent, he appeared alongside some of the biggest stars of the fifties, featuring on the London stage as well as in productions with the RSC in Stratford-upon-Avon. With Miller's help, he'd gone on to perfect his 'Colonel Stick' act, which had been a sell-out in theatres up and down the country. The Korean War had truncated his theatrical career, but he'd resurrected it on his return when he took up the job of theatre manager at the Pavilions. The sixties had been the theatre's golden era, with big-name stars coming to Cornwall to perform, whether in comedy revues, musicals or Shakespearean drama. The list read like a Who's Who of acting royalty: Dame Peggy Ashcroft, Richard Harris, Peter O'Toole . . .

According to his press cuttings, Walter Irvine had been one of the finest actors of his generation, as well as a highly regarded theatrical impresario. So why had he been so completely forgotten, even in Trevay?

Helen could find no answer online. There was no mention of his private life, even on Wikipedia, and she could find only a couple of passing references to his private film collection. It was as if Walter Irvine had vanished into a black hole once the Pavilions closed down.

Helen stretched and sighed. 'I don't suppose I'll crack this in an afternoon,' she said to herself. 'Maybe I should pay him a visit?'

To distract herself she phoned her daughter-in-law, Terri. Helen had been thrilled that her son had found such a lovely wife, and even more thrilled when the newly weds announced that she was going to be a grandmother. Little Summer was a year old now and Helen was totally besotted with her.

Within minutes of Terri answering, the baby – who was sitting in her lap – began breathing heavily down the phone to Helen. She was just starting to talk. 'Gan Gan,' she said. 'Gan, Gan.' Terri prised the phone from her sticky little hands, laughing. 'Gan Gan is you, Helen. We think it's baby-speak for Grandma.'

'Well, I like Gan Gan just fine.'

Helen couldn't wait to tell Piran, who was fonder of his almost-step-granddaughter than he liked to let on. She went into the front garden to wait for him and dead-head the last of the roses. Dusk was settling and the lights of Pendruggan farmhouse twinkled at her from across the other side of the common.

The set of the latest *Mr Tibbs* episode stood in stark relief against the grey sky. Filming was due to begin any day now and the village was enjoying its claim to fame.

She drank in the cool, still air perfumed with the aroma of autumn leaves and sent up a prayer of thanks for this new chapter in her life. Her son happily married and doting dad to a healthy baby girl; her daughter Chloe had finally found her niche working for a charity that helped provide communities in the developing world with clean water, and it sounded as though she'd found love too, with a fellow aid worker. Helen was immensely proud of both of her children. She was quietly proud of herself too, especially now that her first column had appeared in the *Cornish Guardian*. It had been a bold step to end her marriage and start a new life in Cornwall, but she was glad she'd gathered up her courage and taken the plunge. She felt that she belonged in Pendruggan, and with Piran. Theirs was a comfortable arrangement; for all that he was quixotic, untameable and sometimes downright rude, she loved him. She had been a good wife to Gray, who had walked all over her and taken lovers the way an alcoholic helps himself to another drink. Piran on the other hand, had never let her down and she truly believed he never would.

*

Brooke was thrilled with her idea. Once she explained it to them, she was confident that Milo and the Café Au Lait people would be thrilled to. She was going to enlist their help in saving the Pavilions. They could have a small coffee shop bistro in one half of the foyer, while sponsoring great plays, concerts, summer seasons and pantomimes. She would star in many of the productions and Colonel Irvine would resurrect his Colonel Stick alter ego for special performances. The papers would love the story. Trevay was, after all, the St Tropez of Great Britain – Milo had told her so.

She sat in front of her dressing-table mirror, wearing a hotel bathrobe, and made her face up carefully. The smoky eyes, coral lips and tumble of blonde curls that were the trademark of Brooke Lynne looked happily back at her. Finally she was going to make her mark. Saviour of a provincial seaside theatre and a proper actress. She'd give her publicist a call in the morning.

Her room phone rang.

'Brooke? It's Milo. I'm just checking in downstairs. The Café Au Lait guys will be here in twenty minutes. You ready?'

'Almost.'

'What are you wearing?'

'I'm not sure. Maybe a—'

She heard him tut. 'I'll come up and see to it you choose right. I'll be there in two minutes.'

She pulled out a couple of simple dresses and put them on the bed. Nothing too revealing. This was a business meeting, after all.

She answered the door at his first knock and he pushed past her.

'Cool room.' He gave her a sweeping look from head to toe. 'Nice make-up. Good girl. What have you got on under that robe?'

'My underwear of course.'

'Shame. Where are your clothes?'

She showed him the choices on the bed and he rejected them. 'Too daytime. I need you to look glamorous. Sexy. What else you got?'

He chose the tight-fitting scarlet lace dress that she had planned to wear for the press launch the next day, impatiently dismissing her protests: 'It doesn't matter. You can wear it twice. We've got fifteen minutes before they arrive. I've told the front desk to send them straight up. We'll have drinks here in the suite.'

'OK.' Brooke shrugged. To have the meeting in the privacy of the room would be a good idea. Then they could celebrate over supper in the dining room downstairs.

Milo was heading towards the door when a thought struck him. He turned and asked: 'Shoes – what are you wearing?'

'Stilettos?'

'Perfect.'

*

Brooke looked in the long mirror and checked herself out. There was no doubt that this was the Brooke Lynne that Café Au Lait had hired. A blonde bombshell sex siren. She bent over to adjust her stockings and smooth the pile of her scarlet suede killer heels. 'Good luck,' she said to her reflection. 'Tonight's going to be a good night.'

She opened the door to Milo and two men in their forties both wearing sharp suits.

Milo kissed Brooke and introduced her. 'Brooke, this is Rupert Heligan, Chairman of CAL UK.'

Rupert stepped towards her and kissed her hand, holding it just a little too long. He looked into her eyes and smiled. 'I'm so pleased to meet you at last.'

'Me too. Thank you, Mr Heligan,' she replied, turning her bombshell smile up to warp factor seven.

'Please, call me Rupert.'

She smiled and Milo introduced her to the second man. 'Brooke, this is Michael Woodbine, CAL's PR wizard. Without him, you wouldn't have got the gig.'

Michael stepped forward and placed his hands lightly on her elbows while moving in to kiss her twice. Once on each cheek. 'You were the perfect choice. Rupert and I knew you were the face CAL needed.'

'Well, I can't thank you enough. I am so thrilled to be

an ambassador for such great coffee and such a great company. I love your ethos. Fair trade with your growers. Reinvesting in their businesses. I wouldn't want to work with a company that exploited their suppliers.' Brooke knew it was her sex appeal that was her big selling point, and why they were interested in her. She was quite happy to use her charms, but she was determined not to play the bimbo for the sake of it.

The three men smiled at her. 'She's not just a beauty – she has brains too,' said Milo, ushering everyone to the huge sofas.

'Oh yes, I'm so much more than a pretty face.' Brooke turned her smile up another couple of notches.

'Fix us some drinks would you, Brooke.'

Brooke's million-dollar smile froze on her face and she stood still for a moment. She hadn't thought about drinks, let alone being the one who 'fixed' them. She recovered quickly – she was a pro after all. 'Of course. What would you like?'

She went to the cupboard that she'd been told was the bar and opened it. Everything anyone could have wanted was stocked inside.

'Scotch, please. On the rocks,' said Rupert, staring at her bottom as she bent down to search for glasses.

Michael and Milo chose the same. She poured herself a weak gin and tonic.

Once they were all settled and sitting down, Rupert opened up the conversation.

'Milo, what we want Brooke to do tomorrow is go up to the theatre, have a few shots taken by the invited press, do some interviews with the media . . .' He stopped and turned to Brooke. 'Can you do interviews?'

She frowned. 'What do you mean?'

'Can you take a brief? Anything awkward, leave it to Michael. Just keep smiling.'

Brooke felt a stab of annoyance. 'I'm an actress. I can remember lines and I can certainly put across my views.'

Milo surreptitiously raised a finger and gave her a sharp look to stop her from saying more. She stopped.

There was a knock at the door. 'Get that would you,' said Milo, 'there's a good girl.'

Brooke hid her annoyance but did as she was asked. A short, self-important-looking little man in a brown suit was standing outside. 'Hello, can I help you?' she asked.

He held out his hand and, shaking hers, walked in, 'Councillor Bedford – Chris. Sorry I'm late.'

'Ah, Chris – glad you could come.' Milo got to his feet. 'You know Rupert and Michael.' They all shook hands. 'Brooke, get Chris a drink, will you.'

She poured him the lager he'd requested. He had settled himself on the sofa she'd been sitting on, next to Milo. Now there was nowhere but a small stool to perch on. She perched.

The three men discussed business over the top of her head for the next hour. Brooke tried to listen enthusiastic-ally – active listening, she'd heard it called – but the three men seemed to be treating her like a hired servant and it was starting to irritate her. Three times she got up and refreshed their glasses. Not one of them addressed her. Councillor Bedford was an odious creep who hadn't stopped leering at her all evening, staring at her thighs when she crossed her legs and straining his neck to peer down the front of her dress when she stooped to set the drinks on the table. She was so fed up with the whole business it was tempting to tune out completely, but her ears pricked up when talk turned to the Pavilions.

'So, Bedford, you're absolutely sure that we've got this in the bag?' pressed Michael, the PR man. 'We don't want any more interference from those local busybodies. From hereon there must be nothing but positive press – we've got our image to protect, remember.'

'Precisely,' said Rupert. 'We're rewarding you handsomely for your . . . "interventions", and we expect you to deliver accordingly.'

'Yes, yes, absolutely, gentlemen!' Councillor Bedford fawned, rubbing his hands nervously against his trousers. 'I think you'll find that there are plenty of sympathetic ears on the council and I personally guarantee to see to it that any opposition will be silenced.'

Definitely odious, thought Brooke, as their conversation droned on. Her stomach was rumbling. She hadn't eaten since breakfast. It was getting late and she was worried that the kitchen would be closed by the time they went downstairs for dinner. Milo interrupted her thoughts. 'So, babe, how about you tell the boys what being the face of Café Au Lait means to you?'

Brooke's eyes lit up. Here was her chance to tell them her master plan. 'I went up to the Pavilions today and had a look around. It's a fabulous building and I think it's going to be great for CAL.'

Milo gave her a smile of approval. Rupert had his eyes fixed on her legs where her skirt had ridden up as she sat on the stool. He'd had quite a lot to drink. The sooner she said her piece and got them downstairs for something to eat, the better.

'And I've had a great idea,' she ploughed on, ignoring Milo's warning glance. 'The Café Au Lait bistro could run side by side with the theatre. If it were situated in the foyer, it could provide restaurant catering for theatre goers and non theatre goers alike once the theatre is restored. The Pavilions would be transformed into a beacon of high entertainment for the West Country!' She looked around expectantly. Four faces stared back at her, stunned. 'I don't know whether Milo has mentioned this,' she pressed on, 'but I am a trained actress. A good actress. I can not only be the face of Café Au Lait but also the face of the Pavilions!'

There was silence as she finished. Then Milo got to his feet and said, 'Brooke, may I have a word?'

He walked towards her bedroom and she followed. 'Close the door behind you,' he ordered in a low voice. She did so.

'What the fuck do you think you are doing?'

'I . . . was just—'

'You were just fucking me and yourself over. Save the theatre? Be an actress? What the fuck's that about?'

'Well, I . . .'

He grabbed the top of her arm hard and squeezed. 'Don't you ever undermine me in front of a client again.'

'You're hurting my arm.'

He pushed his face into hers and she felt his spittle on her skin as he spoke: 'I'll hurt more than your arm if you carry on spouting out any stupid idea that comes into that pea brain of yours. These are powerful men. They have the money, they have my balls and they have your future in their pockets. Do you understand?'

She nodded, frightened.

'They didn't come down here to hear you speak. They came here to look at you. They came down here so that they could tell their mates they were in Brooke Lynne's hotel room. Now you need to be nice to them – and I mean *really* nice. Am I making myself clear?'

'Yes.' Tears pricked her eyes but she forced them back.

The bedroom door opened behind her. Councillor Bedford stood at the door, swaying slightly, an empty lager glass in his hand. 'Is this a private party, or can anyone join in?'

Milo beamed at him and let go of Brooke's arm. 'I was just saying, we need to get some cocktails sent up. Champagne cocktails, I think. We've got a lot to celebrate.'

Brooke returned to the drawing room. 'Get onto room service would you, Brooke. Have them send up some brandy and half a dozen bottles of champagne.'

As she put the phone down she saw Michael emptying a small bag of white powder onto the coffee table. Taking his wallet from his pocket, he removed a platinum American Express card and began chopping the powder into thin lines. Milo was watching her. 'Come on, Brooke. You're a very lucky girl to be employed by these nice men. Relax.' Michael had just hoovered up the first line. He handed her the rolled-up twenty-pound note he'd been using. 'Ladies first – it's good stuff.'

'No thank you. I don't—'

Rupert put his finger in the residue Michael had left behind and rubbed it on his gums. 'Come on, babe. It's just a little charlie.'

Councillor Bedford's eyes were like saucers. 'I've always wanted to try this stuff. How do you do it?'

Rupert showed him.

As the drug took effect, Bedford's pupils dilated and his manner towards Brooke became more bold. 'I must say,' he smirked, his eyes brazenly roving over her curves, 'This is what I call a nice bonus.'

Brooke's brain was spinning. How had she got into this situation? She felt a hand caressing her bottom. Rupert was behind her, whispering in her ear: 'Why don't we go to your bedroom? The others are happy here. Unless you'd like them to watch?'

He slid his arm round her waist and she felt his breath and hot tongue in her ear.

There was a knock at the door.

'That's room service.' He let her go and she ran to the door. Toby and Marc were there, pushing a huge trolley loaded with six bottles of champagne in a wine cooler and a big bottle of brandy.

'Have you got a phone on you?' she asked in a desperate whisper.

'Yeah,' said Toby.

'Give it to me.' She took the phone and quickly turned around, thrusting the phone towards the table, capturing the lines of coke on the coffee table, the bottles of booze, and the look of stunned shock on the three men's faces.

Marc threw his hands up in horror. 'Oh my God! It's a drugs den!'

Milo ran towards Brooke. 'Give me that phone, you stupid bitch!'

But Brooke was too fast for him. She ran out of the door and into the hallway screaming, 'Help! Police! Help!'

Toby and Marc abandoned the trolley and ran hell for leather down the corridor after her, bundling her into the service lift and taking her down to the sanctuary of the kitchen.

For a second or two they stood in silence, panting and wild-eyed, grateful to be out of that room. Then Marc grinned at her and said, 'You can't half shift in those heels, girlfriend. I'm proud of you!'

10

The taxi pulled up outside Ryan and Jess's flat. The street looked dull and drab after the brightly garish colours of Thailand. The dark and threatening clouds above were only highlighted by the steel grey of the sky. As Ryan paid the cab driver, and signed an autograph for the cabbie's wife, Jess stood on the damp pavement and looked up at the windows of their top-floor flat. She'd soon be alone again. Ryan was off filming in two days' time. The carefree relaxed mood of her holiday was dissolving like an aspirin in water, yet without the benefits of analgesia.

She had asked Ryan, as they'd sat by the pool in Thailand one day, if he thought she might be depressed.

He'd looked at her in surprise, then told her to pull herself together; she didn't have a mental illness, all she needed was to get a job under her belt. When she pointed out that it wasn't that easy and started to list the humiliating auditions she'd endured of late, his response had been to suggest that she give up acting and try something else.

'You're a jolly good organiser,' he told her. 'You'd make an excellent school secretary.'

'Like your mother?'

'Yes. Like my mother. She was always home in time to cook supper for me and Dad, plus she had all those long holidays.' He'd smiled and kissed her. 'It would suit you very well.'

'So you don't think I've got what it takes to make it as an actress?'

'Hey, babe, it's not that.' Ryan put his arm around her and gave her shoulder a squeeze. 'It's just that this business is really tough and I don't want to see you brought down by it.'

Despite the many hours she'd spent torturing herself with the notion that she was a failure as an actress, this unexpected career advice had knocked her sideways. She'd wanted to be an actress ever since she could remember. If that was taken from her, what did she have left? The only thing she could come up with was Ryan. Apart from one (major) indiscretion with a young actress, he'd stuck with Jess for seven years. But there had been no mention of marriage, or children. All they shared was a rented flat at the top of a converted Edwardian house in Willesden and two dachshunds. Lucky girl.

Ryan broke into her thoughts. 'Jess, carry my holdall would you? I'll get the cases.'

Together they hauled themselves and their luggage up the four flights of stairs.

Panting, Ryan put his key in the front door and pushed it open. Jess heard the sound of mail swishing over the stripped floorboards of the small hall.

'Here we are then: home sweet home!' declared Ryan. 'Put the kettle on, love. I'm dying for a whizz.'

While he disappeared into the loo she shoved the holdall and the suitcases further into the hall in order to close the door, then bent down to scoop up the pile of post. She carried it into the kitchen and dumped it on the table, then set about making the tea.

Ryan returned just as she realised there was no milk. 'I'll nip out and get some.' He grinned at her and gave her a hug. 'Happy?'

'Yeah.' She allowed herself to fold into his arms. 'You?'

'What a silly question! Of course I am. Lovely girl-friend, lovely holiday and six months' filming ahead of me. What's not to be happy about?' He rummaged in his trouser pockets, looking for cash. 'Got any change, darling? I've got nothing but Thai baht on me.'

'In my purse.'

Alone in the kitchen she poured the boiling water on to the teabags, then covered the teapot with an old cosy she'd embroidered for her GCSE sewing exam.

Over the next fifteen minutes she emptied the cases, sorted the washing and loaded up the machine. Then she sat down at the kitchen table and began going through the post, sorting it into two piles: one for Ryan, one for her. Bills, catalogues, a postcard from an old school friend, junk mail and a cheque for £27.44 from her agent for a repeat of a television programme in which she'd made a brief appearance. She'd need that to help with the exorbitant kennel bill when she collected the girls in the morning.

She heard Ryan's key in the lock. 'Tea's brewed,' she called.

He came into the kitchen puffing. 'Either those stairs are getting longer or I'm getting older.' He put a carrier bag on the table, its damp edges resting on her £27.44 cheque, smudging the ink. Silently she lifted the bag and slipped the cheque out of the way.

He poured them both some tea and sat down. Jess sipped her tea in silence. His larger-than-life presence was irritating her for no reason. Maybe she should go to the doctor. She was definitely not feeling herself.

'I got a few essentials: cooked chicken, salad, fruit . . . That way you won't have to cook on your first night home.'

'Thank you.'

'I think I'll have a shower and then a nap. Want to join me?'

'Would you run me a bath?'

'Sure.'

The familiarity of their bed and the feel of their own bed linen combined with the light-headedness of jet lag allowed them to sleep the deepest of sleeps.

It was dark outside when Jess woke. They'd slept all afternoon. Ryan was lying on his side, his hand resting under his cheek. His mouth was pursed like a baby's. She left him and went to the living room to turn on her computer.

A message from her agent was waiting for her.

From: Alana Chowdhury
Subject: Availability
Darling Jess,
Tried phoning but you must have it turned off.
Give me a bell soonest.
Alana

Jess reached for her phone and checked the battery. Dead. She found the charger, finally, at the bottom of her handbag and plugged it in.

'Alana Chowdhury.'

'Alana, it's me – Jess.'

'Jess darling, where've you been? I couldn't raise you.'

'I've been on holiday. In Thailand. With Ryan. Remember?'

'You must tell me if you're going away.'

'I did.' Jess knew that she was only one name on a long list of actors represented by Alana, but now she felt as if she'd gone from minor to minuscule.

Alana carried on: 'I've been approached to put some clients forward for a new comedy drama for the BBC. I threw your name in as a last-minute thought.'

'Great,' said Jess faintly.

'And, I've got you an audition. Tomorrow. Nine o'clock. Off the Charing Cross Road somewhere.'

'Nine a.m.?'

'Of course nine a.m. I'll send an email with details. Good luck. And *try* to look the part.'

'How do they want me to look?' But Alana had already rung off.

*

'*Konnichiwa*! That's Thai for hello, isn't it?'

'No, Em, that's Japanese.' Desperate for a friendly voice to lift her spirits and distract her from her woes, Jess had phoned her sister. Emma was younger by three years and lived in rural chaos somewhere in Kent with her musician husband Dan (who never seemed to have an actual paying job) and a headstrong five-year-old son called Max.

'How's my favourite nephew?' asked Jess.

'That's because he's your only nephew. Oh, you know, the usual. I heard one of the mums at school refer to him as Mad Max the other day. Might have been something to do with the little horror locking the reception teacher out of the classroom and leading the kids in a mini revolt.'

Jess laughed. 'Don't worry, he'll be Prime Minister one day.'

'If that happens, I'm emigrating. How was Thailand?'

'It was amazing . . .' Jess's voice wavered.

'You don't sound too sure of that.'

'No, no, no,' Jess protested. 'Ryan was great, really atten-tive, made me feel like a princess.'

'About time too,' said Emma.

'He'll be off shooting *Venini* again soon.'

'Ah. And you're feeling – what, exactly? Wish you were going with him?'

'No, it isn't that.' Jess hesitated, wondering how to put it into words. 'I mean, I will miss him, but . . . I'm feeling so rootless. It's been ages since I had a decent role to get my teeth into and I just don't know if it's ever going to happen for me. Ryan says I should get a job as a school secretary.'

'What?' Emma spluttered. 'Well, that's just typical! Look, I know you adore the pants off the guy and always have – hell, we really like Ryan too; he's fun when he remembers not to take himself too seriously – but selfless he ain't. God forbid he'd have the time or the energy to support you in the same way that you've been there for him.'

'He does support me. He took me to Thailand, didn't he?'

Emma's voice softened. 'Look, Sis, you are a bloody amazing actress. You're not some bimbo starlet, you're the real deal. Remember how Mum and Dad helped you get through stage school, paying for all those extra acting lessons? They weren't just indulging you because it was what you wanted, they did it because they believed in you, because you had a talent that was worth nurturing.'

Despite herself, tears sprang into Jess's eyes. Mum and Dad had been gone over a decade now, both having succumbed to cancer within a few years of each other, but not a day went by when she didn't miss them.

'Don't quit yet, Jess. Something will happen for you, I'm convinced of it.'

Jess swiped the tears from her eyes. She didn't know what she would do without Emma. It felt good to know there was someone in her corner, loving her unconditionally.

'In the meantime,' said Em briskly, 'when are you next coming down? It's been months since we saw you. Dan's got a big jam in a couple of weeks – he and some of the other layabouts have got a mini music festival going on at the local pub. There'll be beer. And possibly fags.'

'Em! I thought you'd quit?'

'Yeah, well, that would make me too perfect. See if you can persuade Big Head to join you.'

'He'll be filming. I'll come though. Can't wait to see Max.'

'OK, but don't put your fingers near his cage. He bites!'

*

By the time Jess came off the phone, Alana's email had landed in her inbox. It wasn't exactly heavy on details: just the name of the casting director, the address of the rehearsal rooms where the audition would take place and the title of the production – *Horse Laugh*. It was based on a series of successful books about a woman called Lydia who inherits a racing stables from her black sheep of an uncle. Despite knowing nothing about horses, jockeys or races, Lydia somehow manages against all the odds to make a success of it, with lots of hilarious adventures along the way. She's aided and abetted by her faithful sidekick, a stable girl called Moira, who's older, wiser and has a cynical one-liner for every occasion.

Jess quickly downloaded one of the books on her

Kindle and spent the rest of the evening speed-reading while being fed chicken salad by Ryan.

'Lydia is a great character, Ryan. I could do a lot with the part.'

'Is she the only female role?'

'No, there's her friend, Moira. But she's quite a bit older than Lydia.'

'What are their ages?'

'Thirty-something and forty-something.'

Ryan put his hand to his chin and rubbed it. Jess could hear the rasp of his stubbly beard on his fingers.

'Why are you looking at me like that?'

'Like what?'

'You think they want me for Moira, the old one, don't you?'

'No, don't be silly.'

'But you do?'

'I'm only thinking it might be a good idea to be prepared to audition for either one, just in case.'

*

The following morning, Jess found the address she was looking for and rang the bell fifteen minutes early. With a buzz, the door unlocked itself and she went into an open hallway, with a long corridor stretching back the length of the building and doors leading off either side of it . . . A young girl with a clipboard and scruffy ponytail was waiting.

'You here for *Horse Laugh*?'

'Yes. Jess Tate.'

The girl looked at her clipboard and found Jess's name. 'You're a bit early, so if you could just wait here.' She indicated four plastic chairs lined up against the wall.

'Thank you.' Jess sat. 'By the way, can you tell me which part you're auditioning for today?'

'Moira.'

Jess smiled brightly. 'Great. Thanks.'

The girl set off down the long corridor then opened the first door on the left and disappeared.

Jess let her smile drop. Ryan had been right. Thank God she'd listened to him and done her homework on both Lydia and Moira.

He'd put his arm round her and given her a pep talk: 'Darling, they'll be casting everyone younger than the book. Lydia will end up as a twenty-three-year-old and Moira a thirty-two-year-old – trust me.' She trusted him.

Twenty minutes later she was standing in Charing Cross Road, dialling Ryan's number.

'I've been called back for this afternoon.'

'I've got everything crossed for you.'

She got the job.

Within ten days the contract came through. Jess was on the up.

*

Ollie parked his old red MG Midget in the car park of Heathrow's terminal five, grabbed the huge bunch of cream roses from the tattered front seat and ran as fast as he could to the arrivals gate. He got there with time to spare. Red's flight was delayed by thirty minutes.

Good-looking young men running breathlessly through airport terminals with vast bouquets of expensive roses inevitably attract attention. He was no exception. Two giggly air hostesses approached him.

'We know you don't want any fuss and this is your

private time, but can we have our photo taken with you?'

He stood and grinned for the picture, conscious all the while of more and more eyes turning towards him.

'You waiting for Red?' a young teenage girl, standing a few feet away, asked boldly and rather too loudly. 'Is all the band coming too? I'm wearing my T-shirt.' She opened her grubby denim jacket to reveal Red and her band Red Zed in action.

'Hmm,' said Ollie, smiling while pulling his baseball cap down further. He felt a nudge in his ribs and turned to find a potbellied man in his fifties, sweating in an over-tight polo shirt and with highly magnifying spectacles, preparing to jab him again. 'You're that actor fella, are you?'

'Um.' Ollie was feeling horribly exposed and uncom-fortable.

'I know it's you. My son here' – he pointed at a gangly spotty boy wearing an 'I ♥ Red' T-shirt – 'is waiting for Red's autograph. She is coming through this way, isn't she?'

'Um . . .' Ollie hated this level of recognition.

'Well, is she or isn't she?' asked Mr Magoo.

At that moment two uniformed police officers, tipped off by the air hostesses, stepped in. 'Come with us if you would, sir,' said the taller one as they positioned them-selves on either side of him, angling their bodies to clear a way through the growing crowd and escort him to the safety of their small office.

'Who are you meeting, sir?' the tall policeman asked, closing the door behind them.

'My girlfriend. Red?'

'Thought so. Our colleagues airside will assist her through Customs and get her out to you in one piece.'

'Thank you. That's really kind.'

'No problem, sir.' The policeman's eyes flicked to his colleague. 'While we're waiting, would you mind giving us a photo and an autograph?'

*

Red's tiny frame, clad head-to-toe in black leather with even blacker sunglasses covering most of her pale freckled face, topped by the trademark scarlet spiky hair, was barely visible within the phalanx of police officers. It didn't stop the fans who were waiting for her, and the wider audience of innocent bystanders, from pressing forward, cameras flashing as they called her name. When Ollie's two policemen manoeuvred him safely inside her secure circle of blue uniforms, Red screamed with joy.

'Oh my God! Isn't this crazy!' She kissed him and held onto the arm that wasn't carrying the bunch of roses. Then, sticking her free arm into the air and waving at the crowds, she yelled, 'Hi, everybody! Red's home!' which encouraged a fresh blast of flashbulbs and hysteria.

'Have you missed me?'

'Yeah!' shouted the crowd, whether they were fans or not. It seemed the polite thing to do.

'Red can't hear you!' she shouted back. 'I said, "Have you missed me?"'

'YEAH!'

By now they were nearing the exit and the police, in one practised and professional move, steered Red and Ryan out of the terminal and into a big black limo parked on the double yellow lines.

Red was bundled into the back and she reached a hand out ready to pull Ollie in after her.

'My car's in the car park,' he said.

'OK. See you later,' said Red. The chauffeur closed the door behind her and hurried round to get behind the wheel. Red's window slid down and she asked, 'Are those for me?' Pointing at the roses.

'Oh – yes.' He handed them over.

'Thanks. I'll call you as soon as I get to the hotel.'

The car moved away from the kerb just as the crowds burst through the terminal doors and out onto the pavement. Seeing them running towards the car, Red tossed her roses into the air for them to catch.

Ollie could only look on in astonishment as two dozen roses at five pounds a stem were torn apart.

*

In the open and very public breakfast room of the Starfish, Brooke took a seat opposite the odious Milo and listened to his pathetic rewrite of the previous evening's events.

'Brooke, babe, you have no idea how upset Rupert and Michael are thanks to your outrageous behaviour.'

'*My* behaviour? Excuse me, but they were off their faces and I was frightened.'

'Frightened? Whatever of?'

'I felt intimidated and threatened. Physically, emotionally and sexually. And instead of protecting me, you tried to bully me into "being nice to them", as you put it.'

'Now you're talking nonsense.'

'I was scared. They were drunk and taking drugs.'

'So what? Everybody does a bit of coke. It's nothing to get your knickers in a twist about.' He picked up his coffee cup and winked at her across the rim. 'Who's to say the charlie wasn't yours?'

'What? I am not some pea-brained idiot, Milo. I felt like a piece of meat last night. "Get them a drink, Brooke. Be nice to them, Brooke." You expected me to have sex with one or all of them, didn't you?'

Milo's face darkened and he leaned forward, glancing around the breakfast room to make sure no one was eavesdropping before lowering his voice and hissing, 'Prove it. Who'd believe a slag like you over someone like me?'

Brooke's heart beat faster as she took in this sudden nasty turn, but she was determined not to show her alarm.

'You forget – there are photographs.'

Milo leaned back in his chair and laughed. 'Meaningless! The boys were just fooling around – a bit of talcum powder and high jinks.'

Brooke played her trump card. 'I'm going to tell Bob. And when he hears how you behaved he'll leave your agency and tell the press why. You'll be ruined.'

'Ooh! She threatens me. I'm so scared!' Then Milo dropped the mock hysteria and hissed nastily: 'Have you checked your phone lately?'

Brooke was on the back foot. 'No.'

'You should.'

She scrabbled in her bag and brought out her phone. One voicemail message: Bob. Very emotional.

'Milo's just called me. Do you really need a job that much? Getting stoned? Drunk? Giving the Café Au Lait guys the come-on? I can't believe it. If Milo hadn't walked in on you, I'd never have known. He's helped you so much and this is how you repay him? And me? Fuck, you've used me good and proper, haven't you? Milo will keep all this out of the papers – for my sake, not yours. As for us? You are not the person I thought you were. I'll send your things

to Milo's office for you to collect. I'm changing the locks and my phone number, so don't bother trying to get hold of me.'

Brooke couldn't believe what she was hearing. Her eyes brimming with tears, she looked across the table at Milo. His mouth twisted in a cruel, satisfied grin.

'How could you be such a bastard, Milo? What have I ever done to you?'

He spread his hands in front of him. 'What can I say? This is business, babe. You don't play by my rules, you're finished. No Café Au Lait contract, no hero boyfriend, and no agent. Oh, and you can kiss goodbye to the magazine column, the make-up range, the handbags – all cancelled. I'll see to it you never work in this industry again. Shame, because you were on the cusp of something good.' He stood and tossed two twenty-pound notes on the table. 'Call that your tip.'

Brooke could only sit fighting back the tears, watching in silence as he walked away, taking her career with him.

11

Colonel Walter Irvine was not accustomed to having visitors. He couldn't remember the last time anyone had dropped by Beach Cottage, his cosy bachelor abode overlooking Shellsand Bay. It was a small two-up-two-down with a tiny kitchen and bathroom tacked on. Those had been Peter's handiwork. Very good at design and building, was Peter.

Walter had already tidied up the shabby sitting room in readiness for his visitors, now he was looking at the uneven walls of the narrow and gloomy hall. How long had it been since he'd painted them in that magnolia eggshell? He thought for a moment. It must have been soon after he'd lost Peter. Goodness – forty years ago. Could it really have been that long? He reached up and brushed a cobweb from one of the numerous photographs of his Glorious Glosters. Not many of the boys left now. He straightened his shiny regimental tie and gave them a smart salute.

'I'm on parade today, chaps. Got a visitor. Save the Pavilions, what. Tell you about the battle plan once briefed.'

Turning away from his old comrades, he marched into the kitchen. He'd no sooner started to lay out a tray of two cups and saucers when there came a knock at the door.

'Come in, come in. Welcome to Beach Cottage.'

His visitor had a kind, pretty face and introduced herself as Helen Merrifield. Walter recognised her from around the village and seemed to recall that she had moved to Pendruggan quite recently.

'Am I right in thinking you are new to these parts, my dear?' he asked, ushering her in.

'Yes', Helen replied. 'I came from London after my husband and I divorced. Fresh start.'

'Ah yes, the big metrollops! You probably wouldn't guess it now, but I hail from London myself. St John's Wood. But Cornwall feeds something in the soul, don't you find?'

'I couldn't agree more. I feel like I've found my spiritual home.'

She followed him into the kitchen where he passed her the cups for their tea and some ginger nuts and fig rolls to arrange on a patterned plate. They both settled in front of the fire in the sitting room. They chatted easily until the Colonel set down his cup and said, 'I don't think you've come just to humour an old man, have you, my dear?'

'Well, no, not quite,' said Helen. 'As you know, Colonel Irvine, the council are planning to sell the Pavilions to a large coffee chain. Many people in the area feel that this shouldn't be allowed to happen and we're mobilising strong opposition to the plans. But we're on the back foot rather, and time isn't on our side.'

The Colonel nodded, encouraging her to continue.

'We've come across something that might just make all the difference to our campaign to prevent the sale going ahead. And that something is you.'

'Me, dear girl?'

'You were the man who opened the theatre and ran it, weren't you?'

For a moment the Colonel seemed engrossed in picking at some invisible fluff on his check trousers, but eventually he looked Helen in the eye, and with some pride, replied, 'I was.'

'You were a performer as well as theatre manager?'

'Indeed. Me and my alter ego – Colonel Stick. I created him during my time in Korea. I was barely out of my teens when I was called up for National Service; drew the short straw and got sent off to fight. Terrible times.' Walter shook his head, then focused his gaze on an old photograph propped on the mantelpiece. It featured a good-looking man in wellies with one foot resting on a garden spade and a cup of tea raised to the camera. 'To liven things up, my friend Peter and I and several of the other chaps formed an entertainment corps. We all needed to take our minds off the horrors that the war was inflicting on us, so we'd put on plays and musical revues. Colonel Stick was my contribution – a parody of some of those blustering army major types. It made the lads laugh, and laughter was something we desperately needed back then.'

Helen could see that they were stirring painful memories: 'We found a photo of you and Max Miller on the opening night of the Pavilions.' She reached in to her handbag and fished out a plastic document case.

'Don't bother with that, dear girl.' The Colonel patted her hand and rose creakily to his feet. 'I've got the original here.' He went out into the hallway and opened the door to the dining room. It was so cold in there, it almost took her breath away. 'Do excuse the mess. I use this room as my office but never seem to get things straight.'

On the old table in the centre of the room were boxes and boxes tied up with string or falling apart where old sellotape had yellowed and lost its stickability. Next to the boxes were piles of letters, theatre programmes and photos. Some had spilled onto the threadbare carpet.

The Colonel indicated the wall to the right. 'There you are. Opening night.'

Surrounding the rusty and empty Victorian grate, were more than thirty framed photographs of a young and extremely dashing Walter with various major stars of the fifties and sixties. Helen noticed that in many of the pictures, posing alongside Walter was another handsome young man, the same one from the photograph next door. In one image, taken in a garden, he had his foot on a spade and a cup of tea in his hand. The Colonel pointed; in the middle was the picture they were looking for.

'Max was a marvellous fellow. He fought in the First World War and entertained us in the Second. He took me under his wing when I was a young assistant stage manager, taught me everything there was to know about performing, about respecting talent and about being generous as a performer. I finished my National Service in 1952 and when I got home, I went to see him backstage at the Hackney Empire, and he took me on again. For a couple of years I honed my craft and performed up and down the country, but I really loved the whole world of the theatre, not just being on stage. When I spotted the advertisement in *The Stage* listing vacancies at a new theatre in Cornwall, Max was the one who encouraged me. He thought I had enough "chutzpah" to go for the top job as theatre manager, even though I was still only twenty-five. "Aim low, you can't miss. Aim high and the sky's the limit," he told me. Anyway, I came down here and got the job. Later, I found out that he'd pulled a few strings on my behalf and promised he'd top the bill on the opening night as long as they gave me the job.'

'That's amazing!' said Helen, completely caught up in the story. 'But this is marvellous. No one could let the theatre close now. You are its star.'

The Colonel gave a sad smile. 'I'm eighty-seven, my dear. Who would be interested in me?'

'Colonel, we've heard rumours of a film archive – a collection of home movies that you made featuring various actors and actresses of the period. Can you tell me about that – is it true?'

The change that came over the Colonel was instant. His friendly face turned pale and he stammered out a reply: 'I can't think what you are talking about, my dear.'

'But, Colonel, our local historian, Piran Ambrose, read somewhere that—'

The Colonel's tone was polite, but it had taken on a distinctly frosty edge: 'I can assure you, there is no such thing – and I should know. Now, please excuse me, I find visitors terribly draining and would be grateful if we could draw this meeting to a close.'

'But—'

The Colonel was already on his feet and off to the hallway, retrieving her jacket and light cotton Liberty scarf, a present from Penny, from the old-fashioned hat stand by the cottage door.

'Please, Mrs Merrifield . . .' the Colonel's steady gaze met her own and Helen thought that she detected more than brusqueness in his face. Sadness? Regret? 'I am an old man and talking of the past tires me. I don't mean to be rude, but I would prefer it if you would leave now.'

'Of course, Colonel. I'm sorry to have tired you. Thank you for taking the time to see me.'

The Colonel bade her farewell and Helen stood on the doorstep for a moment as the front door closed, politely, in her face.

What have I done? she thought. *There's a mystery here. Wait until I tell Piran!*

*

Later that evening, resting her legs on Piran's lap as they lounged on Helen's comfy sofa in Gull's Cry cottage, Helen recounted her visit with the Colonel.

'Mmm,' Piran mulled, as he drank his pot of Cornish Rattler cider. 'Sounds like you 'it a raw nerve there.'

'That's what I thought. What do you suppose it could be?'

'How would I know?'

'I noticed that in a lot of the other pictures of the Colonel at the Pavilions, he was with another man. Perhaps if I could find out who he is and get in contact with him, he might be able to shed some light on the whole film archive thing.'

Piran nodded. 'There's more than one reference to it in the records, so it definitely exists, regardless of what the old boy might say. I'll see what more I can find in the archives. As if I didn't 'ave enough to do – bloody Pavilions!'

'Oh, put a sock in it, you old grumbler. You're interest is piqued – I can always tell, you get that look in your eye.'

'Rubbish.'

Helen stretched over and picked up her iPad from the side table. Piran did the same with his own that has burrowed down behind one of the cushions on the sofa. For the rest of the evening, they must have looked at hundreds of websites relating to the theatre world, many of them run by enthusiasts and featuring plenty of old photographs. There were familiar faces, such as Max Wall and Arthur Askey, and others that Helen had never heard of.

'Blimey, ever heard of Wilson, Keppel and Betty? They were huge in the thirties and forties.'

Piran frowned, 'What are you wittering on about now, woman?'

'Oh, nothing,' she sighed, ready to give up on the seemingly fruitless search. 'Plenty of pictures of the Colonel, but none of the other chap.' She yawned.

'Hang on a minute,' said Piran. 'What's this?'

Helen leaned over to see what he was looking at. On the screen was a picture of the Colonel alongside another man. It was definitely the man she had seen in the photographs at the Colonel's house. The caption underneath read:

Theatre manager Walter Irvine and director Peter Winship celebrate the successful opening of Hats Off, *Trevay!*

Helen grinned like a Cheshire cat. 'Bingo!'

*

The next morning, Helen padded downstairs to make a pot of coffee and spotted a letter on her doormat. She opened it and found a neat handwritten note:

> *Mr Walter Irvine*
> *Beach Cottage*
> *Shellsand Bay*

Dear Mrs Merrifield
Please excuse my unforgivable rudeness yesterday. I fear I am becoming a crotchety old man.

*I can't help you with your other enquiry, but the
Pavilions mean more to me that I can adequately
express. I'll do anything I can to assist.
Yours very sincerely
Walter Irvine (a.k.a. Colonel Stick)*

*

Brooke was curled up on the sofa in her flat, nursing a
gin and tonic and a bad case of self-pity. She was trying
to watch the news but the endless stories of soaring crime
rates and rising house prices made her feel much much
worse.

Milo had been as good as his word. In the next day's
post she had received a recorded letter from Café Au Lait's
legal team, explaining that they would not be moving
forward with the contract and citing grossly unprofes-
sional behaviour as the cause. In her place, the newspapers
crowed, CAL had signed up a pneumatic 'glamour model'
who was looking to change her image.

Despite her many voicemail messages and texts, trying
to explain what had really happened, she'd seen neither
hide nor hair of Bob in the last couple of weeks. Until
this morning, when she'd opened her newspaper to find
photographs of him with his new girlfriend, a beautiful
and bright sports presenter with a satellite TV channel.

So here she was: a stinking cold, no job, no agent, no
boyfriend and no prospects.

Brooke got up and went to the kitchen to pour herself
another gin and tonic. As she came back into the lounge,
a shot of the Pavilions filled the television screen. She
reached for the remote and turned the sound up.

. . . It may look like any other forgotten seaside theatre,

but down here in Trevay the curtain is rising on an extraordinary tale.

The Pavilions made way for a faded photograph of Colonel Irvine, the camera slowly pulling away to reveal Max Miller standing next to him.

Walter Irvine, seen here with comic legend Max Miller, has been keeping a secret. He knows more about this old building than anyone else alive.

Cut to a shot of Colonel Irvine, walking along the headland to the theatre, swinging his stick jauntily, followed by a close-up of him in his dressing room.

'My God! It's him!' Brooke spoke aloud to no one. 'That's the dressing room he showed me.'

'Colonel, what does this place mean to you?'

'A great deal. I ran it for over two decades and during that time we had the cream of British theatre and light entertainment through these doors . . .'

'But now you are fighting to save it. Why?'

'Because the last thing Trevay needs is another coffee shop . . .'

As his short speech drew to a close the Colonel raised his voice and banged his ubiquitous stick loudly on the floor. Watching him, Brooke laughed, but it died on her lips as the faces of Rupert Heligan and Michael Woodbine filled the screen. The very sight of the men from CAL made her feel physically sick.

Rupert was talking in his smooth, oily tones:

'Café Au Lait is committed to bringing jobs to Trevay while offering visitors a place of quality in which to relax. The Pavilions is a great old building, but it's had its time as a theatre. Councillor Chris Bedford has been most helpful in getting our plans as far as he has and he and I feel the people of Trevay will be very pleased with what we'll bring

to the town. I'm a family man with family values and that's what Café Au Lait stands for too.'

Brooke snapped the television off. Family values? The man was a sexual predator and a ruthless conniving shark. Thanks to Rupert Heligan and his cronies, she was out of a job and her career prospects were in ruins – and now he was going to wreck the Pavilions too, and break an old man's heart in the process. Somehow, he had to be stopped. She was damned if Café Au Lait and that cretinous councillor were going to get away with their underhand schemes. First thing in the morning she was going to get herself down to Trevay and join the campaign to save the Pavilions. Milo James might think he'd put paid to her, but he was about to find out that Brooke Lynne could still command a headline or two.

Her head cold and self-pity vanished and she enjoyed the best night's sleep she'd had in ages.

12

Simon stood by the door, agitatedly rattling the car keys in his pocket. Piran had phoned five minutes earlier and told him and Penny to get down to the Dolphin, their local pub: 'Sharpish, mind. We may have found some ammunition to stop those bloody coffee people and the council in their tracks.'

Penny raced down the stairs, trailing her coat behind her.

'So what did he say exactly?' She took a quick look in the hall mirror, and checked her hair.

'Just what I told you,' said Simon, hopping from foot to foot. 'He says there's a woman he wants us to meet. Now.'

The pair of them ran down the vicarage path in the low drizzle and jumped into Simon's old Volvo. In the passenger seat, Penny shook the rain from her hair as she reached round for her seat belt. Simon turned the ignition key. Nothing. He tried again. Nothing.

'This bloody old heap!' Penny muttered under her breath.

Simon, who was very fond of his car, leapt to its defence. 'A bit of damp in her connections, that's all.' He turned the key again. A brief cough and the engine turned over. 'Faith, Penny. Faith can move mountains.' He put the gear lever into reverse and the engine immediately cut out.

Penny shifted herself in her seat to direct a steely glare at her stubborn husband. 'When will you see sense and get rid of this heap of rust?'

'There's nothing wrong with it. I'll open up the bonnet and give her a spray of WD40. It's all she needs.'

'No,' said Penny firmly, then continued in a slow voice as if speaking to a child: 'We are getting out of this car. I am going back indoors to get my keys. Then we shall drive to Trevay in *my* car.'

'But—'

Penny finally lost it. 'Get out of this bloody heap and into my car!'

Knowing better than to argue, Simon meekly agreed.

Halfway to Trevay, behind the wheel of her scarlet Jaguar, Penny broke the tense atmosphere by reopening the conversation. 'Why won't you let me buy you a new car?'

'I don't need one.'

'You do.'

'I don't.'

'I've got enough money to buy you a really nice car. Something practical for you to get around the parish in. Something you can stuff the surfboards in. A Range Rover, maybe?'

'No thank you.'

'You are so pig-headed! What about our marriage vows? With all my worldly goods I thee endow? I've got the money. Let me treat you.'

'It's nothing to do with that.' Simon turned to stare out of his window and missed the face Penny pulled behind his back.

*

The lights of the Dolphin shone warmly on the glistening path. Penny parked the car. She and Simon had barely spoken on the short journey. She hoped this bloody meeting would be worth it.

'Penny, Simon!' They spotted Piran and Helen immediately, but they weren't alone. Piran stood up and welcomed them both. 'Meet Brooke Lynne.'

Sitting on a comfortable armchair opposite the warm fire was the sexiest woman Penny had ever seen. Hourglass figure, tousled and highlighted blonde hair, glossy scarlet lips and smoky eyes. She turned her million-dollar smile at the two newcomers.

'Hello, I'm sorry to have dragged you out on such a horrible afternoon.'

'Not at all,' said Penny, reaching for one of the two stools that Simon was now dragging over from an empty table. Being accustomed to dealing with famous faces, she took Brooke Lynne's sudden appearance in her stride.

The same couldn't be said of her husband.

'Simon and I can't wait to hear what the big news is, can we, Simon?'

She looked at her dear but stubborn husband who was fiddling with his dog collar while trying not to look too hard at Miss Lynne. He found her skin-tight black dress, tanned bare legs and ridiculously high stilettos way too much to take in all at once.

'Simon!' Penny barked at him. 'Stop staring and sit down.' She raised a quizzical eyebrow at Piran, inviting him to explain what was going on.

'I think we may have found another lever to get the Council to think twice about selling the Pavilions,' said Piran. 'They're already on the back foot after the coverage of Colonel Irvine's connection. But just in case things get rougher still, we've got an ace up our sleeve. Miss Lynne here has something that they wouldn't want out in the public domain.'

'That's right,' said Brooke. 'I'm sure you've heard that I was replaced as the face of Café Au Lait, but you probably don't know why. When I saw the Colonel on TV and heard what was happening, I just couldn't bear to sit quietly and let them get away with it. So I did a Google search on opposition to the Café Au Lait plans, and Mr Ambrose's name came up—'

'Ah, that will be Piran's legendary diplomacy skills in action,' observed Helen.

Piran shifted uncomfortably in his seat. 'Can you just tell us what you know, Brooke?'

Brooke recounted her chance meeting with Colonel Irvine at the theatre, the day she'd come down to promote CAL. Then she told them what had gone on in her suite at the Starfish.

'It was horrible. They treated me like some kind of prostitute. I was so lucky that I escaped. But Milo made sure I lost the CAL contract, my agent and my boyfriend.'

'Who was at the meeting?' asked Piran.

Brooke cocked her head to one side and ticked off the names on her fingers:

'Rupert Heligan; Michael Woodbine, his PR man; Milo James, my snake of an agent, and a horrid little lech from the council – Chris someone.'

'Bedford,' growled Piran.

'Yes, that's him. Small, full of himself, with a nasty smug face. I must say, Piran, it was awfully satisfying to see that your fist had connected with that face.' An amused smile played around her full lips. 'Anyway, at the time I wasn't paying too much attention to what they were talking about in this meeting. It seemed to drag on for hours and all I wanted was for it to end so we could eat. But one thing I did hear was Heligan reminding Bedford that they were paying handsomely for his "interventions" and he expected him to sort out the opposition to the scheme.'

Piran clenched his fists and his face darkened. 'I knew that little toe-rag was a crook.'

'I had to come down and help. I'd like to use whatever public profile I have to save the Pavilions. So now I'm here, use me.'

'Do you have any proof?' asked Penny.

'Well, two lovely guys at the hotel – Toby and Marc – helped me out. They saw the cocaine on the table, and the booze. They must still have the photos.'

Simon cleared his throat and spoke first. 'The photos won't prove anything. This is blackmail, Piran. We can't play as dirty as them. And you did punch Councillor Bedford and knock him down. You're lucky he hasn't pressed charges.'

Piran's face darkened. 'He deserved it. In any case, weren't you the one who dragged me into this in the first place? I don't even care about saving the Pavilions – but I do care about our town being run by corrupt, tin-pot, greedy, small-minded dictators.'

'Hear hear!' said Penny.

Simon was about to say something else, but Piran shushed him. 'The point is, not only is Bedford in league with these coffee people, he's obviously being paid by them to push the deal through and to nobble other members of the council.'

Penny frowned. 'When is the final decision due?'

'Ten days.' Piran turned to Brooke. 'Could you get hold of these photos?'

'I'll try. In the aftermath of the whole episode, Milo convinced me that the photos wouldn't be worth anything – that no one would believe a has-been like me. But if you think they'll be worth something . . .'

Simon was a gentle man, but he was first and foremost a man of God. What was being suggested seemed to go against everything he stood for. He swallowed hard. 'That is blackmail.'

'It's the truth!' Piran raised his voice in frustration.

'We're playing with fire.'

'Simon, there are times when you have no choice but to fight fire with fire. These are sleazy men who want to line their own pockets, take drugs and have casual sex with pretty actresses,' argued Penny.

'That may well be the case, but I can't be a party to this.'

'But you're chairman of the Save the Pavilions action group – you have a responsibility, dammit.'

Both Simon and Piran were standing now.

'I also have a duty to my parish and to my faith. I'm sorry, Piran, but if this is the route that you are going down, then you'll need to find another chairman. Penny, it's time we went, I'm needed at a funeral first thing tomorrow.'

With that he grabbed his coat from the back of the chair and set off for the car park. Helen and Penny could only exchange anxious looks as Penny trailed out after him.

*

The following morning over at Gull's Cry, Helen voiced the same argument. 'It all sounds a bit tricky. There's a danger

Brooke could just be out for revenge and ready to say anything – regardless of the damage it might do to the Save the Pavilions campaign.' She passed Penny a large mug of strong black coffee and sat opposite her at the scrubbed kitchen table.

Penny sighed. She hadn't slept well, knowing that Simon was lying wide awake beside her feeling wretched. He'd had an awful time of it yesterday, what with her laying into him about the car and then Piran putting him in such an awkward position after listening to Brooke's extraordinary story.

'Why did we bother to get involved?' she groaned. 'I can't let Simon put his neck on the line. Nothing is that important. Certainly not that hideous pile out on the headland.' She crossed her arms on the table and rested her aching head on them.

Helen had seen Penny in this mood before. When everything was going well, Penny was a powerhouse of positive energy. But one blip and that energy drained out of her like water from a broken fish tank. Looking at her friend's tired and worried demeanour, she decided it was time for a pep talk.

'We've come this far, Pen, we can't give up now and let that odious Chris Bedford have it all his own way. If he gets away with this he'll be selling off the village green next, in exchange for a backhander from some burger bar!'

Penny's lifted her head, horrified at the prospect.

'In just over a week the council will make a decision – this is our last chance, Pen. We need to put everything we've got into galvanising the community into action. I admit I have reservations about Brooke Lynne, but if we went to the *Cornish Guardian* with the story I'm confident they would investigate properly and not just rush to print her photos and allegations. I've got to know the editor a little since I started doing my column and I'm sure he can be trusted. I was also thinking of approaching Brian Simpkins, to see if there's anything he can do to help the cause.'

'Simpkins . . . isn't he that solicitor friend of Piran's?'

'That's right. They're fishing buddies – sometimes Piran takes him and a few of his mates out on boat trips. You know, the kind where they take a fishing rod and six cases of strong ale. He's like a walking encyclopedia of Cornish law – I was thinking that if we could persuade him to take a look at the stuff Piran's dug out of the archives, Brian might be able to find a legal argument against the sale going ahead. It's worth a try, right?'

Helen's pep talk seemed to be doing the trick. The spark was back in Penny's eye and she was reaching for her BlackBerry. 'If we can find a way to save the Pavilions without resorting to sleazy underhand methods, Simon won't have to resign from the action group – I'm going to call him now and let him know you're enlisting Piran's lawyer friend to save the day . . .' Her fingers paused over the keypad as her eyes turned to Helen. 'Well, what are you waiting for – time is of the essence: get onto your editor chum this instant!'

13

I t's incredible what a beautiful, famous face can do for a campaign. Word spread quickly that Brooke had joined the Save the Pavilions action group and a big interview, plus photo shoot, with the *Cornish Guardian* under the headline *WHY I GAVE UP ON CAL TO SAVE THE PAVILIONS* recruited many more supporters. The journalist had asked some difficult questions about Brooke's loss of the CAL contract and the end of her relationship with Bob, but instead of getting into mud-slinging she simply said that she was an actress and her heart lay in saving theatres rather than promoting coffee shops, and that Bob was a lovely guy but things had come to a natural end.

'I wish Bob and Café Au Lait all the very best for their futures while I explore my own.' The journalist bought it.

Penny had set up the Save the Pavilions HQ in the dining room of the vicarage. As soon as that week's *Cornish Guardian* went on sale, the phone began to ring, and ring and ring. Not all the callers were nutters. Some were offering genuine support. The ball was rolling.

Not content with lending her face to the campaign, Brooke showed up at HQ to lend a hand stuffing envelopes.

'How many followers do you have on Twitter?' she asked.

Penny looked nonplussed. 'I don't have a Twitter.'

'OK, how much traffic is there on the website?'

'What website?'

Brooke shook her head and laughed. 'Penny, I'm surprised at you!'

'The IT guy looks after all that,' huffed Penny defensively. 'I'm a creative.'

Brooke was not going to accept this pathetic excuse.

'Social media is where it's all at, these days. Give me the number of your IT man and I'll brief him. But first we need to come up with a name for the campaign that rolls off the tongue a bit better. The "Save the Pavilions Campaign" is a bit of a mouthful, isn't it?'

'Er, I suppose.'

'We need a name that will really stop people in their tracks . . .' Brooke tilted her head to one side in an attractive fashion. 'Hang on – that could be it: STOP! We take the initials Save The Pavilions, and—'

'Where did the O come from?'

Brooke laughed throatily. 'Trust me – I know what works. I'll get hold of your IT man and we'll get him to create a SToP website and Twitter account.'

Within twenty-four hours they were trending, with followers around the globe.

*

Piran and Helen were back at the Dolphin.

'This is beginning to feel more like HQ than Pen's dining room,' she observed.

'I can think of worse places.'

Moments later they saw the jolly, tanned face of solicitor Brian Simpkins come through the door. Piran bought him a drink at the bar and soon they were hunkered down, over a pile of papers that Brian had taken out of his stylish briefcase.

'I think you're going to be pleased with what I've found, Piran,' he said cheerily, arranging the old, yellowing papers into some kind of order. 'Ignore the antiquated language – this document isn't as old as it looks. It might read as if it dates back to the Middle Ages but it's actually from the twenties. When you asked me have a dig around, my first stop was the Land Registry, to see who holds the title to the land that the Pavilions sits on. Unfortunately, it turns out that technically it belongs to the council . . .'

The faces across the table from him fell. But Brian continued as cheerily as ever:

'But when I started to delve further, I kept coming across mention of a covenant that covered the usage of the land.'

Brian paused and took a sip of his Cornish Knocker ale.

'And . . . ?' asked Piran impatiently.

'Is he always like this?' Brian enquired good-naturedly.

'Pretty much,' Helen sighed.

'Come on, Bri, spit it out.'

Brian laughed. 'All right, keep your hair on! As you'll know, being our local historian, in centuries past much of Trevay was common land. The people had ancient rights, permitting them to fish and keep pigs or chickens or whatever, or to help themselves to gravel and sand – I won't bore you with the details. Suffice to say that, by the twentieth century, the commoners, in other words the local people who managed common land for the collective good, had come up with better ways of earning money and so they stopped exercising those ancient rights. But those rights didn't go away. So even though the council have been responsible for managing the land for almost a century, the ancient rights of commoners still stand.'

Helen frowned. 'But what does that actually mean, Brian?'

'The rights of common land are very hard to change or overturn. Think of the New Forest and Exmoor – even today, commoners have the right to graze or keep their cattle on that land. This document in front of us states very clearly that the common land on which the Pavilions stands must continue to be managed by the Board of Conservators for the wider public benefit.'

'So,' said Piran carefully, 'the council are on a bit of a sticky wicket if they sell to Café Au Lait?'

'I'd go so far as to say that there is no way that they can sell, not without a lengthy legal battle – and folk in these parts don't take kindly to politicians messing about with commoners' rights,' said Brian.

Helen and Piran's eyes sparkled as they absorbed this new and exciting turn of events.

Piran rubbed his hands together with relish.

'I definitely owe you more than a pint, Bri.'

*

Back at the vicarage HQ, Brooke was amazed at how much she was enjoying being a part of the campaign.

She was sifting through over a dozen photos of the 1954 opening night that Colonel Stick had brought over. There was the Colonel on stage with Max Miller, surrounded by leggy female dancers in satin shorts and bra tops, clutching enormous ostrich feather fans. No wonder Max Miller was displaying his trademark wolfish grin.

Brooke set about uploading the pictures to the website,

making a note to herself to write a press release around them later.

The phone rang somewhere in the house and was answered by Penny, who walked with it into the makeshift office.

'How lovely of you to call, Julian . . . yes, I'm so sorry I haven't got back to you with dates but it's all been very busy here, what with shooting *Mr Tibbs* and . . . No, no, of course we want you . . . I realise how busy you are, it's been awful of me and I apologise . . . Yes, that's right. She's sitting opposite me right now . . .' She looked across at Brooke, a puzzled expression on her face. 'Yes, she is . . . Is she? I had no idea. Here, I'll hand you over to her.' Placing her hand over the receiver, Penny whispered, 'It's Julian Fellowes. He wants to talk to you.'

Brooke took the phone. 'Hi, Brooke speaking . . . Yes, I'm very well, thank you . . . I know, it has been a long time . . . No, nothing at the moment . . . Gosh, I'd love to. Just let me know when it is all firmed up and I'll be ready. Thank you so much. Bye.'

Penny was goggle-eyed. 'What was that all about? Has he offered you a part in *Downton*?'

'No, but he is offering to write a short play that we can put on to raise money for the Pavilions. He wants me to be in it.'

'Can you act?' blurted Penny.

Brooke took a deep breath and explained once again about the training she'd undergone, both at the Bristol Old Vic and the Actors Studio in New York.

Penny was flabbergasted. 'Darling, I'm sorry. I had no idea you were a bona fide actress – I thought it was just one of those things models say. You know, something to justify swanning about with famous boyfriends.'

'Well, that's what bloody Milo assumed, didn't he?' she answered crossly. 'That was how it suited him to promote me – his clients were all sports stars or TV presenters or models. I don't think he had a clue about the acting world. Biggest mistake of my life, letting myself get mixed up with him.'

'So how do you know Sir Julian?' said Penny, curious.

'He mentored some of the students when I was doing my training. He has a very generous spirit and gave me lots of advice at the time. He must have seen my name attached to the STOP campaign.'

'But how exciting! Julian writing something for you!'

Brooke grinned. 'Yes, it is exciting. By the way, what was he ringing you for?'

'Oh, I called in a few favours from some of my contacts a few weeks ago. He's one of them. He said he could do a night of *Downton* anecdotes for us.'

'Oh, I think that must be the piece he's writing, the one he's just offered me a part in. When's it happening?'

'Don't know. Haven't had time to sort anything out yet. He wants dates; Maggie and Hugh have very full diaries and need to book us in.'

Brooke stopped and gawped for a moment.

'*Maggie and Hugh?* You're kidding? As in Dame Maggie and Hugh Bonneville?'

Penny airily stretched her arms over her head. 'Yep.'

'Bloody hell, Penny! Pass me the diary – it's time we got organised.'

*

Simon was sitting in his chilly car, trying to get the damn thing started. The last thing he wanted was to be late for the meeting he'd arranged with Councillor Goodman. Joan Goodman was a good egg – a well-respected member and leader of the council and, as luck would have it, a member of his congregation. The moment Piran came to him with Brian Simpkins' discovery, he'd got on the phone to Joan and asked if they could come and present their findings to her. Her opinion carried a lot of weight on the council and he hoped that between them Piran and Brian had come up with enough ammunition to persuade her that their case was a sound one.

A sharp knock on the misted side window gave him a start. It was the postman. 'Mornin', Vicar. Didn't make 'ee jump, did I?'

Simon stopped his fruitless turning of the ignition key and wound down the window. 'Morning, Colin. Car's a bit cold.'

'Sounds stone-dead to me,' Colin answered helpfully, thrusting three letters and a charity brochure through the window. 'Mebbe Father Christmas'll bring you a new one, eh? That wife of your'n can afford it. Wish my wife could.'

'No need for that,' hissed Simon. 'I can afford my own car.'

Whether or not Colin heard as he strolled off, still in his summer shorts, Doc Martens kicking at the damp leaves, Simon would never know.

He rubbed his hand across his forehead. 'Please Lord, please let the car start.'

After trying for a further five minutes he finally gave up on looking heavenward for a solution and hurried up the garden path and into the vicarage to find Penny.

She was slouched at her makeshift desk, cradling a cup of coffee and looking at a crossword. At the sound of the door opening, she glanced up, an eyebrow raised enquiringly.

'The car won't . . . er . . . Any chance of a lift to Trevay? I don't want to be late for my meeting.'

It wasn't easy, but Penny rose above the urge to form a sentence combining the words scrapheap and Volvo.

Fifteen minutes later, she deposited him outside the majestic 1930s façade of Trevay Council headquarters.

'Good luck, darling.' She gave him an encouraging smile.

'Thank you, I think we'll need it.'

*

Councillor Goodman scrutinised the document in front of her. In her early sixties, with helmet hair and a penchant for boxy red suits, Joan Goodman looked as if she could give Angela Merkel and Ann Widdecombe a run for their money.

She peered out over the top of her horn-rimmed specs at the assembled faces of Simon, Piran and Brian.

'Well, gentlemen, you do seem to have put forward a most compelling case.'

'But is it good enough to stop Café Au Lait?' asked Simon.

Joan took off her glasses and looked at Simon sternly. 'There are myriad problems to deal with in Trevay and in this part of Cornwall and, for my own part, saving the Pavilions hasn't been a priority . . .'

Simon looked at her, uncertain where this was going. 'But the theatre is such a big part of our local identity—'

She held her hand up. '. . . Which isn't to say that I don't care about the Pavilions. I do. I'm a local girl, and one of my abiding memories from childhood is watching Danny La Rue in panto at the Pavilions as Widow Twanky.

But I am just one member of the council. Whatever else one might say about Chris Bedford, he is tenacious. Once he's set upon some course of action, he will stop at nothing to see it through.'

'Chris Bedford is a lousy crook and shouldn't even be on the council!'

Joan sent Piran a warning look. 'Slander is a serious matter, Piran, and I won't tolerate it in my office – understood?'

Piran fell silent, but his eyes flashed with suppressed anger.

'In politics it's not always a matter of how worthy your cause is, or even whether the law is on your side – such things do not guarantee victory. One can never afford to underestimate the calibre of the opposition. And in Rupert Heligan, the MD of Café Au Lait, you face a formidable opponent. He is accustomed to getting his own way, and he is backed by a multinational company with very deep pockets.' Joan looked at the three dejected faces across the table. 'Heligan and Bedford are unlikely to give up without a fight, which could mean you'll face a costly legal battle – and a lengthy one. Given that the theatre is in such a parlous state of repair, it could crumble to dust before the case reaches its conclusion.'

The three men exchanged sober glances. This wasn't the reception they'd anticipated.

'I'm going to table a motion for a public meeting and I'm sure I can secure enough votes to get you a stay of execution so far as the deadline's concerned. But that still leaves you with a mountain to climb, I'm afraid. The restoration work is going to require millions of pounds of investment – money the council simply cannot afford.' Joan shook her head sadly. 'It would be a shame to see off Café Au Lait and then watch the Pavilions rot away into oblivion. You'll need to have something pretty spectacular up your sleeve if you're going to make good your ambition of saving the old place.'

*

Despite her gloomy prognosis, the councillor delivered on her promise to convene a public meeting. Within a week she was sitting behind a trestle table on the stage of the Pavilions along with five other members of the council, in front of what looked to be a packed house.

'Ladies and gentlemen. Can we have some quiet! Please!' Joan Goodman clapped her hands together to bring the meeting to order. No one took a blind bit of notice. After a moment, she raised her voice – only an octave, but it resonated around the room: 'I am calling this meeting to order.'

There was immediate silence.

Joan gave a satisfied nod. 'Thank you. I would like to begin by welcoming everybody . . .'

From the front row of the auditorium, Helen surveyed the audience behind her. The grimy lights only just illuminated them, but she could tell that virtually every seat in the stalls was taken and the balcony seemed pretty full too.

'. . . As you are aware,' Joan continued, 'the coffee chain Café Au Lait are proposing to buy this building and turn it from a theatre into a coffee shop. However, the SToP campaigners have uncovered some compelling documentation that may prevent any change from the venue's current use. The council's legal team have examined these documents, and it appears that further legal advice will be required before a decision can be taken. We are therefore unable to allow the sale to go through as proposed.'

The SToP campaigners all gasped and looked at each other with happy faces. With the exception of Piran, who was too busy glaring at Chris Bedford. The conniving councillor, sitting to Joan Goodman's left on the stage, had remained poker-faced while she made her announcement. He now sat fiddling with his tie, careful not to meet Piran's eyes.

Joan waited for the murmurs to die down and then went on: 'Which leaves the question of what will become of the Pavilions in the meantime. The SToP campaigners have asked for the theatre to remain open while they prepare their own legal case; they propose that the venue should continue to provide a place of entertainment for the local community, and the monies raised by these performances would got to SToP's legal fund. This is what the committee will be voting on tonight and we are prepared to hear petitions from all interested parties. First, we will hear from Café Au Lait.'

Brooke stiffened as Café Au Lait's PR man, Michael Woodbine, took to the stage. For the next fifteen minutes, he spoke eloquently about how the company would bring jobs to the community and provide a social hub. When he started waxing lyrical about the company's family values, Brooke gave an audible snort, which earned her a frosty glare from Joan Goodman. He was more convincing when he described how they would overhaul the building, preserving some of its original features and making it secure and safe. This was greeted by enthusiastic applause.

The StoP campaigners cast worried glances at one another. They had their work cut out raising legal expenses, let alone funding refurbishment. Only now were they realising that this could prove a significant weakness in their case.

Now it was Simon's turn. Penny gave his hand a squeeze as he walked towards the stage. He gave an impassioned speech about what the Pavilions meant to Trevay: 'Our aim is to make it a thriving place of entertainment once more. The Trevay Players have agreed to stage a pantomime over Christmas and New Year, all proceeds of which will go into the refurbishment fund. My wife has been talking to some very big names and is hopeful we can produce an Easter extravaganza. And Colonel Irvine' – the Colonel stood up to warm applause – 'has promised to revive the first-ever show performed here, in which he appeared alongside the great Max Miller, for a sell-out summer season.'

The Colonel made a comic face and danced a little soft shoe shuffle.

Simon's heartfelt and moving speech concluded: 'The Pavilions aren't just a theatre, they are our past, our heritage. They are Cornwall, they are Trevay. They are us.'

As the audience applauded, some of them rising to their feet to give him a standing ovation, Simon made to leave the stage. He was stopped in his tracks by Chris Bedford.

'Reverend Canter,' Bedford began, his voice dripping with mockery, 'we've heard a detailed explanation from Café Au Lait as to how they are planning to maintain the building. Would you care to tell us how your little band of campaigners and a handful of amateur actors intend to keep this building from falling down? Look around you – the place is falling to bits. The dress and upper circles have had to be closed on health and safety grounds, and the roof has more holes in it than your argument!'

He smirked unpleasantly as laughter rippled around the room.

Simon opened his mouth to speak but no words came out. Piran wasted no time leaping to his rescue.

'It's all about big business and money to you, Bedford, isn't it?' he railed, 'Well, I've got news for you: this town is about more than that. We pull together when things get tough – always have, always will. And there are enough people to get the job done without any help from the likes of Café Au Lait.' He turned to address the auditorium: 'Am I right?'

He was greeted with cheers and clapping. One member of the audience stood up.

'I'm Ray Williams, my mum used to sell ice creams here during the intermission. I run a big building firm and if someone will provide the material, I'll supply the manpower to fix the upper circles.'

More cheers.

Then another person stood: 'My name's Phil Jennings and I'm a roofer. I'll 'appily do what I can – anyone else want to lend a hand?'

Helen was reminded of that moment from the film *Spartacus* as one by one, local people stood up and volunteered their services.

The audience were now ecstatic. Over the noise of their cheers, Piran's deep bass made itself heard:

'You see, Councillor Bedford? Money isn't everything. Trevay is bigger'n you and it's bigger'n Café bloody Au Lait!'

As he sat down, Helen reached for his hand. She thought she had never loved her grumpy, curmudgeonly but heroic Piran more than she did right that minute.

'Order, order!' commanded Joan Goodman, and the room fell silent, though it seemed to Helen that the crackle of tension in the air was almost loud enough to hear. Had they done enough?

'I think we'll put this to the vote now. All in favour of allowing SToP to run the building on a temporary basis?'

Chris Bedford and one other councillor kept their hands down, but four hands came up, including Joan's. The vote was greeted by the biggest and longest cheers of the evening.

*

It was a merry little band who convened that night at the Sail Loft. November seemed to be blowing in with a gale as one by one they fought their way through the door. The wind was so strong it almost whipped the door out of Brooke's hand as she pushed it open. Once over the threshold, she had to lean on it with all her weight to get it to close again. Gone were her glam body-con frocks and stilettos. Brook was adopting the Cornish way. No make-up, jeans, warm jacket and flat boots.

''Tis blowin' a hooley out there, maid,' said Piran, who was standing at the bar paying for two bottles of red wine. 'Sit down with the others and I'll bring over a glass for you.'

'Thanks, Piran.' Brooke pushed her soft honey-coloured curls out of her eyes and made her way to the scrubbed-pine table where Simon, Penny and Helen were sitting.

A moment later Piran arrived with the drinks. Helen shifted her chair so he could squeeze in. 'I'm so proud of you,' she told him. 'You really gave that creep Bedford a good drubbing.'

Piran reached over and helped himself to the chilli chips. 'Very satisfying, even if I do say so myself. Took great pleasure in wiping the smile off that bugger's face.' He poured the velvety red wine into the glasses. 'Cheers, everyone.'

'I hate to be the voice of doom, but the battle's not won yet,' said Penny.

'Come on, darling, we're the dream team – along with all those people who came forward to offer their help.'

'Yes, Simon, the campaign's finally starting to come together, but we've an awful lot of work ahead of us. If we're going to get this panto off the ground then we only have a few short weeks to get everything done.'

'Ah, yes, I hadn't thought of that.' Simon took a thoughtful sip of his wine.

'Less of that,' Penny chided, taking the glass from his hand. 'No sore heads tomorrow. I'll have to get straight on the phone in the morning – and so will you, pinning all those volunteers down so they make good on their promises. People get carried away in the heat of the moment and things can seem very different in the cold light of day.'

'Let me know if there's anything I can do to help,' said Helen. 'I'm sure the Colonel will want to lend a hand too – he didn't want to stay for a drink, he said he was too tired, but I'm sure he'll be a real asset when it comes to organising the panto.'

'What about you, Brooke? When do you have to go back to London?' asked Penny.

'Tomorrow morning.'

Penny's face fell. Brooke's boundless enthusiasm made everything seem possible; she dreaded losing her. 'Do you have to go?'

'I can't afford to stay at the Starfish all the time.'

'There are loads of places to rent down here. Winter rates are quite reasonable.'

'But I've got my flat in London and . . .'

'. . . and down here you've got friends, a cause to champion, work coming up – if Sir Julian is serious.'

'Yeah, but . . . I don't know.'

'Rent your flat out and come down here,' urged Helen.

'Yes,' said Penny. 'Just till the end of next summer. I'll miss your help in the office. We'll all miss you. You're one of us now!'

Everyone around the table nodded in agreement.

'Let me think about it.' She stood up and Piran helped her into her coat. 'Well done tonight, everyone.'

Wishing them all goodnight, Brooke tripped out of the wine bar feeling more positive than she had in quite some time. Maybe she could give it a go down here in Cornwall. A gust of cold air hit her, bringing her to her senses. What was she thinking? She needed to return to London and get her career back on track. Milo James wasn't the only agent in town, and she still had her brain and her looks.

She was so busy musing on this as she made her way to her car that she almost collided with two men weaving their way unsteadily to a waiting taxi. She was dismayed to see that the two men in question were Michael Woodbine and Councillor Bedford. Bedford in particular was rather the worse for wear.

She tried to step round them to get to her car, but it was too late.

'Well, well, well, if it isn't SToP's secret weapon! Can't remember your name – didn't you used to be someone?' Michael Woodbine intercepted her before she could reach her car door.

'I've nothing to say to you, please move out of the way.'

'Ooh, quite the prim and proper little madam now, aren't we? Not quite so prim when your tits and arse were plastered all over the lads' mags, were you?'

Brooke held her nerve. 'I have never done that and at least I come by my money honestly, not by lying and handing out bribes.'

'I've seen your type before,' he sneered. 'You and your tin-pot campaign group. Just wait until our lawyers have finished with you – you'll wish you never started this.'

'I don't think so. You see, even though you think you're invincible, tonight we proved that you're not. And I've still got something on you – underestimate me at your peril, Woodbine.'

At this point, a staggering, drunken Chris Bedford lunged forward unsteadily and thrust his face into hers.

'Yeah, and you tell that Cornish meathead Piran Ambrose that he hashn't heard the lasht of this! I'll show that loser that no one meshes with me!' He poked his own chest with his finger.

Woodbine put his hands on Bedford's shoulders and steered him towards the waiting taxi. When they reached the cab, he turned for a parting shot: 'No one messes with Café Au Lait, love, least of all talentless dolly birds who don't know their place.'

Brooke watched them depart. 'We'll see about that,' she said quietly to herself.

The next morning, Brooke phoned a London letting agent and told him she was moving to Cornwall for a while . . .

*

Brooke found a tenant for her London flat in under a fortnight. In the meantime Penny and Helen managed to negotiate a great deal on the rental of Granny's Nook, a two-up-two-down cottage next door but one to Helen.

'Welcome to Pendruggan, neighbour!' Helen squeezed through the narrow front door carrying armfuls of late chrysanthemums and holly twigs. 'Something to brighten up the place. Simple Tony gave them to me. Have you met him yet? Once met, never forgotten. Sweet lad.' She plonked the homely bouquet in its large kilner jar vase, onto the kitchen table and looked around her. 'Not bad for a holiday let, is it? Furnished nicely. How's the bed?'

Brooke still couldn't believe she'd made the move from London to Cornwall. It had all happened so quickly and she was close to tears at her welcoming present. 'I'm just about to make it up with duvets I brought down from the flat. It looks OK.'

'Here, I'll help you. Have you unpacked everything yet?'

'No, I . . .'

'Come on, let's get you settled.'

By the time Penny and Simon came over, an hour later, with a bottle of champagne and a 'Welcome to Your New Home' card, everything was shipshape. Helen was just giving Brooke some tips on how to light the open fire and filling her in on her own life story, and how she came to be living at Gull's Cry.

'Don't get her onto that shit of an ex-husband of hers. Bloody useless, like all men,' declared Penny, immediately turning to kiss Simon's cheek. 'Except you, my darling. You are the exception.' She turned back to Helen and Brooke, gave them a wink and said, 'I think I got away with it.' Laughing her raucous laugh she instructed Simon to open the champagne.

'I don't know if I have champagne glasses . . .' Brooke went to the kitchen and started banging cupboard doors. 'Will wine glasses do?'

'Jam jars will do if we're thirsty enough.' Penny took the open bottle from Simon and started pouring.

Simon raised his glass. 'Brooke, you are most welcome to Pendruggan. Thank you for your help and friendship.

God bless you and Granny's Nook. May you be very happy here.'

'Amen to that.' Penny chinked glass on glass with Brooke. 'To friends old and new.'

14

Getting the part of Moira in *Horse Laugh* had done Jess the world of good. She'd taken up running and watching her weight in readiness for filming. This was her big break and she was determined to make the most of it.

She was almost pleased that Ryan was off to LA, knowing it would allow her to focus entirely on her new role.

From a dark corner table in Café Au Lait's Heathrow branch, she watched Ryan at the counter, causing a stir among the three young female baristas serving behind the counter. Having ordered their drinks – two lattes, soya milk, decaf – he handed over a ten-pound note and told the girls to keep the change. One of them whipped a phone out of her trouser pocket and took a photo of him. He laughed and then pointed to the corner where Jess was waiting. The girl clamped her hand over her mouth then fluttered it over her face in excitement. Ryan waved at Jess and mouthed, 'They're big fans!' Jess smiled and waved back, praying that they didn't come over to join them. They didn't.

'Nice girls,' beamed Ryan. 'They saw your interview in *Weekend* magazine. They promise they'll be watching *Horse Laugh*.'

Jess smiled and looked across at the girls. All three of them were staring at her. They giggled.

'You gotta get used to it, babe. The recognition embarrasses the hell out of me,' he said unembarassedly, 'but you just gotta go with the flow.' He sipped his coffee and gazed at her with his deep brown eyes. 'And I gotta get used to being with my famous girlfriend.'

She leaned over and kissed him. 'I'm sure you'll cope.' Apart from adopting a slight transatlantic accent (all those gottas and babes) he had been a sweetheart to her since she got the part of Moira. He'd patiently listened to her endless anxieties, telling her that she was more than capable of stealing the show. Gradually, her self-esteem had begun to return. Not only had she told her agent to ask for a bit more money – and got it – she'd persuaded the producer to allow Elsie and Ethel to play Moira's dogs, thus allaying any outlay on kennel fees.

'I'm sorry I've got to leave you, babe, but you know how it is. While *Venini* is hot I've gotta do the casting thing in LA. The series is going down a storm in the States. Wouldn't it be great if I got a movie?'

'It sure would. Then I'd have to get used to being with my film-star boyfriend.' She stroked his familiar cheek and had a sudden pang of emptiness.

'I really will miss you, Jess.' He took her hand and, uncurling her fingers, kissed her palm. 'I love you.'

'Yes?'

'Yes.'

'You won't run off with some young starlet?'

'Several.'

She punched him playfully and he put a strong arm round her shoulder. 'Never. I couldn't lose you. You're everything to me.'

At the departures gate he kissed her deeply for several

moments. A couple of people took photos and one academic-looking woman in her fifties walked by and murmured to Jess, 'Kissed by Venini – lucky you!'

*

Back at the car park ticket machine, Jess, preoccupied with thoughts of Ryan and her new job, barely noticed the young man who had managed to drop a handful of change on the floor and was chasing after a runaway one-pound coin. It stopped at the toe of her boot. The young man bent to pick it up. He looked familiar. She smiled at him . . . He smiled back. 'I've just seen my girlfriend off to New York. She gave me all these coins to lighten her purse. But I still don't think I've got enough.' She smiled at him and held out her hand. 'Count them into here.'

It took a few minutes, but eventually he managed to feed the correct money into the machine and took out his ticket in triumph.

'Thanks for your help.' He hesitated a moment then said. 'You're Jess Tate, aren't you?'

'Yeah, I am,' she replied, frowning. 'I feel I know you too.'

'Ollie Pinkerton.'

'Of course! You've just finished a great season at the RSC, haven't you?'

'Well, you know . . . it was fun, but I'm one of the unemployed at the moment.'

'Your girlfriend is Red, isn't she?'

'Yeah. She's off to play Madison Square Gardens.'

'And you're not going with her?'

'Can't afford it.'

'Oh.' Jess didn't know what else to say. 'Really nice to meet you, Ollie – good luck with everything.'

'Thanks. And good luck with your new show!'

As Ollie walked away to his car he thought how attractive Jess was, for an older woman.

And as Jess fed the ticket machine with an inordinate number of pound coins she couldn't help thinking how charming Ollie was . . . for a boy of his age.

*

As soon as filming got under way, Jess knew that *Horse Laugh* was something special. The script, the cast, the crew – everything gelled. She couldn't put her finger on anything specific. Maybe the stars were aligned in a portentous way, or the angels had decreed the production to be blessed, or maybe it was just good old-fashioned talent and hard work. The star of the piece, a young woman who'd come from a small but meaty role in *Coronation Street*, was super good and without any discernible ego. She and Jess got on famously and their scenes were so funny and so moving that the writer made more of their relationship and added new scenes. It was clear that Jess was not just a supporting actress, she was the show's co-star.

Ethel and Elsie were in their element. They had their own bed in Jess's Winnebago and enjoyed warming up in there when the weather got too cold. Filming in November, in Suffolk, was a chilly affair. The main location was a stables on the coast near Dunwich, and Elsie and Ethel strutted their stuff like two short-legged queen bees round the yard and through the horses' legs. The horses were all local, apart from three stunt horses who were rather beautiful and exceptionally well behaved. Two, Kinkaid and Columbine, had been in *Downton*, the third, Delia, had been in *War Horse*. All the horses loved Ethel and Elsie, but the two dachshunds loved Delia best. She would bend down and tickle their ears with her moustache. They never failed to roll on their backs for more.

At the start, Jess and Ryan would Skype and Elsie and Ethel would woof in recognition of Ryan's voice, but the time difference became a bore for them both. LA was eight hours behind and it was difficult to synchronise the best moment to call. Most days they emailed each other instead. Jess would send an account of her day just before she went to bed and Ryan would read it as he got up. By the time Jess woke up there was always an answer waiting for her. However, as time went on, the less either of them had to say to each other. Ryan was doing the rounds of meeting producers for castings, and two or three times a week had to go to some film studio reception, or a premiere, or a dinner. Jess was tired of hearing about it. Her world had shrunk to the size of a filming day and the unit around her. As for Ryan, he knew how close a film unit got and how intensely Jess was working, so he let the emails drift to four then three times a week. Jess hardly noticed.

She filmed solidly through November and the schedule had her working right through December too. Over Christmas the set would only close for a few days. Ryan invited Jess to spend the holidays with him – a promise of an audition for a huge role in the newest Bond film meant he couldn't fly to the UK – but Jess was too tired to fly there and back and mess up her body clock with jet lag.

'Would you mind very much if I didn't come over?' She was lying in bed with a face pack on and conditioner soaking into her hair.

'Yes I mind, but I understand, babe.'

'Thanks, darling. How's it gone today?'

Ryan began a long story about an actor he'd met who he'd known years ago in rep.

Jess felt her eyelids drooping and allowed them to fall while she listened to him. The script for tomorrow was lying next to her. She had a great comedy scene to play and she really needed to learn it. Ryan's voice carried on in her ear and she hoped she was making the responses he required.

The bed was so soft, the pillow so right. She hadn't felt this comfortable for years.

'Jess! Are you asleep?'

She jolted awake. 'No. Carry on. Are you going to see him again?'

'Who?'

She struggled to gather her fragmented memory. 'Your friend. The one in rep.'

'You *were* asleep.'

'No. Well. Maybe. I'm just a bit relaxed.'

'Have you decided where you're spending Christmas? Going back to the flat or staying in Suffolk?'

She yawned. 'Too exhausting to go back to London. I'm going to stay here. The crew are putting on a Christmas lunch and then I shall just sleep and sleep.'

'OK, baby. I miss you. Speak tomorrow?'

'Mmm. Love you. Night night.'

They shot the last scene in mid January and at the wrap party everyone hoped that they'd be back for a second series.

Jess, Ethel and Elsie went back to London and real life. As she let herself and Ethel and Elsie in through the front door a dark shape stepped out from the kitchen.

'Welcome home!'

She nearly jumped out of her skin before jumping into the arms of a waiting Ryan.

'What are you doing here? You're not supposed to be back for another week!' She hugged him hard.

'I didn't want you coming home to an empty apartment.'

'I love you, Ryan Hearst.' She hugged him again.

'I love you, baby. Let me look at you.' He held her away from him and took in her slender frame and dark circled eyes. 'You need fattening up.'

'I need a cup of tea.'

*

'Gosh, you really have missed me!' panted Jess as Ryan eased himself off her and flopped onto the pillows.

'And it seems you've missed me too,' he chuckled.

She snuggled closer to him and stroked her fingers lightly over his tanned and muscled stomach. 'How amazing life is. Who'd have thought, even two years ago, that you and I would be working like this. Thank you for understanding about me not coming over for Christmas and New Year.'

'You've done it for me,' he said sleepily. 'You let me go and make *Venini* and then head out to Hollywood.'

'It's not about *letting* you. It's about supporting you.'

'And trusting me.'

'Absolutely.'

'As I trust you.'

She laughed wryly. 'Blimey. Nothing to worry about where I'm concerned.'

'I know, darling, I know.' He kissed the top of her head then rolled over to catch up with his jet lag.

*

Ryan was home for four weeks before filming started for the new series of *Venini*. He'd be away for almost all of the next six or seven months. Locations included San Francisco, New York, Boston and St Louis. So during his stay in London he spoiled Jess daily. If it wasn't the cinema or theatre it was cooking her favourite food and making love to her afterwards.

One Wednesday morning he pulled her suitcase out of the spare room and told her to pack for a long weekend in the country. 'Really? Where are we going?'

'Magical mystery tour.'

'When?'

'As soon as you're packed.'

'What about Elsie and Ethel?'

'They can come too. Stop asking questions.' He opened her wardrobe doors. 'Get packing, woman.'

As Jess bumped her case down the steps of their building and on to the pavement, her eye was caught by a young man in a smart suit getting out of a navy-blue Porsche. Both driver and car were jaw droppers.

'Morning,' he said in Jess's direction. She looked around her and saw only Ryan, locking the front door. He turned when he heard the young man's voice and replied, 'Morning. Sorry to keep you waiting. My girlfriend didn't have much notice to pack her case. She's done pretty well, considering.'

The young man walked forward and took Jess's case. 'I'll pop that in for you.'

Jess looked at Ryan. 'What the hell's going on?'

'I know it's an extravagance. Don't be cross with me. I just thought we deserved a little toy.'

'You've *hired* this car?'

'Ah, no. I bought it.'

Jess was thrilled. Ryan had always said a car in London was a waste of money, so they'd had to rely on the bus or the tube, or cabs when they could afford it. Since *Venini* had taken off in a big way, the production company always sent a limo to ferry him around.

'Ryan!' She walked around the gleaming blue beast. 'It's gorgeous!'

'Hop in then, babe. Ethel and Elsie have just about enough room on the back seat.'

Jess sank into the luxury of the leather and inhaled deeply of the unmistakable smell of New Car.

*

They arrived at a small boutique hotel settled on the banks of Lake Windermere. A tall and charming porter in his sixties emerged from the well-lit entrance hall and into the gloom of the car park to help them with their bags.

'Good evening, sir, madam. Welcome to Heron's Pool.'

He checked them in and showed them to their room, which was furnished in traditional English style. Cosy, unpretentious and softly lit.

'It's a bit dark now, madam, but in the morning you'll be able to enjoy the glorious view over the lake.'

He then pointed out the minibar, kettle, WiFi and

satellite television. As he was leaving, he asked, 'Will you be dining with us, sir? Chef has kept a table for you.'

'Actually, I'm starving. Yes please.'

They agreed on a reservation for eight o'clock, leaving them time to walk the girls and get changed.

The dining room was candlelit and the food delicious.

'Why are you spoiling me so much, Ryan?'

'You deserve it, darling.'

'Not a guilty conscience?' she asked playfully.

'Damn! Am I that obvious!' They laughed at this small but significant joke. 'How about a nightcap?'

They took their brandies into the snug and sat together on the deep velvet sofa watching the flames of the open fire licking the red-hot embers.

'All this luxurious living is very tiring.' She rubbed her eyes and yawned.

'You go up and I'll follow in a minute.'

'OK. Give the girls a last wee, would you?'

*

They slept late and ordered a huge room-service breakfast, then went back to bed and made love languidly. Eventually, Elsie and Ethel could keep their legs crossed no longer and Ryan took them out for a stroll while Jess lay in a hot and bubbly bath. It was almost lunchtime by the time they decided they really should get out into the fresh air. A short walk from their hotel, a smart little cruiser bobbed on its pier embarking passengers for a lake cruise.

'Shall we?' Ryan comically raised his eyebrows in a caddish way and offered his arm.

She took it and answered, 'Ooh, sir, I ain't never bin on a boat before. Supposing I feel giddy?'

'Don't worry. I shan't let go of you.' He grabbed her waist (noting how very slender it had become of late) and pulled her to him sharply. 'You're a demmed attractive gal, Letitia.'

They heard the motor of a camera whirr as it took a shot of them larking around.

A woman in her forties, with a very Welsh accent, said loudly to anyone who would listen: 'I knew it was 'im. That bloke off the telly, see.' She walked up and stood very close to Ryan, ignoring any boundaries of personal space. 'It is you, right? What's your name?'

'Ryan Hearst.'

'Tha's right. Ryan. And this is your girlfriend, is it?'

'Yes.'

'Not the one in the paper then. The one I saw today. She's very pretty, mind.'

'What paper?' asked Jess.

'The *Mirror*. I don't like to read them, but it was there like.'

Ryan was trying to steer Jess away from this frightful woman, but she shook him off.

'Who was in the photo?'

'Your fella 'ere. He 'ad 'is arm round 'er.'

Ryan could stand it no longer. In a low voice he told her, 'I am on a private holiday with my girlfriend and would appreciate it if you would just bugger off. Goodbye.'

Then he turned on his heel sweeping Jess, Ethel and Elsie away as smoothly as possible – not easy when the dogs had woven their leads round and through his legs.

Behind them the ghastly woman was declaring loudly, 'Well, there's rude! I was only saying, like.'

Once on board the beautiful little cruiser, Ryan led Jess to a comfortable seat in its bow. Strings of red, white and blue bunting flapped in the wind as the vessel pushed off from the pier and started to putter through the water. Jess had remained ominously quiet throughout.

'Fancy a cuppa?' Ryan asked, his voice artificially jolly. 'I see they have a bar inside.'

'Who did you have your picture taken with?'

He bent down to pick up the girls and put them on the seat between them. 'Hm?'

'You heard.'

'I don't know what the bloody woman was talking about. I've had to go to thousands of parties and dinners and stuff in the last few months. I can't remember much about them.'

'So why has a paper printed a picture of you with your arm around another woman?'

He looked at her, devastated. 'Darling, please don't get like this. I don't know who or what or anything about it.'

'Have you been seeing someone in America?'

'No.'

'Promise me, because . . .' Jess bit her lip. Through her sunglasses Ryan could see a tear shining, ready to drop. He put his arm round her and held her tight. 'Darling, you must believe me: I am not seeing anyone else. I live like a monk in LA. They all laugh at me and think I'm gay.'

He wiped away the tear, which now escaped and was running down her cheek. 'Darling, there is only you. In fact, this holiday is a way of getting you on your own and asking you a big question. I was hoping to do it this evening, but that fucking Welsh cow has forced my hand.'

He slid off the seat and knelt in front of her. 'Darling Jess, would you do me the honour of being my wife?'

15

Ollie rang his agent every day asking about work. His bank balance was spilling into the red and he worried about next month's rent. Though his agent was a sharp operator, his initial interest in Ollie's talent seemed to have waned and he'd gone quiet on him. These days it was hard for Ollie to get to speak to him. He was always 'in a meeting', according to his PA.

On top of all this, Red was being a world-class nightmare. She kept ringing him in the middle of the night, not caring whether she woke him up, to sob down the phone or scream at him or accuse him of being unfaithful, or sometimes to tell him just how great she was and how shit he was. It was doing him no good at all.

He sat on his shabby sofa, the old Spanish shawl that had been his grandmother's thrown over the back, and made his daily call.

'Hi, Trinny,' he said when the receptionist picked up. 'It's Ollie. Is Tim around?'

'Hi, Ollie. Let me check.' The phone went dead and he imagined Trinny checking to see if his agent wanted to speak to him. He was surprised when Tim came on the line.

'Ollie – long time. How's tricks?'

'Great. Yeah. Doing good.'

'Great. How's Red?'

'Still on the American leg of the tour. Sell out. All good.'

'Good. Good . . .' Tim paused. 'So, how can I help you today?'

Ollie thought it was obvious, but stayed with the game. 'I've had a great break after Stratford and I'm ready for a new challenge. Batteries all charged. Eager for work.'

'OK,' said Tim. 'What you got in mind?'

Ollie swallowed his frustration and after a tiny beat said, 'Theatre, telly, voice-overs . . .'

Ollie could hear Tim sucking his teeth. 'Right. Right. If anything comes in, I'll let you know. I'm always working for you, you know that.'

'Yeah. Sure. Of course.'

Tim said nothing more.

Ollie filled the silence. 'OK. Well. Cheers.'

Tim had already gone.

*

At the gym that afternoon, Ollie took his aggression and pent-up frustration out on a punch bag and a heavy set of weights. The man he saw in the mirrored wall was not the man he had been. Yes, he could hold his own with the body builders around him and he knew he was pretty good looking, but something in his eyes had died. Red was sapping the life out of him. He wanted to end it with her but wasn't ready for the emotional onslaught she'd release, or the media frenzy that would surround the announcement. Already the papers were picking up on him not going to the States to see her. The paps followed him constantly, hoping to get a shot of him in the company of another woman. He never obliged. His days were spent at home, in the gym, or at his corner shop grabbing supplies. His friends had stopped asking him out because of the fuss surrounding him. Every week he read in a gossip column that Red was pining for him and that he refused to go to her. Didn't they understand that he was skint? He couldn't afford to jet off to America, let alone pay his way once he was there. And he wouldn't dream of allowing Red to pick up the bill – not that it would ever occur to her to offer. She had no idea when it came to money. Like the Queen, everything was taken care of for her.

That night he rang his mum and embarrassed them both by crying. She listened attentively as he poured out all his problems.

'Why don't you come down and stay for a few days?' she offered. 'You can do your own thing. I won't fuss over you. Just take a break.'

'I don't know . . .'

'Is it the money?'

'No, it's all right.'

'I'll book your train tickets tonight. You're coming down for the weekend.'

*

She was waiting on the platform for him as he stepped off the train in Truro. They hugged tightly. Mum smelled the same as she always had.

They drove the familiar route to the house he'd grown up in. His room was unchanged. His football medals were still on the bookshelf and his old bear Cassius sitting on his pillow.

His father had walked out when Ollie was only seven. A few years later they'd heard he'd died. Liver failure. His Mum had never wanted to find herself another man, she'd been stung once. Instead her world had revolved around Ollie. She'd worked hard and given her only child a good home and the best education that she could afford.

While his favourite toad in the hole was cooking she gave him the tour of her garden. Although it was February, the primroses and daffodils were turning their faces to the sun and purple aubrietia was foaming on the old drystone wall facing the fields where next door's cows were idly chewing the cud and waiting for milking.

He slept soundly that night. The dark and the occasional cough of a cow outside his open bedroom window working its soothing magic on his unhappy soul.

*

'Morning, my love.' Ollie's mum placed a mug of steaming tea on his bedside table. 'Breakfast in twenty minutes, OK?'

'Love you, Mum. Thanks.'

Over bacon, eggs, fried bread and grilled tomatoes, his mum chatted about her plans for the day.

'I've got to nip out for a couple of hours – there's a bring-and-buy sale in the village hall this morning in aid of Save the Children, and I promised I'd help out. I'll be back here by midday though. Then I thought we could go down to Trevay and have fish and chips on the quay like we did when you were little.'

He smiled. 'I'd like that.'

She smiled in return. 'Good. See you later then.'

*

'Salt? Vinegar?' The young man behind the counter was holding a greasy salt shaker.

'Yes please. Mum?' Ollie turned to find his mum already brandishing a twenty-pound note. 'I'll pay for these, Mum. My treat.'

'You hold on to your money. You need it.' She thrust the note towards the young man, who asked again, 'Salt? Vinegar?'

Outside, the watery sun was warm in the sheltered spot that Ollie and his mum found. They sat quietly munching and watching a fishing boat as it tied up alongside the fish market to unload its catch. Seagulls swooped overhead, their beady eyes on the feast below.

'How's Red?'

Ollie internally applauded his mother, who had waited almost twenty-four hours to ask the one question she wanted an answer to.

'Busy.'

'When does she get back?'

'Not sure. Depends on her tour.'

'Are you going out to see her?'

'No.'

'Is it the money?'

Yes, it was the money.

'No. It's work.'

She brightened. 'You've got a job?'

'No. But I need to be in the UK and available for auditions.'

'I see.'

'Yeah.'

*

Helen called Jack to a stop. She had walked him over the headland and onto Trevay's small beach below the

Pavilions. From the beach, Helen could see the progress being made by the volunteer builders. It was beginning to look quite smart; the upper and dress circles were back in action, the windows had been repaired, the roof was now watertight, the heating working and the seats re-upholstered in claret dralon. The Trevay Players had put on a marvellous panto over Christmas and had raised a good chunk of cash for the repairs fund. All in all, things were ticking along nicely.

As Jack stood wagging his tail and sniffing the breeze, Helen's gaze shifted from the theatre to a young handsome man sitting alongside an older woman on one of the many benches dotted round the harbour. The woman had her hands folded in her lap, her eyes closed to the sun, while the young man – her son perhaps? – had got up to put the remains of their takeaway lunch in a nearby rubbish bin. He looked familiar. Helen searched her brain. She got it. He was the actor boyfriend of that hard-faced pop star she was forever obliged to read about in her newspaper. What was her name? She fumbled for her phone and dialled Penny.

'Pen? It's Helen. What's the name of that actor who's going out with that pop star who's touring America?'

'Darling, can you be a tad more specific?'

'You know, the one with red spiky hair.'

'Oh, Red.'

'Yeah. What's her name?'

'Red.'

Helen was blissfully unaware of the irony in Penny's voice.

'Oh yeah! Well, I think I see her boyfriend in Trevay.'

'And?'

'Should I ask him whether Red would be interested in helping the Pavilions appeal?'

Penny couldn't believe the naivety of her friend. 'Great idea. While you're at it, see if she wouldn't do a big concert for us.'

'I think that might be pushing it.'

'I'm joking.'

Helen wasn't listening, 'What's *his* name?'

*

Ollie pulled his neck and chin down into his jacket as he saw the woman with a dog approaching him. It wasn't that he minded being recognised, it was just that today he could do without it.

'Hello, I'm sorry to disturb your privacy . . .'

Then why are you doing it? he thought.

'. . . But I had to say welcome to Trevay. My name is Helen.'

'Hello, Helen. I'm Jan.' The older woman smiled and shook Helen's hand warmly. 'Come and join us – it's lovely out of the breeze.' She shuffled up, leaving a space on the bench between her and Ollie for Helen to sit in. 'I'm Ollie's mum.'

Ollie managed a thin smile but stayed deep inside his collar as this stranger sat next to him.

'What brings you to Trevay?' she asked him.

'He's come home for a break. I'm in Tregleath? Ollie grew up here.'

'Really? You're Cornish?'

His response was a noncommittal 'Yep.'

Helen was on a roll. 'So you know all about the Pavilions?'

Jan answered. 'Yes. Terrible shame, isn't it. Ollie took his first acting classes up there with the Judith Speake school, didn't you, Ollie?'

'Yeah.' He shifted in his seat until he was as far from Helen as possible without falling off.

'It was every Thursday after school. Just two hours. Every Christmas he'd be in the pantomime. Just one of the babes. He did *Cinderella* with Coleen Nolan. She was lovely. *Aladdin* with Brian Conley – he's hilarious. Then there was that summer show. What was it called . . . ?'

'*Dappledown Farm*.'

'Yes. With Brian Cant. What fun he was, and very kind to the children on stage with him.'

'Wow, that's great. So you have a real affinity with the place.'

Ollie, sensing there was no escape, took the course of least resistance. 'Yeah. It's a very special place. It deserves to be saved.'

Helen brightened instantly. 'I'm on the Save the Pavilions committee and I was wondering if you would—'

'Of course, whatever I can.'

'So would you ask Red if she'd help us? Anything at all would be amazing. An appearance at the fundraiser? A concert with her band? Some memorabilia?'

Ollie didn't miss a beat. He was used to people seeing him as nothing more than a conduit to Red. 'Well, I can't promise all of that, but I'll talk to her.'

Helen was scribbling her contact details down on the back of a receipt she'd found in her bag.

'My God. That's amazing. The committee will be so thrilled. I can't believe I saw you. Thank you so so much.' She gave him the tatty receipt. 'Wait till I tell the others.'

16

It was a beautiful March day in Pendruggan. Helen and Brooke were standing in the foyer of the Pavilions, where the exhibition of the Colonel's old photos and theatre memorabilia was finally on display for all to see.

Helen had been so busy the last few months, what with her newspaper column, doing bits and pieces for the SToP campaign, organising the panto, then Christmas and an extended visit from Sean, Terri and baby Summer, that she'd had no chance to catch up with the Colonel. It had been left to Brooke, who seemed to have developed a strong bond with the old veteran, to coordinate the exhibition. Whenever she wasn't helping out at the campaign office, the young actress could usually be found at Beach Cottage with the Colonel, poring over his extensive collection and choosing photographs and theatre posters and programmes to go on display.

The Colonel stood beside them now, gazing at the display with tears in his eyes. 'Oh my dears, look at us all! There's Max . . . and Peter.'

A look passed over his face and Helen wondered if now might be the right time to find out more about Peter. Mindful that the Colonel was careful about his privacy and one needed to tread carefully, she looked to Brooke, willing her to be the one to ask.

'He was a very dear chap, you know,' sighed the Colonel.

'Yes. You've mentioned him before,' said Brooke.

'He was closely linked with the theatre, wasn't he?' prompted Helen.

'Yes, he had a glittering career in London where the name Peter Winship was very highly regarded, but he preferred life here in Trevay. He directed a great many Pavilions productions.'

'You must have worked very closely together?' said Helen.

The Colonel seemed not to hear her. He turned to Brooke: 'You'd have liked him, my dear. All the ladies liked Peter.'

Sensing an opening, Helen probed gently. 'Where is he now? Did he marry and settle down locally? It would be wonderful if we could ask him or his family—'

The Colonel turned to Helen. 'Alas, Peter died many years ago. And the theatre was his only family.'

With that, it was clear that the subject was closed. The Colonel gave a slight bow and turned from them to engage in conversation with some elderly ladies who had come to view the exhibition.

Brooke watched him for a moment, then turned to Helen. 'I've noticed he always clams up or changes the subject whenever Peter is mentioned.'

'I was so hoping he was still alive,' said Helen. 'Now it seems there's no hope of finding out anything more about the film archive.'

'What film archive?'

Helen told her about Piran's research and Brooke's eyes lit up. 'Gosh, that would be a find! I'll see if I can get him to open up to me. You never know . . .'

*

When the reception to mark the launch of the exhibition was over, Helen dropped Brooke and the Colonel back at Beach Cottage. He'd invited both women in for a spot of lunch, but Helen needed to finish her piece on the exhibition for the *Cornish Guardian*'s 'Time Out' and the deadline was fast approaching, so she had to decline the Colonel's offer. Brooke, however, said she would be delighted.

As Brooke laid the table, the Colonel prepared the luncheon and they chatted amiably.

'And when are you going to come out of hiding, my dear?'

'What do you mean? I'm not in hiding, I'm helping keep Café Au Lait at bay. If they get hold of the Pavilions, it would be a disaster.'

'Yes, dear girl, but are you sure that isn't the only reason?'

Brooke's gaze remained fixed on the table. 'I suppose I am hiding in a way. The whole business with Café Au Lait and that rotter Milo really knocked my confidence. It's made me question whether I'm tough enough to make it in this business. Deep down, I'll always be Brenda Foster – there's nothing exceptional about me. Girls like me are ten a penny in the entertainment biz.'

The Colonel patted her hand and Brooke looked up to see amusement dancing in his eyes as he told her, 'No, you're nothing exceptional. I see that now.'

Brooke couldn't help but laugh.

'Come, my dear, no false modesty here. You have an exceptional talent and it would be criminal to waste it. Do you know that the Chinese have the same word for crisis as they do for opportunity? You've a big career ahead of you – and it certainly isn't here in Trevay.'

'But what's wrong with Trevay? You made your life here.'

'Yes, but there were other . . . pressures.'

175

The Colonel's eyes were resting on one of the pictures on the wall. It was a photograph of him and Peter.

'Did those pressures have something to do with Peter?' Brooke asked.

The old man carried on staring at the photo, and at first she wondered whether he'd heard her question, but then he gave a sigh and turned to her.

'I don't regret a single thing. We had a wonderful life together, even though it was cruelly cut short. I've learned that you have to grab life, my dear, before it passes you by.'

She looked at him quizzically.

'All things in good time, dear girl. In the meantime, our lunch is ready.'

*

Once the cottage pie and spring greens had been thoroughly enjoyed, Brooke told the Colonel she needed to head back to Penny's to discuss some campaign business. The Colonel asked if he might accompany her.

'I've been thinking,' he said as they walked the beach path and turned into the short lane leading to Pendruggan. 'I need to talk to the vicar's wife about her thoughts for a general theatre manager at the Pavilions. I'd be happy to show them the ropes. After all, I did the job for many many years.'

'I rather think Penny has assumed she'll be filling the position herself.'

'I hope not.' The Colonel's bushy eyebrows shot up above his glasses. 'It's a full-time job that must be given to someone with experience. The successful candidate must have the skills of a politician whilst being an excellent man manager. In any one day he's dealing with budget, reputation, staff, health and safety. No, no, it's much too big a job for Mrs Canter, who, after all, is skilled only in the art of television. The theatre is a completely different beast.'

Brooke, sensing the approach of one of Colonel Irvine's monologues, skilfully turned the conversation away from the subject, but the reprieve was short-lived.

'Hello, Brooke! Hello, Colonel!' They both looked up to see Penny Canter walking from the vicarage towards her car.

'Ah, Mrs Canter!' cried Colonel Irvine. 'Just the person. Now that your *Mr Tibbs* filming has finished, I wondered if you could spare a moment . . .'

*

'God, why did I get involved in the bloody Pavilions?' Penny put her forehead down on the smooth, warm surface of Helen's kitchen table, a position Helen was getting all too familiar with. 'I've got so much to do. Channel 7 are squeezing my budget till it squeaks, Simon is hassling me over who I have managed to book for the big fundraising show, and now the Colonel wants me to find a theatre manager to run the bloody building.'

Helen quietly placed a mug of tea in front of Penny's head. 'That's a good idea, isn't it?'

'Yes,' Penny grudgingly agreed. 'But I don't have the time to find one.' She picked up the mug and took a sip. 'Got any biscuits?'

Helen passed her an almost empty packet of ginger nuts.

'Got any HobNobs?'

'No.'

Penny blew her cheeks out and ungraciously selected

three ginger nuts. 'We need someone who can manage the cast, and direct them as well. We don't have the budget to pay for both. There is no way on earth I can magic someone like that out of the air. They're like gold dust.' She pushed a hand through her hair. 'There was a great bloke I knew years ago – Jonathan Mulberry. He managed the Du Maurier, just off St Martin's Lane, and was also a great director. Could be a bit mercurial, but he picked some interesting projects; not always commercial ones, but they attracted attention. He came up about the same time as Ken Branagh, but God knows what's happened to him now.'

Helen thought for a moment, 'Didn't you have a fling with him?'

'Yeah. But don't tell Simon!' Penny laughed. 'It wasn't really a fling, I was just grateful to him and let him buy me a couple of dinners.'

'Hussy.'

*

Brooke had on her best secretary/PA voice. 'Good afternoon, I'm calling from Penny Leighton Productions. May I speak to Jonathan Mulberry please?'

Penny hovered next to Brooke, anxious to take the receiver from her when she got through to Jonathan.

'Oh, has he? Do you have a contact number for him?' Brooke scribbled on the pad next to her. 'Thank you. You've been most helpful.' She put the phone down. 'He went to Canada two years ago.'

Penny started pacing. 'Shit.'

'But . . .' Brooke looked smug, 'they think he's just finished his contract and he's back in the UK.' She began to tap out a number. 'They've given me a mobile number for him. Fingers crossed.'

Both women held their breath while the phone rang.

'Hello, am I speaking with Jonathan Mulberry? . . . I'm sorry to call you out of the blue, Mr Mulberry, my name is Brooke Lynne and I am PA to Penny Leighton of Penny Leighton Produc— . . . oh, you remember her?' Brooke arched an eyebrow at Penny. 'Yes, she's just the same. Full of life . . . The thing is, she'd like to speak to you about a new project she's working on. Can I put you through? . . . Great. Just a moment, Mr Mulberry.'

Brooke pressed the secrecy button on the receiver and handed it to Penny. 'He sounds nice – and interested.'

'Penny Leighton speaking. Hello, Jonathan! . . . Yes, it is a long time. How was Canada? . . . Oh that must have been fun. Any plans to go back? . . . Well I may have just the thing for you. Do you know Cornwall at all . . . ?'

*

Jonathan Mulberry had been intrigued by Penny Leighton's call. He remembered her as bright, vivacious and single. He had almost fallen for her, but she was one of those driven career girls for whom life held no space for a partner. Tall, with salt-and-pepper greying hair – luckily all still in place – Jonathan knew he wasn't classically handsome, but thought his face was interesting. Like most men of a certain age he was prone to getting slightly squishy round the stomach, but he tried to keep in shape. His work kept him active. He also appreciated women and their many and varied qualities, but since his marriage had failed more than a decade ago, he'd given serious relationships a wide berth. And he'd completely forsworn relationships with actresses. His ex-wife had been an actress, and he'd decided they were all like her: too needy and with fragile egos. Unfortunately, actresses seemed to be the only women he ever got to meet.

He pulled himself out of the train seat that had held him since Paddington and gathered up the detritus of his journey. Two Twix wrappers, three cardboard cups of coffee dregs and all the day's newspapers.

This train is now approaching Bodmin Parkway. Please take all of your belongings with you when you leave the train . . .

As the carriage twitched and rocked over the track running into the station, Jonathan walked joltingly down the aisle, managing to knock only two people on the tops of their skulls, one a teenager with loud music blaring from his headphones, the other a businessman stirring a Cup a Soup. He apologised to both.

Hopping down on to the platform like a badly coordin-ated Labrador, he pulled his Mulberry post bag (a present from the witty Canadian company of actors he'd just been working with) on to his shoulder and looked about him.

Penny was not there and nor, it appeared, was anyone else who looked a likely candidate to meet him.

He walked to the barrier and pushed his ticket through the slot which opened the turnstile for him. On the other side was the pavement, a turning space and a car park. A sign saying TAXIS stood above an empty stretch of kerb. He turned as he heard the throb of a powerful engine. Behind the wheel of a bright red Jaguar sports car was the unmistakable face of Penny Leighton.

'Darling!' She leapt out and hugged him. 'Typical that the train should be early. Let me take your bag.' Though he didn't disabuse her of the notion that the train was early, it had in fact been running ten minutes late.

He hugged her back and held on to his bag. 'I'll keep it on my lap, Penny. This is so kind of you to collect me. A bit of a treat. I feel as if I'm on holiday, coming down here.'

'Isn't the journey glorious?' Penny was reversing her car skilfully and pointing it towards the station exit. 'So pretty as you go past Dawlish.'

'I enjoyed going over Brunel's bridge over the Tamar. It brought back the excitement of entering Cornwall that I felt as a kid.'

'So, what have you been up to? Last I heard you were doing some whizzy play at the Donmar Warehouse that had all the critics in ecstasies – then things went a bit quiet.'

'God, that bloody play. Nearly finished me off, ha!' Jonathan ran his hand through his short curly hair. A five o'clock shadow was already spreading across his chin.

Penny was reminded, as she glanced at him again while trying to focus on the road, of what she had found attractive about him in the first place. He wasn't an obvious choice, but he had presence. Though he had a reputation as a stern task master, inclined to be sharp-tongued and irascible, Penny knew that he was incredibly loyal and kind and giving to those he cared about. The same ensemble of actors had signed up to work with him again and again, proof that he was capable of inspiring a cast, getting the best out of them and giving them the creative space to explore their characters.

'I just became really disillusioned with the whole London theatre scene at that time. Seemed that the only way to get a play off the ground was to have some big Hollywood name as the star. It started to get to me: all those great actors languishing without work and the rarefied few taking all the credit. When *She Stoops to Conquer* bombed, I'd had enough. Very few Hollywood stars understood the London stage. So I decided to duck below the radar, rekindle my love for the art by doing some community theatre in Canada – thriving arts scene out there.'

'And now you're back.'

'Yep, your call couldn't have come at a better time. I'm ready now to ease myself back in to the UK theatre scene. Canada was great, but . . .'

'Homesick?'

'Exactly.' He gave her a rather wonky-toothed grin.

They both chatted easily and inconsequentially until they reached Trevay. As Penny drove slowly along the narrow harbour road she pointed out all the local land-marks and places of note. 'Great lobster in that bar there. Best ice cream in the west here. And . . .' She followed the bend in the road which kept the harbour on her right, 'as we go up here towards the headland, you'll see the theatre. I just know you're going to fall in love with it.'

The Pavilions stood in all its glory, half covered in scaf-folding with a couple of decorators hard at work resilvering the cupola dome. A team of women were polishing the glass doors and brass handles. The car park still looked like a back lot for a Spaghetti Western, but there weren't as many crisp packets blowing in the breeze as yesterday.

Jonathan said nothing.

'Well?' appealed Penny.

Jonathan nodded slowly, his lips pressed together in a grim line. 'Why do you want to save it?'

17

Jess manoeuvred her left hand, fourth finger, into every glinting, gleeful and glorious position she could think of. The half-carat solitaire diamond surrounded by baby pink diamonds continued to delight her.

'Jess – over here. To me.'

'Jess – in the middle. Straight down the lens.'

The posse of photographers outside their flat were jostling as Ryan and Jess stood at the front door and smiled.

'How did he propose, Jess?' shouted a reporter.

'Romantically,' she called back.

'What's it like to have the sexiest man on TV as your fiancé?'

Jess laughed. 'Not too bad.'

The phalanx of cameras let rip their flashbulbs and shutters to capture the moment.

'Give her a kiss, Ryan.' The blitzkrieg again.

The PR woman for *Venini* stepped forward and spoke to the press: 'That's it for now. Thank you, ladies and gentlemen.' Then she herded Ryan and Jess into their hallway and closed the door.

'Well, that should keep them quiet for a bit.' She looked at Ryan steadily. 'Just be careful. When you're back in LA, in a bar, on set, shopping, they'll be watching you, hoping to catch you out.'

Jess peered questioningly at Ryan, who answered smoothly, 'Diane, I've been in the business long enough to know the tricks. Jess understands.'

'What do I understand?'

He put his arm around her. 'That the press make stuff up.'

'Oh.' She smiled briefly, pushing down the unspoken fear that kept nagging at her. Nothing was going to burst this bubble. 'Right.'

Diane was looking at her phone and gathering her notepad and capacious bag simultaneously. 'Right, my lovelies. I must go. Be good and be happy.'

As they opened the door for her and Ryan planted two extravagant kisses on Diane's cheeks, Jess spotted the last of the snappers outside on the pavement, talking on the phone to his office: 'Yeah. Good shots,' he was telling them. 'She looks happy enough.' Glancing up, he saw Jess and gave her a wave. She waved back and closed the door, not hearing him add, 'Poor cow.'

'Well, that was fun – and great timing for the launch of *Horse Laugh*.' Ryan put his arm round her and together they walked upstairs to the flat. Elsie and Ethel skittered their short legs and tiny claws across the wooden floor and hurled themselves at them.

'Hello, girls.' He bent down to rub their tummies. 'Your Mummy and Daddy are engaged and the whole world knows. Mummy's very happy.' He looked up at Jess, who was watching him. 'Aren't you, Mum?'

'Yes. Very . . .' she paused. Dare she say what she wanted to say? 'Maybe I really could be a mum?'

Ryan stopped the tickling and stood up slowly. He put his arms round her and kissed her. She felt his lips on her neck and then his voice close to her ear. 'One step at a time, Jess.' He released her and walked to the kitchen. 'Glass of champagne to celebrate?'

*

'Do I look all right?'

Jess and Ryan were in the back of a taxi on their way into the West End for the press screening of the first episode of *Horse Laugh.*

Jess glanced over at Ryan and squeezed his hand.

'Ryan, you look gorgeous.'

'Do I?' He studied his reflection in the cab window and played with the collar of his Tom Ford shirt. 'Good shirt, isn't it?'

'Fantastic.'

Still focusing on his reflection, he ran a hand through his carefully crafted floppy hair. 'You never know who'll be there.'

'Do *I* look all right?' Jess asked quietly.

'Hmm?' He was now preoccupied with smoothing his eyebrows. 'What?'

'Do I look all right?' Without taking his eyes off his own reflection he answered, 'Yeah yeah. Lovely.'

The taxi turned left into a narrow street and pulled up outside the discreet screening theatre. There were a couple of taxis ahead of them, depositing other guests into the drizzle. Ryan opened the taxi door and got out. 'How much do I owe you, mate?' he asked the cabbie.

'Seventeen pounds eighty on the clock, sir.'

'How much?' Ryan was incredulous as he rummaged through his wallet for a twenty-pound note. 'Take eighteen pounds – and I'll have a receipt please.'

The cabbie grudgingly gave him one with the two pound change. 'Last of the big spenders entcha, mate?'

In no mood to engage with the hired help, Ryan directed his annoyance towards Jess who was still in the back seat.

'Come on, Jess.'

'Can't we wait till we can pull up outside the entrance? Look, the queue is moving. I don't want to get my new shoes wet in the puddles.'

But Ryan was already striding towards the entrance to the cinema. A flashbulb popped in his face and Jess saw him pose, handsomely, for the autograph hunters.

She got out of the cab and followed him, gingerly stepping through the gutter and onto the kerb.

As she reached Ryan, an autograph hunter thrust a pen into her hand. 'Would you sign this for me, please?'

'Certainly. How kind of you to ask.' She managed a tight squiggle before Ryan, his hand in the small of her back and totally unaware that Jess was having a moment of fame, pushed her into the warmly lit entrance lobby.

'Ryan, I was just signing tha—'

Waving brightly to a young man on the other side of the hall, Ryan cried out, 'Stevie, you old dog!' And strode over to him.

As Jess caught up breathlessly, a waiter cruised past with a tray of drinks. 'Drink, sir? Madam?'

Eyeing the glass flutes of champagne and Buck's Fizz, Ryan said, 'Rather have a Scotch if you can find one.'

'Yes, sir,' replied the waiter. As he turned to start his quest for whisky, Jess managed to grab a glass of Buck's Fizz for herself. She was just raising it to her lips when Ryan introduced her to Stevie by thumping her on the shoulder. 'Have you met Jess? My fiancée?'

Stevie glanced at a Jess, who had champagne down the

front of her dress with small, juicy pieces of freshly squeezed orange on her chin, and said, 'Nice to meet you, Tess.'

'Jess.' She shook his hand but he was already listening to one of Ryan's anecdotes about *Venini*.

Jess spent a rather lonely twenty minutes standing next to Ryan while looking for people she knew from the cast and crew of *Horse Laugh* but she couldn't see them anywhere. Presently a wafer-thin young woman in a smart black dress and teetering heels walked amongst the throng announcing that the screening would start in five minutes if they'd like to make their way to the auditorium.

At the double doors into the cinema her producer was waiting for her. 'Jess!' She hugged and kissed her. 'Where've you been? Was the traffic bad? Why are you so late?'

'We weren't late. I've been here for ages but I couldn't see any of you.'

'Didn't you read the invitation? It said that all cast members were to come to the private drinks reception upstairs. We've been waiting for you.'

Ryan, coming up behind Jess, dug into the inside pocket of his jacket to fish out a bent cardboard invitation.

'Oh shit!' he said as he read it. 'Fuck.'

'It doesn't matter.' Jess put a hand on his arm.

'I'll bet they had a darn sight better selection of booze than the crap we got. I never did get my Scotch.'

*

Horse Laugh was to be transmitted in six episodes, with the first week's show running at a feature-length two hours, and the rest an hour long. Tonight's screening would show-case that first episode. Jess settled in her seat, nervous as a kitten; she glanced down the row towards her co-star and they traded winks and thumbs-up signs before the lights dimmed, the title music swelled and the room hushed.

Two hours sped by. Jess couldn't believe how well the invited audience of critics and TV7 executives reacted to the story. They laughed in the right places, fell silent in the right places and clapped in the right places. Jess allowed herself to believe it might just be a hit. As the last line of credits faded she felt Ryan's head lean affectionately on her shoulder. She turned to take his hand and share a kiss. He had pretended to nod off. She shook him. 'Oh ha ha, darling. What do you think?'

He opened his eyes with a start. 'Hmm?'

'Yes, very funny. What did you think?'

'Has it finished?'

'Yes.'

'What time is it?'

'Did you really fall asleep?'

'No, no. Just closed my eyes. You know what I'm like, left in a warm dark room.'

His words sliced through Jess's heart and shaky self-confidence.

'Thanks a lot,' she said.

She got to her feet, trying desperately not to cry. But as she stood, the room began to applaud. She looked to her co-star, who was also getting to her feet. She seemed as bewildered as Jess. The crowd continued to applaud them both. Their producer grabbed their hands and led them to the dais in front of the screen.

The applause built. Jess looked wildly over to where Ryan was still seated. People around him, standing now and clapping, were nudging him and leaning down to speak in his ear. He smiled his film-star smile and began to applaud his fiancée too.

The ride home in the taxi was a quiet one. Ryan said very little to Jess, though he'd said all the right things to the director, TV7 suits and fellow actors. Now he seemed preoccupied. He nibbled at one of his nails, then pulled off his tie. When Jess leaned over to kiss him he didn't kiss her back, but gave her a tight smile in return. He sat bolt upright and stiff, gazing out of the window with his eyes flickering over any passing object of interest. Not once did he look at Jess.

Elsie and Ethel heard Jess's key in the lock but didn't bother to move from their cosy slumber.

'Cup of tea, Ryan?' Jess asked over-brightly.

'I'm bushed. I'm going straight to bed.'

Jess sat heavily on one of the kitchen chairs. Elsie pulled her short legs up to standing and hopped out of her basket. She trundled herself over to Jess and asked to be picked up.

Jess sniffed the familiar doggy smell and felt the little velvet ears on her lips. 'Daddy's cross with me,' she whispered. 'He's cross that I did all right. Why would he be like that, Elsie? I'm always happy for him.'

Elsie swiped her cold wet nose over Jess's chin and licked her. 'He'll feel better in the morning, won't he? He's such a good actor and I'm just lucky to have got *Horse Laugh*, that's all. It'll be fine in the morning. Won't it?'

Ethel got out of bed and she too asked to be picked up. Their warm bodies on Jess's lap gave her enormous comfort. She cuddled them, staring into space and going over the night's events. A couple of the television critics from the broadsheets had come over to talk to her and paid her some wonderful compliments. The Head of Drama at TV7, a young man who looked about twelve to Jess, came and spoke very gratifyingly of a 'huge success' and asked her agent to book in a lunch with him to discuss a second series, which he was certain he would commission on the strength of this preview.

Jess was so deep in thought that she almost didn't hear Ryan come back into the room.

'Darling?'

She turned to face him, 'Yes?'

'You blew me away tonight.'

'Really?'

'You did stuff on screen that I had no idea you could do.'

She began to shake her head, 'No, no. I just . . .'

He held his hand up to quiet her. 'Listen to me, Jess.' He knelt down in front of her and gazed deep into her eyes as he spoke. 'You were amazing. You wiped the others off the screen. I couldn't see anybody else but you. The others saw that too. Tonight you became a star . . . and I apologise for being such an arse.'

18

'Brooke? Broo-ooke.' Penny, no respecter of others' privacy, and having had no response from the front door of Granny's Nook, was now stepping through the wild back garden and peering through the rear windows. 'Broo-ooo-ooke. Where the bloody hell are you?'

Brooke had been rather elusive lately. Penny couldn't fault her work (voluntary) or the time (unpaid) that she was putting into the Pavilions appeal, and totally understood that Brooke was a jobbing actress who needed to keep up her professional profile, but she was being most mysterious about it.

It had all started a couple of weeks ago when Brooke picked up the latest issue of *Woman's Own*. 'Oh, the bastards!' she gasped.

Penny, who'd been in the middle of sending a tweet about the imminent transmission of the *Mr Tibbs* series, looked up in surprise. Brooke, pale-faced and shaking, was staring down at the magazine. 'What is it, darling?'

'Look at this –' Brooke passed the magazine to Penny. It was opened to show a large photo of Bob Wetherby with a beautiful female sprinter to whom he'd just become engaged.

Penny shrugged. 'I wouldn't worry if I were you. The two of you haven't been an item for months, it's only natural he should find someone else.'

'I couldn't care less about that.' Brooke leaned over and pointed to a photo on the opposite page. 'But why did those bastards have to take a cheap shot at me?'

Penny put her glasses on and immediately things became clear. Opposite the page of gorgeous Bob and his Bahamian beauty was a photo of a bedraggled Brooke walking through Trevay and looking miserable. It was accompanied by an article that read:

Brooke Lynne, once the golden girl of Café Au Lait, was spotted looking dishevelled in the tiny Cornish hamlet of Trevay. Appearing to have the weight of the world on her shoulders, if not her hips and chins, passersby had no idea this was the woman who Bob Wetherby, successful super-rich captain of the English rugby team, once romanced . . . A source close to her former agent, Milo James, alleged, 'Brooke Lynne is a sad case. She had the world at her feet. Milo made her the face of Café Au Lait and even introduced her to Bob [Wetherby] but her unstable behaviour and diva tantrums made her impossible to work with. Milo begged Café Au Lait to bear with her while she sorted out her personal problems, but for a family-friendly company, this was not possible. She hurt Bob very deeply. That is something neither he nor Milo will ever discuss. She was a liability and Milo could no longer represent her.' To see her in such a dowdy and unkempt state upsets all those who care for her. She's a woman of talent and at her best is as funny and sexy as a twenty-first century Marilyn Monroe. Sadly, in this photo, she appears to have taken on some of the tragic star's other traits. Her face is bloated and her roots are growing out. Let's hope she gets back on her feet again soon.

The day after the spiteful article, Brooke had gone to the hairdressers and started to wear make-up again. She took up running and had, in the last ten days, been up to London for private meetings with a publicist, much to the delight of the Colonel, who was the only person in on the secret.

Penny pressed her face closer to the window pane and put her hands up to see better. The cosy sitting room was rather untidy but definitely unoccupied. Her eyes took in a pair of sneakers by the fireplace, an open book face down on the coffee table, a cardigan slung over the back of the sofa, and on the mantelpiece at least half a dozen invitations. She could just make out the logo on two of them. *Hello!* magazine and Stringfellows. What the hell was Brooke up to?

*

What Brooke was up to was 'getting herself out there', as her old friend Laverne would have urged her to do. After all the work Laverne had put into transforming the dowdy Brenda Foster into sexy, glamorous Brooke Lynne, she'd been so shaken by Milo James and his underhand tactics that she'd retreated into her shell. She'd allowed that despicable creep to make her believe she was nothing, a nobody, unworthy of stardom and success. Frightened of being found out and exposed as boring old Brenda Foster, she'd fled to Trevay. Brooke was aware of herself enough to know that Milo had played into all of her insecurities. He fit the same mould as the stepfather who'd always told her she was worthless and would never amount to anything. The Colonel had been right: it was time she came out of hiding and found the chutzpah to recreate her alter ego.

It was ironic that the *Woman's Own* piece should have brought about the reincarnation of Brooke Lynne. Milo James and his Café Au Lait cronies had obviously planted that story in an effort to undermine her. They knew that she could still create a serious problem for them if she were to go public about what happened that night at the Starfish Hotel. They felt so threatened by her that they were trying to neutralise the risk she posed by portraying her as a washed-up has been, so that any claims she made would be dismissed as a vindictive attempt to get back at Milo for ditching her. If, however, Brooke Lynne were to rise from the ashes like a phoenix, oozing star quality and sex appeal – and showing off her talent as an actress – people just might believe her version of events instead of the lies put out by that slimeball Milo.

So while Penny was peering through the windows of Granny's Nook, Brooke Lynne was in London's West End attending the launch of hot new club Wowzer. Since its sister club, Wonker, was a favourite haunt of Princes Harry and William and their circle, the media had turned out in force in the hope that the royals would attend tonight's event. It was the hottest ticket in town.

Brooke had called in a favour from a designer she'd helped promote when her fame was at its peak; he'd been only too delighted to loan her an electric-blue full-skirted dress, cinched in at the waist with a slender mink belt and a breast-skimming, off-the-shoulder, bracelet-length sleeved bodice. Her hair was a rich gold and fell in loose curls round her face, just skimming her bare shoulders.

Her eyes were smokily outlined and her lips shiny in their trademark tangerine. She was standing at the bar drinking a Kite Slinger, accompanied by her publicist, Frank.

'Hi, you're Brooke Lynne, aren't you?' A small blonde in a last season's women's tuxedo suit approached her.

'Hello.' Brooke smiled at the young woman. 'I recognise you from the photo above your column in the *Star* – you're Lucy Nugent, aren't you?'

The woman, thrilled at being recognised, launched into a torrent of questions: 'What are you doing here? I thought you were done with showbiz?'

'I've been working on a new play in the West Country.'

'The West Country? Isn't that rather a long way from the West End?'

'A world away – which is sheer bliss. The place is full of wonderfully good-looking men.'

'Yeah? Anyone special?'

'Now that would be telling.'

'Is he here?'

Brooke gave one of her sexiest laughs and tapped the side of her nose. The journalist tried another tack.

'What do you think of Bob Wetherby's engagement?'

'I'm so happy for him. He's a very nice man.'

'What happened between you two?'

'I never kiss and tell.'

'Well, you look better than you did in those photos I saw the other week. Have you had some work done? Botox? Lipo?'

Brooke laughed. 'I am *au naturel.*'

'So what are you doing here? A high-profile party, journos inside, paps outside, a publicist by your side and a super-hot dress on? Spill, Brooke – what's the news?'

As luck would have it, at that moment the number one boy band in the world walked into the club and made a beeline for the bar – and the spot where Brooke was standing. All five of the boys could only stop and stare at the gorgeous Brooke Lynne.

'Hi, boys,' she purred, smiling at them.

Poor little Lucy the journo was pushed out of the way as they surrounded Brooke, flirting outrageously. Within twenty minutes Brooke had agreed to their invitation to abandon Wowzer and head off to another club where the music was better and the food divine.

Frank stood in silent admiration as he watched his client leave the building to a storm of flash photography.

*

Brooke's mobile rang. 'Hey, babe.' It was Frank. 'Have you seen the front pages today? Congratulations! I've been inundated with calls from journos wanting to know which of those boys you went home with last night!'

'They're all great boys, but every man jack of them is gay.'

'NO!'

'Of course they're not – I'm joking. But . . .' Brooke took a deep breath and went for it: 'Frank, could you get me an interview with one of the sensible papers? I'd like to talk about the Pavilions and why I support the campaign to save the place, and about my hopes for my own career.'

'Honey, I'm not sure. It doesn't sit well with your image.'

'And what is my image? A young, silly, unhinged wannabe actress who can't be trusted?' she asked coldly.

'Babe, I know that's not you, but Milo James slung some mud and it's going to take—'

'Which is why I need you to get me a serious interview with a quality paper. That way I might be able to land a proper job and earn the money to pay your extortionate bill.'

He paused while he thought about it. 'Sure, I'll try, but . . .'

'Pleeeeease?'

'Give me a couple of hours,' he sighed.

It took him two hours and forty minutes, but he did it. 'The *Guardian* will meet you in Trevay, day after tomorrow. Journo and snapper 10 a.m. up at the theatre. Happy?'

The SToP team were ecstatic when Brooke told them the news.

'OMG!' shouted Penny, leaping out of her office chair to throw her arms round Brooke.

'Jolly good,' said Simon, his chocolate eyes beaming.

'Marvellous!' Helen clapped her hands.

Even Piran, though he remained seated, managed a sincere, 'Ideal, maid.'

It was agreed that everyone, including Colonel Irvine, would meet up at the theatre to greet the team from the *Guardian*. The building was starting to look a lot better now that the scaffolding was finally down. A task force of Scouts and Guides had spent a long weekend weeding the car park, and Queenie had assembled a gang of local ladies who'd polished every surface inside until it sparkled.

By 10 a.m. the sun was shining in a periwinkle sky and the welcoming committee were standing by with flasks of tea and coffee and plates of pasties to combat the chill March air, eagerly awaiting the men from the *Guardian*.

'Here they come!' said Penny, grasping Simon's hand as a battered Freelander drew up outside the door.

First out of the car was Graham Mowbray, a journalist known for his love of the arts. He introduced himself then turned to introduce the second man getting out of the car. Tall and rangy, in his late twenties, his handsome features enhanced by a rakish beard, the newcomer turned his bright blue eyes to Brooke and gave her a look that sent a tingle to her stomach.

'And this is my photographer, Louis Suffolk.'

Louis smiled warmly at the welcoming committee then looked again at Brooke.

She knew exactly who he was: Prince Louis of Suffolk. Fighter pilot and royal pin-up.

'Hi,' he murmured.

Brooke noticed a dark Range Rover pulling up a discreet distance behind. The protection officers, she assumed. She looked around her. No one else seemed to have recognised him behind the beard. Well, they weren't going to hear it from her.

19

The *Guardian* article – a two-page spread with photos of Colonel Irvine, past and present, Brooke and her new incarnation as saviour of the seaside theatre, Penny as wealthy television producer/vicar's wife, Simon as miracle worker, Helen as dogged helper and Piran as growly-sexy historian romantically involved with Helen, was newspaper heaven and created an enormous amount of interest locally and nationally.

The SToP office at the vicarage was creaking under the barrage of phone calls and emails. It was a matter of all hands to the pump. Penny drafted in three sixteen-year-olds from the village: Siobhan, who was fond of hot pants, crop tops and tattoos; her friend Tillie, who was quiet with blonde hair that occasionally had a blue or pink streak running through it; and Catty, the mother of a fifteen-month-old son called Watson, whom she doted on.

'Watson? That's very unusual,' said Helen conversationally one morning. 'Is it a family name?'

'No. When I 'ad 'im, I rang his dad from the 'ospital to tell 'im 'e 'ad a son and 'e said, "What son?" So I thought, fair enough.'

'Oh,' said Helen, not knowing how to respond.

Catty laughed. 'Your face! You believed me!'

Helen was confused. 'So what is he really called?'

'Oh, his real name is Watson. After the doctor? Sherlock an' all that?'

'Ah, I see now,' said Helen, though she didn't see at all.

'Actually,' continued Catty conspiratorially, 'I'm expectin' again. Early days an' all, but this time I'm thinking about Jude.'

Helen was tuning into this now. 'As in Hardy's – the Obscure?'

It was Catty's turn to look mystified. 'No. As in Jude Law – 'im what plays Watson in the films.'

Both women looked at each other in some confusion. 'Yeah, well, anyway . . .' Catty jerked her head towards the kitchen. 'Wanna a coffee or anything?'

'Yes. Please. Thank you.'

The awkward moment passed and Helen returned to her desk to find Tillie on the phone.

'You're all right, she's 'ere right now, Jules. No trouble. I'll put 'er on. Catch you later.' Tillie handed the phone to Helen. 'It's a bloke called Jules what writes *Downton*.'

Helen felt her heart miss a beat as she took the receiver and shooed Tillie off her desk. 'Hello. Helen Merrifield speaking.'

'Helen – hello. I was just having a most amusing conversation with your assistant. Very colourful.'

'Oh erm . . .' Helen didn't know if an apology was needed. 'She's a very helpful local girl. Penny and I have taken on three school leavers, who, erm . . .' she struggled to find the right words, 'who are very new to the work place,' she finished limply.

Lord Fellowes boomed with laughter. 'Well, Tillie was marvellous and has quite given me an idea for a new character. Anyway, I was actually phoning to speak to Penny, but I gather she's not there.'

'She'll be back in an hour. Can I take a message?'

'Yes, do. Please tell her that Maggie and Hugh are free on the dates we discussed so it's all systems go. They loved the piece in the *Guardian* and can't wait to meet old Colonel Stick. What a character! And what fun to put on a show at Easter for all the holidaymakers. The *Guardian* story has certainly woken people up to the plight of the Pavilions. I've drafted a little thing I've called *Tales of Downton*, where Hugh and Maggie tell a few anecdotes, as themselves – and there's a part for Brooke Lynne too. Perhaps Penny will call me back later?'

'Yes, yes, of course.' Helen was frantically writing down all this priceless information. 'As soon as she gets in, bye.'

*

Penny had been working like mad on Jonathan Mulberry. Even though he had been so unimpressed by the Pavilions, returning to London the following day with a grouchy promise that he would 'give it some thought', she had set her heart on having him as the general theatre manager. When her phone calls failed to elicit a more favourable response she'd travelled to London for a face-to-face meeting.

'I'm not used to provincial stuff,' he'd told her over dinner. 'I like a nice warm weatherproof building with a guaranteed audience . . . And I've had enough of doing this job for the love of it – I like to be paid, and paid well.'

Penny almost choked on her seabass meunière but managed to stammer, 'I'll pay you . . . well.'

'What with? You haven't any box office yet. And I am not out to bankrupt you.'

'By the weekend the task force of volunteer builders will be moving out. The Arts Council have given us a grant, and the Friends of the Pavilions have raised quite a bit through car boot sales and sponsorship.'

'You're going to need a hell of a lot more than that to get the place open and running. What's your plan?'

'We're not relying on theatrical productions alone for revenue. There'll be the café, for a start, and the foyer can be let out for functions. We'll be applying for a wedding licence so that people can get married up there, but our relationship with the council is a bit sticky so we haven't asked them yet. As for the theatre side of things, Colonel Irvine is brushing off his old script: *Hats Off, Trevay!* It's probably a bit dated, but the show opened the theatre back in . . .' Her voice faded when she saw the look of pity on Jonathan's face.

'It's not good enough, is it? You need a show with huge stars that will knock people's socks off. You need backers with big money. I think you may just have to admit defeat and hand it back to the council. You aren't a theatre woman, Pen. Stick with the telly.'

Penny was outraged. 'How dare you suggest I can't run a business! I know what's needed to build a brand and create success. Look at *Mr Tibbs* – no one else saw the potential in Mavis Carew's old crime novels, but that series has sold in over a dozen countries and—'

Jonathan held his hands up in mock defence. 'OK, I believe you. But you have got to pull something big out of the bag here. That building is a money pit. The repairs you've made are like sticking a bit of Elastoplast over a missing leg.'

Penny couldn't disagree. Maybe she'd spent so much time with her fellow SToP campaigners that she'd lost all perspective on this. Still, she was convinced that getting Jonathan on board was key to making a success of this venture.

She looked him straight in the eye. 'If I were to open the theatre by Easter with a host of star names and a full house, would you be my theatre manager?'

Jonathan returned her steady gaze. 'Yes. But it has to be pretty bloody starry.'

*

Penny had spent the train journey back from London replaying her conversation with Jonathan. By the time she parked her Jag outside the vicarage and walked up the path she was feeling utterly downcast. Before she could put her key in the lock, the door flew open and Helen launched herself at her.

'Pen! Something amazing has happened,' she cried breathlessly. 'I've been waiting for you to get here so I could tell you face to face.'

'What is it?'

Helen told her.

'Oh my God! Julian? Maggie and Hugh? Brooke? Oh my God, my God!' Penny's knees almost buckled and she had to grab Helen for support. 'You're not joking, are you?'

'No.'

'At Easter?'

'Yes.'

Penny closed her eyes and stood in silent prayer, muttering, 'I can't believe it. I can't believe it.' Then she leapt past Penny, rushing down the hall towards Simon's office, shouting his name as he emerged, blinking, from his study.

'What's the matter, Pen? What's happened?' He ushered

her into his study and shut the door behind them. A moment later Helen, waiting in the hall, heard him cry, 'Well done, darling! How marvellous! You must phone Jonathan straight away.'

*

'So, when can I see you again?' His muffled voice in Brooke's hair sent a shiver of pleasure through her.

'I've got to go back to Cornwall tonight. After the *Guardian* piece the whole thing's gone mad.' She propped herself up on one elbow and checked the clock display on her phone: it was three thirty. Prince Louis of Suffolk had cooked her a lunch of spaghetti bolognaise in the tiny kitchen of his apartment. He had a small but very grand annexe of his parents' grace-and-favour London home. Two bedrooms, a cosy drawing room, a dark-room/office and the kitchen. They were lying on a very long, very wide, very squashy sofa in front of his state-of-the-art television.

He kissed her neck. 'Please don't go back tonight. I'll get Hutch to drive you down first thing.'

'That's sweet of you, but I'd prefer not to get into trouble by using royal drivers, thank you.'

'Well, let me take you to Paddington then.'

'And what if we get seen?'

'Stuff it.'

She sat up and pushed her hair from her eyes. 'Louis, I don't want to attract attention by being seen with you.'

He rolled over and rubbed the back of his wrist over his eyes. 'I've told you. It'll be all right.'

'Yes and I get it. You've chosen to be a reportage photographer, you've got a step-uncle who is one of the biggest newspaper barons in the business and now, because you've joined the ranks of Fleet Street, you're "off limits". They don't chase "their own".'

'Exactly. Smart of me, eh? It's like they say – if you can't beat 'em, join 'em. For years my family had to put up with media intrusion and there was nothing they could do about it. Now I have immunity.'

'Is that the only reason you took the job?'

'Of course not. I did photography at university and I got a first, so I do know my onions. War hero stroke playboy prince doesn't cut the mustard as a career option these days. I've got plans. I'm going to open my own gallery when the time is right, but first I need experience.'

'How long will it stay secret though, you and me? It's too good a story.'

He smiled his most beguiling smile and raised his arms to her. 'My step-uncle will buy me some time. It'll probably mean that I'll have to give someone an exclusive at some point – throw them a few bones. But I'm going to make hay while the sun shines. Give us a cuddle.'

He really was a lovely person. Brooke knew it would be so easy to fall in love with Louis, but he was a young man out to have some fun. Before he joined the press, the papers were full of stories about the hero fighter pilot prince and his many many girlfriends. Now that the press no longer hounded him, she had no idea if there were other girls on the scene, or indeed how many.

After the *Guardian* shoot one of the protection officers had slipped her a piece of paper with Louis's number on it. Brooke had put it in her purse but had never taken it out. And then one day her phone at Granny's Nook had rung.

'Brooke?' asked the posh young man. 'We met the other day – I took your photo for the *Guardian*?'

Brooke was suspicious. 'Who is this?'

'I'm, it's . . . Louis. I tracked you down.'

'How did you get my home number?'

'Oh, ah, tricks of the trade. Can't tell you. Would have to kill you. That sort of thing. Fancy some lunch?'

'I'm in Cornwall.'

'I know. So am I.'

'Are you?' She was certain this was a hoax.

'Yeah.'

'Where?'

'Outside your house.'

Brooke had felt a gush of panic flood through her. Was this some kind of prank? She moved slowly towards her front window, keeping to the walls. She peeked round the curtain. Sure enough, out in the road parked between her gate and the Pendruggan village green was a blacked-out Range Rover.

'I can't see anyone,' she blustered.

'I'll get out of the car and show myself, if you like.'

'OK.' At least she'd know who this freak was.

Through the receiver pressed to her ear, she could hear the sound of a door opening and a soft squeak of leather which she assumed meant he had slid off the car seat. She peeked round the curtain again. Shit. It was him.

'Get back in the car! People will see you.'

'There's no one around.'

She watched as he held out one arm and turned full circle on the spot indicating the village with not a soul to be seen.

'Get back in the car!' she squeaked.

'Not until you come outside and let me take you to lunch. I'm hungry.'

'Where would we go? I can't take you to the pub, can I?'

'Have you got anything in the larder?'

'Not much.'

'Eggs?'

'Yes.'

'I make a mean omelette. Can I come in?'

'Is it just you?' She looked to the left and right of his car to find his protection officers.

'I've got Hutch with me. He's good at washing-up.'

The window of the front passenger seat slid open and the smiling face of the man who had slipped her Louis's number appeared. He waved. She waved back. 'Shit. I just waved.'

Louis laughed. 'Can I come in or what?'

20

Ollie had been more depressed than ever after his trip to Cornwall. In the past his mother's face had always lit up with joy whenever they met, but this time it had been obvious that her happiness at seeing him had been tinged with concern and sadness . . . and even pity. It was as if, without meaning to, she'd held a mirror up and shown him the ugly truth: he was stuck in a pointless and horrible relationship and his career had completely stalled.

He hadn't bothered to tell Red about the woman he'd met in Trevay who wanted to get her down for some fundraiser. Did they really think that Red, a global rock star, would drop everything for a shitty little theatre that no one had heard of? He was fed up with being treated as a gateway to Red. He was fed up with being the boyfriend of a woman he never saw and rowed with whenever they spoke. What had happened to them? When he first met her she had been electrifying. A tiny ball of energy, riding the thrilling crest of fame. She had been normal, funny, enjoying this extraordinary luck that had given her so much. They had still been able to nip out to the corner shop together and get the Sunday papers and a bottle of milk, no bodyguards in tow, no smarmy PAs with camp German accents. She'd had her own bank card that she could get cash with. She loved seeing her account balance on the printed receipt, each week adding another nought or two.

All that had changed. Now she was surrounded by security guards, record label publicists and that bloody sycophant, Henrik. She hadn't a clue what she was worth and never carried cash. When he tried to phone her, he couldn't even get to her. His calls were answered by some minion – a new one every time, it seemed – who said they'd pass on the message that he'd called. Had he been dumped? Was he a free man? He hadn't the energy to find out. He felt sucked dry.

His mum rang every day, clearly worried sick about him. 'Ollie, this isn't like you. Please come and stay with me for a bit, just till you get back on your feet.'

'Mum, I've got to be in London. It's where the work is.'

'Have you spoken to your agent?'

'Yes.'

'And?'

'There's a casting next week for a short tour of *Dial M for Murder*.'

'That sounds promising.'

'It'll be shit.'

'But it's a job.'

'It's not what I want.'

'What do you want?'

He wanted to be the Ollie he used to be. The Ollie who hadn't met Red. The Ollie who had energy and saw life as an adventure.

'I don't know, Mum.'

'Have you spoken to Red recently?'

'No.'

'And how does that make you feel?'

'I'm not sure, Mum.'

'Do you love her?' she asked gently.

'I don't know.'

'If you loved her, you would know.'

'How would I?'

'You wouldn't let her out of your sight – you wouldn't be able to stand not seeing her. Tell me something: when was the last time she made you laugh?'

'Can't remember.'

'When was the last time she told you she loved you?'

'Can't remember.'

'And the last time you told her you loved her?'

'I don't know.'

'You're answering all your own questions.'

'Yeah, but . . .'

'Why don't you come down? You can do your own thing. Just take a break for a while, give yourself time to think.'

'I don't know . . .'

'Come and stay with me.'

And so they continued, going round and round in circles.

*

Jonathan got off the train at Bodmin and stepped into the car Penny had sent him. On the seat was a note addressed to Jonathan Mulberry, Theatre Manager, The Pavilions, Trevay.

He opened it and read:

Darling Jonathan,
I promise you won't regret it. Welcome aboard.
All my love,
  Penny

When he had received the phone call from Penny telling him about Julian Fellowes' incredible offer, Jonathan remained cool. So cool that Penny felt the need to tell him again.

'He's written a forty-five-minute piece for us. It starts off as a sort of dialogue between Maggie and Hugh about the incredible and hilarious things that happened during the making of *Downton*. While Maggie and Hugh recount tales from the series, our Brooke will be re-enacting some of the events, portraying some of the characters from the series, like Mrs Patmore and Elsie. She'll have a lot to do on the night. Then, after the interval, he's offering to do an 'Ask the Author' question-and-answer session on his own. It's just incredible!'

'Hmm, not a bad start. Not a bad start at all,' said Jonathan.

'It's fucking brilliant is what it is!' shrieked Penny.

'It's pretty good,' he admitted. 'You know what you've got to do now?'

'Send you a contract to be our new theatre manager?' Penny crossed her fingers and scrunched her eyes up in anticipation of a positive answer.

'Hold your horses,' he drawled. 'First, you need to phone Mavis Carew and tell her what Julian has offered. I'm willing to bet that she'll leap in with an offer of her own – a fundraising evening with herself and the stars of *Mr Tibbs* taking questions from the audience.'

'Ahh!' Penny gasped. 'Do you really think so? Jonathan, you are a genius.'

'I have my moments,' he acquiesced.

'*Then* will you be our new theatre manager?'

Jonathan chuckled down the line: 'You bet your life.'

Penny almost wept with relief before adding: 'All we need

now is a stage management team, lights, designer, sound, wardrobe department, stage-door keeper, and box office manager. Simple.'

Jonathan laughed again. 'Hey, I know a few people and can sort that out – provided you do the rest.'

That night a much happier and more relaxed Penny sat with her feet resting on Simon's lap as they watched the first episode of a new comedy drama called *Horse Laugh*. It was very good. One actress in particular stood out.

'Jess Tate . . . isn't she the girlfriend of that bloke who plays the Italian in that thing about opera and espionage?' asked Simon.

'Blimey. How would you know that?' asked Penny with jokily raised eyebrows.

Simon was a bit annoyed. 'I do read the papers.'

'I know, but . . . never mind. What is his name?'

'Venini something?'

'Yeah . . .' Penny reached for her iPad and tapped a query into Google. After a moment's searching she found what she was looking for. 'Here he is: Ryan Hearst. I'll put a call in tomorrow morning to see if he'd like to join our merry gang.' She typed a short note to remind herself.

*

Ryan was in the pool, having just finished his one hundred daily lengths, when his PA, Jimmy, called him to the phone. 'It's the London office.' As soon as Ryan had pulled himself out of the pool he handed him a towel and then the receiver.

'Hi,' said Ryan as he put the phone to his ear.

His agent gave him all the latest news from the office

and his filming schedule for the next day then said, 'You're probably not interested in this but Julian Fellowes and Mavis Carew are both involved in raising funds for a dilapidated theatre in Cornwall.' Ryan heard the sound of computer keys being tapped thousands of miles away in London and imagined them bouncing off a transatlantic satellite somewhere above him. His agent was looking up the information. 'Here we are. It's the . . .' Ryan imagined him scrolling down the email '. . . the Pavilions in Trevay.'

'The Pavilions? Yeah. I've read about it.'

'Well, they wondered if you would like to join the company for a summer season.'

'With Julian and Mavis?'

'No, as a name for their summer show.'

Ryan laughed. 'Ha! No way! My end-of-the-pier days are behind me now, thank God. Equity minimum and dingy digs with grim landladies. No thanks.'

'Thought as much. You have to admire their balls, though!' The two men enjoyed the joke.

'Chuck it to Jess,' said Ryan. 'She needs something to keep her busy this summer. She's got nothing on till *Horse Laugh* gets recommissioned.'

*

Jess was reading a stunning review in the *Daily Telegraph* for *Horse Laugh* and for her performance in particular when her iPhone popped up with a message from her sister Emma.

See: told you it would happen, you're a bloomin superstar. Call you in half an hour when I'm back home. Xxx

Jess didn't have time to reply before the phone rang again. It was her agent, Alana Chowdhury.

'Darling. Who's my little star then?'

Jess blushed with pleasure. 'Was it OK? Did you watch?'

'Did I watch? Darling, nothing would have moved me from my sofa!' This was a lie. Alana had been dining with another client but had made sure she'd watched it on Sky Plus this morning, fast forwarding through the scenes that Jess was not in. Not that there were many, which had made Alana late for the office. 'You were in-cred-i-ble. I've just got the overnight figures and you won the slot with a 42 per cent share.'

'Really?' Jess tried to sound as if she knew what Alana meant. 'Gosh.'

'Yes, gosh. The network are thrilled. I'm sure we'll hear about a recommission any day. Have you seen the papers?'

'Yes,' Jess replied shyly.

'And?' Alana demanded. 'I haven't had a chance to look yet.'

'Well . . .' Jess stretched out her hand for the *Daily Telegraph*. 'The *Telegraph* says, "an exciting new comedy talent, with divine timing and a real sincerity".' How she wished her parents were alive to read it.

'And do they mean you, little miss modest?'

'Yes, but they mention everyone else too.'

'Forget the others! This is all about *you*!' Alana laughed richly. 'Oh, that reminds me. Want to spend the summer in Cornwall?' Alana filled Jess in on the Pavilions job, carefully not mentioning Ryan chucking it to her as one of his scraps.

'What fun! Yes, please. I'd love a summer in Cornwall and so would Ethel and Elsie. Wait till I tell Ryan. He may even come down to visit. He loves regional theatres and is always talking about how we must back them or lose them.' Jess was thrilled with this new opportunity and rang Ryan immediately . . .

'Hey, babe,' he answered sleepily. Jess looked guiltily at her clock. 10 a.m. in the UK. Shit: 2 a.m. in LA.

'Ryan, it's me.'

There was a clatter on the other end, as if he'd dropped the phone, then a scrunching and things grew muffled. Jess imagined him in the darkness of his room, trying to find where he'd dropped the phone and accidentally burying it under the pillow. She thought she could hear him swearing faintly, but when he came back on his voice was smooth and unruffled. 'Jess . . . darling. It's two in the morning. What's the matter?'

'Oh, darling, I'm so sorry to wake you. It's just . . . you'll never guess what!'

'What?'

'*Horse Laugh* got a 42 per cent share of the audience last night and rather lovely reviews.'

'Did you get a mention?'

'Erm yes.'

Ryan felt a pang of peevishness and didn't ask her to read any of them, but managed, 'Good girl. Any other news?'

She told him about Trevay. 'Maybe you could come down when you get a filming break?'

'Yeah maybe, babe. Listen, I gotta split.' Jess hated this new faux American accent he felt the need to affect. 'I need to get another few hours in the sack. I've got a couple of heavy scenes to shoot in the morning. OK, babe?'

'Yes. Speak later?' But he'd already gone.

Jess spent the rest of the morning answering congratulatory texts from her friends and colleagues from the show and searching the Internet for a picture-perfect Cornish cottage that she and Elsie and Ethel could rent.

*

'Ollie, it's Mum.' Her voice was loud in the receiver.

'Hi, Mum,' replied Ollie in a downbeat voice. 'I was just taking a nap.'

Undaunted, his mum raised her voice even louder: 'Then wake up, boy – I have some good news. They're looking for actors to star in the new summer season at the Pavilions and I've got you on the list for tomorrow morning.'

'Oh, Mum, no, I really don't want to . . . It's very kind of you and all that, but . . . I'm not in the mood and I'm waiting to hear about *Dial M for Murder* and . . .'

'Get yourself on the 14.23 from Paddington – I'll be waiting for you at Truro station tonight. Oh, and I've booked you a haircut first thing.'

She'd gone before he could say a word.

Part Two

21

The Easter production of *Tales of Downton* was a sellout, with tickets changing hands on eBay for many times their face value. The great and the good of Trevay were all out in force, and the Islington Chatterati, many of whom had Cornish second homes, made it their business to secure tickets. Rumours were rife that David and Samantha Cameron would be coming to watch too. They often stayed in neighbouring Rock on their holidays. It all generated a buzz of excitement that equalled anything to be found on a West End opening night.

Brooke was nervously putting the final touches to her make-up. They'd had precious little time to rehearse and she could only hope that her training at the Bristol Old Vic and the Actors Studio had stood her in good stead.

As it was a fairly informal set, with just Brooke and the other two actors on a simply lit stage, she'd opted for an understated but elegant black calf-length dress that wouldn't ride up over her knees when she sat on her stool. Tonight was all about changing the way people thought of her. This wasn't about looking good on the pages of a tacky tabloid; this was about Brooke Lynne – the actress.

Jonathan popped his head around the door.

'Ready? Curtain call in about five mins.' He gave her a calm and encouraging smile. 'Feeling OK?'

'You betcha.' Brooke gave him a wink with more confidence than she felt and put the final touches to her hair.

*

Julian Fellowes did not disappoint his fans. His script for the evening was brilliantly written and perfectly performed by Hugh and Dame Maggie. The anecdotes were hilarious and they held the audience in the palms of their hands. Brooke was a natural. Playing the parts of the other *Downton Abbey* cast members was a perfect showcase for her talents. Naturally funny, she imbued the (liberally exaggerated) stories of behind-the-scenes high jinks and mayhem with humour and intelligence. Her talent as an impressionist was a revelation and the audience were doubled up with laughter at her rendering of the much-loved characters, in particular, her performance as Carson, the butler.

When the three actors took their bows, they received a standing ovation. As they left the stage, the ongoing cheers and cries of bravo brought them back for an encore. Brooke caught the Colonel's eye in the front row and he gave her an approving smile as the audience cheered and clapped their approval.

The night continued in the same enjoyable vein. Sir Julian's 'Any Questions' section was a hoot, and both Lord Fellowes and the audience enjoyed Queenie's good-humoured heckling from the front row, proffering an invitation for Thomas Barrow to drop in and share one her famous pasties out the back of the shop anytime he was passing . . .

The evening ended with an auction. The sale of *Doctor Who* memorabilia and a jacket from Quentin Tarantino, who had worn it while directing *Django Unchained*, made almost £50,000. An awful lot of the money raised would be disappearing into the black hole of building costs and the rent that the council was charging them, but it did a great deal to lift everyone's confidence.

Their next big fundraising gala was scheduled for the autumn. Billed as *A Night with Mr Tibbs*, it was already selling well.

*

Buoyed by the success of the *Downton* evening, everyone involved with the Pavilions was in a buzz of excitement about the summer production, *Hats Off, Trevay!*. By the time the cast assembled for the first day of rehearsals, the theatre had a full complement of staff for the first time in maybe twenty years. For the next five months the Pavilions would be open every day, a proper working theatre once again.

The bustle of the auditorium was what Ollie liked most. He hadn't been in a theatre since he'd left Stratford and the Royal Shakespeare Company. He stood at the back of the newly repaired rows of seats and drank in the smell of paint and fresh wood shavings. On the stage a gaggle of young people were walking about with bits of three-by-one on their shoulders or carrying tins of paint. An older man – Ollie assumed he was the production manager – was barking instructions: 'Ed, stop twatting about and get that bloody ship's rail painted.' A ginger-headed boy with nose piercings sulkily stopped painting the back of his mate's dungarees and got on with his job.

An electrician rattled open a very tall set of aluminium

ladders and shouted to someone in the dark at the back of the stalls: 'Jim? Put up circuit 27.' A voice near Ollie replied, 'Okey-doke!' and a bank of lights lit up the left side of the stage. 'Cheers, mate.' Ladder man climbed up and started adjusting the lamps way up high.

A woman Ollie thought he recognised from his audition walked past him. He racked his brains. Was she the company manager? He couldn't remember. That day had been a blur. The only bit he remembered clearly was going home and telling his mum he'd got the job.

'Excuse me . . .' He stopped the woman.

'Oh, hi,' she said, recognition spreading across her face with a smile.

'I was wondering if you knew where I could put my stuff and where the rehearsals are?' He gestured to his heavy rucksack.

'Of course. Follow me.'

She led him through the auditorium towards the stage and the pass door that separated the audience from the mysteries of backstage. At once he felt himself connecting with the familiar tattiness of the 'actors' side' of the theatre as opposed to the comfort and glamour of the 'audience' side. The woman kept up a steady flow of inconsequential chatter, asking him where he was staying (at his mum's for the time being) and whether he was looking forward to the summer season (yes).

They crossed the stage and went down a short flight of steps to the green room and the dressing rooms leading off it. Several cast members were sitting around on sagging sofas drinking the coffee that a young, female assistant stage manager was making.

Brooke spotted Ollie first and jumped up to greet him.

'Hi, Ollie – Brooke Lynne. So lovely to meet you at last.'

He dropped his rucksack on the floor and they exchanged the two-cheek kiss that is obligatory in showbiz circles.

'Hi.' He beamed round at the others, who all made welcoming noises.

'And this,' said Brooke approaching a shiny-cheeked elderly man who was beaming at everyone from a seat in the corner, 'this is Colonel Walter Irvine. The first manager of this theatre and entertainer extraordinaire.' She bowed with a Dandiniesque flourish of her hand.

The old man chuckled. 'My dear, you flatter me.'

Ollie went to him and shook his hand. 'I'm so pleased to meet you, Colonel. I love your script.'

'Oh, dear boy, I'm afraid the original script, when we blew the dust off it, was very creaky – but young Mr Mulberry has worked hard at bringing it up to date.'

'I think it's wonderful, and so funny,' said the woman who'd led Ollie down from the auditorium. 'Boy meets girl, boy loses girl to heartless baddie, girl realises her mistake, gets back with boy, happy ending.'

'And you, my dear, will be splendid as the girl's best friend.' The Colonel patted her hand.

Ollie looked at the woman again. Bugger. She wasn't the company manager at all, she was Jess Tate. Star of *Horse Laugh* and girlfriend of superstar Ryan Hearst. He'd met her once, somewhere. He racked his brains, trying to remember. It was at the car park machines at Heathrow, when he'd collected Red. 'Yeah. You'll be amazing!' he said, trying to cover his confusion.

It seemed he'd got away with it. 'Thanks,' she said. 'Want a coffee?'

Down the stairs clattered a tall bearded man in his early thirties. He walked towards Ollie. 'Hi, I'm Dan. We met at the audition?'

'Of course. Hi, Dan,' said Ollie.

'You'll find I'm company and stage manager rolled into one. Budget didn't stretch to two of us. I see you've met everyone.' He smiled and turned to the assembled throng.

'Tech crew are just clearing the stage and then we'll go up and have a read-through of the script. It's great to have us all together at last.'

When they finally got up to the stage, Ollie saw that it had been swept and tidied and now had a circle of chairs sitting on it.

Jonathan Mulberry, Pavilions theatre manager and the director of *Hats Off, Trevay!* was waiting for them.

There were lots of kisses and hellos and thank yous as they got settled.

'Lovely to have you all here – and well done on getting the gig,' said Jonathan. There was polite laughter.

'Right, let's get started. Turn to page one, everybody. Ollie, off you go.'

It was clear that Ollie, as the leading man, and Brooke, as his leading lady, were perfectly cast. Jess was both funny and moving as the best friend caught in the middle of the romance. Colonel Irvine was playing his alter ego, Colonel Stick: the jokey storyteller who guided the audience through the tale using dramatic voices, amusing comic interludes and the odd song and dance.

Being a musical, Ollie, Brooke and the cast had songs to learn. At the end of the afternoon, Dan handed round CDs with their music on. From tomorrow they would have a rehearsal pianist joining them. The full band wouldn't turn up till nearer the end of rehearsals.

It was getting dark outside as they all tumbled out into the repaired car park.

'Can I give anyone a lift?' asked Ollie, looking at both Brooke and Jess.

'I've got my car, thanks,' said Brooke. Louis was coming down today. She hoped he'd be at Granny's Nook when she got in.

'OK. How about you, Jess?' Ollie asked.

'I can walk. I'm in the Starfish Hotel. It's only a ten-minute walk.'

'I drive past, if you want a lift?'

Jess hesitated for a moment before replying, 'That would be lovely. Thank you.'

At the Starfish, Ethel and Elsie would be eagerly awaiting her return. The hotel manager, Louise Lonsdale, had so *loved* having Julian Fellowes, Dame Maggie Smith and Hugh Bonneville staying for the high-profile fundraiser for the Pavilions, that she couldn't do enough for anyone connected to the theatre. As a result she'd overlooked the hotel's no pets policy and allowed Jess Tate to bring her two little dogs.

'Miss Tate, Ethel and Elsie are my guests. When you are busy in rehearsals they will work behind the reception desk, adding an extra welcome to our visitors.'

Jess climbed into Ollie's battered red MG Midget and together they set off down the hill into the narrow lanes of the fishing village.

'Where is your mum's house?' she asked him.

''bout ten minutes away. I'm not sure I'll be able to do the whole summer there. I love her and all that, but once you've left home there's no going back, is there?'

He changed gear from third to second, the clutch protesting horribly, and negotiated a tight turn onto the road by the harbour wall before continuing: 'I'd like to stay at the Starfish ideally. I love hotel living, but it's way beyond my means.'

'Oh, I don't know,' replied Jess. 'Louise, the owner, is rather fond of getting "names" into her establishment. If you can put up with doing the odd bit of PR for her, I think she'd probably pay you to stay there. She's given me a really good rate.'

He looked at her with a raised eyebrow. 'What sort of PR?'

'Pose for the occasional photo for the papers and magazines. Have supper with her and her friends, bring Red along. That sort of thing.'

At the mention of Red, Jess felt a distinct chill in the car. She looked over at his now expressionless face. 'I'm sorry. Have I overstepped the mark?'

He gave a rueful smile. 'No, no. It's just . . . well, let's say things are never quite as they seem. I don't know quite how to explain what the situation with Red is, so let's just say it's complicated.'

Jess looked down at her hands which were resting in her lap and turned her left hand to let her engagement ring sparkle under a passing street light. 'I didn't mean to be nosy. I understand how hard long-distance relationships can be. My fiancée is in LA right now.'

He smiled over at her. 'Well, then you and I shall keep each other company. And if you can put a good word in for me with the Starfish's boss – Linda . . . ?'

'Louise.'

'Louise . . . then do. And here we are.'

The MG slowed to stop and promptly cut out. 'Oh shit,' said Ollie succinctly. 'She's a bugger to start when she does this. If I leave her to cool for a half an hour it might do the trick. Can I buy you a drink?'

'That sounds very nice.' But then she remembered, 'I need to walk my dogs round the block first though.'

'I could do with a walk. Can I come with you?'

Jess smiled at him. 'Deal.'

*

The bar of the Starfish was quiet, just a few businessmen chatting over tall glasses of chilled lager after a long day of meetings and a couple with a son around ten years old, Jess guessed, intent on his tablet. Pools of light glowed round the deliciously squashy sofas and low tables arranged in cosy enclaves facing the vast bay windows overlooking the twinkling harbour. A new moon shone on the water and lapped the fishing boats and the yachts that were moored there.

'Evening, Miss Tate. What can I get you?' The bartender was a dear man, almost near retirement age, who'd been with the hotel since its heyday in the fifties and sixties.

'Evening, Jack. May I have a glass of merlot?'

'Large?'

'Is there any other size?'

The man laughed and turned to find the bottle on the long mirrored shelves behind him. After he'd poured the glass and handed it to Jess he turned to Ollie. 'And what can I get for you, sir?'

'A pint please. Doom Bar.'

'Right you are, sir.'

Drinks in hand, Jess led the way to a pair of low armchairs in a far corner. Elsie and Ethel flopped onto the carpet at her feet.

'Are you hungry?' she asked Ollie.

He was unsure how to respond. He was starving and would love to eat here, but he didn't want to overstay his welcome.

'Mum will be expecting me. Chicken pie, I think.'

Jess was disappointed. 'Maybe another time . . .' She looked away and down at the dogs to ruffle their ears. She hoped he didn't think she was trying to chat him up.

'I'd love to stay for supper, but I don't want to impose,' Ollie explained. 'You might feel like an early night and I don't want to be a bore.'

'I'm going to have a bar snack. The macaroni cheese here is the best sort of comfort food. You can eat and be gone within the hour.'

He grinned. 'I'll give Mum a shout then.'

*

It was two hours later when Ollie left. He'd had just the one pint to Jess's three large merlots, and as she said goodnight to him on the front step she hugged him. Over the last two hours they'd managed to give each other a potted history of their lives to date. Jess had skipped over her anxieties about Ryan and Ollie had mostly avoided talking about Red, but they were aware enough of the quiet undercurrents to respect each other's privacy.

'I'm really looking forward to this summer. I hope we can be mates,' said Jess.

Ollie returned her hug and kissed her cheek. He liked this straightforward woman who loved her man and her dogs. 'Mates,' he said, and he turned to take the steps down to his car two at a time.

She watched him as he started the MG first time and the headlights came on to pick out the road ahead of him. He wound down the driver's rickety window and shouted, 'Bye. Do you want me to pick you up on the way in tomorrow, Mrs Mate?'

'My call's at ten. When's yours?' she called back.

'Same.'

'Great.' She smiled and waved. 'See you tomorrow, Mr Mate.'

22

Brooke drove out of Trevay and through the darkening lanes towards Pendruggan. She had given Louis a key to Granny's Nook, on his insistence, and could feel her heart quickening. Would he be there? She drove past the welcoming lights of the Dolphin, the local pub that Louis kept threatening to take her to. She'd love to walk in on his arm and show him off, but then what would happen? Much as she wanted the world to know that this most eligible of princes was taking her out, at the same time she knew that sort of publicity could spell the end of any romance they might be enjoying. Louis was kind and warm and reckless, but he valued his privacy – and, on past history, moved on very quickly as soon as private became public.

Leaving the lights of the Dolphin twinkling behind her, she drove on to Pendruggan and turned left towards the village green. The lights were on in most of the cottages lining the green, but what about Granny's Nook? Yes, yes – the porch light was on, but the curtains were drawn so that she could see only a sliver of light.

She drew up alongside the familiar black Range Rover, turned off the ignition and breathed a small sigh of satisfaction. He was here.

Louis was in the sitting room, grooving to Justin Timberlake and holding a wine glass.

'Hey, Brookie.' He held his arms out for a cuddle and she happily obliged.

A loud cough from the kitchen broke their embrace.

'Hi, Hutch.' Brooke smiled at the policeman.

'Glass of wine, Miss Lynne?' he asked jokily, waving a bottle in front of her. 'I recommend this cheeky little plonk to compliment my world-renowned lasagne.'

Brooke laughed and looked at the two men in mock surprise. 'He shoots to kill *and* cooks to woo?'

Louis burst into raucous laughter. He loved schoolboy humour. 'Darling Brookie, we've been here for hours getting this ready for you. We did a bit of exploring too. We went over to the village shop for the wine and some tomatoes and—'

Brooke's face dropped. 'Oh my God. Did you see Queenie? She'll have recognised you. She'll tell everyone you're here. She runs that shop like a gossip agency.'

Louis took her hands in his and looked down at her terrified face surrounded by its golden blonde curls. 'Darling, darling, I pulled my cap right down and Hutch did all the talking. Told her he was your brother, come to visit with a mate. It's all cool.' He pulled her to him to reassure her.

'Did she believe him?'

'Yes.'

'Sure?'

'Sure.'

'Because if news got out that you were here . . .'

'It won't.'

'Here, drink this.' Hutch passed her her glass of wine. 'He's telling the truth. She hadn't a clue.'

'OK then.' She allowed herself to relax and enjoy the company of these two men who were such fun to be around.

The lasagne was delicious and Brooke complimented Hutch on it. 'Never fails,' he said smugly, sitting back in his kitchen chair. 'All his birds love it.'

There was a moment's shocked silence while they all registered what Hutch had said. It was broken by Louis: 'Time for Hutch to do the washing-up while you and I,' he nudged Brooke in the ribs, 'leave him to it.'

*

Brooke and Louis left the kitchen and he took her by the hand and led her upstairs to her bedroom. As soon as the door was closed she spoke. 'Is that what this is? Lasagne, a shag and a good laugh with Hutch?'

He had the grace to look embarrassed. 'That was clumsy of Hutch – and not true, by the way.'

'He hasn't made lasagne for your other girlfriends?'

'Well, yes. He has.' He was squirming and she admired him for attempting the truth at least. 'But only one or two.'

'One or two lasagnes, or one or two girlfriends?'

'Have you been on the Taliban's interrogation course? You're frightfully good at this.'

'Answer the question.'

'I'm obliged to tell you only my name, rank and number, and I must warn you I have been trained to withstand any amount of terrorist interrogation.' He smiled at her, hoping he could make her laugh.

Brooke was debating whether to create a scene and spoil a lovely evening? Or accept that yes, he had had plenty of girlfriends, that this relationship was leading nowhere and that she'd better enjoy the ride while it lasted. She chose the latter.

'Well done, Squadron Leader Suffolk. You have passed my test with flying colours. Now kiss me.'

*

Something woke her. She looked at her bedside clock: 2.27. She felt Louis, alert, next to her.

'Are you awake?' she whispered.

'Shh,' he replied, before slowly and silently slipping out of bed and going to the window.

'I heard something outside.'

She listened. Her ears straining in the silence. There was a creak on the stair. She moved her head to the sound.

'That'll be Hutch. He's heard something too.'

The bedroom door opened and Hutch's voice whispered urgently: 'Sir, get away from the window.' Louis did as he was told, dropping to the floor. Brooke's heart was beating like a drum.

'The garden is clear – I've checked,' Hutch said. 'But there was definitely someone out there. I heard voices.' He pulled out a mobile phone and made a call that was answered immediately.

'This is Papa Lima Two Zero requesting assistance. We need to clear the area.'

Five minutes later and Brooke was on her own. Two more dark Range Rovers had appeared out of the night and six men, two in uniform and four in plain dark suits, had spirited Louis out of Granny's Nook. Where had they come from? Were they always shadowing her and Louis?

She locked and bolted the front door and checked the back door and all the windows. By the time she got back to bed her clock read 2.36.

Eventually she managed to dose off, but it had been a

restless sleep, her imagination running wild. Had there been someone in the garden? If so who? Press? Kidnappers? Someone looking for a lost cat?

She'd heard nothing from Louis and he hadn't replied to her text. She'd even tried phoning him, but a recorded message told her that the number was not in use. She arrived at rehearsals tired and fretful.

Brooke and Jess were sprawled on the saggy sofas in the green room, drinking coffee from chipped and stained mugs and laughing over a shared joke. Ollie saw Brooke first.

'Hi, Brooke. Sleep well?'

Brooke painted on her best smile. 'Sure did. You guys?'

Jess reached her arms above her head and yawned extravagantly. 'Slept like a baby. This sea air really knocks me and the girls out.'

'The girls?' queried Brooke.

'She has the most adorable miniature dachshunds,' Ollie chipped in. 'Ethel and Elsie.'

Brooke did some mental reframing. Ollie and Jess had clearly been getting to know each other. He'd met her dogs . . . Hmm. Quite an age gap between the two of them – and wasn't he going out with Red? And wasn't she engaged to Ryan Hearst? Brooke made a mental note to watch this space.

*

Jonathan was a good director. He understood actors and was paternal in coaxing out their performances and soothing their fragile egos. He had started the day with a vocal and physical warm-up. The entire cast were asked to jog around the stage while laughing deeply from their diaphragms. A young actress called Rowena did the jogging for the Colonel while he walked, with his ubiquitous stick, and laughed in genuine delight at the ludicrousness of it all. While they were running, Dan the stage manager chucked some bean bags into the jogging mass, telling them to toss them to one another at random, backwards, forwards and across. Ollie threw his repeatedly at Jess, who returned them, aiming at his head or his bottom. The laughing became less forced and more real. Brooke was being targeted by the actor playing the baddie who steals her from Ollie. A huge man with a fake tan and muscles to die for, but for all his testosterone and jockeying for male supremacy, women were not his cup of tea. Brooke liked him though and enjoyed lobbing the bean bags at his carefully gelled hair.

The warm-up over, Jonathan was pleased to see it had had the desired effect. The ice was broken and every last shred of inhibition had vanished.

'Right, everyone. Grab a coffee and a loo break and I'll see you back here in fifteen for Act One Scene One.'

The day progressed with lots of fun and hard work. Brooke was included in the Ollie/Jess gang and their relationship both in and out of character was clearly a good one.

'I say, chaps,' said the Colonel over lunch, 'I think I shall call you the three musketeers!'

By the afternoon tea break, Brooke had still heard nothing from Louis.

So sure was she that she'd never hear from him again, she offered Jess her spare room in Granny's Nook. 'It'll save you a lot of money, and it would be nicer for the girls: their own back garden, the beach just down the lane . . .'

'Would you mind? It would be so nice to live in a

home where I could cook my own food and do my own laundry,' Jess asked hopefully.

'Would you cook for me too? I'm useless.'

'Of course I will.'

'So, when can you and the girls move in? They can be our guard dogs.' She thought about the prowler in the garden the previous night. 'Do they bark and growl?'

'No.'

'Do they yap?'

'Yes.'

'That'll do.'

*

Finally five o'clock came and they broke for the day. Jonathan was pleased with how things had gone so far. He'd forgotten how enjoyable it could be, working on a traditional English production with a maddening, loveable, idiosyncratic group of actors such as he had here. He was particularly intrigued by Jess. She was calm, with a diligent and thoughtful approach to acting and with a remarkable lack of ego, which was a rarity in their profession.

As they collected up their coats and bags, Jonathan managed a quick word with her.

'Jess, how did you find today?'

'Oh, great – exhausting but so much fun. I think all the actors are working really well together, don't you?'

Jonathan gave her a wry smile. 'Ye-e-e-es, so far. But don't forget everyone is on their best behaviour today – including me.'

'Don't pretend you have a hidden dark side, I won't believe it.'

'I'm a wolf in sheep's clothing.'

'Surely not.' She laughed. 'Where are you staying, Jonathan? Has Penny blown the budget and put you up in the Starfish?'

'Sadly not. I've forgone the life of luxury and I'm staying at a small holiday let in Pendruggan – paid for out of my salary, I might add.'

'Pendruggan, that's brilliant! I'm going to be staying with Brooke in her cottage there. You'll have to come over for a drink.'

'I'd love that, Jess. I really would.' And to his surprise, Jonathan found that he really meant it.

'What are you doing for dinner tonight?' he asked.

'I think Ollie and I are going to grab a bite at the Starfish, probably with our old friend Merlot. Would you like to join us?'

The thought of Jess sharing a tête-à-tête with Ollie was less appealing and Jonathan felt a twitch of jealousy.

'Um, no, I'm supposed to be going out for dinner with the Colonel to talk about band calls and choreography.'

'Oh well, another time then. See you tomorrow, Jonathan.'

Jonathan watched Jess trip off to meet Ollie. 'Careful,' he said to himself. 'That was a close call.'

Ollie was in the foyer waiting for Jess to come out of the loo when he had a surprise call from Red. He hadn't recognised the caller ID and was shocked to hear her voice.

'Hey, Ollie. How's it going?' she asked, as if she'd spoken to him only yesterday rather than three weeks ago.

'Red. Hi . . .' He faltered. 'I've been trying to ring you but I guess the messages don't get through?'

'I'm busy, you know. It's not always possible to speak.' She sounded mildly contrite.

'So . . .' Ollie didn't know how to progress the conversation '. . . errr, how's the tour going?'

'Good. Great, actually. We've got a break before the next big push and I thought I might drop into London to see you.'

'That sounds . . . great.' He tried to inject enthusiasm into his voice. 'But I'm not in London. I'm in Cornwall . . . working.'

'You're at the seaside?'

'Yeah.'

'Are there good fish-and-chip shops?'

'Yeah.'

'I'm coming down to get some of them and some of you.'

'Oh . . . ah, great.'

'I'll get Henrik to sort out a schedule and send it to you. I've got to go. Bye, Ollie. I've missed you.'

'Yeah. You too. Bye.' Ollie looked at his phone. What was this? Red, sounding like the old Red, coming down to see him? His thoughts were interrupted by Jess's phone ringing. She'd left it on the seat next to him while she nipped off. Caller ID said RYAN, so Ollie answered it.

'Jess's phone.'

There was a pause. 'Who is that?' The unmistakable voice of Ryan Hearst.

'Hi, Ryan. Jess has just nipped to the loo, I'm—'

But Ryan didn't give Ollie a chance to finish. 'Who are you?' he demanded imperiously.

'Ollie Pinkerton. I'm working with Jess on *Hats Off, Trevay!*'

'Cast or crew?'

'I'm an actor.'

'Tell Jess I called.'

'I will, nice talking to—'

*

Jess was thrilled to hear that Ryan had phoned. 'Did he say why?'

'No. He sounded a bit . . . busy,' Ollie managed lamely.

'That's him! Always busy. He calls when he can . . .'

'Hmm.' Ollie tried to signal agreement.

Jess was watching as Jonathan and the Colonel headed out of the theatre. 'He's a lovely man, isn't he.'

'Who, the Colonel?'

'No, Jonathan.'

Ollie was on surer ground. 'He is – and a really good director.'

'Do you think he's gay?'

'I'm not sure.'

'I think he is. He's just too emotionally intelligent and kind not to be.'

The opposite of Ryan Hearst, thought Ollie.

'Oh, by the way,' Jess continued, 'Louise will be around at the *Starfish* later. If you want to come down with me, I'll introduce you – maybe you could strike a deal with her?'

*

They headed out into the car park and watched as Brooke disappeared into the depths of a blacked-out Range Rover waiting for her outside.

'Wow, she looks happy!' said Jess as she watched the tail lights move off into the dusk.

'Sorry I've only got the old MG, milady.' Ollie ushered her to the car and yanked open the creaky passenger door.

'I wouldn't have anything different, Pinkerton.' She did up her ancient non-inertia seat belt while Ollie hopped into the driver's seat. 'Did I tell you Ryan bought a

Porsche? He drove me and the girls up to the Lakes in it and then proposed.'

'Did he?' Ollie faked a smile, thinking all the while, *What is this lovely woman doing with an ego-driven shit prick like Ryan Hearst?*

23

'You don't mind, do you, Mum?'

'Why would I?' asked Ollie's mother as she folded the last of his ironed shirts and passed it to him.

'At least you know I'm only down the road in Trevay.' He hugged her and she patted his back, enjoying the feeling of his T-shirt and the warmth of his chest against her face.

'I've had enough of you being here, anyway.' She tried to sound light-hearted. 'And the Starfish is closer to work. You'll save on petrol.'

Privately, she was heartbroken and couldn't understand why he'd want to waste money living in a hotel, however good a room rate he'd negotiated. But she was wise enough to keep these thoughts to herself. Just having him back in Cornwall and nearby was enough.

'Thanks, Mum. You're the best.' He gave her a final squeeze and let her go. He picked up his bag, his coat and his keys and walked to the front door. 'Love you, Mum. Come and have supper with me soon? My treat?'

The front door closed and she was on her own again. Her own space. No worrying about when he'd be home and what he'd like for supper. No extra laundry and ironing. She began to realise how much she liked having her own space back . . . and after all, he was only down the road. She went back into the kitchen and made herself a fresh cup of coffee. Now, where was the crossword?

*

'Welcome to Granny's Nook!' Brooke put her key in the lock and threw open the pink-painted front door. 'Come in, come in.'

Ethel and Elsie pushed past both Brooke and Jess and skittered across the polished oak floorboards of the small drawing room.

'Sorry about my girls. No manners,' sighed Jess as she took the handle of one of her three suitcases and pulled it over the threshold.

'Let me help you,' said Brooke. 'Your room is top of the stairs, second left.'

Like most of the older cottages in the village, Granny's Nook was two or three hundred years old, with thick, uneven whitewashed walls. Upstairs there were two small double bedrooms and a decent bathroom. Downstairs, a kitchen, drawing room and small, chilly garden-facing room currently decked out as an office.

Jess got the last of her cases into her room and looked around at the pretty lemon curtains and inviting brass bed. 'It's lovely, Brooke!'

Brooke was standing in the doorway, looking as if she needed to say something.

'What is it?' asked Jess. 'Are you having second thoughts about me and the girls staying here? If you are, that's OK. I can find another place.'

'No,' said Brooke. 'It's lovely to have you here. But I have something to tell you.'

'Yes?' asked Jess, her interest piqued. 'What?'

'Can you keep a secret?'

'I think so.'

Brooke faltered. 'Tell you what, get yourself settled. There are plenty of hangers in the wardrobe. Come down when you're ready, and I'll tell you then.'

*

Jess sat with her jaw dropping. 'Are you serious?'

'Totally.' Brooke had told her the whole story. 'And when I invited you to come and be my housemate, I hadn't heard from him for a bit and I thought it was all over, but since then he's got a new number and everything's OK between us. So you might meet him.'

'Bloody hell!' Jess sank back into her chair. 'When's he coming next?'

'I'm not sure. He's away on a photo shoot in Europe somewhere and then there's a family gig he has to show his face at . . . so . . . maybe next week.'

'Does he know I'm staying here now?'

'Not yet.'

'Is it going to be a problem?'

Brooke rubbed her hand across her forehead. 'I don't know. I shouldn't think so.'

'You'd better tell him.'

'Yeah.'

*

Jess remained on tenterhooks, worrying every evening when she got in from rehearsal that she might find Louis there, and worrying each morning, lest she bump into him coming out of the bathroom. However, her worrying was in vain. Of Louis there was no sight. Apparently he was off on an African jaunt with cousins.

Jess had realised within a very short space of moving in that Brooke's persona was just that: a persona. Underneath the megawatt smile she seemed to be one big bundle of nerves and jitters; it promised to be a tiring combination to live with. To cheer her up, next morning Jess suggested cooking something special for their supper.

'I'll pop into the farm shop on the way home. I thought perhaps a steak? Some salad and a jacket potato?'

'I don't know.'

'Once you smell it, you'll want some.'

'I'm not that hungry.'

''Course you're not – you've just had breakfast.' Jess looked round the small kitchen. Brooke had managed to spread toast crumbs over every conceivable surface. They were not only on the work surface by the toaster, but also on the bread board, the kitchen table and down the front of Brooke's pyjamas. There was also a buttery knife left standing up in the Marmite jar, a cold teabag leaking on the draining board, a milk bottle on the table, its foil lid on the floor, and a congealed dishcloth lying in the bottom of the stained sink. Jess took all of this in and marvelled at how Brooke had managed to wreak such havoc in such a short space of time. She picked up the foil lid from the floor and began to tidy up.

It seemed that her new roommate was oblivious to mugs of cold coffee left by the sofa or the pairs of old knickers stepped out of and left on the bathroom floor. Already Jess was having trouble accepting this level of mess. By nature she was a neat freak and took positive pleasure in swilling bleach round the sink and down the loo. A full washing machine on a hot cycle made her feel everything was right with the world. Her bed was always made every morning and her clothes were hung up each night. She vacuumed every day, concerned that Brooke might spot any stray, muddy paw mark or dog hair of Ethel and Elsie's.

Giving the table a final wipe she rinsed the now spotless dishcloth in hot water and wrung it out before hanging it neatly over the taps. 'So, shall I get a couple of steaks? It'll do you good.'

Brooke stood up and stretched. A blizzard of toast crumbs landed on the floor tiles. 'Can I take a rain check? Only, Louis might call.'

'OK,' said Jess, reaching for the dustpan and brush. 'No problem.'

'Thanks.' Brooke ambled towards the stairs. She turned as she put her foot on the first step. 'By the way, Jess . . .'

'Yeah?' Jess, kneeling down and sweeping up, didn't bother to look round.

'Can you make sure you wipe up round Ethel and Elsie's food bowls? I've noticed they leave bits of meat on the floor and it gets stuck to my feet. I hate a dirty floor.'

*

Despite the compromises and minor irritations that go hand in hand with the business of sharing a living space with someone, the two women got along famously. Brooke had a terrific sense of humour and kept Jess in peals of laughter with her impressions of Laverne and the others she had met while a student in New York.

Rehearsals continued to go well. Jonathan was more than pleased with the performances he was getting out of the cast and told Penny and Helen that the vintage show looked set to be a modern hit.

Ollie came round often to have supper with Jess and Brooke, and the three of them became almost as family. Jess quite enjoyed playing big sister to them both and they treated her as they would any of their friends. On the nights that *Horse Laugh* was on, Ollie insisted on cooking his world-famous corned beef hash so that they could eat from trays on their laps in front of the television.

The three of them recounted messages they had received from their long-distance partners. Jess always had more to tell than the other two, because she and Ryan spoke or emailed reasonably frequently.

'Ryan's filming night scenes all this week. Poor darling, he's exhausted. The press team are insisting he goes to at least one industry party a week. It's crazy. He's getting a break soon, though. Not sure exactly when, but he's going to fly back to London and then maybe nip down for a day or two and meet you guys.'

'Can't wait!' said Ollie.

'No, nor me,' replied Brooke, raising a cynical eyebrow at Ollie over Jess's unseeing head. 'I'll bet he's got some great Hollywood stories.'

'Oh, he has.' Jess's loved-up face shone. 'Working in the States has been such an experience for him. I can't wait to see him.' She twisted her beautiful engagement ring. 'It's been hard, missing him so much. But I couldn't stand in his way. Just as he supported me when *Horse Laugh* came up.'

'Absolutely,' agreed Ollie. 'It's the same with Red. There was no way I was going to be the "touring boyfriend". Like some lap dog, living off her and losing my own identity.'

The two women nodded in agreement, but each privately thinking that Red was a selfish cow who was managing to emasculate Ollie even at a distance.

'Quite, quite,' murmured Brooke.

'She was going to come down to Cornwall as well, but she's shooting the new video so . . .'

'Yeah,' said Jess. 'Tough schedule.'

The three sat in a shared silence, each thinking about their own situation. Brooke was the only one who said nothing about her man. Ollie still knew nothing about Louis and when he'd asked she'd told him only that she had a boyfriend who was very involved in media and was based in London. Sensing it was a closed topic, he had asked no more.

*

It was on one of their evenings together, a couple of weeks after Jess had moved into Granny's Nook, that there was a knock on the old pink front door.

'I'll get it,' said Ollie, and he turned the heat down on his corned beef hash and went to open the door. A tall and muscular man, similar in age to himself, Ollie thought, stood on the step holding a bottle of vodka. He was wearing a battered straw hat, a khaki T-shirt, ripped jeans. And what looked like a crocodile tooth on a leather string round his neck. His smile dropped when he saw Ollie.

'Hi. Can I help you?' asked Ollie.

'Is Brooke in?' asked the man in a posh drawl.

'Louis!' Brooke came bounding out of the sitting room and threw herself into the stranger's arms.

'Hey, sexy.'

Ollie watched as Brooke and the man embraced passionately. As he was taking all this in, he was suddenly aware of another man looming towards the cottage doorway.

'Hello, I'm Hutch – I'm with him.' He nodded towards the stranger.

'Ah, right. Well do come in.' Ollie moved to the side to allow this new man to squeeze past the hugging mass blocking the doorway. 'I'm making corned beef hash. Would you both like to join us?' Ollie calculated that he could stretch the hash out for two more mouths if he added another tin of baked beans.

'It's rather down to the boss,' said Hutch.

Brooke surfaced for air. 'Louis, you should have told me you were coming. My friends are here . . .' She looked at Jess, who was smiling tightly with saucer eyes. 'This is Jess.' Jess stood up. Not knowing whether to curtsey or not, she gave a half bob and a nod of her head for good measure. Louis held his hand out and shook her nervous one firmly. 'Hi, Jess.'

'And this is Ollie.'

'Hi, Ollie.' Louis again offered his hand and Ollie gladly pumped it.

'Hi, Louis. I can smell burning. Would you excuse me?' And with that he dashed off into the kitchen.

*

Ollie's supper went down very well. The five of them crowded round the television to watch *Horse Laugh*. Hutch and Louis insisted on sprawling on the floor and both laughed in all the right places. Jess had never felt so awkward or embarrassed. Ollie, however, was either playing things very cool or he hadn't a clue who these two men were. Jess hoped it was the former but felt sure it was the latter.

When the programme was over, Louis looked over to

Jess. 'That's bloody good, Jess. And the horses all knew their lines.' Brooke laughed and stroked Louis's head adoringly. He took her hand and kissed the palm. 'I'd better tell Granny to watch. She loves all that stuff.'

Jess couldn't speak, so she picked up her supper plate instead. 'I'll wash up,' she squeaked.

'Ollie, that was a bloody good supper.' Louis turned to face him. 'Better than Hutch's lasagne.' He laughed and playfully stretched out his long leg to give Hutch a dig in the ribs with his toes.

'The least I can do,' said Hutch, as he started to get to his feet, 'is help clear up.' As he leaned over to pick up Louis and Brooke's plates, Ollie caught a glimpse of a leather holster sitting neatly between his polo shirt and his jacket . . . There was a gun in it. As Hutch stood up, balancing the plates, his clothing fell back into place and the holster was hidden from view.

Ollie felt fear course through him. Who were these people?

'I'll take those.' Ollie almost snatched the plates from Hutch. 'You're our guests.'

As soon as he got into the kitchen he put the plates down and closed the door.

'Jess!' he hissed. 'I'm pretty sure that man Hutch has got a gun.'

Jess stopped tipping washing-up liquid into the sink and turned to face Ollie. 'I expect he has.'

'What do you mean?' asked Ollie, wild-eyed. 'Who the fuck is he?'

Jess didn't want to spill the beans. 'You'd better ask Brooke.'

'You mean, you know who these guys are? Is Brooke in danger? What do you know? Tell me what's going on.'

Jess turned back to the sink and ran some hot water into the bowl. Ollie put his hands on her shoulders and turned her round to face him. 'Tell me, Jess. I'm scared for you.'

Ollie's jaw dropped to the floor as the news sunk in.

24

'Holy shit!'
    Ollie took two quick paces to the kitchen door and opened it an inch. He put his eye to the crack and stared for a moment. '. . . Is it really him?'

Jess nodded.

'Holy royal moly. How did she meet him?'

Jess told him.

'How come nobody recognises him?'

'You didn't.'

'Yeah, but I'm an idiot.'

'Well, when he was away in the Air Force no new photos of him were released. He went in at nineteen. Out six years later. He's changed quite a bit since then. He grew his hair, put in some coloured contacts and started to mingle with the ordinary people.'

Ollie was still staring through the crack in the door. 'Fuuuck. That's amazing. Bet his cousins are really jealous. Everybody knows their faces.'

'Quite.'

Ollie closed the door and Jess handed him a tea towel. 'Now don't go saying anything stupid. Just act like you did earlier.'

'But I didn't know who he was earlier.'

'Exactly.'

'Hey, I'm an actor! I can just play the part of the man

who doesn't know that the man he's talking to is like four-teenth in line to the throne.'

'Good thinking.'

The two of them finished the washing and drying and Jess went back to the sitting room. Louis and Brooke were stretched out on the sofa. Hutch was in the armchair and all three were watching a rerun of *Blackadder*.

'Coffee? Tea?' asked Jess.

She took their orders and returned to the kitchen, where Ollie was still looking gobsmacked.

'Put the kettle on. They want coffee. There's some fresh ground stuff in the cupboard above your head and a cafetière on the shelf by the cooker.'

Ollie did as he was told and then insisted on taking the tray in himself.

'Here we go.' He picked his way through the furniture and sprawled legs to the low stool by the fire. 'I'll put the tray down here and you can help yourselves.'

'Cheers, buddy,' said Louis, smiling at him.

'My pleasure.' Ollie sat on a large cushion on the floor. Jess came in carrying a tartan-patterned biscuit tin with a picture of Balmoral on it.

'Biscuit, anyone?'

Ollie clocked the tin and watched as Jess passed it to Louis.

'Thanks, Jess,' said Louis. 'I love shortbread. All those holidays in Scotland, I suppose.'

'Oh, really?' said Ollie. Jess shot him a warning look but he carried on. 'My mum has a tin a bit like that one. She's a member of the National Trust and loves going to visit castles and stuff.'

Brooke gave Ollie a daggers look.

Silence settled over the small group as they watched

Hugh Laurie, as stupid Prince George, fall victim to Rowan Atkinson's ridicule. Louis and Hutch laughed. Both Jess and Brooke stared hard at Ollie, willing him not to say anything.

'Once my mum and I went to Windsor Castle and we had tea in the café – which was very expensive, by the way –' shooting Louis a look – 'Mum stole the tray that the tea came on. She reckoned she'd paid enough to have it.'

Hutch shifted uncomfortably in his armchair and gave Ollie an unamused look. Remembering the holster hidden under the man's clothing, Ollie stopped talking. Jess blurted through gritted teeth, 'Ollie. There's no sugar on the tray. Please go and get some.'

Ollie looked at the tray. 'No, there's a bowl right there – look.'

Jess stared desperately at him and then said, 'Ollie, oughtn't you to be going soon? You have an early call in the morning.'

'Not till ten.'

'Then would you take the dogs round the block with me?'

Ollie looked at her, mystified. She'd never asked him before.

'What, now?'

'Yes, now.'

Ollie stood and gave Jess a mock bow. 'OK, Your Majesty.' But Jess was already dragging him out of the room.

'What do you think you're doing?' She was furiously trying to put her cardigan on but one of the sleeves was inside out and she was flailing pathetically.

'What do you mean?' asked Ollie, pretending to be hurt. 'I was just making conversation.'

'Why mention your mum nicking the tray, and why call me "Your Majesty"?'

'Well, you started it by bringing in the bloody shortbread biscuits in the Balmoral tin.'

'I told you not to say anything stupid, and BAM in you go, up to your neck.'

'He didn't notice.'

'Hutch did.'

Again, Ollie thought of the gun and gulped. 'Oh yeah. Maybe I'd better head back to the Starfish.'

'Can I come with you?' asked Jess.

'Why?'

'I can't stay here. Hutch will want my room and I can't bear the idea of bumping into HRH on the landing in the morning.' She looked at Ollie beseechingly. 'Please?'

'They may not have any spare rooms.'

'Can I stay with you? I know I can trust you.'

Ollie felt mildly insulted. 'Oh. Can I trust you, though? I know what you cougars are like.'

Jess punched his arm. 'I am a respectably engaged woman.'

She finally found her way into her cardigan and, whistling up the dogs, they left the cottage.

The two of them walked in peaceful silence arm in arm around the green. Ethel and Elsie trotted along, sniffing and peeing happily. The Dog Star shone brightly over the little village of Pendruggan and in the distance they could hear the sound of the sea breaking gently on Shellsand Bay.

'That's one Christmas present ticked off the list then,' Ollie said. 'It's the shortbread for Granny.' And he and Jess dissolved into helpless laughter.

*

'Darlings . . .' Brooke was holding her arms out, inviting hugs from Jess and Ollie. 'Where did you go last night?' She was sitting cross-legged on one of the green room sofas, cradling a mug of black coffee. 'Lou was so worried that Hutch had chucked you out of your own bed.'

Jess bent to accept Brooke's embrace, then stepped back. 'I stayed with Ollie at the Starfish. You and Louis needed to be alone. You haven't seen each other for weeks. Did you have a good time?'

Judging by Brooke's impossibly sexy tousled blonde 'bed-head' hair, she could guess what the answer was.

'Mmm,' purred Brooke. 'He's just soooo . . . wonderful. In all departments.'

Jess unzipped her warm fleece and put her hands out to fend off any more information. 'Don't tell me. I have my memories.'

'You mean Ollie didn't jump your bones?' Brooke laughed throatily.

'I,' said Ollie, standing tall, 'am a gentlemen. I didn't look once as she undressed down to her polka-dot bra and pants.'

Jess stuck her tongue out at him. 'Well, I wasn't going to tell anyone, but now that the gloves are off, do you know how loudly you snore?'

'I do not!'

'Oh really? Then why were the windows rattling?'

Brooke sat up straighter, 'Oh yeah. Jess, there's a message for you at the stage door. I saw a note with your name on it, pinned up on the board.'

'Really?' Jess looked at her watch. 'I've got a few minutes before we start.' And she walked out of the green room and down towards the stage door.

The note was from Ryan and it was in his handwriting.

*Jess, darling, where are you? I'm here in Trevay. Flew
in from LA last night and got a car down to surprise
you. Stage-door man tells me you aren't in till 10.00
a.m. I'm at the Starfish having breakfast. Delightful
woman there. All over me. Loves* Venini. *Given me the
Sea Horse suite, very comfy bed. God, I've missed you.
Bell me as soon as you get this. R x*

Jess felt a shot of pure happiness rush through her
veins. She ran back to the green room to get her bag and
find her mobile. Jonathan was there, talking to Brooke,
Ollie, Colonel Stick and the cast.

'We're going to run the whole of Act One this morning,
Act Two this afternoon. Try not to stop for anything. Keep
going, even if you dry. I want to get a timing on it so I
know where to make cuts if we need to.' He saw Jess at
the back panting a little and looking around for her bag.
'Jess, you OK?'

'Yeah, I just need to pho—'

But Jonathan wasn't listening. Like all directors, once
he'd given the orders he expected the cast to jump to it.

'Right, everyone on stage. Mobiles off. No distractions.'

Jess wondered if she could quickly send a surrepti-
tious text to Ryan, but Jonathan was approaching. 'Jess,
I want you to really work the scene with Brooke when
she breaks up with Ollie. You are angry with her. You
can see she's making a mistake. But play the anger quietly.
Dangerously. That way, when you get to the number,
you can wrench the audience's heart out with the lyrics.
Yes?'

Jess put her phone back in her bag and turned her full

attention to Jonathan. She had work to do. Ryan would understand.

*

The run-through went well. Nearly everyone remembered their lines and Jonathan was pleased.

Jess was eager to phone Ryan, but Jonathan had other ideas. He clapped his hands to get the cast's attention.

'We're having a working lunch. I've sent out for soup and sandwiches. No one is to leave. I don't want your concentration broken. This afternoon we'll run Act Two.'

There were groans. 'Knew you'd be pleased. If you don't know all your lines, you have an hour to settle in a quiet corner with some lunch and go over them. We'll start at two fifteen sharp.'

*

The afternoon went badly. Brooke burst into tears when she forgot an entire song and Jonathan, frustrated, shouted at her in front of everyone. Ollie and Jess could only mutely support her and get on with their bits. At last they'd finished and Jonathan was going through his notes.

'Well, everybody . . .' he leaned back in his rehearsal chair and rubbed his eyes with his thumb and forefinger '. . . that was bad. Really bad. I am disappointed in the lot of you. I'm not sure we'll be ready for opening night.' He leaned forward and put his arms on the table in front of him. His head followed. In a muffled voice they heard him say. 'Now piss off and learn your lines.'

In the subdued quiet, people got up from where they

were sitting and gathered their bits together, shooting worried glances at each other.

Dan the stage manager, who had been having a whispered conversation with the desolate-looking Jonathan, called out, 'Listen up, everyone. Call time tomorrow is coffee at 8.30 a.m. On stage and rehearsing at nine. We'll finish when we finish.'

No one dared to groan as they shuffled quietly off stage and away to the green room.

Jess retrieved her bag and turned her phone on. No messages from Ryan. Brooke, her sexy tousled hair now hanging in rat-tails around a face streaked with tears and mascara, looked broken. Ollie, pale-faced with anger and exhaustion, put his arms round both women.

'We need alcohol.'

25

Ollie squeezed the girls into his MG with Brooke sitting on Jess's lap. As they headed down into Trevay, Jess tried to feel for her phone to ring Ryan, but it was in an awkward position in her bag and with Brooke on her lap there was no way she could get to it. Never mind, she'd be there any minute.

As they climbed the steps up to the hotel Louise Lonsdale was waiting to greet them in reception. 'Miss Tate! Welcome back. I understand you stayed with us last night?'

'No, she left me alone last night, Louise.' Ryan approached, looking impossibly handsome. His blue eyes sparkling. His longer hair shining. His clothes sexy and expensive. 'Jess wasn't here.'

Louise looked confused for a moment and then, seeing Jess and Ollie's look of panic, put two and two together and made at least twenty-three.

'Oh my goodness! Yes, of course. I meant to say welcome back, Miss Tate. We are looking forward to having you stay with us again. Where are your delightful dogs?'

Ryan walked towards Jess and she leaned into his arms. She had missed him so much. He tilted her head up to meet his face. 'Yes, darling, where are Ethel and Elsie?'

'They're at Rowena's, in Pendruggan. I left them when I came back with Ollie last night.'

Too late she realised what she'd said. Louise Lonsdale, with a tiny gasp, made off to welcome some non-existent guests and left the frozen quartet standing.

'So you *were* here, in the hotel, last night?' He smiled quizzically and held the top of her arm a little too hard.

Ollie stepped in and, leaving out the identity of Louis, told Ryan the truth. Brooke backed him up.

Ryan smiled charmingly. 'Oh, that's all right then! That's what we merry band of actors do, isn't it! That's what mates do! It's great to have *mates*.' He let go of Jess's arm and put his arm round Brooke's waist instead. 'You look as if you could do with a drink. Coming to the bar, anyone? Drinks with mates. What could be better than that.'

Jess, didn't like the attention Ryan was showering on Brooke and tried to talk to him. 'I'm so sorry I didn't call as soon as I got your message. It was impossible to use the phone. Jonathan was watching us like a hawk.'

'I understand, Jess.' He patted her leg. 'In the same way you understand when I'm sometimes pictured with beautiful starlets. It's just work. Means nothing.' The cocktail waitress approached and Ryan made a show of ordering a jug of margaritas whilst flirting with the poor girl. Once ordered, he turned his full attention to Brooke and Ollie and listened attentively to their day in rehearsal.

'Directors get power mad. Sounds as if he's full of insecurities. I'll come down tomorrow and watch.'

Jess was alarmed. 'Oh, darling. Better not. It might aggravate him.'

'I'll be as quiet as a mouse. Won't say a word. He won't know I'm there. Promise.'

'But . . .'

'No buts, Jess. He won't have the balls to throw *me* out.'

'Perhaps you'd like to have a word with him now, let

him know you're coming?' Ollie pointed to the entrance of the bar where Jonathan had just entered with Dan the stage manager. They were talking intently and carrying folders which were probably full of scripts and set designs. Jess guessed that they were planning to have a working dinner in the restaurant.

Jonathan waved at the table of actors and came to say hello.

'Evening, all. Hope you're not planning to get plastered. Big day tomorrow.' He said it good humouredly, all earlier stresses put aside for now and Jess saw his eyes twinkling at her.

'Hi – Jon, is it? The name's Ryan, Ryan Hearst.'

Ryan stood and thrust his hand towards the director.

'It's Jonathan, pleased to meet you, Ryan. I've been enjoying *Venini*, it's a great show.'

'Yeah, thanks. Just thought I'd pop down and see Jess, see how she's getting on out here in rep. Working in the provinces is good for keeping your hand in, I suppose, but no substitute for London or LA – that's where the action is really happening.'

Jonathan saw Ryan glance slyly at Ollie when he said this.

'Well, we've got a top-notch cast here and this is a production that everyone will be talking about by the time we're finished,' said Jonathan firmly.

Ryan gave a wry smile. 'You hope, anyway. Whatever – good luck and all that. Thought I might pop down and see you in action tomorrow.'

'Thanks, but I find friends and family a distraction in the early weeks. Anyway, I don't think luck will have much to do with it. Hard work, dedication and commitment are what usually work in my book. Enjoy your evening, all of you.'

Ryan had already turned back to Brooke and Ollie and was continuing his anecdotes.

'Bye, Jonathan, enjoy your evening.' Jess smiled weakly; she couldn't suppress an uncomfortable feeling as Jonathan met her eyes with a puzzled look of his own.

*

The rest of the evening went by in a warm tequila haze as at least two more jugs of margaritas appeared then disappeared down their throats. Ryan regaled them with stories of Hollywood and how ghastly it was to be recognised by all the British tourists holidaying there.

'I've even been given my own security team. Great guys. On location it can be so hard not to be recognised. If someone comes up and says hello, you've got to be nice to them hoping that, if they pull a hand gun, the guys will get them before they get me.'

Brooke, thinking about Louis and Hutch said, 'It's a dangerous job.'

'Yeah, but I'm prepared to take the risk.'

Ollie shot Ryan a look of amazement. Did he really think actors did a dangerous job? Or was Ryan sending himself up? Nope. Ryan was not smiling.

They had supper together in the bar and it was midnight before they knew it. Ollie saw the sozzled Brooke into a taxi before staggering off to his room.

Ryan took Jess's arm and together they negotiated the lift to the magnificent Sea Horse Suite. In the super-king-size bed, Ryan was more loving and tender than he'd ever been to Jess. He buried himself in her and she wrapped her arms round him as he made love to her. She was surprised to see tears in his eyes.

'What's the matter?' she asked.

'I've missed you. Seeing you tonight, after so long . . . You haven't been sleeping with Ollie, have you? It would kill me if you were. He's a pretty boy. Younger than me. You might have your head turned.'

She held him and reassured him and all too soon it was morning, last night's events only vaguely remembered and she had one hell of a hangover.

Ryan lay half dead in the ruin of the bed. His eyes tight shut and his face squashed against the pillows.

'Are you coming to rehearsals later?' she asked, leaning over him to kiss the nape of his neck.

'Would you mind awfully if I didn't?' he mumbled into the Egyptian cotton. 'Jet lag and all that.'

'And a tiny hangover?'

'Possibly. You?'

'Possibly. I think it's best you stay here. See you later, my love.'

'Yeeahh. I'll just have a little sleep first.'

Jess tiptoed out of the room, hoping to pick up some paracetamol in the Trevay pharmacy on her way up to the Pavilions.

She stood waiting for the lift, thinking over last night. She'd never known Ryan to be jealous before. It rather pleased her. The lift doors opened and, standing in the corner, wearing sunglasses and hanging on to the handrail was Ollie.

'Nice look.' She smiled at him.

'I can't drive. I'm still pissed.'

'Fine. We'll walk. I need to stop at the chemist anyway.'

'Me too.'

*

The morning was hard work. Brooke, Jess and Ollie were distinctly below par. Ollie kept fluffing his lines, Jess wasn't her usual self and Brooke was completely out of step when she was doing her dance numbers. The fluffs built up and it was clear that their hangovers were seriously affecting everyone's ability to rehearse properly.

Jonathan's stretched patience finally snapped.

'What a bloody shower the three of you are. Opening night is looming and we're going to have to go at it full tilt to be anywhere near ready, and may I remind you that you are doing this because there is something important at stake! We're trying to save the Pavilions! Everyone here is working their bloody arses off and all the three of you can do is come in half-pissed from the night before and cock it up for the rest of us!'

Ollie and Jess hung their heads, suitably shamed. Brooke attempted a sulky pout but soon dropped it when she got a thunderous glare from Jonathan.

'We're really sorry, Jonathan, and everyone,' said Jess. 'We just got a bit carried away, it won't happen again. Promise.'

'It better bloody not!' But Jess thought she saw Jonathan's face soften a little. 'Now, let's break for lunch. Perhaps some food will help to dry you all out.'

*

Feeling slightly revived after a lunch of egg sandwiches, salty crisps and sugary Coke, Brooke and Ollie found themselves outside the stage door taking in some sea air.

'How are you feeling now?' Ollie asked.

'Bit better, but had to concentrate hard on not throwing up during the dance number.'

'What did you make of Ryan?'

'Yeah. Nice.'

'Really?'

'Why, what did you think?'

'Slimy shit.'

Brooke laughed into the wind. 'Me too! He kept putting his hands on my legs. Every time a little bit higher. And all that stuff about how big and important he is in LA – he's just another English telly actor. Not exactly George Clooney.'

'What does Jess see in him?'

'God knows. She's such a sweetie and he's such a big head.'

'How long is he staying for?'

'Dunno.'

'If he hurts her, I'll kill him.'

Brooke turned to look Ollie in the face. 'You said that as if you mean it.'

'I do.'

*

'But why have you got to go now?' Jess couldn't understand. She'd just got back from the Pavilions and here was Ryan packing.

'Bloody PR. They've heard I'm back in the UK and I have to "be seen"' – he made the sign of two quotation marks with his fingers – 'at a few parties in town. The new series of *Venini* goes to air here in the next couple of weeks, and—'

'Golly. So soon.'

'I did tell you,' he snapped.

'Did you? Sorry, Ryan, my head has been full of this show and—'

'Yeah, well – yada yada. And they want me to promote it before going back to the States and promoting the first series which airs on NBC next month.'

'Does it? Oh, congratulations.'

'I have told you all this.'

'Sorry.'

'So, much as I'd like to stay to see you in your small-town show . . .'

His words stung her like a slap on the face.

'Ryan, that's a horrible thing to say.'

He was gazing in the mirror, playing with his hair. 'Sorry, darling. But *Hats Off, Trevay!* is hardly *A Chorus Line*, is it? Hm? *Venini* is huge and I have a responsibility, as the name above the title, to get out there and be seen.'

'I do get that, Ryan. I'm not stupid. In fact *Good Housekeeping* are looking for a date when they can come down and do a feature on me for *Horse Laugh*. It looks like we've definitely got a second series. I'm just waiting for the contracts.'

'*Good Housekeeping*? Hardly *Vanity Fair*, is it?'

'No, but its readership are our viewers and . . .'

Ryan looked at his watch. Then crossed the room and hugged her.

'Well, darling, it's been so lovely to see you. Gotta go. Love you.'

*

That night, back at Granny's Nook and playing Scrabble with Brooke, Jess thought about the last twenty-four hours. Ryan had been so wonderful and then so awful. Had she done something to upset him? She must be more understanding. After all, he had come straight off the flight and down to Cornwall to see her. He was jet-lagged and had so many commitments at work. She couldn't remember him telling her anything about *Venini* being shown in America, or the second series coming out early here. Maybe she had been too wrapped up in her work to listen to him properly. Mind you, he hadn't been very excited to hear about *Horse Laugh* being recommissioned. But, compared to the global success and pressure of filming he had with *Venini, Horse Laugh* was just a simple little job. He was tired and she must be more understanding.

'Xanadu on a triple-word score.' Brooke crowed with pleasure. 'Beat that, Miss Tate!'

Jess marshalled her thoughts back to the here and now. 'Not bad, Miss Lynne. Not bad at all.' She'd apologise to Ryan tomorrow, Sunday, her day off.

*

You've reached Ryan Hearst's phone. Please leave a message.

'Hi, Ryan. It's me. It was great seeing you and thank you so so much for taking the time to come down. I know how busy you are, darling. Call me when you can. I hope the PR stuff is going well. I'm just walking the girls on the beach. They love paddling and they say they miss their daddy. I miss you too. Love you so much. Bye.'

Jess felt really low. She was tired from working so hard, she had a cold coming and her relationship with Ryan was just too long-distance. Maybe she should give up the idea of her own career and support Ryan. Travel with him. Be a proper partner to him. She needed to talk to him about setting a wedding date. A small affair in a registrar's office would do . . .

But then she recalled how miserable she'd been when she had no work, and now her career was just taking off . . . She loved *Horse Laugh*. She didn't want to give it up . . . but if it meant that she and Ryan would be a proper couple again, it would be a sacrifice well made. Wouldn't it? And if she didn't have to worry about a career, she could start the job she really wanted: to be a mum.

She stopped at the water's edge and watched Ethel and Elsie splash about in the wavelets. The sea was calm today and the sky a real Cornish blue. Three gulls were playing on the air currents made warm by the early June sun. She turned her face to the heat. With her eyes closed she could see the pink of the blood in her eyelids. She heard a shout coming towards her on the breeze and opened her eyes to see who it was. Ollie was bounding over to her.

'Brooke told me you were here. Are you OK?'

'I'm fine, thanks. Bit of a cold, that's all. What are you doing here?'

He looked anxious. A bit uneasy. 'Err, have you seen the papers?'

'Not yet. I was going to pick them up from Queenie's when I get back. Why?'

'It's probably nothing but . . . there's a story about Ryan.'

26

'Here –' Back at Granny's Nook, a white-lipped Jess took the newspaper from Ollie.

'But it's the gossip page.' Jess was shaking with fear and anger. 'Nothing in here is ever factually correct.'

'I know, but . . . I just thought you ought to see it.'

Which English actor, currently filming and hustling for movie projects in Hollywood, is playing away behind his fiancée's back? Who's going to tell her? It's only a matter of time.

Alongside, under an engagement photo of Ryan and Jess was a malicious snippet: 'Isn't this a super photo of Ryan Hearst and Jess Tate on their engagement day?'

Jess's phone rang. 'Jess, babe, It's me. Just got your message. You OK?' It was Ryan.

'Yeah. I'm fine. Ollie's just shown me something from today's paper.'

Ryan looked down at the same article in front of him and his palms grew sweaty. 'Oh yeah? What's it about?'

She frowned and bit her lip. 'Oh, it's nothing.'

'Sure?'

'Yeah.'

'What paper?'

'The *Sun on Sunday*.'

'Oh. I think I have that. Let me look.'

'Don't bother.' But Ryan was already adding fake sound effects of searching, by rustling the paper in front of him.

'Ah yes. Here we are. What page?'

'Nineteen.'

Ryan rustled and paused, then, 'The little shit.'

'How do those people sleep at night, writing lies like that?'

'Agreed. But I meant Ollie. Put that toe-rag on the phone.'

Jess did so, happy to prove Ollie wrong.

Ollie put the phone to his ear and swallowed. 'Hi, Ryan.'

'Listen, you wanker, I don't know why you want to make trouble between me and Jess, but back off. I've already given you the benefit of the doubt after you shared a bed with her last week. And if I get even a sniff of you trying it on with her again, I'm going to hurt you where the sun don't shine. Geddit, sonny?'

'Ryan, I wasn't doing anything, I just thought it better that Jess should know . . .'

'GEDDIT?'

'I get it. Yes.'

'Good. Pass me back to my fiancée.'

Ollie did as he was told. Ryan sounded very angry. 'I don't want you mixing with that man.'

Jess, always the peacemaker, said, 'He's a mate. Just looking out for me, that's all.'

'Well, I don't like him. I want you to come up to London tonight.'

'I can't. I'm working tomorrow.'

'You've got a cold, haven't you? Tell that bloody director you're ill and need to have a couple of days off.'

'I can't let him down. Besides I'll feel better tomorrow.'

'OK. I'll phone him myself.'

'No, Ryan!'

'You are coming up to London and I am going to spoil you. I'll take you to the Ivy for dinner. Pack something sexy. Now get on the next train and I'll pick you up from Paddington. Tell them you'll be back when you're better.'

*

The Ivy Club was soothingly warm and friendly. The waiter escorted them to a table where they could both see and be seen by the great and the good who were members here.

'You look lovely, Jess,' said Ryan, reaching across the table to hold her hand.

She smiled. 'Thank you. You don't look too bad yourself.'

Ryan picked up the menu. 'What do you fancy?'

'You.'

He raised the lids of his dark, almond-shaped eyes and gave her a look that melted her heart.

'Not Ollie?'

'Not Ollie.'

Jess couldn't remember the last time they'd had a dinner like this. She'd never been to the Ivy Club before. More exclusive than the world famous Ivy restaurant, it was star spotter heaven. Underneath an enormous canvas of Damien Hirst butterflies, Jess recognised Cara Delevingne, Kate Moss and Harry Styles laughing and enjoying themselves. Everyone in the place was a butterfly, drawn to the heady mix of fame and fashion. Membership was very expensive but had been a present to Ryan from his agent when he'd landed the second series of *Venini*. The waiter was diligent but not intrusive, the smoked salmon followed by the saddle of lamb was fragrant and melting. Jess was starting to think the time was right to mention marriage plans when a tall, very thin dark-haired woman in a Donna Karan dress walked past, stopped and then draped herself all over Ryan.

'Darling!' She left blood-red lipstick on his top lip. 'Haven't seen you for ages. How's Serena? I thought she looked a-may-zing in LA.' She glanced towards Jess and feigned surprise. 'Hello.' She held out her bony hand. 'I'm Amanda. I've been working with Ryan in the States.'

She turned back to Ryan. 'You and Serena are coming to the *Huffington Post* fundraiser, aren't you?'

Jess was watching Ryan carefully. He was completely unruffled. 'I think so, yes.'

'Good. See you there. I'm sure it will be ghaaastly.'

She kissed him again and nodded at Jess. 'Byeee.'

Ryan picked up his napkin and wiped away the lipstick. 'Sorry about that. Horrible woman. That's why I didn't introduce you.'

'Who's Serena?'

Ryan was cutting into the last of his steak. 'What, darling?'

'Who's Serena?'

'Oh, she's been in a couple of the new *Venini* episodes. Young actress. Quite good. Sweet.' He eyed Jess warningly. 'The equivalent of your Ollie, so nothing to worry about, is there?'

*

Two days later and Ryan had gone back to LA and Jess was back in Trevay being bawled out by Jonathan. 'Where's your sick note?'

Jess blushed. 'It was a cold, that's all.'

'If it was just a cold you should have stayed here. Not

been outside the Ivy Club being photographed on the arm of your boyfriend wearing next to nothing.'

Jess bit her lip to stop the tears that had started to blur her vision. Jonathan was becoming meaner and more unpleasant to work with as the opening night drew closer.

'I . . .' a thousand excuses whirled through her mind before she decided on, 'I'm sorry, Jonathan. I really wasn't feeling well and Ryan insisted I went home to rest. The night out was supposed to be a treat.'

Jonathan stared hard at her, frowning, before turning away with a sigh. 'OK, you're here now and you've got a lot of catching up to do.'

Colonel Irvine, watching this exchange from the side-lines, beckoned her over to where he was sitting. 'My dear, he's got his knickers in a twist. You are wonderful in the role and you've missed very little. Ignore him. I suspect his annoyance is based on something other than a couple of days off.'

'What do you mean?'

But the Colonel gave her a sphinx-like smile and said only, 'Youth is wasted on the young!'

Jess couldn't think what he meant, but she was worried that she had got on the wrong side of Jonathan. She liked and respected him and she didn't want him to think that she was a shirker. She resolved to work harder to make up for it. Perhaps she could take him out for a drink when he was less cross?

*

At the end of the working day, she and Brooke prepared to go home to Pendruggan.

'Thanks for looking after Ethel and Elsie. Were they all right?'

'Completely fine. I think they missed you. Ethel kept jumping up at the window, I think she was looking for your car.'

Jess looked around for Ollie.

'He said he had to shoot off,' said Brooke.

'He's hardly said a word to me all day.'

'After what Ryan said to him, I'm not surprised.'

'What?'

'Well, Ryan kind of told him to back off from you, didn't he?'

'Did he? When?'

'On the phone. Ollie doesn't want any trouble. He's got enough trouble with Red coming down.'

'Is she?' Jess felt a cloud of disappointment dim the room. Everybody was deserting her. Ryan back in the US. Jonathan shouting at her. Now Red coming to upset things.

'Yeah. Tomorrow, I think. Can't wait to meet her. A proper bona fide rock star! If she's a bitch to Ollie I'll give her a piece of my mind. Louis says he met her backstage at a Prince's Trust concert in the park and . . .'

Jess tuned out as Brooke gossiped with gusto all the way back to Granny's Nook. She needed to think. Ryan had told Ollie to back off? Red was coming to Trevay? Her little Cornish applecart was well and truly being upset.

27

Ollie felt sick with nerves. Red had called from Heathrow and was on her way down the M5 in a blacked-out people carrier. She had sounded tired but was unusually upbeat.

'I'm home to see my man!' she'd whooped down the phone. 'Get yourself scrubbed up and ready for me. I need you, Ollie, babe. And I mean neeeeed you.'

'Great, honey. I'm looking forward to seeing you too. It's been such a long time.' He added a little joke. 'How will I recognise you?'

'Google me, babe, I'm the hot mamma with the great arse.'

He laughed with what he hoped was conviction. 'Can't wait, Red. Can't wait.'

There was the sound of a muffled conversation between her and someone in the car.

'Who's with you?' he asked.

'Only Henrik and Bibi and Bango and . . .' She pulled away from the mouthpiece to ask, 'What's your name, babe?' Back into the phone: '. . . Oh yeah, and Mezz,' she laughed, 'and the fucking driver, who's directly related to the slowest man on earth.' Again she pulled the receiver away from her mouth: 'Henrik, tell the twat to put his foot down or I swear to God I'll drive myself.'

'Where are you?' Ollie asked.

'Fuck knows. Henrik, where are we?'

More talking that Ollie couldn't make out. She came back on the line. 'Just passing Lifton Down.'

'Oh shit, you're about an hour away. I'd better get a move on.'

'Yeah, baby, you get a move on before I make a move on you.' She laughed hysterically and Ollie wondered if it was due to jet lag, alcohol or something altogether less palatable.

They said their goodbyes and he checked his watch: 6.30 a.m. He was due into rehearsal mid-morning. He hoped Red wouldn't be too awkward and clingy when she arrived. With luck she'd want to sleep and he could leave her in his hotel room. But what about the entourage with her? He couldn't stand Henrik – and who the hell were Bibi, Bango and Mezz? He needed to talk to someone who'd calm him down. He called Jess.

*

Jess was up and out on the beach with Ethel and Elsie. The warm sun was promising a perfect June day. The sea was flat calm and the cornflower sky reflected on its surface. The concerns of the last few days she put down to nerves. Her nerves, Jonathan's nerves, Ryan's nerves. The opening night was looming and rehearsals were getting more intense. It wasn't just the cast on stage any more. Now, they were rehearsing with the band and the juvenile dancers from the local theatre school, along with their principal, the fearsomely glamorous Miss Coco Parry, who ruled her young pupils with an icy glare and plenty of praise – and they adored her.

Miss Coco, as she was known by one and all, was an

ex-Bluebell dancer and one-time Tiller Girl. Now, surely pushing eighty, her face was still beautiful despite the wrinkles, her figure lithe and slender, her hair in a glossy raven pleat and her make-up immaculate. She held everyone spellbound with her charmingly colourful stories – told in her smoky, deep, elocuted voice – of dancing at the London Palladium in the Tiller Girl line-up.

'Darling, I must tell you that high kicking in a synchronised line of girls is much harder than it looks and takes its toll on one's digestive system. We had to be awfully careful about what we ate before a show. Certainly no baked beans. The blowing off that went on as we danced was nobody's business! I remember one trombonist almost swallowed his mouthpiece he was laughing so much.'

Jess was chuckling to herself, recalling Miss Coco's reminiscences, when her phone rang. It was Ollie.

'Hello . . .' she answered tentatively. Ollie was still being rather cool with her, almost avoiding her, and she couldn't think why he'd be calling at this hour.

'Hey, Jess.' He sounded rather down. 'Just wondered if you had a moment to talk?'

'What's wrong?' She settled herself on a barnacled rock and tickled Elsie's ears as she brought the ball back ready to be thrown again.

'I dunno. I'm just . . . it sounds stupid . . . but Red's arriving in the next hour and I'm just not . . . ready for her, I suppose.'

'What do you mean?' She chucked the ball and wiped the dog saliva and seawater off her fingers.

'Just that, really. I don't think I want her here.'

'Ah.'

'Mm.'

They both sat in silence, pondering this. Jess staring

out to sea, watching a cormorant dive and wondering where it would surface. Ollie in his boxer shorts and T-shirt, sitting on his crumpled bed and feeling a rising, overwhelming anxiety.

'What is she going to do when she gets here?' asked Jess.

'Fuck everything up.' He wanted to crawl away and hide.

'No, she's not. You're being overdramatic. Let's be practical. Is she staying at the Starfish?'

'I suppose so.'

'Is she on her own?'

He groaned. 'No. She's got some hangers-on with her. They'll be awful.'

'How do you know that?' Jess had an urge to kick the self-pity out of him.

'Because one of them is Henrik, who hates me, and the others will all be like him.'

Jess went for tough love. 'Stop sounding like a sulky teenager. Your girlfriend is on her way. So are her friends. Get on to reception and book some rooms for them. While you're at it, book Red into a room of her own so that she can have her own space.'

'She'll go mad,' he said fearfully.

'Tell her you've done it as a thoughtful gesture for her, knowing she needs to chill after all that travelling. Get the room filled with flowers and have them stock the mini bar. Book a masseur and anything else she likes.'

'Maltesers.'

'How very rock'n'roll,' Jess said drily. 'Order Maltesers by the sackload. That should keep her busy and out of your hair while you're rehearsing. Oliver Pinkerton, you've got work to do. Get on and do it.'

*

The receptionist was super efficient; as soon as she heard who the rooms were for, she was straight on the phone to Louise Lonsdale. Ever on the lookout for a PR opportunity, Louise immediately vacated her personal suite and rounded up the housekeeping team with orders to have everything spotless within forty minutes.

There were three other single rooms available. They weren't the best in the hotel, but by the time Louise's gang had filled them with flowers, the latest DVDs, iced bottles of Krug and gift sets of exquisite Cornish gifts, they were suitable for royalty.

Ollie was showered, shaved, dressed and waiting at the top of the Starfish steps by 7.28. Louise came out to give him the once-over.

'Nice shirt,' she said.

He hugged her. 'Thank you for getting everything ready at such short notice.'

'The Starfish is always ready.' She smiled at him. 'I may have given you preferential rates on your room, but believe me, I'll make a profit on the deal when word gets out Red is here.'

'Louise!' He stepped back, feigning shock. 'You mean you're not running this place as a charity?'

She put a manicured fingertip to her lips. 'Shh.'

Three motorbikes slewed to a halt at the bottom of the steps and three pillion passengers dressed in black leathers and with black helmets leapt off. Out of the bike's panniers they pulled fearsome-looking cameras with huge lenses. Twenty seconds later a red-and-white Fiat 500 with blacked-out windows joined them. The driver, with a hoodie covering most of his face, jumped out brandishing a similar camera.

Within seconds a black people carrier escorted by two

further motorbikes and a couple of VW Golfs skidded to a halt.

Ollie reached for Louise's hand. 'Oh shit. This is it.'

Louise shook his hand away and called to her doormen: 'Please help our guests into the hotel.'

The four doormen ran down the steps in their regulation black linen trousers and shirts, barged through the phalanx of flashing cameras and bodies – followed by Louise and Ollie, who was somewhat surprised to find himself being steered by Louise's very strong hand in the small of his back.

The side door of the people carrier slid open and Henrik emerged. Several cameras went off in his face. He flapped his hands about and swore at them, before leaning into the dark interior and offering his hand to a tiny woman dressed in skin-tight black leather trousers and a white silk blouse undone to her navel. One small breast, its nipple pierced with a glinting diamond, escaped for a moment and the cameras went wild. Her dramatically kohl-lined eyes sparkled mischievously and she ran a hand through her tomato-soup-coloured spiky hair.

'Hi, guys – Red's home!' She posed and preened for a couple of minutes before finally spotting Ollie. She pointed a finger at him and beckoned him to her. The photographers parted to let him through.

'And here's my baby boy.' She put her hands either side of Ollie's face and kissed him deeply and fully. Again the flashing of cameras was like a mini-blitzkrieg.

Finally she pulled away. 'Have you missed me, baby?' She reached for his hand and placed it inside her shirt while simultaneously grabbing his crotch. 'Hmm. I see you have!'

The photographers laughed and leered and took the picture.

'How long you here for, Red?' asked one of them.

'As long as it takes. But now my boyf and I have a lotta catching up to do. Carry me, baby?' She pulled on a cute little girl expression.

'What?' Ollie asked.

'Carry your little Red to bed.'

She hung her arms around his neck and he was obliged to pick her up and carry her up the steps and into the hotel.

Several guests were gathered in the large hall, on their way to breakfast, and they broke into spontaneous applause as they watched the handsome actor carry the rebel rock star into the lift. As soon as the doors closed he put her down.

'Are you tired?' he asked her.

'Not too tired.' She leaned against him suggestively.

'I've got a great room for you.'

'Yeah? What's the bed like?'

'Comfy, I think.'

'Good. I need some comfort, Ollie.' She opened her blouse to expose her breasts. 'Don't you?'

*

Incredibly, Ollie was only six minutes late for rehearsal.

'Has she arrived?' asked Brooke, fully au fait with all the gossip thanks to Jess.

Ollie put his coat on the hooks by the door and answered, 'Yes.'

'And?' asked Jess, sidling up.

'Your plan has worked. She's having a massage right

now and then a few hours sleep. Tonight she wants to meet you girls.'

'Oh my God! Really? Where? The Starfish?' Brooke was clearly rather excited. 'No. That'll be too busy. Unless she likes the attention? Or would you both like to come back to Granny's Nook and we could get a takeaway? Is she vegetarian? Would she mind if Louis were there? He thinks he might come down tonight.' She stopped talking and looked at Jess and Ollie. 'Am I gabbling?'

'Yes,' said Ollie. 'Look, she's cool. She just wants to say hi to you both because I've told her quite a bit about you, that's all. She'll be tired anyway. A quick pizza at Granny's Nook sounds perfect.'

*

Ollie returned to the Starfish aglow with satisfaction that the evening was sorted. He was in for a rude awakening.

'Where the fuck have you been?' snarled Red, the moment he walked in. 'I didn't fly halfway round the world for you to ignore me.'

'Ya,' flounced Henrik, blowing on his newly varnished nails. 'Vere haf you bin, Actor Boy? Red iz zuperstar and she not liking ze ignoring from anyone.'

Ollie walked over to Red and kissed her angry little mouth. He needed this like a hole in the head, but experience had taught him that the best way to deal with her was to turn on the charm. 'Did you have a nice massage and a sleep?'

'Yes,' she replied grudgingly.

'Would you like to meet my friends for supper in their proper little Cornish cottage?'

'Who are they?'

'Jess and Brooke – I've told you about them.'

'Oh yeah. The dykes who've been smothering you.'

Ollie paused, wondering whether to contradict her or not. In the end he confided, 'Well, actually one of them is dating someone who is pretty famous.'

'Am I supposed to be impressed?'

'God no! No!' improvised Ollie. 'I just thought a quiet, fun evening, all of us together, and then an early night would be what you needed.'

'They'd better not ask me to sing or sign anything for their cousin's workmate's friend's daughter who's raising money for charity.'

'I promise that won't happen.'

Red looked over at Henrik. The puffed-up PA was looking daggers at Ollie. 'Hen, be a doll, get Bibi and Mezz and Bango up here. I need to look my best.'

Ollie moved towards the door. ''Kay, babe. I'll leave you to it and I'll come back in an hour.'

*

An hour later he returned to the suite to find the retinue of stylist, hair designer and make-up artist in a drama of discarded clothes and hairspray. Red stood in the centre of the room surrounded by them, each doing their thing. Once they stepped back, and Ollie could see her, he gasped. She looked exactly as she had when he left her.

'Whaddya think?' She took on a rock-star stance: hand on one hip, other hand pointing to the ceiling and flicking a V sign.

He did some serious nodding, inwardly laughing at all the bollocks surrounding Red's lifestyle. 'Babe, you're every inch a star.'

'Ya, you bet she iz, Actor Boy. Too goot for you.'

Red giggled. 'Oh, Hen, you are so naughty.'

'Iz true! No von iz goot enough for you, Red.'

She swatted away the hair designer, who was fiddling with the back of her head. 'Yeah, well, see you all later. And clear up this shit' – she pointed at the piles of cosmetics and clothes – 'before I get back.'

*

The evening went better than Ollie had expected. As soon as Red had determined that Brooke and Jess were no threat to her, she dropped the attitude and became quite chatty. She loved Elsie and Ethel and they, much to Jess's annoyance, wouldn't leave Red alone. She kept them all amused with stories of life on the road and Ollie found himself relaxing and enjoying her company again. The old Red was still in there. Somewhere.

She didn't go so far as helping collect up the plates after the pizzas were eaten, instead she went into the sitting room and played with the dogs while the others tidied and washed up. This left Brooke free to whisper that Louis wasn't able to get over that night after all.

'Probably better this way,' whispered Jess back. 'It could have got a bit too much with two superstars in a confined space.'

*

Instead of heading straight back to Trevay, Ollie drove the MG Midget, with the top down and Red by his side, along a short narrow diversion to the sea. Once he'd killed the engine the two of them sat listening to the sound of the breakers rolling onto the sand. Red snuggled into Ollie's shoulder.

'This is nice. Can we paddle?'

'Sure.'

The clouds were gently pushing their way over a waxing moon, which was doing its best to reflect its silver path on the ocean.

Standing with the cool sand between their toes, Ollie and Red held each other as if for the first time.

'This is really nice,' Red said again.

28

Someone was banging on Ollie's bedroom door. Red was still sleeping next to him. He checked his phone: 8.15. Hurriedly he swung his feet out of bed and pulled on a luxurious dressing gown supplied by the hotel.

'I'm coming. Shh,' he said as quietly as he could. Outside in the corridor stood an impatient Henrik. He barged past Ollie and walked straight to the bed, where he stood over Red's sleeping form.

'Vake up! Vake up!' He clapped his bony hands by her ear.

Ollie walked to him and pulled him away from the bed. 'Leave her alone. She's tired.'

'Don't touch me, Actor Boy,' Henrik snarled at him. 'You are not in charge of her.' He once again stepped towards the bed and started shaking Red awake. 'Get up, you bitch, ve haf to be in London.'

Ollie saw red. 'Don't speak to my girlfriend like that.'

Henrik turned to face Ollie with his hands on his hips. 'Girlfriend? Your girlfriend? I don't sink zo. She is a little whore who needs to get up for verk.' He turned back to Red and now started slapping her awake.

Ollie grabbed the ghastly man and spun him round while bringing his arm up behind Henrik's shoulder blade and twisting it as hard as he dared.

'Ow! Get off me! You're hurting my arm!' squealed Henrik.

Ollie did not let go until he'd marched Henrik out of the room and slammed the door in his face. Red was trying to sit up in bed.

'What the fuck's going on?'

Ollie told her. Red rubbed her sleepy eyes as she listened and then got out of bed and went to the bathroom without saying a word. She turned the shower on.

'What are you doing?' asked Ollie.

'Getting ready.'

'For what?'

'I have to go to London. There's a big meeting with the record company. They want me to write the next album.'

'But you're in the middle of a world tour.' Ollie was confused. 'You've been on the road for almost a year. You need a holiday.'

There was no response. He watched as she soaped herself behind the glass door of the shower. She had never carried much flesh on her bones, but now he could see her ribs and hips, the vertebrae sticking out along her spine.

He closed the loo seat and sat down, waiting for her to come out. He thought back to last night and how desperately she had clung to him as they made love in the dunes. She had needed affection rather than passion from him. The scary rock star had reverted to a needy little girl. Ollie was no idiot. He understood that something had shifted in their relationship last night. She had moved on and away from him as a lover, but a deeper understanding had been conceived. Friendship?

She got out of the shower and shivered. He stood and wrapped a huge warm bath sheet round her and hugged her to him. Her bones pressed uncomfortably into his body. Without her make-up, her skin was spotty and drab. Her eyes, once so clear and lively, were yellow-tinged and dull.

Ollie was worried for her. 'Henrik called you a whore and a bitch.'

'Yeah. He does that.'

'And you let him?'

'He's my PA. He has to make sure I get everywhere on time.'

'By calling you names?'

'It doesn't matter.' She started to clean her teeth. Her face in the mirror looked defeated.

'Red, what's happened? Last night you were like your old self. Jess and Brooke really loved you. This morning you're a different person.'

She spat into the sink. 'I'm on duty. That's all.'

There was another knock at the door. 'If that's Henrik, I'm not letting him in,' said Ollie as he marched off to open it.

It was Bango the hair designer, clutching something in his tattooed hand. 'Is Red in 'ere?' he asked in a Cockney accent.

'Yes, I am,' called Red from the bathroom. 'Have you got my stuff?'

'Yeah.'

Red appeared, still wrapped in her towel, and held out her hand to Bango. He passed her something that Ollie could only guess at before leaving the room.

Ollie sat on the bed and asked wearily, 'What has he given you?'

'Nothing.' She went back into the bathroom.

Ollie could hear her drinking from the tap. 'What have you just taken?'

She came out again, shrugged off her towel and started looking for her clothes. 'Don't freak out. It's just a little something to get me going.'

'Drugs.'

'Nothing bad. Everybody has a little helper. It's nothing.'

'You were always so dead against drugs. What about your fans? What if you get caught?'

She pulled on her leather jeans and turned to him in a fury. 'Fuck off, Ollie! Just fuck off. I'm not a junkie. The record company make sure I have all the good stuff. Their doctors wouldn't give it to me otherwise, would they?'

'The record company knows about this?'

She stared at him insolently. 'Duh! Of course they do. As soon as I've got the new album down, they've said I can take a year off and I won't need it any more.'

Ollie couldn't take in what he was hearing. Whatever Bango had given her, it was working very quickly. She was getting agitated and frustrated, struggling with the simple task of slipping her feet into her trainers.

'Let me help you with those.'

She threw them at him. 'God, you are such a loser!' She found her phone and keyed in a number. 'Hey, Henrik. I'm done. Get me out of here.'

Henrik was there within the minute.

'Call me later?' Ollie asked.

She looked at him bleakly through dilated pupils, vulnerable in her bare feet. 'Nah. I don't think so.'

Henrik passed her a huge pair of glasses, which she put on. 'Zere's plenty paps out zere. The record company do zere job vell.'

Red nodded acceptingly.

Ollie picked up her discarded trainers and passed them to her as she and Henrik walked to the door. 'You know where I am if you need me,' he told her.

*

Jonathan gestured to Jess to join him as they drank their coffees in the mid-afternoon break. 'What's wrong with Ollie?'

Jess followed his line of sight to where Ollie was sitting on his own, staring into space.

'Red had to go back to London this morning.'

'So he's lovesick?'

Jess shifted her weight slightly more towards Jonathan and said, 'Confidentially, I think they've split up.'

Jonathan raised his eyebrows. 'Again? Rock stars tend not to have stable personal lives and Ollie seems like a person who'd prefer a stable relationship.'

'He's young. He'll survive.' Jess took a sip of her coffee. 'Brooke and I will keep an eye on him.'

Jonathan turned his gaze towards Brooke. 'And what about our gorgeous starlet? She's had a bumpy ride in her short time in the business.'

Jess filled Jonathan in on the Café Au Lait episode. 'I admire her. She's taken a lot of shit, kept her head down and worked hard.'

'Hmm. She's certainly got talent,' Jonathan agreed. He lowered his voice, 'Tell me, is it true about the royal boyfriend?'

Jess looked at him in alarm. 'What?'

'Ah. So it is true then.'

'I don't know what you're talking about.' Jess was blushing.

Jonathan laughed. 'Don't worry. I am very discreet. No one down here knows anything, but I have friends in London who know him and let the cat out of the bag a few days ago.'

Jess turned pleading eyes towards him. 'Please don't let her know you know.'

'I'll say nothing, but tell me one thing . . .' He looked around to make sure no one could hear him. 'Is he coming to the first night?'

Jess could answer this truthfully. 'I have no idea, and neither does Brooke.'

'Good. We could do without any distractions. Now,' he sat back and spoke in a normal voice. 'How are you and Ryan? Is he coming down for opening night?'

'I hope so. He's really busy, but I know he'll do his best.'

'I hope so, Jess. You deserve the best.'

Something about the way Jonathan was looking at her unnerved Jess.

'When is the wedding?'

Relieved to be back on safer ground, Jess replied, 'Actually, you may be able to help me with that. Are we rehearsing on Saturday?'

Jonathan sighed. 'I'm thinking you'd like the weekend off?'

She nodded.

'Ryan is a lucky man. I just hope he realises it.' Jonathan appeared to be weighing something up. 'You know what, we could all do with two days off. I'll break the good news to everyone in a minute.'

'Oh, that's fantastic! Thank you.' Jess kissed his cheek, but failed to notice the blush that crept up his face as she did so. 'I shall go home on Friday night and surprise Ryan. He's on a short stopover from LA to do some dubbing in a voice studio, then he goes back on Monday. He won't be expecting to see me. I intend to nail him down to a date, a church and an invitation list. I rather fancy a Christmas wedding. What do you think?'

'Very romantic.'

'What about you, do you have a partner?' Jess asked. He had never mentioned one.

'No.'

'How liberating,' she said, with what she hoped was a dash of *joie de vivre*.

'So some would say.'

Jess stopped smiling. 'I'm sorry, I didn't mean to intrude on your privacy.'

'No apology needed.' He touched her shoulder fondly. 'I travel hopefully, so don't worry about me. Now shall we get on with this last scene?' He stood up and called the room back to work.

*

The Friday night train from Penzance to Paddington was full. Jess got on at Bodmin Parkway and was grateful that she'd reserved a seat in first class. At Plymouth a large group of uniformed Royal Marines boarded. With very few seats left, they found themselves places in spaces between carriages and enlivened the quiet of the train with military banter. One of them recognised Jess as he walked through her carriage to the loo.

'You're off the telly!'

Jess was embarrassed but polite. 'Yes.'

'Thought so. I'm Whitey.' He held out his hand. She shook it.

'Jess Tate. How do you do.'

'Would you mind saying hello to some of my mates?'

Jess looked around apologetically to her fellow passengers, who by and large ignored her. 'Not at all.'

Over the next ten minutes she was introduced to several of the men from 42 Commando based in Plymouth. 'This is Smudge, Bomber, Techy, Spesh and Matron – don't ask why: it's a bit rude.'

Jess shook hands with all of them. 'Where are you going?'

'A bit of a do at the Admiralty. Some of the lads here did rather well in Afghanistan.'

Jess was thrilled. 'Can I ask what?'

'Not really.'

The man sitting opposite Jess, who had hitherto behaved as if he could neither hear nor see any of these brave fighting men, put his newspaper down and said, 'Can I buy you chaps a drink?'

'That would be very nice. Soft drinks only though, sir. We don't drink in uniform.'

From then on a party atmosphere pervaded the carriage and when the ticket collector came through he knew not to ask if any of them had first-class tickets.

At Paddington, Jess was escorted off the train by Whitey and the lads and placed in a black cab with smart salutes. Her spirits were running high and she couldn't wait to see Ryan and tell him all about her journey.

Arriving at their Willesden flat she let herself in quietly. It was almost midnight and she could see a soft light coming from under the living room door. Lying in the hallway was Ryan's suitcase, its contents carelessly spilling out across the corridor.

Jess tiptoed in, leaving the flat in darkness rather than alert him to her presence. She couldn't wait to surprise him. In the kitchen she silently undressed and, on a whim, pulled open a kitchen drawer which housed tea towels and a chef's hat Ryan had given her for Christmas last year. Across the front, 'Kiss My Baubles' was spelled out in red sequins. She put it on.

As she trod stealthily towards their living room door, it opened and a stunning woman in a short satin dressing gown walked out. Behind her, Jess could see Ryan lying on the sofa with a glass of whisky in his hand.

The woman screamed long and loud, her red lipsticked mouth forming an enormous O. Ryan leapt from the sofa wearing – even in her shock Jess was grateful to see – a T-shirt and a pair of boxers.

'What the fuck!' Ryan stumbled towards her. 'Jess! What are you doing here?'

Jess pointed at the woman who had stopped screaming. 'What the fuck is she doing here?'

Ryan stood where he was and started to laugh. 'Oh, my darling. How sweet you look in that hat. Here . . .' He passed her an over-sized cardigan that was draped over the sofa, 'Put this on and let me introduce you to Serena.'

29

It was not an easy evening. Ryan explained that Serena and he had arrived in London on the same flight and he had offered her their room for the night. He was planning to sleep on the sofa but she had come into the living room for a chat while he was getting ready for bed. They'd were just having a friendly natter before they both turned in.

'I feel so awful,' Serena gushed. 'You must have thought the absolute worst when you saw us together like that, but I was just saying goodnight on my way to bed.'

'Not at all,' said Jess, assuming an air of nonchalance she really didn't feel. 'It's absolutely fine. I'm just so sorry I inflicted my nudity on you!'

Both women laughed actressy laughs. Ryan looked from one to the other. His male brain sensing that a primal, female, territory-marking ritual was being performed here, but he couldn't quite get a handle on it. Instead, he went to the airing cupboard to grab spare bedding and left them to it. When he came back they were in the same positions chatting about some soldiers Jess had met on the train. He dumped the duvet and pillow on the floor and scooped his clothes off the sofa.

'Right, girls. Time for your beauty sleep. I'll have the sofa and you two can take the double bed.'

Jess stiffened but Serena answered first:

'Oh no, I bags the sofa! You two get into your own bed and I'll see you in the morning. Night night.' She shooed them out of the sitting room and closed the door.

*

Ryan fell into an easy slumber. Jess, lying next to him, stared into the dark. A small white-hot flame of jealousy was burning in her gut. She had to get control of it. Since that one time, almost six years ago, he had never been unfaithful to her. She trusted him. As he trusted her. She had quite liked it when he'd warned Ollie off. It was nice to know he was a bit jealous. But there had never been anything going on between her and Ollie. And nothing was going to happen between Ryan and Serena, she told herself. Even if she hadn't turned up. Absolutely not. Ryan would never jeopardise what they had. Ever. The heat in her stomach cooled a little. By the morning it would be extinguished. Serena was just a gorgeous young actress whom Ryan was friends with. And that was that.

*

Serena stayed all weekend. Both she and Ryan had to go into Soho to dub their voices on to the latest episodes of *Venini*, so it made sense for them to hang out together until their flight back to LA on Monday night.

Jess rather enjoyed playing hostess. While they were out, she shopped for food. She had missed the coffee and bacon smell of the local deli, and the staff had missed her. Marco, the owner, plied her with nibbles of cheese and ham and a perfect cappuccino while she decided what she would cook for dinner. He recommended a beautiful bottle of crisp Frascati to go with the melanzane sott'olio, caprese salad and focaccia that she had chosen as a starter. And with the veal scalloppine a bold Montepulciano red. Jess was an enthusiastic cook and what she lacked in expertise she hoped she'd make up for in flavour. For pudding she bought one of Marco's fresh-made tiramisus.

Marco placed all the lovingly wrapped parcels into Jess's round wicker basket and kissed her cheeks three times.

''E willa lova youa fora eva, Signora Jessa. And ifa hea doesa notta. I willa tella hima offa.'

'Thank you, Marco. I'll certainly let him know.'

As she strolled back to the flat the sun shone warm on the Willesden pavements. This would be her last visit to London until after *Hats Off, Trevay!* came to an end in September. She shut her eyes for a moment and thought of Cornwall. How at home she was feeling there. How happy Elsie and Ethel were, sniffing in the rock pools and paddling in the wavelets. She knew Brooke would be spoiling them rotten back at Granny's Nook, but she wished she could have brought them with her to London. She missed their tappy claws trotting after her and the way they'd come to her for a snuggle. They could be ring bearers at the wedding. Would that be too horribly cute? Oh, what the hell, she told herself, if you can't be cute on your wedding day, when can you!

Just two streets away was a very chi-chi bridal shop. Although she couldn't resist gazing in whenever she passed by, she'd never had the courage to actually stop and stare. It wouldn't do any harm today though, would it? Over supper tonight she would talk to Ryan about it, and get some input from Serena too. That would draw a fence round Ryan and signal to Serena that he was taken.

Hefting her fashionably artisan but super-heavy and rather awkward wicker basket from her right hand to her left, she made the detour to the wedding dress shop. It was called LOVE IS FOR ALWAYS and the window was glistening with crystals and marabou feathers. In the centre of the display a mannequin was dressed in the gown of Jess's dreams. As if in a trance, she put her hand to the door handle and entered.

The middle-aged woman behind the counter greeted her warmly. With kindness and efficiency she had Jess out of her clothes and into the dress in five minutes.

It fitted perfectly.

*

Supper was delicious and Serena a very appreciative eater. She and Ryan spent the entire evening talking with each other about people Jess hadn't heard of and laughing at anecdotes she didn't understand. When the last drop of wine was poured into Serena's glass, she and Ryan got up and made their way into the sitting room, leaving the table and the washing-up to Jess. She had tried to tell them about her day and the magical, wonderful dress that was hanging up in a special bag in her wardrobe, but there just hadn't been a moment when she felt it appropriate to open the conversation.

Never mind, she told herself, there's always tomorrow.

*

Tomorrow was Sunday. A lie-in, the newspapers, coffee and croissants sitting outside the café across the road from the flat. All these things Jess did on her own. Ryan and Serena had had to get to Soho early to finish the dub.

'What time is your train tonight, darling?' asked Ryan as he left.

'Three minutes to six.'

'Great. I'll be back in time to give you a lift.'

He wasn't. He phoned at four to say there had been a technical problem with the recording equipment and he didn't know when he'd be home.

Jess's black cab rattled its way from Willesden to Paddington, the driver keeping up a long monologue listing all that was wrong with the country today and what he'd do if he met Boris Johnson. Jess sat quietly in the back responding with the odd nod of assent but feeling very insecure. She longed to call Emma, to ask her what she thought. But she didn't. Jess had a horrible feeling that she knew what her sister would say.

*

'Poor Jess, what a horrible weekend. How could Ryan be so thoughtless?' Brooke was hurt on Jess's behalf. 'You should have stayed here with me and the girls. We had lots of fun. Didn't we, ladies?' Brooke tickled both Elsie and Ethel, who were flat out next to her on the sofa. 'Ollie came over and we played cards and watched telly and ate popcorn. The weather was glorious. We took pasties down to the beach and even had a swim. Bloody cold, mind, but I think it cheered Ollie up. Flashed his muscles on the beach, which were greatly appreciated by every woman down there.'

When there was no response to her chatter, Brooke looked over at Jess. It was obvious that she was feeling utterly miserable. 'Come on, bird. It's just a blip. He's busy, you're busy. Long-distance love ain't easy. Look at Ollie and Red.'

'Exactly,' said Jess. 'How are things between them?'

'All off. They've talked a bit on the phone, but she's out in a different world. Even though Ollie hasn't been happy for months, it still hurts when you're the dumpee rather than the dumper.'

'Poor Ollie.'

'He'll be fine. He's a good-looking twenty-eight-year-old with a set of pecs to die for. Don't worry about him.'

'Speaking of pecs – how's Louis?'

Brooke looked away and fiddled with the remote control on the arm of her chair, 'Oh, you know. He flies in and out on the breeze. There's a bit of family stuff he's got to show his face for and then he's got an assignment with his cousin and a group of injured servicemen . . .'

'Will he make it to the first night?'

'He says he'll try.' Brooke brushed her blonde fringe out of her eyes and looked again at Jess. 'What about Ryan?'

'He says he'll try.'

'Good.'

'Yeah . . . good.'

30

I t was ten days to opening night.

The weather had warmed up and holidaymakers were filling the streets and B&Bs of Trevay before the school holidays got into full swing.

Liz Parker, the Pavilions' glamorous new publicist, had lined up interviews with all the local media, plus some big guns from the national press. Jess, Ollie and Brooke were excused from morning rehearsals to fulfil their quotas of interviews.

Journalists, no matter how original they thought they were, asked only the obvious questions:

'Jess, when are you and Ryan getting married?' And, 'Is he coming to the first night?'

Answer: 'It'll be a private affair. We'll let you know when we've done it.' And, 'It would be great if he can make it.'

'Ollie, have you and Red split up?' And, 'Is she coming to the first night?'

Answer: 'We are good friends.' And, 'Maybe.'

'Brooke, you lost a big job with Café Au Lait a few months ago amid rumours that you were out of control. Was it drugs?' And, 'Do you have a boyfriend?'

Answer: 'Don't believe all you read in the papers.' And, 'Are you flirting with me?'

'Colonel, what does it feel like being back on stage?'

Answer: 'Like coming home, old chap. Like coming home.'

Jonathan was interviewed by the arts reviewers of the *Guardian*, the *Observer* and *The Times*. When they appeared in print, the interviews were prefaced by subheadings in bold type: 'Once touted as a great director in the making, why is Mulberry now officiating at an end-of-the-pier-show?' And 'Jonathan Mulberry, the man the West End forgot. Can he save a seaside theatre and his career in one season?' And 'A likeable man, but he's no Trevor Nunn'.

These painful articles served to make the rehearsal atmosphere nervy, to say the least. The only man to keep a perspective on it all was the Colonel. One afternoon after Jonathan had lost his temper spectacularly with Miss Coco and her youngsters, he stepped in.

'Mr Mulberry, kindly sit down and be quiet!' he commanded.

Jonathan, his cheeks puce and a vein throbbing in his throat, took a second before sitting.

In a softer voice the Colonel continued: 'Brooke, dear, would you take our young dancers out to find refreshment.'

Brooke duly gathered up the white-faced and teary dancers and led them out of the theatre and into the welcoming warmth of the foyer café.

The Colonel then made his way to Miss Coco, who was standing ram-rod straight, her mouth pinched and her hands trembling slightly at her side. Determined to maintain her dignity, she hadn't moved since Jonathan had started bellowing.

'Mr Mulberry,' said the Colonel, 'I believe you owe Miss Coco, and indeed the entire cast, an apology.' He glowered sternly at the director.

Jonathan shifted in his chair and cleared his throat. 'I apologise, Miss Coco. My behaviour was unjustifiable.'

She took a deep breath and said. 'So you withdraw the remark about my dancers moving like three-legged camels on a plate of snot?'

Jonathan had the grace to blush. 'I do. Wholeheartedly.'

'And that I am to choreography what a bucket of paint is to a fur coat?'

Jonathan brushed an invisible crumb from his corduroy trousers and said, 'Yes. I do.'

Miss Coco waited a beat, then inclined her head in acknowledgement. 'Apology accepted.'

Jonathan spoke again. 'And to the whole company, I apologise for my lack of professionalism.'

This was greeted with murmurs from the cast of 'That's all right', 'Quite understand' and 'It's all a bit tough at the moment.'

The Colonel looked around the room. 'I think we should take a short tea break for the troops to rally themselves. Back here for half past, chaps.' He turned to Jonathan: 'Would you stay behind with me for a moment?'

Once everyone had left, and the stage and the auditorium were their own, the Colonel took a seat next to Jonathan, who was leaning back in his chair, his eyes fixed on a spot on the ceiling.

'What's the matter, dear boy?'

Jonathan lifted his head and looked at the Colonel. 'I can't see the wood for the trees. Am I a useless director? Is the whole thing shit? Are we heading for disaster?'

'Ah.' The Colonel smiled kindly at Jonathan. 'You've lost faith in our strength as a platoon. Perfectly normal, old boy. I've seen it many times. Felt it myself once or twice. Now look here, you are their commanding officer.

You've trained them well. They know their job and what has to be done. Victory is in our grasp.'

'Colonel, with all respect, this could end my career.'

'And?'

'And that's the end of my reputation.'

'How very selfish of you. You put your own life and reputation above those of your men?' A pause and the Colonel added, 'And women?'

'They'll be all right. They're all talented and young. They have families to go home to.'

'Not true of all of us.'

Jonathan looked ashamed. 'So what should I do?'

'My dear boy, what we all do in these circumstances – man up! Feel the fear and do it anyway. Isn't that what today's popular psychology tells us? In my day it was "Pull yourself together or face a court martial in the morning." That usually sharpened us up.'

Jonathan managed a small laugh. 'I can see that it would. No one's going to shoot me, are they?'

'I might, if you bugger up my script. Now go fetch yourself a cup of coffee and let's get this show on the road.'

*

That evening, the cast were preparing for their first technical dress rehearsal and a long night lay ahead. Jess and Brooke were readying themselves in their dressing room.

'Hey, you look great,' said Jess, stunned by her first view of Brooke in full make-up and costume. There was a big opening number and Brooke got to wear a stunning dress of vibrant green satin that perfectly set off her blonde hair and accentuated her hourglass figure.

'Ooh-boo-bi-do.' Brooke gave her friend a wink. 'Thanks, girlfriend. I'm as nervous as a virgin on her wedding night, though.'

'Those were the days!' Jess teased.

'No, really, shall I light this candle Miss Coco gave us? It's supposed to help calm your nerves. I can't stop worrying about getting the steps right in the first number.'

'You'll be brilliant, and remember this is only a stagger through.' Jess watched as Brooke lit the lavender and camomile candle. 'It smells lovely, we musn't forget to blow it out.'

Jess gave Brooke a final good luck embrace and then hurried off to look in on Ollie and the Colonel.

'Beginners Act One on stage, please!' came the tannoy call.

'Oh, God!' Brooke blew out the candle and dashed out into the hallway. As the door fell shut behind her, the resulting gust of air caught a tissue, half pulled from its box and sent it floating through the air until it landed on the smouldering candle wick.

The entire company of actors and dancers had gathered in the wings and in the front seats to watch the dress rehearsal. It wasn't until just before the end of the first act that the flames took hold and smoke began to drift along the corridors to the stage.

Stage manager Dan was the first to notice it. He got on his headset and asked the lighting desk operator if he could see any smoke in the auditorium.

'Negative,' came the response.

Dan made a call to the stage-door man: 'Dave, I can smell smoke. Would you check backstage, please?'

Within moments, a serious Dave was back with Dan in the prompt corner. 'Bring the iron curtain down.

Dressing two is alight! Put a tannoy out to Front of House and tell them Mr Brown is paying a visit. Then dial 999.'

Mr Brown was the code word used by many theatres to warn the staff that there is a serious emergency. If fire and smoke alarms went off in the auditorium, panic could ensue and someone could get injured in the rush to get out.

Dan got on his headset and spoke to the men manning the fly rigging backstage. 'Bring the iron in. Repeat. Bring the iron in. Now.'

Mrs Coco's girls were halfway through their end of Act One number and now found themselves on a darkening, smokey stage.

'Get the girls off and outside.' He ordered the perplexed Miss Coco before calling over the tannoy again. 'Mr Brown is in the building. Would all staff and guests please leave the building quickly and calmly and gather outside in the car park until further notice.'

Jonathan, sitting at the back of the dress circle could smell smoke and knew this was no practice drill. He reacted quickly, his deep voice booming out authoritively across the auditorium.

'Everyone, move quickly and calmly out of the building. Those of you in the front of the stalls use the exit straight out through the front foyer, the same for those of you on stage. Those backstage need to take the exit through the side door.'

By this time, the sprinkler system had kicked in and a fine mist was now falling from the ceiling.

Jonathan made his way backstage. Word had filtered through and all of the actors and crew were filing out quickly towards the stage door. Here the water coming from the sprinkler system was heavier and there was a slightly more chaotic feel to the cramped and crowded corridors.

Madame Coco was marshalling her tearful and anxious charges to the exit: 'Now, now, Pippa, do stop snivelling. Chloe, stop gawping – do keep up, dear.'

'Good work, Madame C,' said Jonathan as he hurried by. 'Do as Madame Coco says, and keep calm, girls.'

He spotted a worried-looking Colonel Stick being helped out by Ollie.

'This is terrible, my dear boy, after all we've done – to lose the Pavilions now . . .'

'Let's just make everyone safe, Colonel, and worry about the bricks and mortar later.'

'Have you seen Jess?' asked an anxious-looking Ollie. 'I don't know where she is, was she out the front?'

Jonathan felt a tremor of panic in his stomach. 'No, now that you mention it. Look, you get the Colonel out and I'll see if I can find her.'

He hurried down the narrow passageway to the dressing rooms. It was here that the smoke was at its thickest. Before long his eyes were stinging, it was hard to breathe and the water from the sprinklers was making the floor slippery underfoot.

'Jess, Jess, where are you?' he shouted between coughs. Nothing. He made his way further down the row of dressing rooms. 'Jess, can you hear me?'

It was becoming hard to see. He stood still and listened, straining to make out sounds. At last he heard a muffled response: 'Help, I'm in here, in the loo. I can't get the door open, it seems to be jammed.'

Jonathan ran to the loo next door to the burning dressing room and tried to turn the door handle. It wouldn't budge.

'Oh God,' cried Jess from the other side of the door.

'Don't panic, I'll try and break it down. Stand back.'

'OK, I'm not panicking. I'm standing back.'

Jonathan put his shoulder against the door and pushed. The door held firm. 'One more time,' he told himself.

He took a step back and, with an almighty effort, hurled himself against the door. To his huge relief, it gave and he was through. Grabbing Jess's hand, he led her back the way he'd come.

By this time the corridor was thick with smoke and it was impossible to see a hand in front of them. In the enveloping darkness they completely lost their bearings and Jess felt the panic start to overwhelm her.

Then they heard a voice through the smoke.

'Thank God! Here, take my hand.'

It was Ollie.

With Ollie to lead them in the right direction they were outside within minutes, gratefully breathing in the cool, clear air.

'That was a close shave,' said Jonathan.

'That door had been sticking for ages. I kept meaning to mention it, but never got round to it. Jonathan, if you hadn't come back for me, I might . . .' Unable to finish the sentence, Jess took his hand in hers and squeezed it. 'Thank you.'

Jonathan found it hard to meet her gaze. 'And thanks to Ollie – without him we might both be toast.'

Ollie shrugged nonchalantly. 'Hey, I'm just an ordinary, run-of-the-mill superhero, right?'

The wail of the fire engines cut through their reunion. They watched as the firefighters poured from the engines and set about their work capably and with no fuss.

It was then that it dawned on the entire cast and crew that their dress rehearsal might just be the one and only performance of *Hats Off, Trevay!*.

*

Mercifully, the fire had only destroyed Brooke and Jess's dressing room. But the water from the sprinklers and the damage from the smoke had caused almost as much devastation as the fire.

Colonel Stick's dressing room, which was next door, was in a terrible state, along with the wig room and wardrobe room directly above. The sprinklers in the auditorium had saturated everything and the tip-up seats were dripping miserably.

Brooke was distraught and was quick to tell the fire officers about her candle. They took down her details and thanked her for her honesty while making it clear what they thought of her stupidity. 'As soon as they can gain access, our investigating officers will determine the cause of the fire. Candles should never be left unattended.'

'But she blew it out, officer,' said Jess, holding on to a sobbing Brooke.

'I'd better take your details too, miss.'

Ollie, Jess, Jonathan and Brooke drove back to Pendruggan together. As Jonathan and Jess sat in the back, he felt her shiver. Instinctively, he put his arm round her and kissed the top of her head. She leaned in to him.

'Are you cold?' he asked.

'No. But I was thinking, what if someone had died in there? What if I had had the girls with me tonight? They would have been shut up in the dressing room.'

'Stop with the "what ifs". Nobody died. Everyone's fine. Ethel and Elsie were at home.'

She turned and looked behind her at the Pavilions, illuminated by the emergency services' arc lights and the flashing blue lights of the fire engines.

'But the Pavilions – after everyone's hard work. We didn't even make it to the first night.'

*

As soon as she'd heard the news, Penny had got in the Jag and driven to Trevay. There she joined Piran and Helen, watching their dreams going up in smoke. There was no need for words. When she eventually got home, Simon made her scrambled eggs on toast and apologised for not coming out to join her. He had been holding a confirm-ation class in the church and hadn't known about the disaster until he came home and found Penny's hastily written note on the table.

'The bloody car wouldn't start or I'd have been there.'

He was expecting her to have another go about his clapped-out car, but instead she patted his hand, finished her glass of milk and took him up to bed.

*

The following afternoon, Penny held a council of war.

All of the SToP campaigners were present, except for Brooke. She was too upset to come, blaming herself for the fire, though all of her friends had been completely supportive. Jonathan and Jess were there, along with the Colonel and Dan the stage manager and Liz Parker the publicist.

It was Penny who voiced what they were all thinking: 'What on earth do we do now?'

'I've spoken to the fire brigade and the council this morning,' said Simon. 'According to the fire brigade, most of the damage is superficial. The building is quite sound structurally, but the cost of the repairs will run into tens of thousands of pounds.'

'Our coffers are running on empty as it is. We needed the box office income to pay the next round of bills.' Penny bit her lip, her eyes brimming with tears. 'But now . . .'

'This venture's been doomed to failure from the start, if you ask me. That building is an eyesore and a money pit. Even if we could raise the money, it'd be like throwing good money after bad. Might as well go and toss your money off the harbour at Trevay—'

'Piran, darling, that really isn't a very helpful attitude,' chided Helen.

'It's the truth.'

Helen ignored him. 'There must be something we can do. If we had the money, could we get the theatre open in time?'

'Where there's a will there's a way – but the company don't have anywhere to rehearse now,' said Jonathan.

'We have the church hall. It's seen many a performance in its time and could certainly accommodate you all, if you didn't mind roughing it,' replied Simon.

'I hate to be the voice of doom, but we have NO money,' said Penny. 'All of this is academic.'

'Well, yes . . .' Simon took a deep breath. 'And I've got more bad news, I'm afraid. I spoke to Councillor Joan Goodman this morning and she tells me that if the company were found to have been negligent or to blame for the fire, then we could lose our right to use the building.'

'That's downright unfair!' Penny was incensed.

'Maybe, darling, but as the SToP campaigners are managing the building, we should have made sure that all Health and Safety regulations were enforced. They'll blame us for it, I'm afraid.'

'And bloody Chris Bedford won't cut us any slack, will 'e?' added Piran.

This threw them all into silence.

'What we need right now,' said Helen despondently, 'is a bloody miracle.'

Colonel Stick said nothing. He was deep in thought.

31

Helen and Brooke were sitting in Colonel Stick's cosy sitting room, wondering why he'd invited them over. Helen had noticed that he'd been unusually quiet at yesterday's meeting, and when she got the call asking her to come over for a cup of tea, her first thought was that the old boy was feeling bereft and in need of company. Instead it was Brooke who looked to be in the depths of despair, as if she hadn't slept a wink since the fire.

'You really must stop blaming yourself,' Helen told her. 'It was a complete accident and the whole building is like a tinder box anyway. Right, Colonel?'

'Indeed, a complete accident. Retreating into yourself won't help anybody, my dear girl. We must all do our bit. Which is why I have asked you both to come here today.'

'Have you had a bright idea?' asked Helen hopefully.

'Better than that. Follow me, both of you.'

Helen and Brooke followed the Colonel down the corridor into his cold study. Much of the clutter had been cleared away and in the centre of the room a projector and screen had been set up. Helen noticed a box that appeared to be full of reels of old 8mm film. Two seats had been set up in front of it.

'Please, take a seat if you would. I'm terribly sorry about the cold in this room. Never seems to warm up, no matter what the time of year it is.'

Helen and Brooke looked at each other, not sure what to expect.

'Helen, my dear, I owe you an apology. Some time ago, you asked me if I knew anything about a film archive. I'm afraid I was lying when I said I couldn't help. Nothing could be further from the truth.'

The women looked at each other and then back at the Colonel. 'Go on.' They chorused.

'Yes. I didn't tell you what I knew because . . . well . . . I suppose I have become so used to part of my life being secret that old habits die hard. You see, I never married, but if I could have married . . . it would have been Peter.' His eyes wandered to a photograph of the young and handsome man. 'We were soul mates. He and I met many decades ago and bonded for life. The London theatre scene has always attracted . . . shall we say "flamboyant" gentlemen, but in the fifties and sixties it was still very dangerous to be openly homosexual. It was illegal; we could have gone to prison, so relationships were conducted in secret, away from prying eyes. Even in the permissive sixties exposure could prove very damaging to one's career. Peter was a respected director, but jealousy and spitefulness are universal, I'm afraid, and some unkind and cruel colleagues had started a whispering campaign against him. He and I decided that life in Trevay would be infinitely quieter and happier. We moved here and never regretted it. The Pavilions and the people of Cornwall gave us a wonderful life together.'

'What happened to Peter?' asked Brooke.

'The same thing that will happen to us all, child, but Peter was cruelly struck down by cancer well ahead of his time.' His voice started to break. 'I've been without my love for nearly thirty years now.' He took a clean hanky from his trouser pocket and wiped his eyes.

'I'm so sorry,' said Helen, getting up and kneeling beside the grief stricken Colonel.

'Thank you. But these past couple of days have been a wake-up call for me.' He blew his nose and sat up straighter. 'One can't go on living in the past, and I've kept silent for far too long already. The survival of the Pavilions is at stake and I have something that may just help . . .'

He stood, placed his handkerchief back into his pocket and went across to draw the curtains, then moved to the ancient projector and clicked a switch. In front of them a creaky black-and-white home movie started to play.

They were looking at a theatre stage, where a man was moving chairs around a table. Brooke recognised him at once.

'It's Peter.'

'Correct,' said the Colonel. 'Keep watching.'

From stage left, a man and a woman appeared and started to chat with Peter. They all laughed at something the woman said and then Peter offered a packet of cigarettes to each of them. The woman took one, lit it and inhaled deeply as the camera moved in towards her face.

Helen and Brooke both let out gasps of astonishment.

'It can't be!' exclaimed Helen.

'It is!' said Brooke.

They were looking at Elizabeth Taylor and Richard Burton. Burton was craggily handsome, captured in his prime, before all the drink had taken its toll. Taylor was surely as beautiful as she had ever been. Other figures appeared at the edge of the stage and the two actors began reading from a script. For the next fifteen minutes, Brooke and Helen watched as Burton and Taylor rehearsed, relaxed and laughing with the other cast members, teasing and affectionate with each other.

When the reel finished, Helen and Brooke sat transfixed.

'There are sound tapes too,' said the Colonel. 'But I don't have the technology to play them here. I expect someone somewhere will know what to do to get them working.'

'Where on earth did this come from?' asked Helen.

'Burton performed *Doctor Faustus* in Oxford in the sixties. His wife, Elizabeth, had a part in it too. It has become the stuff of legend.'

'But the film . . .' interjected Brooke.

'Peter was involved because he was a friend of the director.' He stood and began to thread another film reel into the machine. 'By the way, your friend Piran was wrong about one thing,' said the Colonel, his eyes twinkling mischievously at Helen. 'It was Peter who was the film buff, not me. He loved making home movies of his work, and this box here is just one of many. All the greats of the London stage are there: Alec Guinness and John Gielgud, Laurence Olivier and Ralph Richardson . . . And then there are the comedy greats like Morecambe and Wise – who came to Trevay for a summer season at the Pavilions – and Peter Sellers, Joyce Grenfell, Kenneth Williams. They're all here.' He indicated the box of film reels. 'There's such a wealth of material, I've rather lost track.

'Colonel, this is incredible! This is something that people would pay good money to watch,' said Brooke.

'That is what I am hoping. Peter filmed these for his own pleasure, but he loved to share them and never would have wanted them to be locked away, gathering dust. I haven't been able to watch them since he died. Too painful, too many memories. But if Peter were here, I know what he would want me to do. Helen, do you think Piran would be willing to help me organise these?'

'I'm sure he will,' said Helen.

'I'll help too,' said Brooke.

'You have both already helped me more than you can imagine,' said the Colonel, his eyes misting again with tears.

*

Helen was on the phone to Piran immediately.

'And here's me not believing in miracles,' he told her.

Once word was out, it didn't take long before Piran's mobile was ringing non-stop. Representatives from institutions all over the world had heard about the archives and a bidding war had started.

'But do you want to sell them?' Piran asked the Colonel as the two of them sat in the small study, working through reel after reel of footage. Piran had lost count of the many gems that they had rediscovered.

'If selling some of the films helps to keep the Pavilions going, then I know that is what Peter would have wanted. He loved the place as much as I do.'

Piran and the Colonel agreed on selling two or three movies of Laurence Olivier and Vivien Leigh to a wealthy Japanese film school. The money was wired overnight.

Penny was on cloud nine. 'The Colonel's films have raised enough to pay a professional shop-fitting company to come in and replace the damaged flooring and carpets, as well as paying for the material to repair the damaged dressing rooms and corridors and mend the stage curtain.'

With seven days to go until *Hats Off, Trevay!* was due to open, Simon and Piran went to see the bank. Thanks to the Colonel's contribution to the fund, the bank agreed to give them an extension on their overdraft against future ticket receipts.

Penny phoned Jonathan and Simon with the news: 'It's time to rally the troops.'

*

Over the next few days, Trevay showed what it was really made of. The whole town turned out to help and Brooke was able to pull a few strings with Louis, who turned up at the theatre and took lots of great photographs. The story of the Pavilions and the bad luck which seemed to be dogging the theatre had now made national news. BBC South West ran a feature on its early evening magazine programme and Louis' photos made the *Daily Mail* under the headline '*Last Chance Café for Seaside Landmark*'. And that was just the beginning; Liz Parker had got plenty more publicity lined up.

In the meantime, while the cast continued their rehearsals at the church hall, Piran had been supervising the building work. He certainly seemed to have succeeded in galvanising the team of shop-fitters, the dehumidifiers were on full blast and within days the dressing rooms had been repaired, new carpet and flooring were in place – everything seemed to be coming together nicely.

'Do we dare hope that we can pull this off?' said Penny.

'I daren't jinx it by even hoping,' Helen replied, as they sat watching the frenzied activity in the theatre auditorium. 'I spoke to Queenie on the way in. She's doing wonders in the box office. Apparently, tickets are selling like hot cakes.'

'Even though we haven't officially got the go-ahead from the council?'

'Seems that way.'

'Speak of the devil.' Penny had spotted the square, businesslike bulk of Joan Goodman walking up the central aisle.

'A word, if you please, Reverend Canter.'

Simon, who had been lending Piran a hand directing the works, welcomed the councillor and offered her a newly refurbished seat next to Helen and Penny.

'I must say, Vicar, I'm amazed at what you have managed to achieve in so short a time.'

'Colonel Stick's contribution was the miracle we were waiting for. God moves in mysterious ways.'

'Indeed He does,' said Joan. 'I think He may have been moving for you in another department too. I've had word from the fire service investigation team this morning. Apparently, they've discovered that the fire was caused by an electrical fault and was nothing to do with the candle. The wiring in the whole building is a problem. It should all have been replaced years ago – by the council.'

'So Brooke is in the clear? She'll be thrilled!' Helen clapped her hands.

'Completely in the clear. And the council have been found liable for making good on the work, since it was something they should have been doing all along. So that's one item that won't have to come out of your funds. We, the council will have to find the money.'

Simon was beside himself. He even gave Joan a hug – which she received rather unenthusiastically.

'Remember, though, you're not in the clear yet. This is only a temporary respite. You still have to win your case against Café Au Lait and find the funds to keep the theatre running as an ongoing concern.'

With that, Joan Goodman departed, her shoulder pads bearing all before her.

'Oh, stuff all that for today – we're finally on the up!' cried Penny, and she and Helen leapt up, unable to resist a little jig of joy.

*

Five days to opening night. Penny put the phone down and pushed back her office chair. 'Helen, we are sold out for the opening night!'

Helen gave a whoop of joy. 'All seventeen hundred and fifty seats?'

'All seventeen hundred and fifty.'

'And the rest of the week?'

'Not too bad, but I think much will depend on the reviews. Can't wait to see the final dress rehearsal.'

'I bumped into Jess in Queenie's the other day. She reckoned it was going well, but apparently there have been some tense moments.'

'Bound to be with these arty types. Jonathan's keeping things close to his chest, but he tells me he has every confidence.'

'Really? Brooke told me the Colonel had to give Jonathan a pep talk.'

'I expect she's exaggerating. We'll see for ourselves soon enough, won't we?'

*

Two days later a large delegation of SToP personnel took their seats for the theatre dress rehearsal. Penny had made certain that anyone who had helped in any way to get the theatre back on its feet was invited as a special guest.

The lumpy old seats had been dried out. The huge dome above their heads looked resplendent now that the soot had been washed away. The bar, the loos and the foyer had all been thoroughly cleaned and dressed with cheerful 1950s ephemera. Backstage, the dressing rooms had been restored. According to the cast, they were a big improvement on the state they'd been in before the fire. Just a waft of smoke remained in the air – like an autumn bonfire.

Rehearsals had moved from the church hall to the theatre and Jonathan was seen walking from the pass door to the stalls. Keeping his head down so he wouldn't have to acknowledge any of the expectant faces in the audience, he settled himself at the back of the stalls where he could chew nervously on his pencil and write last-minute notes for the cast and crew.

Slowly the house lights dimmed leaving the 'tab warmers' to glow on the velvet of the old red curtains which had been clean, patched but were now a little singed. From the orchestra pit the band struck up a merry overture, the curtains flew open and *Hats Off, Trevay!* took off.

*

Jess was talking to Ryan on the phone. 'The flight's delayed? . . . When will you know? . . . But you should make it? . . . Of course I understand . . . I know, and you won't be letting me down . . . these things happen . . . OK . . . fingers crossed . . . I love you too . . . bye . . . bye.'

She put the phone down on the bed covers and looked

at her alarm clock. It was 9.00 p.m. The show opened tomorrow at 7.30 p.m. and Ryan was still in LA, which is eight hours behind the UK. He was at LAX airport now, at the start of a journey that should take eighteen hours door-to-door, so providing the plane took off in the next eleven hours he should make it. She found a pen and some paper and started scribbling the calculations. She was tired and she wasn't sure if any of it was right. Tears pricked her eyes in self-pity. All she wanted was for Ryan to be there for her.

She got out of bed and went downstairs to let the girls out for their last wee. Brooke was typing an email. She pressed 'send' as Jess opened the back door to let the girls out.

'Bloody men,' sighed Brooke.

'I couldn't agree more,' replied Jess tartly. 'What's happened?'

'Louis doesn't know whether he's coming or not. He wants to, but he's working in London tomorrow and he doesn't know what time he can get away.'

'Oh.' Elsie and Ethel trotted in from the garden and Jess locked the back door. 'Ryan's stuck in a departure lounge. His flight has been delayed.'

'Oh.'

'Hmm.'

'Fancy a drink?'

'Shouldn't really. I need to sleep.'

'Me too.'

'But a glass of whisky maybe . . . ?'

'Can't hurt.'

'I'll get it.' Jess went to find the bottle and two glasses.

As she walked back into the drawing room, Brooke's phone buzzed, signalling a text.

'It's from Ollie.' Brooke opened it and read: 'Can't sleep. Can I come over?'

Jess turned and walked back to the kitchen. 'I'll get another glass.'

Within seconds Ollie was knocking at the door. He hugged them both. 'I was outside when I texted. Went for a drive and found myself here. I saw your lights were on. Don't mind, do you?'

'Not at all.' Jess made space for him on the sofa. They sat in silence. Subdued. Nervous.

'I heard from Red.'

The girls looked up sharply.

'She says she's coming.'

32

On opening night the buzz in the foyer was incredible. Outside, the car park was filling up and the great and the good were pushing their way through to the bars. Penny spotted Piran and Helen near the steps to the circle. She pulled Simon towards her and shouted above the noise: 'There they are. Helen's in a white dress. See?' She pointed and Simon saw them. He leaned towards his wife's ear and said, 'I'll get the drinks and bring them over.' She gave him a thumbs up in answer and squeezed her way towards her best friends.

In dressing room one, the Colonel was applying his make-up carefully and without undue haste.

The tannoy crackled into life: 'Good evening, ladies and gentlemen.' It was stage manager Dan. 'This is your half-hour call. Half an hour please.'

The Colonel checked his watch: 6.55. The 'half' in a theatre is always called thirty-five minutes before a performance and the Colonel was pleased that Dan was spot on.

One of the runners popped his head round the door. 'Shall I check your personal props, Colonel?'

'Yes, please do,' replied the Colonel.

The runner checked that he had his cigar, large silk handkerchief, pocket watch, silver half a crown, magician's bouquet made of feathers (which would be stowed up his sleeve), and small replica pistol.

Brooke and Jess were sitting in front of their mirrors in dressing gowns, having their wigs fixed by the wig mistress, Julie (proprietor of Julie's Hair Boutique, just off Trevay's Fore Street) and her assistant Dawn. They had made a pact not to mention the name Louis or Ryan or whether either man would make it to the show or not.

Jess had received a text from Emma:

Break an arm or whatever it is you're supposed to do! We'll be down to see your sure-to-be legendary performance for ourselves soon. You're all over the news! xxxx

'I can't find my eyelash glue,' said Brooke.

'I've got some. I bought a big tube. Here.'

She pushed it over to Brooke as Dawn secured the wig with a final pin and push. 'Thanks, Dawn.'

Dawn put her hands either side of Jess's head and gave the wig a final squish and wiggle. 'Does that feel secure?'

Jess gave her head a rapid shake. 'Yeah. Feels fine.'

Julie was doing the same to Brooke's platinum Marilyn Monroe-style wig, and after a final spritz of hairspray Dawn and Julie left them on their own.

Jess watched as Brooke took the longest, thickest pair of eyelashes she had ever seen out of their box. 'Blimey, what size are they?'

'Eyelure Two-o-two's. Miss Coco wore them in the fifties.'

Jess shook out her rather puny lashes from their box. 'I've only got one-o-ones.'

The tannoy made them jump. 'Ladies and gentlemen, this is your quarter-hour call. Fifteen minutes, please.'

*

Outside in the foyer, Queenie had been rushed off her feet in the tiny box office, but it had quietened down and there were just a few stragglers left, rushing through the foyer to make sure that they got their drinks and made it to their seats before curtain up.

'Couldn't 'alf do with a cuppa,' she said to herself. 'Only ten minutes to go.'

Just then, the main doors opened and in walked an incredibly handsome, tanned and fit-looking man. Dressed in perfectly fitting jeans, a white polo shirt and with a loose cardigan draped over his shoulders, he bore the unmistakable look of an out-of-towner. While Cornishmen were unquestionably handsome and rugged, Queenie couldn't remember any of them looking quite so striking as this man.

'Allo, can I 'elp?'

'Good evening, ma'am.' His accent was American. That explained it. 'I'd like to buy a ticket for tonight's performance.'

'Sorry to disappoint you, sir . . .' For some reason, Queenie found herself putting on her best voice and patting her blue rinse just to make sure that every hair was in place. 'Tickets sold out days ago. 'ottest ticket in town, y'know. Not got any seats until next week. Been all over the news, this theatre 'as.'

'Yes, ma'am. I've been reading about it and seen the news on TV. This is a great building. It deserves to be saved.'

'In the theatre business yourself, are you?'

'In a way, ma'am, you could say that.'

Queenie was beginning to feel sure that she had seen this man before.

''Aven't I seen you about somewhere?'

'I don't believe we've had the pleasure. But I hope we will. Good evening.'

And with that, he left. Just as Helen came out to see how it was all going.

'Who was that, Queenie?' she asked, watching the retreating back.

'Can't remember. But you wait – it'll come to me. I know I've seen 'im somewhere.'

*

Penny put her hand to her mouth and handed her glass to Simon. 'Excuse me a minute . . .'

She rushed to the ladies closest to the bar, knowing she was going to be sick. There was only one loo and the queue was long. There was nothing for it but to be sick in one of the hand basins.

'I'm so sorry,' she said to the faces staring at her in the mirror. 'Nerves, I suppose.' She ran the tap, rinsed her mouth and cleaned the sink. 'I really am so sorry.'

*

Jonathan had been to all the dressing rooms and delivered an uplifting speech in each one. It had been a nerve-wracking week, but he'd got his emotions back under control and was now in the wings taking deep breaths. He patted the shoulders of the backstage crew as they walked by and thanked them for all their hard work.

As he looked on, Miss Coco took her brood of dancers through their warm-up and stretches. He smiled at her and she gave him a wave in return. Things had improved immensely between them after he'd discovered that her favourite perfume was L'Heure Bleue by Guerlain; he'd presented her with a huge bottle by way of apology for his outburst. A trail of it was pervading the wings right now.

Ollie was feeling the fear. Nothing from Red. Her phone was registering number unavailable and he had no idea whether she'd be out front or not. He almost hoped she wouldn't be. The fuss and distraction of having her in the audience would be too much to bear. To calm his nerves, he decided to take his presents in to Jess and Brooke.

'Come in,' sang Brooke as he knocked on their door. He entered and found her smiling dizzily with her arms round a huge silver ice bucket containing tequila, peach schnapps, vodka and gin. 'It's from Louis,' she explained. 'And those.' She nodded towards a floral display so vast it would have fitted in at a horse-jumping event.

'Very nice!' said Ollie. 'Is he here then?'

'Don't know. Better not to think about it.'

'God, yes. I feel the same way.'

'Oh, is Red coming?'

'Best not to think about it.'

Jess remained quiet and was re-powdering her nose. Ollie mimed to Brooke, 'Any news from Ryan?'

Brooke opened her eyes wide and gave a subtle shake of the head.

Ollie remembered the packages in his hands. 'Presents for my best girls.'

For Brooke there was a pure silk dressing gown and for Jess a necklace of silvered seashells.

'Ladies and gentlemen, this is your five-minute call. Five minutes please.'

*

'Are you OK, Pen?' asked Helen. 'I've just overheard someone saying you were sick in the ladies.'

'Oh God. Don't. I'm so embarrassed. It must be nerves. I've never felt so sick in my life.'

'Have you had anything to eat?'

'Not since breakfast. I think the wine on an empty stomach did it.'

'I'll ask Piran to get you a soft drink.'

'I'll be fine, honestly.'

'If you're sure . . .'

'I'm sure. Come on, let's find our seats. It's nearly time.'

*

In the wings, Jonathan looked out through the small patch of gauze which allowed him to see the audience but kept them from seeing him. In the stalls he counted the faces of at least four major theatre critics from London. They could make or break a show. He prayed silently to a God he wasn't sure existed.

Stage manager Dan, sitting at his desk in the prompt corner, script opened up in front of him and headphones on, was talking to the sound and lights team in their positions at the back of the auditorium. 'Stand by, please,' he warned them.

'Standing by,' came the reply.

Dan made his final call to the dressing rooms: 'Ladies and gentlemen, this is your Beginners Act One call. Would Miss Lynne, Miss Tate, Colonel Irvine, Mr Pinkerton and the dancers please make their way to the stage. This is your Act One Beginners call. Good luck, everyone.'

33

The curtain calls went on for ever. The audience gave the young dancers and the juvenile leads appreciative whistles and catcalls, and when Jess, Ollie and Brooke bounded down the grand staircase at the back of the stage, the entire theatre got to their feet in a standing ovation. Ollie kissed the hands of Brooke and Jess in turn, then stepped back and gave them the chance to have their own moment's applause. They then pulled him downstage to take his roar of approval. The final and loudest cheer went to Colonel Walter Irvine. He stood at the top of the stairs, tall and still, acknowledging the accolade with dignity and humility. With ineffable timing, he started the long walk to the front of the stage, gave a deep bow and raised his hands to quieten the theatre.

'Well, I must say, I have enjoyed myself tonight,' he declared. This produced a gale of laughter. He silenced them again. 'In 1954, when I was a young man fresh out of the army, I came to this theatre as its first manager. Our opening show was this one, *Hats Off, Trevay!*, written by me with some help from the marvellous Mr Max Miller, and of course my partner, the late Peter Winship, the original director.'

Some cheers of recognition from older members of the audience.

'Max and I had a ball that night too. I never imagined I'd be here again, and among so many talented performers and our wonderful director, Jonathan.' He looked round at the cast gathered behind him. 'I want to thank them all for breathing new life into an old show and an old man.' His voice cracked, and as he reached in his pocket for his handkerchief to wipe his eyes, the band struck up the theme song of the show, 'The Trevay Tattoo'. As the crowd once again got to their feet and started to clap in time to the beat, the cast gave one more rousing rendition of the song that would follow them throughout the rest of the summer.

*

A fleet of minibuses took the entire cast, band and crew to the party, which was being held on the roof of the Starfish Hotel, where the roof terrace offered a stunning view of the harbour with the twinkling lights of Trevay reflected on the water. It was a cool, clear night with a new moon.

Ollie came back from the bar laden with a tray of drinks for himself, Jess and Brooke, and also Penny, Helen, Piran and Simon.

'Here we go. The barman has made some gruesome cocktail called "Trevay Tipple". I couldn't say no, but I've also smuggled' – he reached into the inner pocket of his jacket – 'a bottle of this.' It was gin, which he splashed into each of the vile green 'Trevay Tipples' on the tray. 'Here's to us and those that love us. Down the hatch.'

The others laughed and gasped as he put the cocktail glass containing the grim-looking drink to his lips and swallowed in one, then wiped his mouth with the back of his hand.

'Quite gruesome – but it hits the spot,' came the verdict.

''Aven't they any beer?' asked Piran, eyeing his glass suspiciously. 'I'd rather have a pint of Doom Bar.'

Helen nudged him. 'God, you're such a traditionalist! I promise I'll get you a beer after you've drunk this. Come on. We'll do it together. One, two, three . . .'

Helen linked arms with her stubborn boyfriend and together they drank it down. After a moment they looked at each other and spoke as one: 'Disgusting.'

'I need a pint to take the taste away.' Piran was wiping his beard and moustache. 'Is that what you drink in London, young Ollie?'

'All the time,' giggled Ollie, who was pouring neat gin into his glass and offering the bottle to Jess and Brooke. 'Come on, Penny. Your go.'

Penny put her hand over her glass. 'No, no thank you. I've had enough. I'll stick to soft drinks from now on.'

Ollie didn't hear her answer as he was being swamped by a gaggle of teenage girls who all had their camera phones out wanting to have their pictures taken with him.

Helen looked at Penny's face and thought she looked a bit tired. 'Are you OK, Pen? Still feeling sick?'

'A bit, but I'll be fine.'

'Have you told Simon?'

As she said this, she watched as the colour drained from Penny's face and a look of panic crossed her features. 'I'm going to be sick.'

'Let me take you to the ladies.'

'No time . . .' Penny had turned and was retching into the pot of a conveniently placed fig tree.

Helen dug in her bag for a packet of a tissues and a piece of chewing gum. 'Here.' She offered them to Penny, who took both appreciatively.

'I'm going to tell Simon that you need to go home,' said Helen, expecting opposition from Penny, but none came.

Over at the bar, Helen caught Simon's eye and explained what had happened.

'She never said anything.'

'Didn't she mention that she was sick before the show?' asked Helen.

'Was she?' Simon was looking really worried now. 'I'll get her home and tuck her up. Do you think I should call the doctor?'

Helen thought for a moment. 'I think she'll be all right. Until the morning anyway. Just get her into bed and then I'll come over tomorrow and see how she is.'

'Thank you, Helen.' Simon squeezed her hand and kissed her goodnight before collecting Penny and walking her slowly to the exit.

'What's the matter with them?' asked Piran, returning with a pint in his hand and froth on his moustache.

'Penny's got a tummy upset. She's been a bit sick tonight. She'll be fine. Just the build up of nerves over the last few months, I suppose.'

*

Outside the Starfish, Simon placed Penny carefully in the front passenger seat of his old Volvo. 'There, I'll have you home in a jiffy.'

He climbed into the driver's seat and, after fiddling with the keys for a moment under the interior light, he put them in the ignition and turned. Nothing. Penny sat very still. He tried again. Nothing.

Penny looked straight ahead. 'Don't tell me the bloody

thing isn't going to start.' She said it in her special quiet but dangerous voice that Simon hated.

'It's going to be fine.' He tried again. Still nothing. And again. No. And yet again. No.

Penny heaved a big sigh and unclipped her seat belt. 'Well, you can keep at it all night, but I'm going home in a cab.'

'Darling, please. Just give it a couple more minutes.' He tried smiling at her.

'I need to go home.' She opened the car door and stepped out. 'There're a couple of taxis on the rank by the harbour. Come on.'

Simon wouldn't budge. 'No. It will start in a minute. Patience is a virtue, and I'm not wasting money on a taxi.'

That did it. Penny slammed the car door in his face and set off for the taxi rank. Just as she crossed the road to the harbour wall, Simon saw her lean over the railings and vomit into the water below.

'Oh shit.'

In the taxi home, Penny leaned her head on Simon's shoulder. 'Thank you for coming with me, Simon. I'm sure I'll be fine in the morning.'

*

Back at the party, Ollie was downing drinks like a man on a mission. He was flirting with every girl there. Jess and Brooke watched him do his thing.

'He's really cut up about Red not being here. That's what this is all about. She didn't call him. Not even a text.'

'And what about you, Jess?' Brooke looked at her friend. 'Anything from Ryan?'

Jess looked down at the glass in her hand. 'No.'

'Still hopin', tho?' Brooke said in her best Monroe voice, pulling a girlie face to make Jess laugh.

Jess did so reluctantly. 'Yeah, I suppose so. Maybe he's going to turn up any second and surprise me. Or maybe he's at Granny's Nook?'

'Has he got a key?'

'Yes.'

'Hmm. Well. Maybe.'

They stopped talking and watched as Ollie hit the dance floor. His muscled thighs looked good in his tight jeans and his T-shirt accentuated his abs to perfection.

'He's not a bad-looking bloke, is he?' offered Jess.

'If he wasn't Ollie, I'd definitely have a go.'

'Would you?'

'Yeah.'

'But it would be odd, wouldn't it? Him being Ollie and all.'

'Weird.'

'Yeah. Really weird.'

*

Jonathan approached them through the throng and kissed them both. 'Congratulations! You were both amazing tonight. You deserve your success. Here's to you both.' He stopped a passing waiter who was carrying a tray with a bucket of champagne and four glasses.

'Ah, sir – I couldn't see you in the crowd. Where shall I put this?'

'On the table here, please.'

The three of them watched as the waiter expertly opened the champagne without spilling a drop and poured the bubbling liquid into the glasses. 'If you need anything else, sir, just give me the nod.'

'Thank you.' Jonathan handed the girls a glass each and made a toast. 'To my two leading ladies, with love and gratitude.'

At some parties every minute feels like an hour. Fortunately, this wasn't one of them. The hours slipped by until only the hardcore revellers were left. As the night gave way to a soft sunrise in the east, Miss Coco was on the dance floor trying to teach Jonathan the quick step. The Colonel, Piran and Helen were drinking large cups of hot chocolate, wrapping their hands round them for warmth and discussing the history of Trevay and the Pavilions in particular.

Ollie was draped all over Jess, telling her how bad he felt over breaking up with Red. 'I never saw her, but I miss her,' he slurred.

'I know.' Jess stroked his head.

'I'm not good at picking girls. I need someone who's just normal and nice. Not these fricking head cases. Where are all the normal girls, Jess?'

'There are lots of us about.'

'How do I spot one?'

'Well, we're just . . . normal.'

'Is Ryan normal?'

Jess had to consider this for a minute. 'Yeah. I think so. As normal as a bloke gets. He doesn't hear me when I ask him to put the rubbish out and he thinks farting is acceptable in front of me, so . . . yeah. He's normal.'

'But he's a superstar. Red's a superstar. That's not normal.'

Jess was distracted from this line of conversation by the look of pure shock that had crossed Brooke's face.

'Brooke, what's the matter?'

'Turn round.' Brooke instructed.

Jess did as she was told and almost knocked Ollie to the floor as she leapt to her feet in shock.

'You didn't think I'd miss my baby's first night, did you?'

It was Ryan, looking impossibly handsome in a Tom Ford evening suit and carrying a dozen peach roses.

'Ryan! Oh, Ryan.' She walked into his arms and melted into the feel and the smell of this man she loved so much.

A couple of journos who hadn't been able to tear themselves away from the party or the free booze found themselves with a scoop on their hands. With no photographers on hand, they snapped some shots with their smartphones and asked excitable questions.

'When did you get here, Ryan?'

'Did you see the show, Ryan?'

'What did you think of the missus tonight, Ryan?'

Ryan stood in the glow of the rising sun and answered their questions politely, all the while hugging and kissing Jess. She felt she'd never loved him more. But his place in the sun was not to last. A shadow fell over Ryan's ego as Louis, obviously the worse for wear, staggered out of the roof terrace lift with two boxes of Maltesers in one hand and a box of Twister in the other.

'Hey, gorge.' He pointed at Brooke who giggled with delight. 'Wanna have some fun?'

She ran towards him and he pulled her into an alcoholic snog.

'How did you get here?' she asked breathlessly.

Louis tried to locate Hutch by spinning on one foot and almost falling over. 'Aha! There he is. My man Hutch.

He got me in the car and he drove all night.' He kissed her again. 'That's a good name for a song.'

The journos deserted Ryan like rats from a sinking ship, and were now swarming all over Louis and Brooke. This was the Big Story.

34

Hutch must have radioed for assistance because six plainclothes officers appeared on the roof terrace and bundled the small group into the lift and down into a fleet of waiting people carriers.

All Jess knew, a few hours later, was that she was lying in her own bed, in Granny's Nook, next to the sleeping form of Ryan.

She got slowly out of bed and pulled on her dressing gown. Downstairs the kitchen clock said 8.35. She could only have been asleep for a couple of hours and yet last night's adrenalin was still coursing through her body.

She put the kettle on and rustled up a couple of mugs.

'Hi.' The voice behind her made her jump.

'Oh. Ollie! What are you doing here?'

'I slept on the sofa. You just walked past me.'

'Did I? Sorry. I was miles away.' She reached up for another mug. 'Is Louis here?'

'I don't know. I was in the last vehicle. I think we dropped Jonathan at his place and then Miss Coco at hers. My memory's a bit of a blank.'

'Why didn't you stay in your own room at the Starfish?'

'Oh yeah.' He thumped his forehead with his hand. 'Doh. In all the excitement I suppose I . . . it was like being in an action movie, wasn't it?'

Jess laughed. 'Yeah. When all those guys appeared and grabbed us . . . who were they anyway?'

Ollie shrugged. 'No idea, but what fun for Louis to have those kind of people looking out for you.'

Jess went to the fridge to get the milk. 'There's no milk – see if the milkman has left some on the step, would you?'

'Sure.' Ollie walked out of the kitchen and towards the front door. Jess heard him scream in fright and the door being banged shut. He skidded into the kitchen, empty-handed, and said, 'I think Louis *is* here.'

Jess lifted the kitchen blind half a centimetre and peered out. The garden was full of reporters and photographers. One young woman in a pencil skirt and stilettos was approaching the front door. Jess let the blind drop just as the knock came.

'Leave it,' she hissed at Ollie as he dropped to his knees in fright.

'But they know we're here,' he whispered.

'We've got the kettle, a fridge full of food, a loo and the telly, so we can hole up for days,' she whispered back, kneeling beside him.

'We've got to get out to do the show though.'

'Not till later . . . they won't stay all day, will they?'

Both of them froze at the sound of the back-door handle rattling.

'Oh my God. Who's that?'

'It's me, Hutch.'

Jess and Ollie slowly straightened up.

Hutch, dressed in camouflage trousers and jacket with a black woollen beanie on his head, slipped through the door and bolted it behind him.

'OK, here's what we are going to do . . .'

Apparently, on the night they had heard noises in the garden and Hutch had spirited Louis out of the village, the perpetrators had been extra security officers who were recce-ing any escape route that their vulnerable charge might one day need. Hutch had been briefed shortly after and had just now been checking it out. The garden of Granny's Nook backed onto the old church and its graveyard. To the left ran the narrow lane leading to Shellsand Bay and a dead end. To the right were the neighbours' back gardens and the lane to Trevay.

'We're going to create two diversions. I've got a vehicle parking in the lane to Trevay as we speak and another is due to arrive outside the cottage. Jess, is Ryan awake?'

'I can wake him.'

'Good. Tell him to get dressed and come down straight away. Ollie?'

'Yes?'

'I want you to get dressed too. You are both about to play the role of Prince Louis.'

There was another knock at the front door. Jess flinched.

Hutch looked at her urgently. 'You're going to open the door and tell them he's not here. Don't be too good an actress. I want them to think you are lying.'

Jess held her hands to her chest and pulled her dressing gown round her more tightly. 'OK.'

'Wait till Ollie and I go upstairs before opening the door. We'll get Ryan and Louis ready. Just keep them talking. You'll know when to stop.'

'Oh. OK.'

She watched as the two men slipped up the stairs, grateful that she'd got into the habit of shutting all the curtains at night in case Louis dropped by and any nosy neighbours came peeking.

The knock on the door sounded again, louder.

A young woman's voice called through the letter box: 'Brooke? Louis? I just want a quick word with you. I'm from the *Daily Mirror*. I can make all these other people go away if you just let me in.'

Jess took a deep breath to prepare for one of the scariest performances of her life. She opened the door just a crack. The photographers picked up their cameras and let off a volley of flashes.

'Good morning.' She tried to look friendly and innocent. 'It's awfully early. We had a very late night last night. How can I help you?'

The female journalist, who was trying to see round Jess into the cottage, replied, 'Miss Tate, I am so pleased to meet you. I think you were wonderful in *Horse Laugh*, by the way.' She was offering her hand. 'My name's Julia. How did the show go last night?'

Jess looked at this seemingly nice, well-mannered young woman. She had no pen or notebook in her hand, so she wasn't making a note of this conversation. All she was holding was her phone. Curious, Jess took a closer look at the phone. 'Are you recording our conversation?'

Julia smiled, unabashed. 'Of course. Always recording.'

'Isn't it polite to let people know you are recording them?'

'Well, you do know, so that's all right.' She looked over her shoulder at the press pack behind her. They were clearly in cahoots. Send in the least dangerous-looking of them to get a foot in the door and then go in like a pack of wolves. She turned back to Jess. 'Don't worry about them. They'll back off just as soon as we get a quick word and a photo.'

'Of whom?'

Julia gave a snort of derision. 'Who do you think, Miss Tate? My editor will make sure that you, personally, get some great reviews for the show and a healthy donation to your favourite charity. Let me in and we can have a chat.'

Julia put her foot over the threshold, but Jess stood fast. 'How much?'

'Aw, that's better. Like I said, let me in, Jess – I can call you Jess, can't I? – and we'll have a cuppa. I take it Louis is in bed? With Brooke?'

Out of the corner of her eye, Jess could see a black saloon car turning into the village from the Bodmin road. It slunk along the edges of the village green before stopping, silently, opposite the gate of Granny's Nook. So quiet was it, that the press pack didn't hear it.

Jess switched into acting mode, looking more nervy than she felt: 'Well, I've been told to say nothing and I really don't know much but—'

She couldn't say more because a tall figure with a blanket covering him ran past behind her and out towards the back door. There was the sound of the door opening and then a gust of wind blew through the house.

Julia immediately dropped the pleasantries and turned to the pack: 'The bastard's just gone out the back way,' she yelled.

Half the press corps turned, stumbling through the front gate, some turning left, some right. The other half stayed put, guessing that this was a ruse.

Julia stayed with them and turned back to Jess. 'We will get him and the story, you know. We always do.'

Before Jess could answer, a strong hand gripped her shoulder from behind and pulled her back into the house. She saw two men, one covered in a blanket, the other was Hutch. They ran through the pack as two police cars, sirens and lights blaring, turned onto the village green. The officers kept the press gang at bay as the two figures jumped into the black saloon and drove off towards Bodmin.

When the car had disappeared from sight, the police officers cautioned the company of press men and escorted them away from the village.

Jess slammed the front door shut behind her.

The phone rang. It was Hutch.

'Well done. You all right?'

'Yes. Is Louis OK?'

'Go upstairs and ask him.'

'You mean he's still here?'

'Yeah, but not for long. I've got your boyfriend with me. Want a word?'

'Hi, babe. That was rather thrilling, wasn't it? Can't talk – there's a suspicious motorcyclist following us. Hutch has offered me a lift back to town . . .'

'Town? You mean Trevay?'

'No, honey, London town, so I'll get out of your hair. Speak later, babe. Love you.' She heard the receiver being passed over. 'Jess? It's Hutch. You've got a job to do. Listen . . .'

*

When Jess went upstairs, she found Brooke and Louis lying in bed watching the news. There were photos of Louis, three sheets to the wind, arriving at last night's party. And then they cut to a picture of him hugging and kissing Brooke, while some pompous old commentator intoned, 'The Queen will not be amused. Yes, this boy may be a lesser member of the royal family but he is a royal. This is a major embarrassment for the Palace.'

The camera cut away from the photos and back to the studio where a pretty young woman was arguing in Louis' favour: 'Look, this is a young man the country has taken a real shine to. He's brave, he's dashing and he's behaving like one of us. Why shouldn't he go to a party and have some fun with his girlfriend?'

The male presenter chipped in: 'Ah, but is she his girlfriend? There are reports, not denied by the palace, that she is an old family friend and that Louis turned up to support her at the opening night of *Hats Off, Trevay!* – a show that's been staged in the hope of saving a theatre in Cornwall from demolition. And from the reviews in today's papers, it is a hit.'

Jess found the remote control and pressed the mute button.

'Look you two, I'm on a mission – Hutch's orders. Louis, get up. You have five minutes before the press pack come slithering back and in that time I've got to get you down to Shellsand Bay. We have to walk down – all three of us, ideally – as if we're just taking a stroll. On the beach, there will be a boat that'll get you to safety.'

Neither Brooke nor Louis moved. 'I've got a hell of a headache,' Louis groaned.

Jess had had all she could take. On the floor she spotted a pair of jeans, which she assumed belonged to Louis; she picked them up, threw them at him and shouted, 'Just DO IT!'

*

The second performance of any show usually lacks the lustre of the opening night. It was certainly the case for *Hats Off, Trevay!*. Poor Ollie, having been bundled out of the back door and into the car parked in the lane at the side of the churchyard, had been driven off towards Newquay, where the driver, who needed to get back to Hutch, had to leave him. It had taken Ollie over an hour to get back to Trevay and his hotel room.

Once Jess had managed to get Louis to do as he was told, she and Brooke had joined him for the walk to the beach with Elsie and Ethel in tow. They'd watched as Louis was whisked off to safety in his boat. It was all just in the nick of time, because as the girls returned to Granny's Nook the photographers were already gathering in their cars.

A few reporters had hung around all day and followed them to the theatre, but most abandoned the stakeout, knowing the story had gone cold.

The green room was agog. As Brooke walked in, a hush fell over the company.

'It's OK,' said Brooke. 'Yes, he was here. No, he's not here now. And that's all I'm going to say.'

Miss Coco was the first to speak. 'My dear, I think it's all very exciting and marvellous publicity for the show. Have you seen the reviews?'

All the critics, even the sniffier ones, had agreed that the show was perfect for a seaside audience and offered the hope that other crumbling end-of-the-pier theatres would save themselves in a similar fashion. Ollie, Brooke and Jess got sparkling critiques, but the undisputed star, all the papers agreed, was Colonel Stick. He'd been giving interviews all day and there was talk of an important publisher wooing him for his autobiography. When he arrived at 6.45 p.m. prompt, the Colonel was met with a resounding three cheers from the entire company.

35

Things settled down over the next few days. Ryan was back in LA, Louis had been given a dressing down by the powers that be and was on a very short leash. He was not going to be allowed out for some time. And Red made the papers declaring she was in love with a talented young female comedienne and that they intended to adopt children from around the world.

'Hey, babe. I haven't woken you, have I?'

Jess, who had been in bed only five minutes, shook off her sleepiness. 'Of course not, darling. Are you OK? You don't normally call me at this time.'

She could hear chatter and laughing coming through the satellites all the way from Hollywood.

'Everything's fine. I'm just off to the big studio do. You know the one I told you about?'

Jess didn't know but blamed her tired memory. 'Oh yes?'

'Yeah. I just wanted you to know they've paired me up with Serena again. They're going large on the PR for *Venini* and they want to milk our working relationship for all it's worth.'

Jess settled back on her pillows. Bless Ryan for thinking of her and reassuring her. 'That's OK, honey. Have a great time. She's a nice woman.'

'Actually, she's right next to me and wants a word.'

'No, it's OK—'

'Hi, Tess! Thanks for lending me your man. I'll look after him for you. I really need to get a Ryan of my own.'

'Someone as gorgeous as you will have no problem.'

'Oh, you're sweet. I'll pass you back. Bye!'

'Bye . . .'

'Jess, babe.' It was Ryan again. 'Gotta go. We're at a pre-party and the limos are arriving.'

'OK. Have a good time.'

They said their goodnights and Jess put the phone back on her bedside table. She rested her head on her soft pillow and allowed herself to drift off again. Her last conscious thought was, 'Did Serena really just call me Tess?'

*

The following day was a Saturday and Trevay was heaving with holidaymakers. School was out for the summer and children and adults alike were as horses out of the trap: eyes shining, mouths grinning and feet, thrillingly, galloping to the box office.

The matinee was full and the audience appreciative. In the break between the afternoon and evening performance, the cast and crew decided to order in fish and chips and sit round the small television in the green room. There was a football match on, and Brooke and Jess, not being particular fans, took their food back to their dressing room and stretched out on their uncomfortable couch. As they were chatting there was a knock at the door and Jonathan stuck his head round. He'd taken a couple of days off to recharge his batteries and he was looking tanned and lean.

'Jonathan, you look like you've had a holiday,' said Brooke. 'Did we knacker you that much?'

He laughed. 'Yes. You are torture to work with!' He plonked himself in a free chair and leaned over to pinch a handful of Jess's chips. 'Actually . . .' he bit into one and fanned his mouth. 'Cor, they're hot! Actually, I nipped across to the South of France to meet a man about another job.'

'Oh?' chorused both women, more interested in their cod than anything else.

'Yes. I've been asked to direct a revival of Noël Coward's *Blithe Spirit*. It would start out of town and, with luck, go into the West End. It has two cracking female leads and one male lead, and I was thinking . . . who could I possibly cast?'

Neither woman spoke, not wanting to make fools of themselves if he meant them. Which they hoped he did.

Jonathan continued with mischief in his eyes, 'So I wanted to ask you both . . .'

'Yes . . .'

'What you thought of . . . Ollie to play the male lead? Do you think he'd say yes? Of course it would be dependent on who he wanted to play the two female roles. It has to be someone he likes. Trusts . . .'

Both Brooke and Jess were sitting up a little straighter with wooden chip forks poised between greasy paper and greasy lips.

'So . . .' He leaned forward to pinch a bit of batter from Brooke's portion. 'So, Jess . . .' Brooke's eyes turned from Jonathan to her friend or rival. Jonathan continued, 'When do you start filming again for *Horse Laugh*?'

Jess swallowed and put her fork down. 'October to January, I think.'

'So you'd be free February to May?'

'Yes.'

'And would you consider the role of Madame Arcati? Because I really couldn't think of anyone who'd play her better.'

'Gosh. Yes, I'd love to. I'd really love to.'

Brooke scrunched up her food in its paper and polystyrene package and threw it into the bin. 'Congratulations!' she said, trying to mean it. Then she added, 'Jonathan, you'll have another hit on your hands.'

'Oh, I don't know.' He looked at her teasingly. 'It's very much an ensemble piece, and if I don't get the right actress to play Elvira, the ghost of the dead wife, it'll be a disaster. . . . Brooke, I want you. You and Jess and Ollie are my dream team. Please say yes.'

Ollie found them all hugging and kissing. 'I love a group hug.' He put his arms around them as best he could. 'Do I gather we've got our two leading ladies?'

'We sure have,' laughed Jonathan.

'When did you hear about this?' Brooke asked.

'About five minutes before he came in and asked you. I'm thinking that tonight we need to celebrate. Dinner at the Starfish?'

'On me,' said Jonathan.

*

It was late and the restaurant was quiet when the happy party arrived. A very handsome, very camp waiter settled them into the table overlooking the familiar harbour view. A warm westerly wind ruffled the water and blew gently through the doors leading out to the terrace.

Brooke's phone rang and she excused herself to take

the call outside. Ollie left the table to go to his room and drop his bags. It left Jess and Jonathan together with Adam, the waiter. Jonathan ordered a bottle of Camel Valley Champagne.

Adam returned with the bottle and ice bucket and while he went through the rigmarole of showing the label to Jonathan and preparing to remove the cork he started to chat. 'How's the show going, Mr Mulberry?'

'Very well so far, thank you.'

'I'm hoping to see it on my day off.'

'Let me know when that is and I'll get you a pair of complimentary tickets.'

'Really? That would be amazing. Thank you. I love the theatre.'

'Do you go much?' asked Jonathan.

Jess watched their conversation and body language very carefully. Was Adam flirting with Jonathan? Jonathan was showing no signs of discomfort. He was getting out his wallet and was passing Adam his business card.

'Give me a call and we'll sort something out.'

'Thank you so so much.'

Adam, poured the champagne and touched Jonathan's hand. 'I can't believe it.'

'My pleasure,' said Jonathan.

Jess was in no doubt now about Jonathan's sexuality. She knew that she should be happy for him now that a little romance might be on the cards for him, but instead she felt annoyed. Before she had time to wonder why she might feel this way, Brooke appeared from the terrace, her eyes shining and her face flushed. 'Do you mind awfully if I run out on you? Louis has just phoned. He's going to be in Pendruggan in half an hour . . .'

'Oh, how lovely!' beamed Jess.

'The only thing is . . . darling Jess . . .' Brooke was starting to wheedle and Jess guessed what was coming.

'Yeeees?'

'Do you mind not coming home till a bit later? I haven't seen Lou for such a long time . . . it would be nice to pretend we were on our own . . . even though Hutch will be there.'

Jess and Jonathan waved her off with their blessing.

'You can always bunk in with me if it gets too late,' said Jonathan with a smile.

'Thanks. I might just have to.'

A few minutes later Ollie arrived and all they could talk about was *Blithe Spirit*.

It was Jonathan who couldn't stay up any longer and he said his goodnights first, leaving Jess and Ollie to it.

They wandered to the comfortable bar and ordered two large brandies.

'Jonathan's a good bloke, isn't he,' said Ollie stretching himself out in his vast armchair.

'Do you think he's gay?' asked Jess.

'Don't know. Don't care. Why do you ask?'

Jess told him what she'd witnessed between Jonathan and the waiter.

'Really?' Ollie yawned. 'Does it honestly matter?'

Jess felt embarrassed. 'No, of course not. I'm just wondering. Such a nice man. I want everyone to be happy. As happy as I am with Ryan.'

'Are you really happy, Jess?'

'Yes.' She flashed her engagement ring. 'I'm engaged, dontcha know.'

'Ah. Yes. And when are you getting married?'

'I was hoping Christmas.'

'Does Ryan know this?'

'He's been a bit distracted with work and stuff, but we'll find a quiet couple of days and do it.' She smiled shyly and put her hand to her lips. 'I've bought the dress.'

'Have you?' He shook his head disbelievingly. 'Miss Tate! You dark horse. Does Ryan know about that?'

She shook her head.

'He's a lucky man,' Ollie continued. 'If you didn't have that ring on your finger, I might make a play for you myself.'

She reached a leg out and kicked him.

'No, I would.' He rubbed his shin. 'We'd be great together. I like Ethel and Elsie. You like Cornwall. Ideal couple.'

'Yeah, right. I'm a bit old for you.'

He gave her a comedy wolf face. 'Oh my dear, but the older woman has so much experience.'

Jess was enjoying this banter. 'You're, what, twenty-eight?'

'According to my CV, yes. And you are . . . ?'

'According to my CV, thirty-five.'

They looked at each other for a moment and started to giggle.

'How old are you really?' asked Ollie.

'Thirty-eight.' Jess looked shame-faced. 'How old are you really?'

'Nearly thirty-four.'

'NO!'

'Yep.' He put out his foot and stroked Jess's ankle with his toes. 'If ever you want a toyboy . . .'

36

The taxi rattled its way from Trevay to Pendruggan and Jess, swaying in the back seat, smiled at her reflection. So Ollie lied about his age too? How hilarious. And how she had enjoyed his gentle flirting. She thought about him as a potential lover and just as quickly stopped. She couldn't imagine taking her clothes off in front of anyone other than Ryan now. She was slim but she had touches of sag and droop that she'd prefer to keep to herself, and Ollie was used to Red, who was only twenty-four. Red's body was fresh out of the cellophane and still made of lycra. Bone-hugging, soft and wrinkle free. Jess's was losing its elasticity and as for the pencil-under-the-boob test, well she could get a whole branch of Ryman's under hers. She stuck her tongue out at her reflection in the window and giggled. God, she was pissed. Supposing she'd stayed at the Starfish tonight; would Ollie have made a move? She closed her eyes to imagine him kissing her. It was a nice thought. How would his muscled arms feel through his shirt? She snapped her eyes open again. *Jess Tate, you are as good as married*, she told herself. *But it's rather nice to think someone as young and nice and gorgeous as Ollie could . . . Stop it, Jess!* she scolded herself. *He's in bed now, laughing at how he made a fool of you. Forget it. He's a friend. That's all.*

''Ere you go, my love.' The taxi driver pulled up outside Granny's Nook. 'Seven pounds twenty, please.'

She paid the cabbie and lurched her way up the garden path as quietly as she could. As she turned to shut the front door, she spotted on the other side of the green a familiar dark Range Rover. Louis was still here then. She flicked on the sitting-room light to illuminate her path across the floor to the stairs. Hutch was on the sofa in his sleeping bag. She'd woken him up.

'Hey, Jess. What time is it?' he asked, rubbing his eyes.

She looked at her watch. 'One thirty. Sorry, I forgot you'd be here. I wasn't supposed to come back.'

'That's all right.'

'Hi,' said another voice from the rug in front of the hearth.

Jess saw a man with his head on an armchair cushion and his body covered in the old throw that usually covered the sofa.

'Oh, that's Chris. Chris, this is Jess – Brooke's flatmate. Jess, this is Chris, my new partner. Since the last brouhaha, Louis needs two of us.'

'Is security that high for him?' Jess asked, trying to sound totally sober.

'Something like that.' Hutch looked at her carefully, 'Are you pissed, miss?'

'I don't think so.'

'Oh good. I like your shoes.'

'Thank you.' She looked down at them. They were on the wrong feet. No wonder she'd had trouble getting up the path.

'Just as long as you're OK then,' said Hutch, turning over to face the back of the sofa. 'Turn the light out on your way up.'

Upstairs on the landing she crept past the closed door of Brooke's bedroom. There was no light coming from under it and no sounds either.

When she was finally curled up in her own bed she wondered whether she ought to phone Ryan to check how the party had gone. It occurred to her that she hadn't heard from him in twenty-four hours. 'No news is good news,' she told herself, and immediately fell into a deep sleep.

*

'Jess! Jess!' A man's voice, close to her ear. It was him. She was sure of it. He mustn't come into her bedroom.

'Go away, Ollie,' she told him sternly, keeping her eyes tight shut. If she didn't look at him he'd go away.

'Jess, it's Chris. It's important.'

Chris? Who the hell was Chris and what was he doing in her room? My God, she was a man magnet!

'Chris, you're very sweet,' she mumbled into her pillow, 'but I'm engaged to Ryan.'

'Jess, wake up. Now.' He was shaking her awake.

She opened her eyes and slowly focused on the face of Louis' new detective. 'What's the matter?'

'We've got a bit of trouble.'

Jess pulled herself to wakefulness. Hutch was on the landing talking on the phone.

'What's happened?'

Hutch, finishing his call, came into her room pocketing the phone. 'We should have got Louis out of here before dawn, but . . .' He looked sheepish. 'We all overslept. Our friends from Fleet Street have been tipped off and they're starting to gather outside. Only two or three at the moment, but I've had to tell my bosses and four types of shit is about to land on my head. Would you do me a favour and go outside and tell them he's not here? It'll give me a chance to think of something.'

The door to Brooke's bedroom opened and she came out with Louis. They were both fully dressed and Louis was on his phone.

'Ma, listen to me . . . I'll get out of here . . . I know what I promised . . . there aren't many of them outside yet . . . I'm sorry . . . we'll talk about it when I get home . . . gotta go, Hutch is here . . . OK, Ma, see you soon. Bye. Bye.'

Jess's head was fuzzy from lack of sleep and excess booze, but she knew enough to realise that the royal boyf had just had a dressing down from his royal mama. What the hell had happened to her peaceful life?

She turned her attention to Chris and Hutch, who were looking very uncomfortable.

'So,' she said. 'You have all fucked up. Royally, if I may say so.' She laughed at her own joke but as no one else did she continued as soberly as she could manage: 'You want good old me to go out there, lie through my teeth and let you slip out the back way again. Am I right?'

Hutch shuffled a bit. 'In a nutshell.'

Jess swung her feet out of bed. 'OK, I'll do it. But this is the last time. They probably won't believe me anyway. I have done this before, remember?'

Brooke took Jess's dressing gown off the back of a chair and helped her into it. 'Thank you,' Jess breathed.

'Phwoar! You stink of booze.' Brooke wafted her hand in front of her face.

Jess gave her a withering look as she did up her robe. 'Do you want me to save your skin or not?'

'I do, I do. I'm sorry.'

Louis stepped forward and embraced Jess. 'Thank you, Jess. I promise this will never happen again.'

Jess ran a hand through her hair and set off down the stairs.

By the time she opened the front door she had her speech, all irate but dignified, prepared. She wasn't given a chance to use it. A grim-faced reporter shoved a photo in front of her as the usual flashbulbs popped. She frowned and pulled the photo closer. It came into focus. It was a picture of Ryan and Serena at a party.

Ryan and Serena kissing.

Ryan with his hand up Serena's skirt, caressing her be-thonged arse.

She dropped the picture and gave a little cry. She tried to slam the door in the face of the wretched reporter but he held it open with the palm of his hand.

'Sorry to have to break the news to you this way, Miss Tate, but Ryan has been a bit of a naughty boy. He and Serena Metcalfe are engaged. What's your reaction?'

Jess felt nauseous. Last night's brandy was making its way up her throat. 'I . . .'

'Let me read you the statement Miss Metcalfe's publicist released early this morning.' He reached into his pocket for another piece of paper. 'It says, "Serena Metcalfe is thrilled to let the world know of her love for *Venini* star Ryan Hearst. Love has bowled them both over and last night at a star-studded party Mr Hearst proposed to her and she accepted."'

Jess felt nothing as she hit the floor.

*

The shock was so great that when Jess came to, as she was being carried to the sofa, she didn't know what had happened. Brooke was being kind to her and stroking her hand, Hutch was brewing some strong coffee and Louis was apologising over and over.

'What do you keep saying sorry for, Louis?' she asked. 'Have you hurt me? I don't feel hurt. It must have been an accident.'

Brooke looked anxiously at Jess's pale face and placed a hand on her forehead to test her temperature. 'Darling, you've had a nasty fall. I think you may have bumped your head.'

'It does ache a bit, but I think that's because Ollie and I had a bit too much to drink last night. He flirted with me. Bless him.'

'Did he? He's coming over soon.'

'Why?'

'He heard about . . .' Brooke checked herself and came up with an alternative ending: 'He heard you had a fall.'

'Oh.' Jess still didn't understand. 'What's happened to me? Why are you all looking so worried? If there's something serious, Ryan had better know. He's in LA at the moment.'

'Yes, we know,' said Brooke, kissing Jess's fingers as a mother might a child's.

A thought crossed Jess's mind. 'Is Ryan all right? Has something happened to him?'

Hutch brought the tray of coffee in and put it on the low table by the sofa. 'Here you are, Jess. Sit up a bit and get this down you.'

The coffee was very strong, hot and sweet. Jess took a sip and pulled a face. 'That's horrible. What are you giving me this for?'

Hutch sat down next to her and very gently told her why.

It all came flooding back. Jess had never known pain like it. She almost couldn't breathe for it. She clung to Hutch like a drowning woman to a piece a driftwood and sobbed.

At the peak of her exhaustion, Louis and Brooke helped her to bed.

The minute they left her alone, she found her bag and her mobile phone in it. She dialled Ryan's number. She left the worst kind of message on it. Vitriolic, disbelieving and teary. She redialled and repeated a similar message every few minutes until Brooke looked in on her and confiscated the phone. 'He's not going to pick up,' Brooke told her gently.

'Have you tried?' sniffed Jess.

'Yes. Several times. And I've emailed – but nothing.'

Jess, clutching at straws, checked the time. 'It's the time difference. He's asleep. He always turns the phone off when he's asleep. Or . . . maybe he's on the plane. That's it. He's flying home to tell me it's not true. I must check the flights.' She tried to get out of bed, but Brooke held her and wouldn't let her go.

'Darling, it's over. There's no mistake.'

Jess looked at Brooke with hatred and almost spat in her face. 'How dare you say that! You haven't a clue what Ryan and I feel for each other. It's that witch Serena who's putting out these lies.'

Brooke let go of Jess. 'OK. I think you'd better come downstairs and watch Sky News. They're running the story every fifteen minutes. Come on.' Angrily she grabbed Jess's hand and pulled her out of bed.

The television was on and it only took a few minutes

before they ran the story of Ryan and Serena's engagement. The happy couple had been filmed emerging from the Beverly Hills Hotel for a press conference. Serena said little but stood next to Ryan, leaning on his shoulder and looking up at him adoringly. It was Ryan who spoke: 'I am genuinely amazed that this beautiful woman could love me as I love her. I can't wait to make her my wife and have lots of little girls who look just like her.'

'What about Jess Tate. Does she know?'

'Jess is a wonderful woman, but we've grown apart and moved in opposite directions. I wish her nothing but happiness.'

Jess lost consciousness for the second time that day.

*

The doctor, when she came, was very kind and suggested that Jess take a few days off work and do relaxing things like walk the dogs and snuggle on the sofa in front of some old films. She wrote a prescription for a few days' supply of Diazepam before leaving.

When Brooke returned from seeing the doctor to her car she found Jess ripping the prescription up and chucking it in the grate.

Hutch, Chris and Louis had to go. Parking the Range Rover on the opposite side of the village had been a simple ruse that had worked. Brooke was glad to see them leave. In situations like this, men weren't always the best help. Hutch and Chris left first in order to bring the car round so that Louis could jump in quickly without drawing attention. The grim-faced hack and his mates, having delivered their devastating news and got their pictures, had gone.

As Louis held Brooke and kissed her, he apologised again for bringing so much disruption to her and Jess's lives.

'It's been fun,' said Brooke, somehow knowing that this was the last time she would see him.

He kissed her lips gently. 'It has been fun. You are a very special girl, Brooke. I won't forget you.'

The Range Rover was at the gate. He gave her one more lingering kiss then walked away. He didn't look back.

*

Brooke watched as his car moved off and out of sight. She leaned her forehead on the door jamb and allowed a couple of tears to slide down her cheeks and splash on the flagstones.

Jess called to her from upstairs. 'Have you got any decent scissors?'

'Yes, in my dressing-table drawer.' Brooke called up.

'Can I borrow them?'

'Of course.' Then a cold fear gripped Brooke. 'Oh my God, what are you going to do?' She raced upstairs, fully expecting to have to grapple the scissors from a blood-soaked Jess, but instead she found her on the landing with a long cream dress bag in her hand.

'What the hell are you doing?' shrieked Brooke.

'I'm having a moment's liberation.' Jess unzipped the bag and pulled out the most beautiful wedding dress. 'I bought this for my wedding to that bastard Ryan. Now I am going to cut it up into tiny pieces.'

'No! It's lovely – someone else would love to have it. Give it to charity. Auction it on eBay, but please don't destroy it,' begged Brooke.

She was too late. Jess had the scissors in her hand and Brooke could only watch as the swathes of satin and silk were snipped, ripped and chopped into nothing but rags.

37

A form of insane sanity settled over Jess. The shredded
dress was now in the dustbin, the threads on the
landing all hoovered up. And she was in her bedroom, calmly
filling black bin-bags with anything associated with Ryan.

Ollie drove over with Jonathan, bringing camomile tea,
lavender oil and a box of Nurofen Plus.

Brooke let them in and called up the stairs brightly,
'Jess – Ollie and Jonathan are here.'

'I'll be down in a minute,' Jess called back.

Brooke pulled a worried face at the boys and beckoned
them into the kitchen, pulling the door shut so that they
could talk without being overheard.

'What happened?' asked Jonathan. Brooke told them
the full story, including the possibility that she might
never see Louis again.

'Are you OK?' Ollie asked.

'I think I probably am. I mean, it's not like I was ever
going to be Princess Brooke, is it.' She began filling the kettle,
purely as an excuse to turn away from them so they wouldn't
see the tears forming in her eyes. 'I'll miss him a bit, but . . .
well, it'll be something to tell the grandchildren, won't it?'

'Does Jess know?' asked Ollie.

'No. Not yet. I'd prefer to keep it to myself at the
moment. It's easier to handle . . . if you don't mind not
saying anything.'

'Understood.'

'In the meantime, I'm much more worried about Jess,' said Brooke. 'In the last three hours she's been through all the stages of shock, denial and anger, and now appears to be in acceptance.'

'That was quick,' said Jonathan, spying an open packet of chocolate HobNobs and helping himself.

'Yeah. Worryingly so.'

'What's she doing up there?' asked Ollie, eyes looking ceilingward.

'Well, after she stopped trying to phone Ryan, ripping up the prescription the doctor gave her and cutting her wedding dress into shreds, she went pretty quiet. I think she's chucking all his stuff away at the moment.'

They heard footsteps on the stairs and the bumping of something heavy being dragged down.

'Shh,' said Brooke, and the three of them arranged their faces into natural expressions as if nothing out of the ordinary was occurring.

The kitchen door swung open and Jess lugged in three heavy bin-bags. 'Hi, guys.'

'Hi, Jess.' Jonathan smiled at her.

'Want some help with that?' offered Ollie, nodding to the rubbish sacks.

'Great. Thanks. Can you put them out by the dustbin. The binmen collect tomorrow.'

Ollie and Jonathan took the bags out. Once out of sight of the kitchen, they had a quick peek.

'Tom Ford shoes!' admired Jonathan.

'Put them back,' hissed Ollie.

But Jonathan continued: 'Cashmere jumper . . . Vivienne Westwood shirt . . .'

'Yeah. I bet she bought them all for him.'

They piled them into the dustbin and went back to the kitchen.

Both girls were at the kitchen table sipping camomile tea. Ollie pulled out the chair next to Jess and sat down beside her. 'How are you doing, old friend?'

Jess sighed. 'Honestly? I feel as if I've been punched very hard and I'm numb all over.'

Jonathan offered her a HobNob. 'You don't have to do the show tonight if you don't want to. But, in my opinion, it might just be the best thing you could do.'

Brooke disagreed. 'She needs to have a couple of days off to get her head together.'

Ollie put his arm around Jess's shoulder and hugged her to him. 'I think Jess needs to make her own mind up.'

The four of them sat in silence, listening to the hum of the fridge and the dachshunds snoring in their basket. Jess sat still, staring ahead and thinking.

The clock was creeping round to the time they should be leaving for the theatre. Summer season meant never having a day off, even a Sunday.

Eventually Jess spoke: 'Let's go. What would I do, sitting here by myself tonight?'

*

Jess didn't know she had it in her. She got through the show on autopilot and only once broke down in the wings. It was Colonel Stick who shared a few gentle words and Ollie who held her steady with firm eye contact whenever they were on stage together.

After the show, Ollie offered the girls supper but Brooke declined. 'I think I'll go home. Things to do . . . and stuff.'

Ollie understood.

'Well, that leaves you and me, Miss Tate. Fancy a bite to eat?'

*

By the time they got to the Starfish, Jess knew she didn't want to do anything but crawl into bed and cry herself to sleep. There had been a short email from Ryan, waiting for her after the show, saying he'd speak to her soon to explain. She had immediately phoned him back but got voicemail. She made one more call, to her sister Emma, who had been frantically trying to reach her and leaving messages offering to come to Trevay to be by her side. Having sworn to Em that she was OK and there was no need to worry, she turned her phone off and left it in the dressing room. She didn't want the temptation of trying to call him through the night.

As Ollie parked up his red MG outside the Starfish and extended a hand to help her out, she told him, 'I'm sorry, Ollie. I really am not great company tonight. I'm going to take a cab back to Pendruggan.'

He looked at her with such concern that she laughed. 'I'm all right, honestly. I just need to . . . oh . . . I don't know, I just need . . .'

'To walk into this beautiful hotel, check yourself into a luxurious room, sink into a bubble bath and eat something from room service in front of the telly, wrapped in a huge white robe. Am I right?'

She nodded. 'You're right.'

He offered her his arm and escorted her up the steps where she checked in to the best available room.

'No bags, Miss Tate?' said the receptionist.

'Nope. I'm baggage-free tonight. Baggage-free from now on, I think.'

The receptionist was embarrassed. 'Oh, I am so sorry. I didn't mean . . . Well, I saw the news today and I'm so sad to hear that you and Mr Hearst . . .'

'It's OK. It's fine.'

'Would you like a complimentary washbag with tooth-brush and stuff?'

'Yes please. I have nothing at all with me.'

Her room was adjacent to Ollie's and had a view over the narrow streets of Trevay. She stood at the window looking down at the people who were making their way back to their B&Bs or holiday apartments. One couple, in their forties she guessed, with two teenage children in tow, walked hand in hand talking and laughing together. She drew her curtains on them. That was never going to be her future.

Ollie was fiddling with the huge television at the end of the bed.

'Why don't hotel tellies just turn on and off?' He was juggling two remote controls. 'You have to get through all this "Welcome, Miss Tate" and "Hotel information" guff before you get to . . . ah, here we are. Back-to-back episodes of *Frasier*. That's what you need.' Satisfied he'd beaten the technology, he went to the bathroom and came back bearing a big white fluffy robe. He put it on the bed. 'Put that on and order some room service while I run you a bath.'

'Ollie, stop. I can look after myself.'

'It makes me feel better to know I'm doing something,' he called above the running of taps. 'You're doing this for me, you know. Not the other way around.'

When he was satisfied that Jess had everything she needed he left her to it with these words: 'Night, sweetheart. You'll get through this, trust me.'

In the empty room she felt at peace. The bath was the perfect temperature and the steak sandwich and glass of Merlot just the ticket. She even managed to laugh at the television. 'I'm going to get through this,' she said to herself several times. Finally she got into bed . . . and couldn't sleep.

*

Ollie couldn't sleep either. What on earth was happening in his life? A few months ago he was a Royal Shakespeare Company actor with a rock star girlfriend and a flat in London. Now he was a single seaside entertainer, living close to his mum. Good old Ollie. How life and its various chapters can lower one's opinion of oneself. He thumped his pillow into a more comfortable shape and tried to sleep again.

He was lonely. He'd been lonely for months. Or even longer. In fact, all the way back to the start of his relationship with Red. What had she ever seen in him? And God only knew what he'd seen in her. They were like two lost souls who'd collided. He had loved her creativity and her energy. He'd never known a performer who could give so much of themselves to an audience. He'd done his training around actors who were intense and introverted. 'Up their own backsides,' as his mother would have said. Unlike Red, who truly loved her audiences and was loved by them in return, actors felt that their public hated them. 'See that woman in the third row with the green jumper? She's not laughed in any of my scenes. I played the whole effing thing to her and she hates me. What's she here for?'

That was the kind of conversation heard daily in the angst-ridden dressing rooms of our nation's theatres.

The strange thing was, Ollie was really loving *Hats Off, Trevay!*. The comedy, the schmaltz, the people who paid hard-earned cash to be entertained. The kids at the stage door with their scruffy bits of paper and a dried-up biro, wanting an autograph and a photo. It made their holiday. It wasn't Shakespeare or Beckett or even Alan Ayckbourn, but it was fun and he had made some good friends. He truly valued Brooke and Jess – and Jonathan too, although he didn't know him so well. Actors had to fall into comradeships quickly. Their lives were made up of relationships that were intense, utterly revealing and brief. One day you were bosom buddies then the final curtain came down and you might never see those people again. A travelling band of minstrels, all too many of whom were morally incontinent. Bloody Ryan Hearst. How dare he hurt Jess! Ryan had known all along he was bad news. What a bastard. Where would that prick be without Jess? She had supported him and trusted him, and he couldn't even summon the decency to let her down gently. Poor cow.

He hoped she was sleeping peacefully. As he turned his pillow and plumped it up, he vowed to keep an eye on her.

*

Jess's bed was too big. She wished she had Ethel and Elsie with her, to squash her up a bit. And to offer her some distraction. She couldn't stop torturing herself with thoughts of Ryan and sodding Serena. What time would it be in LA now? Mid afternoon? It would be warm and they'd be stretched out on a double sunbed, holding hands and rubbing sun cream into each other's backs. OK, they couldn't be holding hands *and* rubbing sun cream into each other, but they'd be together. Jess found the sorest spot in her mental anguish and started to press it hard. It would be so hot in the sun, that they'd dive into the pool, Serena creating barely a splash, and Ryan would caress her flawless body under the water, pulling off her bikini bottoms. She would squeal and be mock shocked but he would grab her and make love to her and . . .

Jess sat up in bed. She needed a drink. The minibar was well stocked but the bottles were too small. She wanted a big bottle of wine. No, champagne. And she needed someone to drink it with. She thought about phoning Brooke and asking her to get in a car and bring the dogs too, but it was late and Brooke would be asleep by now. Who could she ring? Her heart leapt painfully as she thought about Ryan again. No. She wasn't going to ring him. Not if he was the last person on earth. She'd ring . . . Ollie. Of course. He was only next door. She rang room service and ordered a bottle of really expensive champagne and asked to be put through to Mr Pinkerton's room.

He answered on the second ring. 'Hello?'

'Ollie. It's me. I can't sleep and I wondered . . . if you're awake, would you like to share a bottle of fizz with me?'

'As a matter of fact, that sounds just the ticket. I should love to. Is it a pyjama party?'

'Most definitely.'

'Give me two minutes.'

*

Jess made the most of her two minutes. Brushed her hair, cleaned her teeth. Wondered why. Then rubbed some of the complimentary body lotion into her legs and arms in lieu of perfume.

There was a knock on the door. It was the waiter. He pushed over the threshold a trolley holding a bottle of champagne which was rattling in an ice bucket. Two glasses were chilled and dewy. There was also a plate of smoked salmon sandwiches and a bowl of crisps. 'Compliments of the kitchen.'

As the waiter took his leave, Ollie slipped into the room. Freshly shaved and minty breathed.

'Hi,' he said, suddenly feeling a bit awkward.

'Hey,' said Jess. 'This seemed like a good idea five minutes ago. If you've changed your mind, it doesn't matter.'

'No. It's a great idea. Shall I open the champagne?'

'Yes please.' Jess pointed to the sandwiches and crisps. 'And please don't think I ordered these too. They're compliments of the Starfish, apparently. Might give me heartburn this late.'

The champagne cork popped softly in Ollie's hand and he deftly poured the foaming liquid into a glass and passed it to Jess before pouring his own. 'Well, I'm willing to risk one.' He picked up one of the tiny triangles and munched. 'It's delicious – and no bad effects yet.'

'Ryan hates smoked salmon.'

'He's a prat.'

'Says it repeats on him.'

'How romantic. Now stop talking about him and eat one of these babies before I scoff the lot.'

Jess ate two and had a top-up of champagne.

'Shall we watch a movie? There must be some old black-and-white thing on TCM surely?' asked Ollie.

'I can't remember how you turned it on.'

'God, women are pathetic.' He shook his head in mock exasperation. He found the remote and eventually found TCM. 'Do you like Bette Davis?'

'Of course.'

'How do you fancy *Now Voyager*?'

'Oh wow! Is it on? I love that movie.'

Ollie made himself comfortable on top of the covers of the enormous bed. 'Come on, we'll watch it together – and bring the bottle and the crisps with you.'

They sat up next to each other, quite relaxed, as the movie played and the bottle got emptier. When the film came to the end they spoke in unison with Bette Davis as she said the immortal line, '. . . Oh Jerry, don't let's ask for the moon. We have the stars.'

Ollie turned the volume down and looked at Jess intently. 'Do you think we could have the stars?'

'I think maybe it's late and that's the champagne talking.'

'Maybe. But I'd like to kiss you.'

'That's definitely the champagne talking.'

'No. It's me, honest.'

'Don't make me laugh.'

'Why not?'

'I can't kiss properly when I'm laughing.'

38

It had been decided that the annual village fête, due the Sunday after next, would have a theatrical theme.

Pendruggan pulled out all its stops. Side shows included a hoopla stall called LORD OF THE RINGS, a baby shower tent called MAMMA MIA and, Penny's particular favourite, a horse-betting game called STRICTLY COME PRANCING. Other attractions included old favourites such as bowl for a pig and guess the weight of the vicar.

This year the celebrity fête openers would be the cast of *Hats Off, Trevay!*.

The morning dawned warm and bright. Penny was in her bedroom at the vicarage, stepping into a nifty little Cavalla dress from last year. 'Zip me up, would you, darling?' she asked Simon.

It turned out he had to put in quite a bit of effort tugging at the fabric to make the fastener pull up over her bust.

Penny was annoyed. 'Bloody thing must have shrunk at the cleaners.'

Simon agreed, tutting at the poor standards these days, although privately he thought his wife had put on a bit of weight recently.

'Does it look too tight?' Penny asked him.

'No. It looks perfect, and so do you.' He asked God's forgiveness for this tiny white lie.

Across the village green at Gull's Cry, Helen was gathering up her purse and the dogs. She had three today: Ethel, Elsie and Jack, Piran's terrier. His master had gone on ahead to help Simon with the BBQ and the tea and beer tent.

Ollie's MG had its top off today and was growling its way to Pendruggan through the lanes. Jess couldn't remember when she had last felt so relaxed. With Ryan she had always been slightly on edge, never quite knowing whether she had pleased him or pissed him off. Ollie was so much easier. He had barely left her side since the night of champagne and salmon and Bette Davis.

The next morning they had woken up with crisps in the bed but no other discomfort. No heavy discussions. No need to spell things out. They were together and that was that.

When they went to work that night, Ollie had insisted that they walk into the theatre together. He held her hand while they made their coffees in the green room and he kissed her lips when she went to get ready. All this was witnessed by their colleagues and universally, tacitly, happily blessed. Well. Almost.

While Jess was alone in her dressing room, she received a visit from Jonathan.

'What's going on with you and Ollie?' he asked, covering up the hurt in his voice with an accusatory tone.

'What's the problem? We're two consenting adults. I didn't think we needed to ask permission.'

'You've just gone through a really painful break-up. You're not ready.'

'Says who?'

'A decent man would have given you a bit of space before moving in on you. Ollie is way too insecure to give you what you need. You need someone more solid. Besides, if something goes wrong, it could be very bad for the production.'

'Well, if that happens, feel free to come to my dressing room and give me a bollocking. Right now, I'm busy – curtain call's in ten minutes.'

When she heard, Brooke was surprised: 'I'd never have put you two together, but now I see it . . . it's just right.'

Jess had hugged her and thanked her and then asked about Louis. Ollie had told her the news.

Brooke was upset but sanguine. 'He rang this morning, which was sweet of him. He couldn't talk for long. The family firm have decided that he's had his fun in the real world but now they want him to face up to who he is. He's jacking in the photo journalism. He's jacking me in. Now the castle gates are clanging behind him.'

'Poor guy. What a future,' sighed Jess.

'Yeah, but look at the positives: endless opportunities, flunkies, gorgeous, suitable princesses throwing themselves at him . . .'

'You gave him more fun than any old princess ever would.'

Brooke smiled ruefully. 'I hope so . . . Anyway, cheers to Prince Louis!' She raised her mug of tea. 'And up yours, Ryan!' She raised her mug again.

Jess couldn't help but laugh.

*

And now she was looking at Ollie's dear profile as he concentrated on driving. His left hand reached for the gear stick as he took a narrow corner and then searched for her thigh, which he gently squeezed. 'You OK?' he asked.

Her hair was blowing on her face and as she reached up to grab it into a ponytail she nodded to him, her smiling eyes letting him know the answer.

The village had turned out in force and Jess, Brooke, Ollie and Colonel Stick were treated like stars.

Jonathan had kept things on a strictly business footing with Jess and Ollie since he'd found out, but even so he took pride in standing back and watching his cast charm everyone that Penny and Helen introduced them to.

Brooke had been in the village long enough to have met most of the locals already, and thanks to the time they'd spent rehearsing in the church hall while fire-damage to the Pavilions was repaired, the rest of the cast had encountered Mrs Audrey Tipton and were doing their best to steer well clear of her. Both she and Mr Audrey Tipton were easy to spot in their matching red sailing trousers and Guernsey jumpers; in Geoffrey's case this ensemble had been accessorised with a jaunty sailing cap, three sizes too small, balanced on his wiry grey hair.

Queenie, the old village shopkeeper, was another familiar face as a result of her volunteer work in the box office, but the cast had never seen her in her off-duty attire: a full-skirted original 1950s sundress and white peep-toe stilettos. Though she was wobbling a bit on the precarious heels, it didn't seem to be preventing her doing a brisk trade on her Cornish pasty stall.

At the stall next to hers, Tony Brown – or Simple Tony as he was affectionately known to the locals, many of whom relied on his green-fingered expertise in their own gardens and vegetable plots – was selling tomato plants and runner beans.

Psychic Polly came out of her tent just as Penny and her retinue were walking by.

'Ask me your future and I shall show you the way,' said Polly, making the delegation laugh. 'Come on, Colonel – I see a golden future for you. Cross my palm and I'll tell you more.'

'That's awfully sweet of you, Polly, but not my cup of tea, you know. Better for the ladies, I think. How about young Brooke here?'

Brooke was eager to give it a go and followed Polly into the candy-striped tent while the others moved on.

'Sit down, my dear,' said Polly kindly. 'Crystal, palm or cards – which do you fancy?'

Brooke stuck out her hands. 'Palms, please.'

*

'And to judge the dogs in fancy dress contest, would you please welcome our very own Colonel Walter Irvine!' Mr Audrey Tipton had not let go of the microphone all afternoon and had no plans to do so in the foreseeable future. Without waiting for the applause to die down, he began booming over the PA system: 'Dogs and owners to the centre of the show ring, if you please.'

The show ring was a small affair but big enough for the four dogs and humans who assembled there. There was a pug dressed as Rhett Butler, a spaniel as Cameron Diaz in *There's Something about Mary*, a black Labrador as Will Smith and finally, an arthritic greyhound as Audrey Hepburn in *Breakfast at Tiffany's*.

The Colonel made a good show of talking at length to each dog and owner about their choices and costumes. Just as he was getting to Audrey Hepburn there was a small flurry by the microphone and Mr Audrey Tipton made a fresh announcement:

'This is most irregular, but as a gesture of goodwill I am accepting three late entrants to the competition. You may enter the ring!'

Helen and Piran then walked in with Ethel and Elsie dressed as *Hats Off, Trevay!* chorus girls, and Jack as Colonel Stick. The crowd roared with laughter. Rhett Butler immediately trotted off to mount Ethel, who sat down very firmly. Jack barked furiously, his straw boater falling fetchingly over his left ear. Rhett sloped back to his embarrassed owner.

Colonel Irvine continued his judging with enormous dignity and after a short deliberation gave the prize of a huge bone to Will Smith.

All dogs got runner-up bags of treats and Jack made sure he shared his with Elsie, for whom he had a soft spot.

The actors were loath to tear themselves away, but the time had come for them to return to the theatre. By this time the real fun was just beginning. The beer tent was heaving, the local boys got some guitars together and started an impromptu gig, and Penny went to have her fortune told, just for a bit of fun, by Polly.

*

Since Jess and Ollie had got together they had split their time between sleeping at Granny's Nook and the Starfish. Brooke loved having them around, but it was getting a little tiresome never knowing when she'd have the place to herself so that she could lie in the bath with a face pack on, or walk around naked without worrying about anyone barging in on her.

She'd been waiting and waiting for the right moment to broach the topic with Jess, but now she'd reached the point where it couldn't be put off any longer. As she stepped out of her final costume she asked in what she hoped was a casual tone, 'Are you coming home tonight, Jessie?'

'I'm not sure. Depends on how tired Ollie is. Why?'

'I'd just like to know so that I can do things I need to do.'

'Like what?'

'You know . . . just things. Things it's good to do on your own.'

'I didn't know you needed to do things on your own.'

'Not major things. Just stuff that . . . hey, let's not get into an argument.'

'We're not having an argument.' Jess brushed her hair just a little too vigorously. 'Maybe I've been insensitive. Is it difficult seeing Ollie and me together when you're . . .'

Brooke pursed her lips. 'When I'm single?'

'No. I just mean . . . I'm sorry if I've been so wrapped up in my own happiness that I haven't taken your feelings into consideration.'

Brooke started to pull on her jeans. 'All I'm saying is, it's nice to know when I have the cottage to myself so that if I feel like burping loudly, I can. That's all.' She yanked the zip of her jeans up huffily.

'All right,' said Jess, mystified that this silly tiff had come from nowhere. 'I'll stay with Ollie tonight and you can have some burping space.'

'Good. Thanks.'

'And tomorrow we'll go through diaries and fix nights I'm there and nights I'm not.'

'Right.' Brooke picked up her bag and slung it over her shoulder. 'See you tomorrow night then.'

'Oh, I was thinking I might come back tomorrow to do some laundry.'

'OK. But let me know, would you?'

'Sure. I'll call you.'

'Thanks. Night.' And Brooke walked out, closing the dressing door just a little too loudly.

'Night,' said Jess.

'Maybe she's premenstrual,' said Ollie. They were sharing a bath at the hotel and Ollie had gallantly taken the tap end. 'Or not getting enough how's your father.' He took a swig of his ice-cold gin and tonic.

Jess was not amused. 'How very New Man of you. Why do men always think that if a woman is upset it's something to do with her womb?'

'Eugh. Please. I hate that kind of talk.'

'Womb. Womb. Womb. Period.' With each word she flicked soapsuds at him. He at least had the grace to laugh.

'Brooke will be fine. She's had a tough year. Remember all the trouble she had with losing the Café Au Lait contract and being dumped by Bob the rugger bugger. Now she's lost the RB . . .'

'RB?'

'Royal Boyfriend.'

Jess took a deep glug of her gin and tonic. 'You're right. I haven't been a very good friend to her, have I?'

Ollie's mobile phone started to ring in the bedroom.

'You've been a brilliant friend.' He heaved himself out of the steaming water, leaving it to lap over Jess's chin. She watched him wrap a towel around his gorgeous physique before he set off to answer the call.

'He-llo?'

Jess listened, wondering who would phone him this late. She hoped it wasn't something wrong with his mother.

'Where are you?'

The urgent tone of his voice sent anxiety coursing down her spine.

'No! Don't come up. Give me five minutes and I'll come down . . . I'm in the bath . . . just wait where you are . . .'

Jess stayed where she was and waited to hear what he was going to tell her.

He came into the bathroom looking very uncomfortable.

'Darling Jess, I'm sorry to do this to you, but would you mind leaving and going back to Granny's Nook tonight?'

'Why?'

He rubbed his hands through his hair, looking miserable. 'It's Red. She's in the lobby. Very upset. I have to go to her.'

'No you don't.'

'Please don't make this difficult.'

'Difficult? What's difficult? Maybe Ryan'll call in a minute and I'll go off to see him. How would that make you feel?'

Ollie was looking utterly wretched now. 'Darling, please. Let me just sort this out and we'll talk tomorrow.'

*

Jess put her key in the lock of the ancient front door to Granny's Nook. Brooke was sitting on the sofa with her hair in cling film, painting her toenails. She looked up in surprise. 'What are you doing here?'

39

'I can't believe it! I thought Ollie had more backbone than to run back to Red the minute she clicks her fingers!' Brooke was angrier than Jess. 'After all that's happened. How horrible she's been. How great you two have been together. It's unbelievable.'

Jess was more philosophical. 'He's a young man. Red's a very sexy young girl. What can you do?' She shrugged her shoulders and dipped her hand into the family-size bag of Twiglets.

'What the bloody hell is she doing back in Trevay anyway?'

'He'll tell me tomorrow, he said.'

'And you believe him?'

'Well, he's not going to do a runner, is he? And I can't see Red hanging around here for too long.'

'I wouldn't be so sure.'

*

After a fitful night's sleep, Jess woke early and took the dogs down to the beach. What a year this had turned out to be. A hit TV show, getting engaged, saving a theatre, getting unengaged, acquiring a toyboy and now . . . What? She checked her phone. Nothing. She had made a promise to herself not to call Ollie.

As she stood at the top of the beach she saw a familiar figure with a small Jack Russell bounding in and out of the waves. Ethel and Elsie had seen them too and scooted off to say hello.

'Mornin',' said Piran, his black curls dancing in the wind.

'Good morning. The Pendruggan fête went well, didn't it?'

'Aye.'

For all his buccaneer good looks, Piran was a lousy conversationalist. Jess couldn't help wondering how Helen put up with him.

She tried again. 'How's Helen? It was good of her to have the girls while I toured the stalls with "the team" yesterday.'

He grunted, picked up a stone and threw it into the sea for Jack to retrieve. The little terrier ignored him; his whiskered nose was busily sniffing Elsie's posterior. Piran got his boot under Jack's chest and lifted him out of the way. 'She don't want you sniffin' round, boy.'

'Oh, I don't know.' Jess smiled. 'A good-looking boy like Jack must have a lot of success with the ladies.'

'Yeah, but 'e hasn't the money to support any offspring.'

Jess laughed again. 'But how sweet would they be?'

'You sound like my Helen. Always wanting a happy ending with fluffy little bunnies. Life ain't like that.'

His words stung Jess. The reality of losing Ryan and now Ollie hit her afresh. Not wanting this great oaf of a man to see the tears in her eyes, she turned her face to the wind and whistled up the girls. 'Come on, girls. I need a cup of tea.'

She hoped that Piran would stay by the water's edge playing with Jack, but instead he caught up with her and looked into her eyes.

'I 'aven't upset 'e, 'ave I, maid?'

'Goodness me, no!' Jess attempted a bright voice. 'This wind is strong. It makes my eyes water, that's all.'

He stood in front of her, blocking her path, and pulled a handkerchief from the pocket of his jeans. 'You might need this then.'

She took it and properly burst into tears.

Piran took her straight round to Gull's Cry and the welcoming arms of Helen.

'I found this poor maid on the beach. And before you say anything, I didn't upset 'er.' He turned to Jess. 'Did I?'

She shook her head.

'Well, that'll be a first!' Helen helped Jess to a bright patchwork chair by the fireplace in the sitting room. 'I'll get the kettle on and, if you want to talk, then feel free.'

Helen was a good listener. Without offering any advice, she managed to patch up Jess's wobbling self-esteem.

'My ex-husband was hopelessly unfaithful. I don't know why I put up with it for so long. For the children's sake, I suppose. But one day I woke up and became my own person. He couldn't control me any longer. That's how I came to be here in Cornwall. As soon as I'd made the break, my life changed dramatically. Piran and I have been together for a couple of years now, but I could never live with him. We're both happy the way we are – he can do his thing, I can do mine. But we trust each other, which is amazing because, after my husband, I thought I could never trust anyone again.'

Jess blew her nose. 'I've always trusted too much. First Ryan, now Ollie.' She felt the phone in her pocket vibrate. 'Oh, that'll be him.' She fished the phone out. 'Hello, Ollie?'

Helen saw Jess's face blanch.

'Ryan? Why are you calling me? . . . Oh . . . I'll get

them to contact your agent . . . I wish you every happiness, but please . . . don't call again.' She hung up and put her phone back in her pocket.

'Dare I ask what he wanted?'

'He wants the name of my solicitors so that he can buy me out of our flat. He and Serena are going to use it as their London base.'

Piran, who'd been eavesdropping while reading the paper, said succinctly, 'Arsehole.'

At that moment, Helen's mobile rang.

'Sorry Jess, I'd better get this.'

Penny seemed to be beside herself. 'Have you seen the paper?'

'No, not yet, Piran's looking at it now.'

'Quickly, turn to the centre pages and then call me back.'

Helen rang off. 'Penny says turn to the middle.'

'What the 'ell for?'

Grudgingly, while Helen and Jess looked over his shoulder, Piran did as he was asked.

The headline screamed out in bold letters:

CAFÉ AU LAIT CHIEF IN COCAINE SHOCKER!!

The three of them looked at each other in disbelief as they read the article.

'Brooke has got to see this,' said Jess.

*

Back at Granny's Nook, with Jess by her side, Brooke read the article, barely able to keep the excitement out of her voice:

Café Au Lait Managing Director Rupert Heligan has been caught in an orgy of sex and cocaine by our intrepid undercover team. Preserving their anonymity behind the code names the Prince and the Pauper, our photographer and reporter have once again succeeded in uncovering something nasty at the heart of the establishment.

Rupert Heligan, who claims his company prides itself on wholesome family values, was discovered holed up in a hotel with two hookers and a pile of premium-grade cocaine. When challenged to provide an explanation, Heligan responded with a string of expletives and attempted to attack our courageous reporters . . .

And so it went on. Across the centre pages were photographs of Heligan, sitting on a sofa next to a topless woman with large breasts who was draping herself over him as he focused on the glass table in front of him, where he appeared to be arranging a pile of white powder into neat lines with a platinum credit card.

Last night, Heligan was unavailable for comment but a spokesperson for Café Au Lait gave us this statement:

"We will be carrying out a full and thorough investigation in the light of these allegations. We completely disassociate ourselves from those whose activities would bring our name into disrepute and we will act rigorously and decisively if we discover evidence of wrongdoing by any employee."

Brooke's eyes were shining. 'The Prince and the Pauper. That must be Louis. I just know it. He didn't let me down.'

'What now?' asked Jess.

'I think it might be time to pay a visit to a certain councillor.'

*

Ollie phoned later that afternoon as Brooke and Jess were setting off from Pendruggan to the theatre.

'Ollie! Are you OK? What's happening?'

'It's a bit complicated.' Ollie was whispering. 'Red's in the loo. She's very upset and can't be left on her own. She's coming into work with me tonight.'

'Oh. So you want me to keep a low profile and stay out of your way?'

'Would you?'

Jess hung up before she could give him both barrels.

*

To Jess it seemed that each new day brought a fresh kind of hell.

Red clung to Ollie like a limpet. He couldn't go on stage without her standing in the wings and waiting for him. She allowed no one to get near him, least of all Jess.

On the second day of her appearance in Trevay, Red's management team organised a press conference from the Starfish board room.

Jess, against her better judgement, had slipped into the back to watch as Red and Ollie were ushered into the room to take their places behind a long table. 'God,' thought Jess, 'it's just like a *Crimewatch* re-enactment.'

Red, looking pale and frail, began reading from a prepared script.

'Good morning, ladies and gentlemen. Unfortunately I have had to abandon the Far Eastern leg of my world tour because doctors have found nodules on my vocal cords. I shall have to undergo exploratory tests soon. This is clearly a very worrying time for me and my singing career as I have been told I may never sing again. I have also been diagnosed with severe exhaustion and I have come home to my partner Ollie Pinkerton for the love and care that only a boyfriend can give.'

A reporter shouted a question. 'Are you still gay? What's happened to your girlfriend?'

'My "friendship" with a particular female comedienne was just that. She's a great girl and we remain the best of friends. She is now busy pursuing her own dreams and we don't have any plans to see each other in the near future.'

Red stopped talking for a moment. Choking back tears, she grasped Ollie's hand. 'I am beyond happy that Ollie trusts me and knows the truth and that our relationship is as strong as ever.'

Jess wanted to march to the front of the room and let everyone know what a charade this whole performance was, but Ollie saw her and pleaded silently with such loss in his eyes that she did nothing.

He was a big boy who had got himself into a big mess. She was not the one to get him out of it.

*

'It took me a while to track them down, but I was lucky. Louise at the Starfish had kept in contact with Marc. He does seasonal work for her and comes and goes. He's back in Exeter now, but he couldn't have been more helpful when I contacted him.'

Brooke was sitting outside the council offices with Piran and Helen. In the light of the revelations about Rupert Heligan, she had decided to track down the photos that had been taken on the disastrous night she'd spent in the company of the men from Café Au Lait. She was in luck. Marc had the photos and was more than willing to allow her to use them:

'No problem, girlfriend. I'd love to wipe the smiles off the faces of that bunch of toe-rags.'

Hence the decision to go head-to-head with Chris Bedford.

'Come on, then,' said Piran. 'I've been looking forward to this for a long time. 'Ere's our chance.'

The three of them were just getting out of the car when Chris Bedford came down the steps of the council offices, puffing on a cigarette. He had a hunted expression on his face. When he saw the three of them approaching, he visibly paled.

'What do you want? I'm very busy, don't have time to see you now – make an appointment through the usual channels.'

'Busy, eh? We'll see about that!' growled Piran. 'Let 'im 'ave it, Brooke.'

'Perhaps I should go through the official channels, Mr Bedford?' she said. 'I'm sure your colleagues on the council would love to take a look at these.'

She thrust her iPhone in his face, displaying the image of Bedford and Heligan with white powder under their nostrils and a pile of the stuff on the table. Bedford was in the frame too, clearly the worse for wear, bleary-eyed and blotchy.

'I'm sure this'll go down a treat in the run-up to council elections in the autumn. Don't you agree, Chris?' Piran thrust his face close to Bedford, who was sweating and pulling at his tie.

'Café Au Lait's case is dead in the water. Heligan's name is mud and I'm sure even you won't be wanting to continue your association with that slimeball. Now, how about you just make sure that there'll be no further bids, no court case and that the Pavilions remain protected, as they should have been all along?'

'Wu-wu-well . . . I'm not sure . . .'

Brooke gave him her sweetest smile. 'We're relying on you, Chris. You won't let us down, will you?' She patted his cheek. He gulped.

'We'll be seeing you,' added Piran, with menace.

Chris Bedford shot off to his car, almost tripping over himself in his hurry to get away.

'Mission accomplished?' asked Helen, who'd watched the exchange from the car . . .

'Let's hope so,' replied Brooke.

Piran eyes were glinting. 'He's a bloody slippery eel, but this time, we've well and truly caught him in our nets.'

*

When troubles come, the most surprising people step forward to help. In Jess's case that help came from Jonathan.

She had been walking the dogs on the beach in Trevay on a beautiful sunny August morning when she saw him waving from the harbour wall. As she got closer he called down, 'Fancy a coffee?' Over the days and weeks that followed they fell into a pattern of walks, swims, lunches and occasional matinees at the cinema in Wadebridge.

He was an erudite man who had studied Shakespeare as a young director. He would read the sonnets to her as they sipped their cappuccinos and together they'd analyse the wordplay and debate whether Shakespeare was indeed the author or whether there was merit in the argument that the sonnets had been penned by Marlowe or Bacon.

These conversations fed an undernourished hunger for knowledge in Jess and she was amazed that this clever man could be interested in her opinion. Ryan had never even read a book and was interested only in himself.

Jonathan was uncomplicated, unthreatening and the gay best friend every woman needs.

*

Ollie had to take a week off the show in order to accompany Red to the London clinic where a world-famous throat specialist performed an exploratory operation on her throat.

That week was a joy. Ollie's understudy stepped up to the mark and the entire theatre company could breathe again. A Scrabble board appeared in the green room and a league soon formed. The wonky telly was showing football matches again and the sound of laughter filled the backstage areas.

Colonel Stick started a bridge school. Every day from noon till three he could be found in the green room teaching anyone who cared to join in.

Then Red came back. The tests on her throat found nothing more serious than a bit of a strain to her vocal cords. No further surgery required. No threat to her singing career. No centre of attention. She was furious. The atmosphere back at the Pavilions was ten times worse than before . . .

Until one marvellous night when at last the unshared, unspoken prayers of the entire company were answered and Red stormed out of Trevay. Her Twitter account revealed that it was all over between her and Ollie, who was 'not the man he thinks he is', declaring, 'Red is back on the road, people!!!'

Ollie preferred not to speak about any of it. The whole subject of Red and the misery she'd caused was the elephant in the room. He looked thin and pale, but on the surface was as easygoing as ever, chatting to everyone and working hard on stage. But after the show he'd slip back to the hotel, barely saying goodbye to anybody.

Where Jess was concerned, Ollie was pleasant but impersonal, keeping her at arm's length. She decided not to hassle him over it. He knew where she was if he wanted her. All the same, it made her sad. She still had strong feelings for him and couldn't work out if it was because he'd been so kind to her after the whole Ryan disaster or whether it was just a summer romance or whether they could really have a second try.

*

One evening, not long after Red left town, Jonathan invited Jess out for a light supper. A new restaurant had opened overlooking Silver Beach, which was on the road to Newquay.

The evening was cool and the moon was hiding behind dense clouds as they climbed into the taxi waiting for them by the stage door. Jess was pleasantly surprised when she saw the restaurant. It was painted in soft *eau de nil* with silver chairs and twinkling lights, with a perfect view over the moonlit bay.

They ordered oysters followed by turbot, with sticky toffee pudding for dessert.

Jess had had a wonderful evening. Raising the final glass of Pinot Grigio, she toasted Jonathan: 'You are the best gay friend a woman could ever have, and I love you.'

Jonathan leaned forward and said quietly, 'That's very sweet of you, Jess – but I'm not gay.'

'Have I turned you?' She giggled merrily.

'No, darling. I have always been straight.'

'Really?' Jess was astonished then horrified. 'Oh my God – I'm so sorry. What a terrible thing to say.'

'It's OK. You're not the first. I'm definitely in touch with my feminine side.'

'I should say. Fooled me. So . . . do you have a girlfriend?'

'I'd like to.'

'Anyone you've got your eye on?'

'Yes.'

'Ooooooh! Who?'

Jonathan held her gaze.

The penny dropped.

'Oh.'

Jess didn't know what to say. She wanted to tell him: 'Would you take me home now please, because this is really awkward,' but she couldn't very well do that without sounding rude or pissed or both.

'Bad timing,' he said. 'Sorry.'

They sat in the taxi and she held his hand, not wanting him to feel that she was anything other than still a friend.

They kissed chastely as he got out at the Starfish and she waved to him through the back window as the taxi drove off towards Pendruggan.

After a couple of minutes she changed her mind.

'Driver, would you turn round and drop me back at the Starfish.'

'No problem.'

Walking into reception she could see no sign of Jonathan. She asked the young man behind the desk if he had a room available for the night.

'Yes indeed, madam.'

In the lift she held her key firmly and marvelled at how she had the balls to do this.

Once in her room she gave herself a good talking to in the bathroom mirror. 'You've got one life and one chance at getting it right,' she told herself. 'It's now or never.'

She left her room and walked the corridors to a familiar door and knocked.

'Who is it?'

'Me. Jess.'

'I'm in bed.'

'It's OK. Nothing terrible is going to happen. I just want to talk to you.'

She heard the rustle of bedclothes, of clothing being pulled on and of feet padding towards the door.

Ollie opened it.

40

He was wearing pyjama bottoms. His eyes were full of concern and anxiety.

'Jess, what's the matter? It's late.'

'I just want to talk to you.'

He stepped aside to let her in. The room was softly lit by a small bedside lamp and the bed was rumpled. She deliberately chose to sit on a tub-style armchair at the foot of the bed. There was a small pile of soft clothes on the seat and he watched as she picked them up and put them gently on to the floor before making herself comfortable.

He sat on the edge of the bed looking unhappy.

'I'm a bit pissed,' she said. 'And it's probably inappropriate for me to be here with you, but I wanted to see how you are.'

He shrugged. 'I'm fine.'

'Are you?'

'Sure.'

'How are you feeling about Red?'

'I don't know.' He shrugged again. 'She's gone for good and that's it.'

Jess shifted from the chair to the floor and sat on her knees looking up into his eyes, which he kept downcast. 'Are you in love with her?'

He ran his hands over his eyes. 'Oh God, Jess . . .'

She ploughed on: 'What am I to you? I'm not your

mother, I'm not your girlfriend but I care about you and feel that it would be such a shame if we lost what we had.'

'Jess, you're a lovely woman and you mean the world to me. I've never wanted to hurt . . .'

Tears pricked her eyes. 'But why would you hurt me? No one could hurt me as much as Ryan did, and I've been so miserable watching Red smothering you and knowing she was not what you wanted. You made me so happy and I want to make you happy again. Next year we've got the play with Brooke and Jonathan to look forward to. Why not go forward as friends, if not lovers, into next year – or has that changed for you?'

He still couldn't make eye contact. 'No, Jess, it's not that. I don't know who I am. I just . . . I don't know . . . I want to spend time as a single man with no responsibility, I need to figure out where I'm going with my work and what I want from my life.'

'That's fine by me, as long as we can still be friends.' Her fingers reached out to the tops of his bare feet and stroked them. 'Please?'

There was the slightest of noises from the bathroom. So slight that Jess wouldn't have paid it any attention if Ollie's eyes hadn't flickered.

She let go of his feet and sat up. He looked hard at the floor. She got up and went to the bathroom.

He said quietly, 'No, Jess. Don't.'

The door was not fully shut and she pushed it gently open. Sitting in the dark on the closed lid of the loo was Brooke, wearing nothing but a sheepish smile.

Jess felt her body drain of heat but her heart was leaping in her chest. She felt sick and her breathing started to come in short gasps.

'Hi,' said Brooke.

'Hi,' said Jess in shock. 'I think it must have been your clothes I put on the floor by the chair.'

As she stepped slowly backwards, Jess bumped into Ollie who was now behind her.

'I'm so sorry,' said Jess. 'Silly me. How humiliating. The older woman is always swapped for the younger model. I've been ridiculous. Forgive me. I hope you'll keep my stupidity to yourselves. Please don't tell anyone. I'm fine. I'll be fine. Good night.'

Fumbling with the handle, she opened the room door and it slammed shut behind her on its sprung hinges.

She took a couple of steps down the corridor before the patterned carpet started to make her feel giddy. She put a hand out to the wall to steady herself. It took her a few minutes, but slowly she found her way to her room and the horror of solitary humiliation.

*

It was three in the morning and Jess had been lying, still dressed, in a heap on her bed for the best part of two hours. Letting the tears fall on her pillow and staring blankly at the wall. Her life was in turmoil and it was too late to phone Emma. If her mother was alive, Jess knew what she would have told her: 'It's better to be an old man's darling than a young man's fool.' Her mum had known all about that. Jess's biological father had been a charming and feckless younger actor. Quite a feather in his cap to bed the older leading lady.

As soon as he found out Jess was on the way, he had done a runner. Her mother had remarried a kind, loving man who'd been a wonderful dad to Jess and her half-sister, Emma.

Like mother like daughter.

Jess's tears started to flow again. At least her mother had had two children. What did Jess have? Two dogs.

The future stretched ahead of her. Loveless, childless, desolate.

She needed a drink.

Jess stepped out of her clothes and splashed some cold water over her swollen, make-up smeared face. She rubbed the worst of the mascara tracks off onto a big white fluffy towel, leaving it stained and sad.

She pulled on the robe hanging behind the door and made her way down to the bar to find the company of the night porter and a drink.

The lobby was silent and beautiful with its glittering fairy lights. And squishy sofas. She padded into the bar, the deep pile of the carpet comforting on her feet. She heard the rustle of someone walking towards her. 'Good evening, madam,' said the night porter, completely unfazed by this devastated and crumpled-looking woman. 'Can I get you something?'

'Thank you, yes. I'd like a bottle of brandy and a pot of strong coffee.'

'Certainly, madam. Shall I serve it to you here in the bar? Or maybe the lounge?'

'Erm . . .' Her mind was too bruised to make a decision.

A voice came from the depths of a high-backed winged armchair overlooking the harbour lights. 'You can always join me . . .' Jonathan looked round the side of the chair and smiled. 'If you'd like to?'

She nodded gratefully and sank into the chair opposite him.

'I've been a complete fool tonight,' she said.

He raised an eyebrow. 'Really?'

She remembered the early part of this terrible evening when she'd assumed Jonathan was gay and then rebuffed him. 'Oh, not just with you . . . I've humiliated myself in front of Ollie and Brooke too.'

'Well done.' His blue eyes twinkled mischievously. 'Do tell. Just think of me as your gay best friend.'

She hung her head in shame. 'Oh fuck, I'm such an idiot!'

The night porter arrived with the cheerful rattling of coffee cups and ice cubes being carried on a tray.

Jonathan poured her a large brandy, adding several chunks of ice.

'There you go,' he said. 'Now, let it all out to Uncle Jonny.'

*

As she told the story of turning the taxi round and heading to Ollie's room, Jess felt the embarrassment drench her again. She covered her face with her hands and kept on with all the details, right up until she found Brooke in the bathroom, naked. Jonathan listened intently but when she got to the denouement he couldn't help but laugh.

'It's not funny,' wailed Jess.

'Oh, it is. It's hilarious! Bloody actors are all the same!' laughed Jonathan. 'Can you imagine how shit they feel now? You punctured their little bubble of seduction perfectly.'

'Don't be mean. They're my friends and I don't want them to be unhappy.'

'You are too nice, Miss Tate.' He poured her another

brandy and a cup of coffee. 'Look at it this way: Ollie and Brooke were prepared to hurt you, and now you've embarrassed them. I'd call that quits.'

'Would you?'

'Yes. Because tomorrow, or rather, today, you have to work with them. Now, this can go one of two ways. You can be all embarrassed and polite and not discuss what happened tonight. Or get it all out into the open and move on. You and Ollie were very good together, because you are friends and because you like each other. Whether Brooke and Ollie are in for the long run . . . who knows? I doubt it. I've met enough actors in my time to know what happens. You live in each other's pockets, get all cosy, and in the seclusion of an intimate set, friendship can seem like something else entirely.' He looked her in the eye. 'You're not a typical actor, Jess. You take everything at face value and you're too honest by half. But, being practical, I hope that Brooke and Ollie last for another twelve months – that will see us safely through to the end of *Blithe Spirit*!'

It was Jess's turn to laugh. 'You selfish but clever man.'

'Thank you. Do you fancy some breakfast? I smell toast coming from the dining room and I see guests drifting around.'

'I'm in my dressing gown.'

'Darling, you are an actress, you can arrive wearing whatever you like. Come on. I'm starving and you're tired. Let's eat, then you can sleep for the rest of the day.'

*

Jess was nervous when she showed up for work that night, but not as nervous as Ollie and Brooke, who were waiting for her in the dressing room.

It was Brooke who immediately apologised. 'Darling Jess, I feel so awful and can't imagine how you must be feeling. I never meant to hurt you or go behind your back . . . it just happened last night and—'

Ollie cut in '—it was just last night. We had a few drinks and—'

Jess shushed them. 'I'd be lying if I said that seeing you together last night didn't hurt me. It did, but I think it was more the shock of it than anything. I've done a lot of talking and thinking and . . . well, what's happened has happened. Water under the bridge and all that. I've been paddling in the shallows of life for thirty eight years. Too scared to make waves. Not wanting to get splashed or fully commit myself to living. I pretended I was happy with Ryan, but actually I was the one who was keeping him afloat. When he and I broke up I almost drowned, until Ollie saved me.'

'You saved me too,' he said.

She smiled. 'So now, shit scared as I am, I'm ready to go swimming in the deep. Way out of my depth, with my chin firmly out of the water and looking at the sky.' She pulled out the chair by her dressing table mirror and dropped her bag on the floor beside it. 'Friends?'

'Friends,' Brooke and Ollie agreed.

'Good.' Jess sat down and began to pin her hair away from her face, ready for her wig and make-up, then remembered something. 'By the way, Jonathan isn't gay.'

41

Summer was turning to autumn and the holidaymakers were leaving like the swallows.

Penny was sitting at her desk wondering how she was going to spring her surprise on Simon. It was his birthday tomorrow and the garage had promised to deliver the new Volvo by 8 a.m. The secret was getting harder to keep, but keep it she must. It was too good a surprise to spoil. When Polly had read her palm at the fête, everything had fallen into place.

The car salesman had given her one set of keys which she'd wrapped in a small box that was now burning a hole in her desk drawer. She had told no one. Not even Helen, who was, after all, her best friend.

She opened the drawer to have one more look at the snazzily wrapped package. Before she could take it out and give it its umpteenth rattle, a ping signalled an incoming email. She rammed the drawer shut, glad to be distracted.

The email was from a film production company in California. She'd had dealings with them a year or so ago . . . They had wanted to buy the US rights to *Mr Tibbs*, but she had turned them down. She looked at the subject line. It read: The Pavilion Story and *Hats Off, Trevay!*

Intrigued, she opened the email. After reading the first couple of lines she knew this had to be a hoax. Why would a production company in LA be interested in buying the rights to *Hats Off, Trevay!*, for goodness' sake? She googled the name of the production company and nearly choked when she saw who it was owned by. No two ways about it, someone must be playing a practical joke on her.

She told Simon about the email.

'Why don't you give them a ring, make sure one way or the other?' he suggested. 'God does move—'

'—in mysterious ways. Yes, I know, it's what you always say.'

'Well, it's true.'

Penny thought about the surprise she had in store for her husband tomorrow morning and decided that maybe he was right.

*

Queenie was sipping on a cuppa, enjoying a ten-minute break after the morning rush. She'd left Simple Tony in charge of the shop downstairs, with orders to give her a shout if any strangers came in. He could manage just fine, serving the locals, but some of these holidaymakers could be a bit demanding.

'I wonder what's on telly?' she muttered to herself.

She picked up the remote and flicked through the channels: *Jeremy Kyle* – 'Bloody loudmouth!'; *Bargain Hunt* – 'Load of old crap, who'd wanna buy any of that rubbish?'; *Come Dine With Me* – 'God Almighty! What a shower, 'oo'd want to 'ave anythin' they cooked?'

After much flicking, she finally came to rest on a channel showing nothing but films. Credits were rolling down the screen, signalling the end of a movie. Wondering what was coming next, she reached for her copy of *TV Quick*. It had fallen down the side of her battered old armchair. As she leaned down to pick it up she saw just how threadbare the chair was getting, but there was no way she'd ever replace it. It had been her husband's favourite chair. She'd come to Cornwall as an evacuee from London's East End; after her parents had been killed in the Blitz, she had nothing to go back for. Seventy-odd years she'd been in Pendruggan, yet there wasn't a hint of Cornish to her accent and she still sounded as if she'd just stepped off a bus on the Mile End Road. Her husband, Ted, had been dead nearly fifteen years, but sitting on his chair kept him close.

Queenie lit a roll-up and pursed her lips at the sight of Ant and Dec on the front cover. '*Britain's Got Talent*, my arse. Right, what's this then: "*Runaway Bride*. Richard Gere and Julia Roberts star in romantic comedy about a woman who has left a string of fiancés at the altar."'

Queenie stared intently at the small TV screen. A light bulb popped in her head.

'I knew I'd seen him somewhere before!'

Queenie stubbed out her fag and legged it down to the shop as fast as her birdlike legs could carry her.

'A'right, Queenie,' said Tony. 'Can I go now? Got to start on the weeding in Miss Helen's garden.'

'You stay where you are, Tony. I've got to see Penny – and this won't wait!'

*

Queenie rushed into Simon and Penny's kitchen, where Penny was just putting the phone down – a look of shock on her face.

''Ere, listen,' said Queenie. 'Opening night at the Pavilions, there was a fella came in wantin' a ticket – all tanned and gorgeous 'e was, an' I knew I'd seen 'im somewhere only I couldn't think where. Well, I've remembered.'

'Hang on a minute, Queenie. The most extraordinary thing has just happened. Simon, you were right, it seems that God really does move in mysterious ways. You'll never guess who wants to buy the rights to *Hats Off, Trevay!*.'

'Who?'

'Bloody Richard Gere – bloody Hollywood legend, that's all. Star of *Pretty Woman*, *Officer and a Gentleman* – I could go on. It defies belief.'

Queenie was flapping her hands. 'But that's what I'm trying to tell you – he's the Yank who came in on opening night. Came later the following week, an' all. I wasn't on the box office meself, but I saw him sneak in at the back a couple of minutes before curtain up. Then he left just before the end.'

'He obviously didn't want to be seen.'

'But 'e didn't count on old Queenie, did 'e? I knew it'd come to me.' Queenie grinned a self-satisfied smile.

'So what happens now?' asked Simon.

Penny could barely bring herself to say the words – the universe was on its head.

'He wants to meet us. Holy shit, I've got to call Helen!!'

*

Backstage at the Pavilions there was a party atmosphere. It was the last night and preparations for the crew's after-show party were in full swing. The stage management team had already strung bunting and balloons around the green room and a small table was accepting bottles of donated booze.

Someone had organised a Secret Santa-type gift collection. Everyone had drawn names out of a hat and for ten pounds had to buy that person an amusing gift without them knowing who it was from.

Jess couldn't believe that it was nearly over. So much had happened in the last couple of months. Her life was completely different now. The last couple of weeks had passed in a blur. Emma and Max had been down for the weekend and it had given her a real lift. There was nothing like a sister to put some perspective on things.

'Look, Sis, Ryan leaving is a blow. But he was holding you back, not the other way around.' They were sitting outside at a fabulous new fish restaurant that had opened on the harbour. 'You'll see, it will all be great now. I can feel it. Ryan didn't want the same things that you did. Or if he did, it was with a layer of fake Hollywood veneer slicked over it.'

'Do you think he and Serena will get married and have kids?' Jess asked. It still worried her that she had left that side of things too late. Forty wasn't that far away.

'Maybe, but who cares if he does? They'll only spawn another generation of selfish bastards like themselves.'

Jess laughed. 'Come on, let's have another glass of wine – d'you think Max will let us?'

Max was sitting between them and seemed to be engrossed in drawing pictures of a rather frightening-looking scarecrow. 'Look, Mummy – I've drawn Daddy!'

'Oh dear, poor Daddy.' Emma and Jess laughed at Max, his face screwed up in concentration.

'Let's risk it.'

'And what about Jonathan?' Emma asked as the waiter brought them each another glass of Cabernet Sauvignon.

'I don't know what you mean,' Jess replied, a blush creeping into her cheeks.

'Don't come the innocent with me. I've seen the way he looks at you. You could do worse than give him a try, you know. I wish someone would look at me like that, once in a while.'

'I don't know what you're talking about! Anyway, I seem to have made a mess of everything. I don't want to mess it up for Jonathan as well, he's too good.'

'Time waits for no woman, my girl. Remember, you're not going to be scared of life any more. Promise me.'

'I promise.' And Jess decided that this time, she really meant it.

*

Sitting in her dressing room, Jess looked at the photograph of herself with Ollie and Brooke that was propped up on her dressing table and smiled. The Three Musketeers. She didn't know whether they would stay friends for life. Or even if they would be friends this time next year. But those two had got her through some pretty sticky moments.

There was a tap on the door and Jonathan popped his head round.

'Ready for the final curtain call?' Registering her pensive face, he came in, shut the door and sat down beside her. 'Something wrong?'

'No, not wrong exactly.' Jess took Jonathan's hand in her own. 'Jonathan, I know how you feel about me and I just want to say something.'

Jonathan's steady gaze met hers. 'I think I know what you're going to say.'

'Jonathan, I'm not sure that you . . .'

He held his hand up. 'Look, we've had a wonderful, crazy rollercoaster of a ride and I wouldn't have missed it for the world, but I realise that I'm not what you're after and I understand. My offer still stands to work on *Blithe Spirit* and I won't get in your way or bother you – we'll be complete professionals, OK?'

'But, I was going to say—'

'Jess, you don't have to decide right now. Let's talk at the party.' He gave her hand a quick squeeze and then got up to go. 'By the way, I don't know the details, but I'm told something pretty spectacular is on the cards for later, so prepare yourself.'

With that he was gone.

Jess sighed at her reflection in the mirror.

'Men!'

*

The final performance of *Hats Off, Trevay!* was a resounding success. The loudest cheers and the longest standing ovation was saved, of course, for Colonel Stick. Jess found that she had tears rolling down her cheeks as the cast took their lengthy encores.

Ollie started a call for 'Director, Director!!' and Jonathan was hauled up on stage, against his wishes. Jess saw his chest swell with pride as his loyal team of actors and crew cheered him until they were hoarse.

Backstage, the atmosphere was like a carnival. All of the actors were hugging and embracing each other, making short-lived declarations of lifelong friendship. In the hubbub, Jess felt herself clasped in a huge bear hug, arms all around her. It was Ollie and Brooke.

'You're just amazing, Jess. Promise me that we'll always be friends. I know I've been a wanker – forgive me?'

'Of course. I couldn't ask for two better friends.'

Brooke hurried them along. 'Let's get out of these costumes, I need a drink!'

*

After putting in an appearance at the crew's party, the cast decamped to the Starfish, where there was more partying. It seemed that Trevay's great and good had turned out in force for the occasion.

'Here's to us!' said Brooke.

'Hear hear!' agreed Ollie. 'One for all and all for one, right?'

'You bet!' agreed Jess, draining her Cosmopolitan and swiping another one from a passing waiter with a full tray.

Jonathan and the Colonel came over to join them.

'You're a triumph, my dear boy,' the Colonel was telling Jonathan. 'You've done almost as well as my Peter. Almost, but not quite!' His eyes twinkled.

'He's an impossible act to follow.'

Miss Coco interrupted them. 'You're more of a triumph than you realise – here look at this.'

He thrust an early edition of tomorrow's newspaper in front of them.

'Here, let me read it out,' said Jess.

Hats Off, Trevay! *playing at the threatened Pavilions in the eponymous Cornish seaside town is nothing short of a triumph. Under the excellent direction of Jonathan Mulberry, Hats Off has reinvented the musical tradition. By turns funny, uplifting and poignant, the age-old cliché of boy meets girl has been given a new lease of life by a cast and director who are at the top of their game. It's Hats Off indeed, and let's hope that we'll soon see a transfer to the West End for this superlative production . . .*

'Oh, Jonathan – you're a genius!!' Jess threw her arms around him and gave him a full kiss on the mouth. He blushed, but before he had a chance to speak, a tinkle of metal on glass signalled that the speeches were about to begin.

'Hush now, let's listen,' said Jess as she squeezed his hand. Simon Canter took the stage.

'Thank you all for coming tonight, and thanks to all of the cast and crew for making *Hats Off, Trevay!* such a roaring success. We couldn't have done any of this without the help and support of the people of Trevay. We've shown that when push comes to shove, we're made of true grit.'

This was greeted by a chorus of whoops and whistles from the packed Starfish terrace.

'I'm sure you're all wondering what is going to happen to the Pavilions now. Well, today we've had some wonderful news that will take us one step closer to securing the future of the Pavilions for decades to come. Penny, would you like to tell us what this is all about.'

Penny stepped on to the stage and addressed the familiar faces.

'Yes, Simon. As you know, the big problem has always been finding the money to keep that amazing building going long beyond the life of *Hats Off*. I'm delighted to tell you all that today, with the blessing of the Colonel, I have secured a deal for the film rights. As of next summer, *Hats Off, Trevay!* will be going into production – and I'd like you to meet the director and star.' Penny paused for dramatic effect.

'Mr Richard Gere!'

There was a moment's stunned silence as the audience drank in what Penny had said. They watched, stunned, as an impossibly handsome, silver-haired screen icon took to the stage and gave them a friendly wave.

'Ladies and gentlemen, it's an honour to be here and I hope to do justice to this great play and the story of how a small group of people can take on and beat big business.'

The Starfish erupted in cheers and shouts, and soon Richard Gere was surrounded by the people of Trevay, eagerly pumping his hand and desperate to get a sprinkling of his Hollywood magic.

'Mr Gere, there's someone I'd really like you to meet,' said Penny, gently leading him away from the throng and introducing him to a flushed and flustered Joan Goodman, whose legs were shaking like a schoolgirl's.

*

Jess was feeling pleasantly piddled as she chatted to Jonathan and Ollie.

'Who would have thought it! Richard Gere, a Hollywood film, a West End show and the Colonel's film archive. We're going to be the talk of the showbiz world.'

'Let's hope so. We asked for a miracle and now we've more than one! Here's to the power of prayer.' Jess clinked glasses with them both.

'Where's Brooke, Ollie?' asked Jess.

'Over there.'

They followed Ollie's finger as he pointed to Richard Gere, engrossed in conversation with a sparking and animated Brooke, who seemed to be giving it 'Brooke Lynne' for all she was worth.

Eventually he extricated himself and came to say his quiet goodbyes to Penny, Simon and the Colonel. He took Penny's hand and looked into her eyes with a warm gaze that melted her tough business heart.

'Penny, I can't wait to work with you guys. We're gonna have a lot of fun.' He kissed her on both cheeks then turned to the two men.

'Simon, it's been a pleasure to meet you and the Colonel, without you I wouldn't be here. Hold on to your hat, you're about to be a big star all over again. Are you ready for it?'

The Colonel stood upright and proud. 'Mr Gere, I'm of the generation that goes down fighting.'

'Glad to hear it, but we're not going down, we're going up – all the way to the Oscars, I hope.' The small group laughed and shook hands with the Hollywood legend before he slipped away, unnoticed.

Penny leaned against Simon. 'Oh my God, he's gorgeous!'

Brooke came over, slightly tiddly, 'Where's Richard gone? We were getting on really well. I want to buy him a drink.'

Penny, pulling away from Simon, put her arms around her ambitious friend. 'You and me both, Brooke, you and me both.'

*

Ollie, sitting with Jonathan and Jess, watched Brooke gather up her bags and walk unsteadily out of the room.

She saw Ollie, blew him a kiss and a wink before walking out of his life forever. He sighed and took a long slug from his Manhattan cocktail.

'*Hats Off, Trevay!*. Boy meets girl, messes it up, meets another, gets messed up, then the circle begins all over again. Just another crazy day in the acting profession. Right, Jonathan?'

Ollie slapped Jonathan good-naturedly on the back then rose unsteadily towards the bar, where a number of pretty and tipsy young women threw themselves at him.

'Actors, eh? Present company excepted, of course.'

'Jonathan . . .'

'Look, Jess, what I said earlier: let's just try and behave like nothing ever happened . . .'

'Nothing has ever happened.'

'I know . . . but . . . well, what I'm saying is—'

'Jonathan, please be quiet. There is a time for talking and a time for being quiet.' She took his face in her hands. 'Guess what the time is now?'

'Er?'

'Men! You're never ready, are you?'

And with that, she gave him the kiss of his life.

42

Penny was awake early and brought him his birthday tea and toast in bed. Simon was astonished. In all the time he'd been married to her, this had never happened before.

'Thank you,' he said, taking a sip of tea.

'Well, it is your birthday. And here's something else . . .'

She handed him the gaily coloured box containing the keys to his new car.

He took it and she crossed her fingers ostentatiously.

'Why are you doing that?' he asked, picking at the sellotape.

'I'm a bit scared you might be cross with me.'

He gave her a funny little frown and continued to unwrap his present. He found the keys and turned them over in his hand. Eventually he said, 'I hope these aren't what I think they are.'

Before she could answer there was the toot of a car horn in the vicarage driveway. Penny looked worried. Simon got out of bed and walked to the window. Looking down he saw the roof of a gleaming, black, brand-new Volvo estate.

'Is that my present?'

'Yes.'

'I see.'

He put his dressing gown and slippers on and Penny

followed him as he went downstairs and opened the front door. The garage man was on the step, about to knock.

'Ah! Mornin', Vicar and 'appy birthday.' He held out the second set of keys. Simon walked past him and towards the new car. He stood looking at it and then tentatively opened the boot. 'It's very big,' he said.

'Yes,' said Penny.

He walked to the driver's door, opened it and got in.

'All 'lectric seats. Fully adjustable and heated. Your missus wanted the best for you,' said the delivery driver.

'It's very comfortable,' said an expressionless Simon. He reached towards the rear-view mirror and adjusted it. Then he stopped, astonished at what he could see. He turned round and looked at the back seat. Fitted snugly behind the passenger seat was a baby's car seat. He frowned. 'Does that come as standard?' He looked at Penny.

'Ah. No. I have another little surprise for you.' She took a deep breath. 'We're going to be parents.'

It took a moment for the penny to drop, then he leapt out of the car and hugged her tightly, all the while saying, 'It's a miracle. Oh, thanks be to God! It's another miracle.'

'All right, all right,' protested Penny. 'I'm not that old.'

'You must get back into bed. You need to rest. How long have you known? When is it due?'

'Firstly, I do not need to get back to bed. Secondly, I am fourteen weeks into a forty-week pregnancy, so we should have this baby around Easter.'

They turned at the sound of Simon's old Volvo coughing and spluttering to life. The delivery man had somehow managed to get it started first time and with a cheery wave he drove it away, eager to share the baby gossip with his wife and colleagues.

*

Penny and Simon couldn't wait to share their good news. First to hear were Helen and Piran, who came round immediately for a celebratory cup of something non-alcoholic.

Simon was so excited about the baby he couldn't stop asking Penny questions and jumping up and down with offers of tea or water or a blanket to cover her legs.

'Darling,' she said, 'I do hope you're not going to be like this for the duration. It's exhausting me more than being pregnant.'

'I hope you're going to make me a fairy godmother,' said Helen over a Jaffa Cake.

'Of course, who else?' The two friends exchanged a hug.

'It will be wonderful to have a child around the vicarage.' Simon's eyes suddenly lit up. 'Do you think it could be twins?'

'Don't even suggest it.'

There was a rattle at the front door signalling the arrival of the post.

Simon gave Penny a kiss on the top of her head and went to collect it. Back in the kitchen, he looked at the letters in his lap. Two rather smart-looking ones for Penny, a brochure with a desperate-looking African farmer sifting through barren dry soil for him, and one addressed to the Chairman of the Save the Pavilions Committee.

God had moved in a mysterious way.

'Today of all days! Look, we've had a letter from the council.'

The others stopped their excited chatter.

'Well, stop gawping, man! Read it out,' urged Piran.

Simon smoothed the letter between his fingers and read:

Dear Reverend Canter,

  We the Council write to you in your capacity as Chairman of the Save the Pavilions Committee.

  As you know, the planning committee held every Thursday of each second month was preparing to pass judgement on the appeal your committee had lodged, re the new usage of the Pavilions Theatre Building Trevay . . .

Penny huffed impatiently. 'For God's sake, their letter writing is as pompous as themselves.'

'Wait, my love. It gets better.' Simon carried on reading:

Café Au Lait, the multinational coffee chain and prospective buyers, have informed us that they have decided against coming to Trevay. The reason for this needs no explanation.

  The council are now in the position of having to determine what the future of the Pavilions will be. We are aware of further developments that will impact on this decision. Not least the success of the recent production, coupled with a cash injection that has been provided by the sale of the film rights to the production, kindly donated in their entirety by Colonel Walter Irvine.

'Good old Colonel Stick!' Helen clapped her hands.

It has therefore been decided, by a unanimous vote, that the management of the Pavilions should stay in the hands of the Save the Pavilions Committee for an interim period, to be decided, then pass to a committee of trustees, the representatives of which will be appointed by public vote. This is subject to certain caveats and legal procedures. We also expect that the committee will apply for lottery funding to further secure the future of the site.

We hope that you are in agreement that this is a satisfactory conclusion for all parties.

Yours sincerely

Joan Goodman

Leader of Trevay Council

Simon looked up and smiled at Penny. 'Darling – our prayers are answered!'

'You'll have to put yourself on that board of trustees, Simon.'

'And you, Piran,' said Simon.

Piran rolled his eyes. 'Never wanted to save the bloody thing in the first place. Still think we should let the 'ole lot fall into the sea.'

Before he could carp any further, Helen threw a tea cosy at his head.

*

By March, spring had sprung and Penny was as big as a house, due to give birth in a matter of weeks. She and Helen were in the bar of the National Film Theatre in London's South Bank, with Colonel Stick, Jonathan, Jess and Ollie. It was a momentous occasion. The NFT had bought Colonel Stick's remaining unsold archive and saved it for the nation. Such was the importance of the rare and fascinating footage, a sixty-minute documentary had been made and was now on limited release. Tonight was its premiere and a glittering array of actors and industry people had turned out. Colonel Irvine was barely able to take a sip of his drink, such was the interest he generated. Every few minutes a famous actor or director would come over and shake his hand like a long-lost friend.

'Did you see Dame Judi, just going in? And I'm sure that was Michael Gambon.' Penny rubbed her swollen belly. 'I'm still not sure this was a good idea. I never realised how uncomfortable your car could be for a woman who is eight months pregnant.'

'Stop grumbling,' said Helen.

'And now I've got to sit still for the best part of an hour. What if I need a wee?'

'You can sit near the aisle. Honestly, Pen, you know you wouldn't have missed this for the world.'

'None of us would, would we, Jess?' added Jonathan, hugging his girlfriend.

Jess kissed him on the cheek and patted her own bump, smaller than Penny's but definitely noticeable. She was positively blooming.

'Of course not, darling. We're all here except for Brooke. Ever since she left Trevay, her star has been on the rise. We're not even sure she's going to be able to do *Blithe Spirit*. Word is that she's going to be Miss Moneypenny in the new Bond movie. Her last film, *She's Got It*, was such a huge hit on both sides of the pond, I reckon she's out of our league now.'

'She was always destined for great things. She is a fine actress and a canny girl. I'm proud of her,' said Colonel Stick.

'Me too,' said Ollie. Ollie had just appeared in a critically acclaimed production of a cutting-edge new play at the Royal Court and his career was back on track.

'I'm sorry to miss being in *Blithe Spirit*,' said Jess, 'but Jonathan has got a plan B and I just can't wait to be a mum. It's all I've ever wanted really. Elsie and Ethel are going to make great big sisters.'

'I saw that Ryan and Serena had broken up,' said Helen.

'Yeah, shame.' Jess shrugged. 'But the only person that Ryan really loves is himself. I hope one day he works it out.'

The announcement came for the audience to take their seats.

'Piran and Simon send their apologies,' said Helen to the Colonel. 'Simon has got Lenten duties and Piran just isn't the London type. Said he'll wait for the documentary to air on BBC Four.'

'That's quite all right. My dears, would you both like to take an arm?' Colonel Stick offered his elbows to Helen and Penny, who linked arms either side of him.

'Don't go too fast!' warned Penny. 'This cannonball is weighing me down.'

*

The lights dimmed and the audience fell silent.

The film rolled and the audience sat rapt over the next hour as the greatest names of stage and screen were captured in front of them. The sound had been restored and the quality of the prints was excellent. Best of all, these old home movies captured the various legendary icons in all their humanity: Laurence Olivier joking with a stage hand, Vivien Leigh playful and ravishing as ever, Orson Welles majestic and brooding.

At the end of the film, the credits rolled. The last image that the audience saw was of Peter and Walter, arms around each other's shoulders, taking a bow after the first opening night of the original *Hats Off, Trevay!*.

The caption beneath read:

In loving memory of Peter Winship, 1927–1985

Colonel Irvine didn't speak. He held tightly to Helen and Penny's hands and stayed that way long after the rest of the audience had left the theatre.

Epilogue

The house jazz band struck up the familiar theme tune to the TV show as its glamorous star, Laverne Washington, vamped her way down the long and twinkling staircase to greet her ecstatic studio audience.

She laughed her raucous, sexy laugh and then hailed the audience. 'Good evening and welcome to *The Laverne Show*. Tonight, we go live to the new Brangelina film set where Brad has promised to take us on a tour of his new Winnebago!'

This was greeted with whoops from the audience.

'And – Will Smith is in the house!!!' More audience hysteria. 'But first, I am delighted to welcome to Laverne's Lounge . . .' The cheers and applause increased in volume, '. . . the girl on eveybody's lips. The one and only, the fabulous Brooke Lynne!!'

Brooke appeared at the top of the stairs in a Victoria Beckham scarlet dress. Her golden curls were pinned loosely on top of her head; her smokey eyes smouldered and her glossy, coral lips were parted in her trademark searchlight smile.

As she walked down the steps, she was accompanied by the house band, playing a jazzed-up version of the *Hat's Off, Trevay!* tattoo. Laverne waited for Brooke at the bottom of the stairs and they greeted each other like the old friends they were.

Laverne guided Brooke over to a sumptuous couch. 'Hey, girlfriend, what's happened to you since we were roommates in Manhattan?'

With great charm and humour, Brooke allowed Laverne to tease out the story of Brenda Foster and the low rent days of their lives as drama students.

'And now,' encouraged Laverne, 'tell us about *Hats Off, Trevay!*? When does the movie open?'

'At the weekend.' Brooke replied. 'I'm as nervous as a kitten but it's such a good film. And behind it is the true story of a theatre and of the man who saved it, but if it's alright with you, Laverne, why don't we let him tell you the story for himself.'

'Is he here?' Laverne did an excellent job of looking as if she didn't know what was happening next.

'He certainly is.' Brooke stood up. 'Ladies and Gentlemen, the man you've read all about, the man who wrote *Hats Off Trevay* . . . Colonel Walter Irvine!'

To the amazement of the audience, a sprightly Colonel walked out in front of them and gave a deep bow.

After lapping up the warm applause, he turned to Laverne and asked sweetly. 'I have brought a friend with me. May I bring him on too?'

Laverne nodded her rehearsed assent, bracing herself for the crowd's reaction.

Then with no fuss at all, Richard Gere stepped out in front of the lights.

*

The opening of *Hats Off Trevay*, the movie, was a glittering and starry event. Sitting in their stretch limo waiting their turn to pull up on to the red carpet, were

Brooke, the Colonel, Ollie, Jess and Penny. Penny was holding her mobile phone to her ear and talking to Simon.

'I can hear her crying – is she hungry? There's a bottle in the fridge . . . I've been expressing all day . . . Well, maybe her nappy needs changing . . . Perhaps I'd better come back to the hotel?'

Half a mile away, Simon was sitting in their luxury hotel suite cuddling his daughter, Jenna, and juggling the phone.

It was his sixth call from Penny since she'd left twenty minutes before.

'Darling, she's fine. I'm fine. Don't worry. Jenna and I are watching the live pictures of everyone arriving on the red carpet. Richard's just turned up. I think this one is . . . yep, Emma Thompson.'

'She's in the car ahead of us!' said Penny, looking through the tinted windows as the British star stepped out of her car into the glare of the waiting flashbulbs.

'So, you're next?'

'Yes, oh God. Here we go. The car has stopped. I'd better hang up. Love you both.'

Simon and Jenna sat rapt as they saw their friends disgorge from their limo. Brooke came out first, followed by the others, then after a small tussle with her shawl that had got stuck in the heel of one of her stilettos, out stepped his beautiful wife.

'Look, there's Mummy!' He pointed to the screen. Jenna gave a hiccup and a big, gummy smile. Simon watched as Penny blinked under the pop of the photographers' flashbulbs, but then she steadied herself, hitched up her skirt and stood in the blaze of light, grinning and putting two thumbs up for the camera.

A reporter stuck a microphone towards her and asked, 'Any messages for the folks back home, Miss Leighton?'

Penny thought for a moment, before saying joyfully, 'Not a bad turnout for a seaside affair!'

The End

Make sure you look out for
Fern's brilliant new novel,

A Good Catch

Available to buy from April 2015

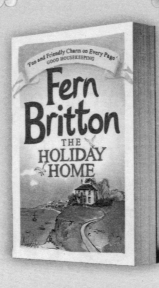

THE WONDERFULLY WITTY NOVEL
BY FERN BRITTON IS AVAILABLE NOW!

Each year, the Carew sisters embark on their yearly trip to
the family holiday home, Atlantic House, set on
a picturesque Cornish cliff.

Prudence, the hard-nosed businesswoman, is married to
the meek and mild Francis, but she's about to get a shock
reminder that you should never take anything for granted.
Constance, loving wife to philandering husband Greg,
has always been out-witted by her manipulative sibling,
but this year she's finally had enough.

When an old face reappears on the scene, years of
simmering resentments reach boiling point, but little do
the women know that a long-buried secret is about to
bite them all on the bottom. Is this one holiday that
will push them all over the edge, or can Constance
and Pru leave the past where it belongs?